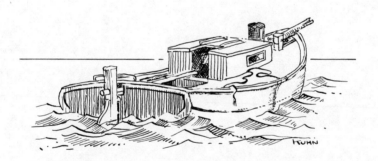

The Adventures Of
JEREMIAH DIMON:
A Novel Of Old East Hampton

The Adventures Of
JEREMIAH DIMON:
A Novel Of Old East Hampton

By EVERETT T. RATTRAY

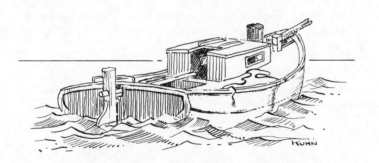

Introduction by Wilfrid Sheed
Afterword by Helen S. Rattray

PUSHCART

The Pushcart Press
Wainscott, New York

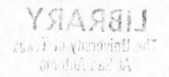

Copyright © 1985 Helen S. Rattray
Library of Congress Catalog Card Number: 85-060911
ISBN: 0-916366-34-0

First printing, April, 1985
Printed in the United States of America

East End map: cartography and general research
by Thomas M. Thorsen, Town Planner;
Place name research by Norton W. Daniels, special consultant;
Consultation and review by Carleton Kelsey, Town Historian.
Prepared for the Town of East Hampton Bicentennial 1776 - 1976

Manufactured in The United States of America
by RAY FREEMAN and COMPANY, Stamford, Connecticut

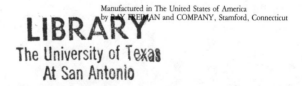

Introduction

*"He does not die
that can bequeath
Some influence to the land he knows,
Or dares, persistent, interwreath
Love permanent with the wild hedgerows;
He does not die, but still remains
Substantiate with his darling plains."*
Belloc, *"The Four Men"*

Such a man was Everett Rattray, and his spirit lives out here in the coves and hollows of Long Island. Ev could, in fact, have bequeathed his influence to most any place he chose. As a graduate of Dartmouth and the Columbia School of Journalism, and a superb journalist by nature, he could have named his ticket. But he chose instead to donate his heart and his talent to a flat, skinny strip of land known as the South Fork of Long Island, with which he had fallen fatally in love as a boy.

It was an interesting choice. Bonackers, as all South Forkers call themselves, don't go in much for great men. It may have something to do with a fishing economy -- you don't want people standing up in the boat. So Everett, a great man if ever I met one, hunkered down into being a regular small-town newspaper guy. Nor did he flash any signals about it to the outside world -- look what a great small-town editor am I! -- which might have made him famous in the manner of Vermont Royster. The East Hampton Star was for Bonackers and about Bonackers, and that was universe enough for Rattray. In the process, he turned the Star into a national-class weekly, but that was a byproduct. Everett simply couldn't help doing things well.

The love affair that generated such dedication to a place is the subject of this book, and those of us who live out here will need no further invitation. Just to hear the place names, from Napeague to Amagansett to Montauk, rolled lovingly off the tongue, gets the blood moving. And then -- to imagine how it looked on a bright blue day to a 16-year-old in 1887, when the Fork was even more unspoiled than it is today, and when it took a good three hours by horse to get from Bridgehampton to Amagansett, so that you treasured every inch of ground, especially the ones you lived on.

This novel is obviously not your usual autobiography, unless we project Everett into his late 90s, but it is the autobiography of a mood. Jerry Dimon seems to spend at least half his life on the water, from which a man can strike out in any direction. Some of his Bonac neighbors have seen the East Indies but not Manhattan; young Jerry settles (in this book at least) for an impromptu trip to Cuba. But even if you went nowhere at all, the possibility was always there, the dream was part of the heritage. Ev's tight little corner of the world had a roving imagination second to none.

Sometimes the roving got no further than Sag Harbor which, in Jerry's eyes, is one of those flashy, sinister seaports like Shanghai with its street lights and whorehouses and foreigners. In real life Ev always seemed mildly sorry that Sag Harbor had lost this raffish quality. He felt there should always be ONE town like that, though not necessarily his own (Ev could be playful about his local loyalty; it was not a great weight that he carried).

Readers should perhaps be warned in this novel that

Everett Rattray is only intermittently a novelist. Just as he gets something going, his eyes land on an old tool shed and he drops everything to describe a flintlock musket and other paraphernalia therein at rapturous length. Throughout the book, the historian, the geographer, the plain old Long Island lover keeps elbowing the story teller aside, or else getting him to write scenes in which THEY can strut their stuff.

Never mind. He gives us sharp characterizations and vivid situations and, for now, I'm just as happy to hang around the tool shed with him, absorbing his sensuous wonder at manmade objects or back on the water again learning that lobster back then was not worth the trouble it took to fetch it and that clamming was, as always, just like "weeding a cornfield."

The past and the present were single tense to Ev as they are to all true historians, and the place he lived in, if studied wisely enough, was everyplace.

When Ev died bravely and tragically at 47, he had already fashioned his own testament in the form of this book and another (COMPLETELY non-fiction) called "The South Fork: The Land and the People of Eastern Long Island" -- not to mention a thousand newspapers. Anyone who has read Rattray will thereafter see the South Fork slightly differently, slightly in a sense through Ev's eyes. And this for a writer is a far greater bequest than slapping one's name on some high school or playground. To be merged with the very landscape is what Belloc was talking about and what Everett Rattray achieved.

Wilfrid Sheed

Sag Harbor, February 3, 1985

The Adventures Of
JEREMIAH DIMON:
A Novel Of Old East Hampton

At his all-conquering decree, the forest that had stood for ages steps aside to let him build his cabin and cultivate his farm. The sea which raved and foamed upon the race has become a crystal pathway for commerce to march on. The thundercloud that slept lazily above the mountain is made to come down and carry mailbags. Man, dissatisfied with his slowness of advancement, shouted to the Water and the Fire, "Come and lift!" "Come and help!" And they answered, "Ay, ay, we come!" and they joined hands -- the fire and the water -- and the shuttles fly, and the rail-train rattles on, and the steam-ship comes coughing, panting, flaming across the deep.

The Rev. Dr. T. DeWitt Talmage
"Thanksgiving Day"

Prologue

Heading Out

Easy there; I just paid to have that door painted. It'll lock itself, if it swings shut. You'll remember to have somebody come and drain the pipes? Heat's off, and they'll burst for sure before I get back, if I do, with one flipper out of operation and the left side of my face like it was full of Novocain. Can't understand me? Well, that's too bad, and you ought to know better than to call me Doc. This is the first time I ever rode in the stern of one of these things on my back, though I've rode in front often enough, yes and before either of you was thought of, when an ambulance was pulled by a horse.

Been in back then, too, but with a nurse from Blackwell's Island and we wasn't going anyplace in particular, and I wasn't on my back. For God's sake don't start playing games with that siren. Siren I said; leave it off. There's no use giving satisfaction to them are glad to see me go, nor upset to them that aren't. I've had my time, and if I'm going to go, why that's all right. They say when you're close to it you remember your whole life, but that isn't so. I've seen a couple of thousand die, held their hand a lot of them, and there's no telling what most of them are thinking about but generally you know damned well it's not their whole life. Almost drowned once myself, and what I was thinking about was what a damned fool I'd been, doing what Father had told me a dozen times not to, that is swim alone. The summer I was sixteen, '87 it was.

Slow down! My God I wish I could tell them. Not that these young louts care but what I'm thinking is how fast the years have gone. How young the country is, when you get down to it.

Thinking. Remembering. Where am I? What difference does it make. Or how old? You cipher it out. Born in '71. In Amagansett. Five years before the Centennial and five years before Custer lost his hair. A hundred something? Sounds likely, close enough. Who wants to know? The business office? You'd think they'd know without asking. I helped build this damned hospital. Before the First War. First War? I was grown up and married before the Indian wars really ended.

One of the things about growing old in the medical trade is getting interested in other old crocks. Maybe if I'd tried using one of those see-saws my tubing wouldn't have burst. Know a guy in his eighties uses one, head down and feet pointed at the attic and all the blood rushing to his brain. It's that or plastic arteries, he says. And three ounces of happiness at five o'clock. I concur in his treatment, that last part of it. Old Benjamin Cain, in Sag Harbor, it was his hundredth birthday six or seven years ago; I went around to say hello. He was in fine fettle, a little arteriosclerotic, except his niece, the one he lived with, couldn't get him to change his trousers for love nor money. Somebody'd given him a quart of wine, and he had it jammed in his hip pocket and he went around all day pulling on it. Nobody in the Harbor had ever seen Cain drunk, except the day he heard his grandson had been killed in the Argonne.

When I visited him we talked about getting old, and he said he didn't mind so much except that he didn't have any friends left. "All gone," he said, "and I see them go." The house backed up to Oakland Cemetery, and he had to watch the plantings over the fence. Didn't really have to, but he did. He had tears either side of his nose when he told me.

What in Christ's name is that noise? A television? No,

I do not want to be cranked up to see it. Drag that screen across here. I'm willing to share a room but I'll be damned if I have to share the low tastes of those others.

Progress. That's the reason I've lived so long, with the bad tubing that got Father laying me low half a lifetime later than it did him. Been lucky too. That summer I was sixteen, like they say, it's clearer in my recollection than the day before yesterday.

Chapter
I

June, 1887

It was the end of spring, the beginning of the summer, of '87. I'd finished my first year at the Literary and Commercial Institute in Bridgehampton -- boarded there with the Hallocks. There was no way except about three hours on a horse to get back to Amagansett, but I used to come home Saturday noon for a day. The railroad turned off at Bridgehampton for Sag Harbor then. It was another eight years before the cars came through to East Hampton and Amagansett and Montauk. That, the railroad coming through, made all the change in the world. It was, for us, what the year I was sixteen had been for me. The year I saw the elephant, you'd call it.

Swimming in Hook Pond one Saturday the beginning of May, coming back from Bridgehampton, I'd swallowed a lot of water, come close to drowning, and that went to pleurisy and the rest. Well, I was over it, a bit unsteady after six weeks and my birthday in bed, and the first cigar came near killing me. Oh, yes, I smoked, but not in front of Father or Mother. They knew it, I guess, but they didn't say anything. If it had been cigarettes, coffin-nails they called them, that would have been a different story. That was the way they were.

The summer was ahead. The summer before, 1886, a bad year for business but a good year for bunkers, moss-bunkers, menhaden-fish, I'd gone in the steamer Narragansett with Father. After the season, she'd been turned over to a Southern captain, to take down there for another crack at the bunker fishing, but the engineer was green and she caught fire and burned off the beach at East Hampton. Hopping & Topping, the house movers, got her boiler up next spring. So there wasn't a vessel for Father in '87, though the Company was dickering for one from a Rhode Island outfit, and he thought that after being sick I deserved a chance to rest up. He was going off on a mackerel-seiner, a schooner. I was to go to Third House, on Montauk, for a month or so, to help with the chores for my keep and get some fresh air.

Third House was run by my Aunt and Uncle Stratton. It was a farm, like home; either place there'd be plowing and feeding hogs and milking and the rest of it. Boys of sixteen generally prefer to take their orders from anyone but their parents, so on June 17th, a Friday, I set out, intending to stop at Fresh Pond for the first part of the East Hampton Sunday School -- Presbyterian, there wasn't much else -- picnic before walking across Napeague Beach to Montauk. If I left Fresh Pond by noon, I could get to the Hither Plain Life Saving Station well before dark, and spend the night there before walking on to Third House, another five or six miles, the next morning. I'd always wanted to stop with the Life-savers. The crews had gone off for the summer the first of May, but there were ordinarily one or two men living in the Stations and fishing all summer.

I set off from the Sunday School picnic at the end of the morning, after eating but before the ball game. Walking down the Bay beach toward Albert's Landing, I could see Gardiner's Island off to the left and Promised Land, with its docks and red buildings, around the sweep of beach to the right. The sails were set on the Gardiner mill, arms going around to light airs from the southwest, grinding corn probably, you might as well grind it, and eat it yourself, at twenty-eight cents a bushel. It was hot, for June.

The little steamer Jud Field was running down through the Bay, bringing freight and passengers from Greenport for the fish factories at Promised Land and Hicks Island and Napeague. The bunker season was just getting started, and back of me, at Deep Hole, Springs, the schooner Marshall Wells, a two-master, was unloading coal to run the boilers at the Sterling Oil Works. The Fred Smith, a bit bigger, was there too, loading what was left over after the oil was squeezed out of the bunkers, fish scrap for fertilizer. The two vessels off toward the horizon, to the northeast, were the Portland, Captain George Smith, out of the James Smith Works at Promised Land, and the Hudson, Captain Josh Edwards, fishing for the Sterling Works. The two vessels were as nearly alike as two peas, eighty-five or ninety-foot steamers with high bows, but we could tell them apart, just the same, as far as we could see them.

Promised Land was a joke name, though we were not quite sure what the joke was. Promised Land because the place smelled so bad, until you got used to it, with the factories going full steam? Or Promised Land because it was the destination of the gangs of foreigners we would see each year just before the season started? Groups afoot of Italians, Ginnies everybody called them, or Swedes, or what we didn't quite know, odd men with odd ways and odd names we never heard.

Sag Harbor was back up the Bay, around past Cedar Island Light, a foreign place to us. The last whaler had sailed from there seventeen years before. People were talking about a revival, but none of them really believed it. Sag Harbor captains, most of them really from Bridgehampton or Southampton, still commanded whalers out of San Francisco or Honolulu for the Arctic fishery. You could still see

Kanakas, and Indians, and Chinese too, on Sag Harbor Main Street, and you could see saloons and such social eyesores. Sag Harbor had Irish, too, working in the watchcase factory, and a Catholic church, a candle shop. Sag Harbor made me nervous. So did the Italians going to the fish factories, dark men with mustaches and clothes cut foreign who would stop at the store in Amagansett and buy round loaves of bread shipped over from the Harbor just for them, and onions and cheese, and sit on the stoop using their sheath knives to make big sandwiches, chattering to themselves. At the factories, they shoveled the fish, pushed the hand-carts, bagged scrap, and fought among themselves, sometimes with the sandwich knives. The crews aboard the boats were local, though; Father and the other captains wouldn't have foreigners.

I cut across from the Bay to the Ocean as soon as I could, after passing the pond at Cranberry Hole, a mile or so shy of the fish works. Long Island is only about three-quarters of a mile wide there, all sand and deerfeed flats once you get east of the Highlands. Napeague Beach is the low ground between the Highlands, which are part of Amagansett, and Nominicks, the first high ground at Montauk. I paused on the first line of sandhills and could see sails and smoke off-shore. To the right was Amagansett, most of its houses hidden by the Highlands but Gabe Edwards's and some of the others on the bluff just visible and the roof of the Life Saving Station sticking up south of them. To the left, in the dunes two miles east of me, was Number Nine, the Napeague Station, flag flying. Someone was there, then, probably George Eldredge, like just about everybody else in Amagansett a cousin of sorts. George was an old Navy man, a widower. He was a fisherman, but he hadn't done well enough in that line to be called Captain or for me to hesitate much before calling him plain George. I liked him, though. He wore the round cap with the LSS badge winter and summer and fish-ed from the Station off-season, and in-season too, and was hardly ever at his house in Amagansett.

I hung my shoes by their laces around my neck and ran the hundred yards from the sandhills to the edge of the water. The white sand was hot underfoot. It was low tide, and there was no more than a gentle surf sloshing up cool around my ankles. The walking was easy on the wet packed sand. After a mile or so, I went up and sat on the break of the beach. The air was clear enough to be able to tell from the topsails sticking up over the horizon which way the vessels out of sight below were headed. There was just enough breeze to make up dimples of chop on the low swells. I reached into the pocket of my old canvas coat and pulled out the slab of fried pork Mother had wrapped in oil paper. I ate and thought about school, and the recess last winter. Father had decided I was big enough to go whaling off the beach. My first winter of whaling, though, turned out to be the first in a decade or so that the five Amagansett boats hadn't fastened to a whale. We made a rally once, just after New Year's, when I was home, but the creature, a right whale bull, was one of the knowing kind, and set off to eastward into a head sea and we soon gave up. I'd hoped to come ashore splattered with blood, as I'd seen older boys do, to strut for the girls. Girls was a subject I knew little enough about, though I had a pretty good idea of the workings of male and female; I'd never applied the idea to the actuality. It was hard to imagine people doing such things and impossible to imagine my parents. Nat Bennett claimed to have laid one of the Cuffee girls, part black and part red, mixed Montauk and Shinnecock, but I doubted it. He was seedy enough but he showed no signs of the fleshly corruption and mental disintegration I'd read about in the papers. That Nora was bound to have some loathsome disease. I'd better stop thinking about this, because it led to self-abuse and tremors, insanity, spots on the face, shadows under the eyes, fits, and various other marks of the Sin of Onan. I ran my fingers over my upper lip and thought about letting a mustache grow.

A black speck came up on a swell, four or five hundred yards east and back of the bar, disappeared, and appeared again. A whale? Late in the season. The speck was going in and out of sight too fast, and in time with the seas heaving up under it, swells peaking a bit as they neared the shallow water on the bar. I ran along until I was opposite whatever it was, and climbed the dune to get a better look. It appeared to be wreckage, wood, perhaps a cabin or cuddy top. Either side, swirls on the water as the object rose and fell signaled more wreckage, a piece twenty or thirty feet long. It was slowly drifting eastward. The Station was only a half mile or so away now, and I set off toward it at a trot, my heart pounding.

George was mending a gillnet on the grass out front. He laughed when I arrived out of breath, and let his seine needle dangle from the twine.

"I saw it, too. No need to get all worn out, I figured. She's coming this way in any case, and whatever she is might fetch up right here without me getting all gallied."

I was impatient. "Can I borrow your dory, George?"

"Sure," he said. "You can borrow me, too."

We dragged his dory down the beach on wooden rollers. He pushed her in, swinging his body over the coffin-shape of the transom, and I rowed. Neither of us had boots, and I was wet to the thigh and he to the waist. The water was cold -- the ocean doesn't really warm up until the Fourth of July -- but the sun and rowing would dry us out. George stood facing me now, me pulling and he pushing the single pair of oars. He was eager, too, though he didn't want to let on. He was chewing, and spitting more than he had to. We didn't have far to go; the set had brought whatever it was almost down to the Station, and the surge had worked it in over the bar, maybe a hundred yards off the beach.

"Let 'er run," he said, squirting a brown stream of tobacco juice to leeward. I craned around and looked. Two or three rods away, the top of a hatchway was bobbing up and down. To the left about fifteen feet was, now and then, a broken stub, a bowsprit probably. To the right, the top of a curved counter showed. What we had was a derelict some twenty-five or thirty feet long. Even with the gentle surf, she'd be in the wash before long, and filled with sand and buried, to be pounded into pieces as soon as the breakers built up. George took our anchor warp to the dory's stern. I backwatered in, and he jumped over onto her deck, which showed a foot or so down in the clear water. What little of her could be seen settled under his weight. He made the warp fast around the stub bowsprit, and I backed in again for him. George didn't have to tell me to pull offshore, and when we fetched up at the end of the twelve-fathom warp, he helped at the oars again, standing and using all of his weight. It took us a quarter-hour to work beyond the bar. Then he made the dory anchor fast to our end of the warp, and hove it overboard. "That'll hold her, long enough," he observed, wiping his forehead with his sleeve. We drifted back toward the wreck, and looked. "You know what that is? That's a Bahamas sloop. I saw enough of them, down by Nassau and the Keys, in the War. What's she doing up here?" he said. We could see her mast broken off just above the deck, and rigging dangling down in the water.

"We might find somebody below," George went on, "but I doubt it. Don't know what happened but I'd bet she was run down, at night, and like enough some steamer passed right over her and carried away her spars, and whoever she belonged to. We'll soon find out, with some luck."

We rowed ashore and walked up to the Station. George rounded up a hammer, nails, some light lumber, line, bits of canvas, caulking cotton, and a long tin pump. We rowed out and made fast to the derelict's stern. George hopped aboard again, stepping careful in his bare feet. He tripped over a hatch on deck but grunted with satisfaction when his fingers told him its cover was firmly in place. He forced the top board of the three sliding ones in the companionway up and out, leaving an opening in the cuddy a foot or so above the water. I passed him the pump, and he jammed it down the hole at an angle, swinging it back and forth until he was satisfied it was as far down as it was going to go.

He primed the pump with the dory's bailing-scoop, gave it a few strokes, and waved me in. "I'm an old man," George said. "Let the younger generation find out if she's sound, or if they are going to have to pump the whole damned Atlantic Ocean through her." He climbed back into the dory, spit out his cud, wiped his whiskers with the back of his hand, and pulled his pipe and some tobacco, by now about the only dry thing on him, from an oilskin wallet in his shirt pocket. The pumping wasn't easy, but I put my back into it. After fifteen minutes George said he believed she was coming. I couldn't tell if he was joshing, probably not, so I kept a poker face. He let me pump another quarter-hour, and had another pipe, before spelling me. George was a slave to Lady Nicotine, he was.

"Once we get her deck clear, we're in business," he said. This took close to an hour more, the two of us taking turns. Then we took the other boards out of the companionway. George stripped to his wool underwear and slipped down in alongside the pump. He passed me his cap and pipe, and ducked to feel around. "Nobody there," he reported, water dripping from his whiskers. "I can't find any holes, but that don't mean she don't have some. Tell you the truth, I don't know how she could have got full of water like this even if she was run down and over, unless she was holed." We looked around on deck and over the sides.

"Here," said George. "Feel." There was a deep gash in the sloop's planking on her starboard side, running diagonally down as far as either of us could reach. George put his clothes back on. I guessed she'd been struck while under sail, on the starboard tack, probably at night; that didn't take much deducting. George agreed, but said he began to think she had been carried along, her rigging caught some way. "Crew on deck, drunk or asleep or something, that's my speculation. If 'twere a steamer, he like enough wouldn't stop anyhow, and if 'twas a vessel under sail, by the time they roused the watch below and went after them they'd all have parted their cables. This didn't happen long ago, that is she didn't drift up here in the Gulf Stream from the islands. There'd be grass all over her, were that so. Like enough off here and not too far off at that. She couldn't have drifted long without someone seeing her, but they must have figured she was just wreckage, nothing but that little bit showing."

We pumped some more. She rose slowly and we found that some of the planking where she had been struck was sprung, and that two frames were cracked. We drove caulking cotton into the seams, necessarily from the wrong side, the inside. It was getting on toward supper when we rowed ashore.

"Got to get her out of here," George said. "If you were a Bahamian snowball you could scull her around Montauk, but you ain't. You get on home and harness old Ranger to the wagon and get the spritsail from your father's whaleboat. Get some food and anything else you think you need, and if you know anybody who can swim and hasn't anything better to do than chase around Robin Hood's barn in somebody else's sloop with you bring him along. Meanwhile, I'll get back out there and pump some more."

George had never had any children, but he understood boys pretty well. Off I went, and got home after dark. Mother was braiding rags for a rug, by the light of the coal-oil lamp in the kitchen, a big basket either side, one full of scraps and the other one with a length of finished braid long enough to go clear around the house. She had her needlework face on, that purse-lipped look women get as if they were aiming the stitches with their mouth.

She kept right on piecing the wool scraps together and

adding them to the braid, and I explained things.

She thought a while before speaking. "Your Father's up at the Pines. One of those no-goods is dying, and Mr. Dimon, Christian that he is, is sitting with him. There's few that would." We had a doctor in Amagansett, but Father, who when he went cooper in the Ontario when he was young had had to combine his barrel-making with being dentist, barber, and doctor -- he pulled our teeth when we needed, still -- was sometimes called to the bedsides of the near-dead. The Pines was the little settlement at the far end of the village, near the Roses' hotel. So-called hotel, Mother said.

"I suppose it's up to me to decide, and I suppose you are old enough to take care of yourself. You have George bring Ranger back tomorrow, though," she said, tugging the strands of the braid to work them tight.

It was ten o'clock by the time I had got Ranger's tackling on him and him hitched to the wagon, and had jogged around to Nat Bennett's. I took some gravel and threw it up against his window. He poked his head out, elbowing aside three of his little brothers, got dressed, and left home by way of window, shed roof, and a branch. Nat was my age, and hadn't been to school for two or three years. He'd tried clerking in the Harbor, but he didn't like that, and he didn't like farming, either. He was fishy, though, and paid his board at home with what he earned fishing, working with this crew or that. Just now he was between flatfishing and poundnetting. He didn't have to worry about leaving home without notice to his mother, that was the way things were in his family. His father was working on Gardiner's Island, tending sheep, he said, curling his lip at the word sheep.

On the way down to the beachbanks I told Nat about the sloop. I'd never seen a Bahamian sloop before, nor Nat either. We'd heard of them, and just about everything else that floated, from whalemen who'd been around the world two or three times. Some of us knew from them more about the

Sandwich Islands than we did about Brooklyn on the far end of Long Island.

The little sloops from the islands southeast of Florida were handy. The one anchored off Napeague was about twenty-six feet, with a beam of maybe nine feet, and might draw three or four. She had a small standing well aft, and the hatchway in the little cabin trunk was just big enough for a man to squeeze through. George had said there were bunks or benches either side of the mast, two of them. There were cleats for a sandbox, to cook in, on deck.

All of us had grown up with boats, from little pumpkin-seed gunning skiffs to whaleboats, the most graceful of them all. Father's was in a shed half-buried in the sand on the north side of the beachbanks, bottom-up on big saw-bucks, white and shiny in the light of our lantern. She'd been built for him two years before I was born. The whaleboat was a foot longer than the sloop, but only a quarter the displacement. She was flush-planked, in cedar, up to the last strake or plank below the gunwhale. That one was lapped over and clinkered down with brass rivets. She was light enough for a half-dozen men to carry upside down over their heads, like Red Indians a canoe. That was what we thought they'd grown out of, the canoe; most of what the first white men to go whaling off Amagansett knew about the chase they'd learned from the Indians. They used to kill whales from their canoes -- harpoon-warps fast to wooden drags, to tire the whale out so the red men could prick him to death with their lances, or, some said, hop on his back and hammer a plug into his blowhole to smother him, something I'd have to see to believe. The settlers, Dimons among them I guess, had used pretty much the same tools at first, save for the plugs, Englishmen having more respect for their hides than that. They took what they learned from the Indians, and some of the Indians too, out to sea with them, to the South Atlantic and Pacific and finally the Bering and the Arctic, and when the deepwater whaling played out, they were right back to where they'd started, whaling off the beach like the Indians. Except that the Indians didn't seem to have the urge any more. It was as much for old times' sake as anything, that and perhaps a thousand dollars each winter to share amongst a dozen or two men, which was not anything to sneeze at, cash being in short supply on eastern Long Island.

Either side of the long shed, slung on the walls, were most of the tools of the whaler: fifteen-foot killing lances, their sharp ovals of cutting edge sheathed in wooden scabbards, smaller than a man's hand but big enough to kill the world's biggest animal if rammed deep enough and in the right direction; lance-warps of nine-thread manila, five fathoms long, neatly coiled and hung from the butt-ends of the hickory lance-shafts; harpoons, their toggle-ends at the end of three-foot lengths of slim, soft Swedish iron made to bend but not break, harpoons shorter than the lances, made to fasten, not to kill; cutting-in spades and boarding knives and mincing knives and axes and hatchets, for stripping the blubber on the beach to be sent to the potworks up on the Bluff for trying-out, where the trypots and skimmers and dippers and more gear were kept inside another shed, the pots perched atop brick furnaces.

On the packed sand of the shed floor were the two line tubs, the hundred-fathom warp carefully coiled in larger imitation of Mother's rug-braid. One snarl with the line running out could mean a man's life, or six lives. Overhead, on the open beams, were the oars, many more than the five, three starboard and two port, carried by the whaleboat. Some were spares, some were strays picked up on the beach. The good set was painted with a green stripe around the blade, and numbered, because they came in different lengths to fit the position in the boat. There were three steering oars, too, longer than the boat itself. We pulled down the mast, sail, and sprit, made up together in a long bundle with the halliard around it and stowed with the oars, and put its

peak-end on the grindstone to keep the canvas off the floor.
The grindstone was as much a part of the whaling gear as
anything else in the boathouse, for the cutting tools had to
be kept sharp enough to shave with.

We gathered up a coil of old inch manila line, put it into
the wagon, and lashed the mast, sail, and sprit to the wagon
box, one end under the seat and the other sticking up and
out astern.

I shut the shed doors, replacing the bar and the heavy
leaning timber that kept them tight enough that the sand
didn't drift through. Inside there was everything you needed
to go whaling except the whale and the bomb gun and the
darting gun, what Father called the bomb gig. Bumb, he
said it. The latter armaments, with their powder, were kept
locked up at home by Father, who knew what boys would
do with them, given the chance, around Fourth of July or
New Year's. The bomb gun was a muzzle-loader; the darting
gun was a harpoon with a short gunbarrel, to fire a bomb into the whale when the harpoon struck his hide. Greatuncle
Sylvester didn't approve of either weapon.

Under the wagon seat was an old carpetbag from our attic, with my clothes, food, and traps. Nat was sailing light --
underdrawers and shirt combinations, old cotton shirt without a collar, an older coat, a pair of canvaseen trousers, his
pipe, and no tobacco. Most of his outfit was hand-me-down
from his father, but so was mine. As for the rest, "The Lord
Will Provide," Nat said. He had a habit of taking the Name in
vain, something he'd picked up working in the store in the
Harbor. It was my Christian duty to say something about it,
but I couldn't seem to.

Nat took the reins, and I dozed after we had jolted down
the deep cut through the bluff at the Highlands out onto
Napeague Beach. There was breeze enough to keep most of
the bugs away, out of the southwest, but not enough to
cause us to fret much about the sloop. We made the Station
away past midnight, put Ranger into the lean-to stable be-

hind the boathouse, and walked down onto the beach. We could make out the shape of the sloop, riding to her anchor right where I'd left her. We turned in; George stirred but didn't wake.

A clatter at the stove routed us out in the morning. George was cooking our breakfast, corn in Egypt -- pork-chops, hash, mince pie, coffee, bread, jam, and butter. We could see the sloop through the windows on the beach side, now riding bow to us and to the surf. The wind had come around northwest. Clear weather and a breeze, that means, and the wind off the land flattens down the surf, not that there was much. We ate fast, and talked of what we would do that morning.

"Mainly, you've got to get her out of here and around Montauk while you can," George told us. "That means get-ting the stub of that mast out and your rig in, and some caulking and maybe some more pumping. This breeze, you'll have to get out of here around noon to catch the flood at the Point before dark. Full sea's about seven. Otherwise you'll have to spend the night either anchored in under the beach or running off and on, and no offense is intended but I don't think you ought to be doing either, not alone and with a jury-rig."

Neither did I; in fact I felt a little funny in the belly at the possibility: "You're not coming with us?"

"Not by a damned sight. I've got more to do than fool around all summer on something like this."

"That's your sloop, as much as mine, or ours."

"I know it. But I'll make you a proposition. You get her back up on the Bay, and get her rigged proper, and want to do some fishing with her, I'll take twenty-five per centum off your net for the first season, my lay, and call her yours, and call it quits. That agreeable to you?"

It was, and we fed and tethered out Ranger. Then we carried out traps down from the wagon and loaded the dory. George waited for a slatch of smooth water following three seas a bit bigger than the general run before shoving us in. "Pull," he grunted, and we were off, Nat and I each with a pair of oars and George steering over the stern, a single oar held in the shallow cut at the top of the transom by the pressure of his right forearm.

The sloop had taken on some water during the night, but she did no more than roll a bit as we swung aboard and let the dory drift back on her painter. We knocked out from belowdecks the wedges around the stump of the mast where it went through the deck. The butt of the mast, though, had been squared off where it fit into the step. We could wiggle the stump like a loose tooth, but she'd take some pulling. "Blind wedges in there," George grunted. "Give me room to swing." He struck the mast a horizontal blow with his ax, followed by another upward, neatly chipping away the pine to leave a lip about a foot and a half above the step. We used two hatchboards, one as a fulcrum and the other as a lever fitted into the lip, and the stub rose up easily. Free of the step, we swung the butt aft and lowered it into the bilge. In the step-hole, as George had predicted, were four narrow bits of tapered hardwood, big ends down: blind wedges. "Look here." He held up a tarnished copper coin, and then rubbed it against his sleeve. "An English penny, 1885, and that tells you when she was built, if not exactly where. Didn't bring her the luck it was supposed to, though."

The new mast was stepped, and it swayed, being considerably smaller around than the old. The wedges wouldn't be enough to clamp it in place at the deck level. At its butt, though, it fit nicely into the step. We'd put the penny back.

"Not much of a rig for something the size of this," George said. "You're no longer'n a whaleboat, the same length, but it'll take a good deal more to drive this." We unrolled the sail and the sprit dropped back. George went ashore for more light line, some blocks, and a small jib, all from the collection of flotsam and jetsam every Station had at the back of the boathouse, except when the District Superintendent made his quarterly rounds. Then they had to move it out and hide it, and move it back in afterward. We unstepped the mast again, and set up the running rigging. She would be all right if we didn't press her, George said; there was nothing left worth using of the tarred manila shrouds that once took the strain off her mast. We'd cut free what of them was left, and were squaring off the stump of the bowsprit, just for looks, when we heard a long Hellooo and saw a man standing on the bank alongside the Station, waving his hat. Nat volunteered to pump the sloop while George and I went ashore to see who it was.

Chapter
II
Around Montauk

He came down the beach to help drag the dory up, and I recognized Charles Stuart Homidy -- clawhammer coat, vest with gold chain and moose tooth, paunch, and the usual ratty Homidy whiskers. He was an East Hampton man, around Father's age, fifty or thereabouts, but no friend of his. "There's something about those Homidys," Father said, and he was right. They'd come to Long Island just before 1700, maybe thirty years after everybody else. If that weren't enough, nobody knew where they'd come from, though the story went that they, the Homidys, knew, the secret being passed down from generation to generation in the male line. It was pretty much thought they were of French origin, their name maybe being from L'Hommedieu or something of the sort, though some held they were gypsies. They married into the other families, but they remained the same, mechanics and windmill makers and gunsmiths, farming and fishing and whaling only incidentally, sticking to themselves and their precious secret, wearing a family face that couldn't be mistook. There was Patience Mulford Homidy, a widow twenty years when she went up around

Albany, and stopped at an inn up on the Hudson somewhere and saw a portrait and fainted dead away. 'Twas her
husband's spitting image, except for the old-time clothes. It
turned out to be the innkeeper's wife's great-grandfather, a
Homidy who'd moved or been run out at the time of the
French wars and who must have been great-great uncle to
Patience's departed, who was Thomas Jefferson Homidy,
another sample of their queerness, Thomas Jefferson being
no more popular in these parts in the early years of the nine-
teenth century than Charles Stuart had been in the seventeenth.

We explained what we were up to and you could see
right away that, being a Homidy, he was calculating how he
could get involved in it. "You say you were on the way to
stay with the Strattons, at Third House, my boy? As I am
wending my way to the Point, booted but not spurred
aboard my faithful plug, there to transact some business
with the Light House Service, in reference to the repair of
the intricate and costly mechanism which rotates the Fres-
nel lenses of the coastal Cyclops, it would be an easy matter
for me to leave word at Third House of your whereabouts,
and perhaps I will observe your passage around Montauk
from my aerie above Turtle Hill, known to the resident red-
men as Wamponamon and immortalized by Whitman,
great bard for all that he is a Sodomite, and run out of
Southold for it, as all the North Fork knows, in his 'Seawanhaka.' " We had heard about Whitman at the Institute,
some, and I had thought he was a native-born American.

There was more of this as we walked up to the Station, a
fogbank of oration hiding a mind that, as Father said, would
rather connive for fifty cents than work honestly for half as
long for five dollars. Mr. Homidy followed us into the boathouse, and seeing nailed to the walls the nameboards of the
schooner Rose Brothers and the ship Margaretha, began to
describe the wrecks in detail. George, who had been on
hand for one of them, and I, knew that what sounded like

the deposition of an eyewitness was not. Through the open doors I could see north across the pines to Napeague Harbor, where a piledriver was driving spilings, lifted by last winter's ice, back into the bottom off the Falcon works. There would be a thump, and then a little puff of steam, not much bigger a cloud than a Dutchman's breeches, then a thump, then another puff, and a thump, and a puff, and, the distance being a mile or more, you couldn't tell which puff belonged with which thump.

Puff was Charles Stuart Homidy's nickname. Puff he had been since his first day at the school Down Hook in East Hampton, back in the '40s, when the old maid teacher asked him his name and he piped up:

"Charles Stuart Pufferson Homidy, Puff by Name and Huff by Nature. Takes twelve barrels of water to make a steamboat run; Elephant tool to make your Grandma come."

He was thrashed within an inch of his life and sent home; they wouldn't let him back for another term. I suppose his older brothers had put him up to it. Only the winter before, at an oyster supper in Clinton Hall, Mr. Homidy's family inclinations had made a show of themselves again. After the meal, a dozen or so old whalemen had gathered at one long table, and begun to gam over their coffee. We heard tales of swamped boats, smashed oars, men drowned. Nantucket sleighrides so fast boats came right out of their paint, and there'd be a paint-boat bobbing in the wake. Wrecks. Cannibals. Charles Pufferson sat more and more uneasy. He'd never made a voyage, and of all the men at the table, he alone had never been in the boat when a whale was ironed off the beach here. Not his fault, to be sure, just chance. Nobody thought him a coward; the Homidys had a whaleboat, one of the three East Hampton crews, but they hardly ever killed a whale, didn't really know how to, and the few times they had, Charles hadn't happened to be along.

The tales grew livelier. A bunch of us youngsters crowd-

ed closer, and the ladies stopped their chatter at the other
tables to listen, too. There was a pause, and Mr. Homidy
coughed to get attention. He slowly reached around into his
pistol pocket, flipping up his coattails and leaning forward.
His right hand came up slowly and dropped a something,
smooth yet shriveled, dark, two or three inches wide and
four or five inches long, a bag perhaps, yes, maybe skin, a
gasp went up as several of the ladies guessed it might be
some sort of scrotum, an animal perhaps, certainly not a
whale but something else.

"Ye know what that is?" No one spoke. "That, gentlemen, is a beavertail, captured just over the New Hampshire
line from our North Woods hunting camp, near the conflu-
ence of the Dead and Swift Diamond Rivers, in that tract of
wilderness known to students of the late Daniel Webster as
the Dartmouth College Grant." And he was off, couldn't be
stopped, on his own tale of adventure, the hero being himself, and beavertail became a local watchword.

Mr. Homidy walked down the beach with us, talking all
the way. He helped drag the dory toward the water, but he
didn't get his feet wet. "I shall see you at Montauk, d.v.," he
shouted. I knew what that meant; perhaps the Homidys
were secret Catholics, as some believed. He was out of sight
behind the beachbanks, riding off toward Montauk, before
we reached the sloop. It was noon and hot, and we were in a
sweat to get under way.

With the mainsail up and the sheet free, we bent on the
jib and hoisted it. George got back into his dory and drifted
clear. "You've got my anchor," he observed as we were
stowing it on deck, one fluke over the rail. "Keep her, but
don't lose her." I trimmed the sheets, and we paid off on the
port tack, headed toward Montauk, Nat at the tiller. We tin-
kered with the sails until all was full and pulling, made the
running rigging fast, and settled down, jogging along to the
eastward in the gentle breeze, following the beach and the
breakers, each long low swell raising us up gently and low-

ering us down again. We were inside the bar, and, as always, we felt like we were above the level of the beach, as if it were all downhill from us to the wash along the breakers, a little dizzying.

Nat and I talked about the summer. We'd try to fish the sloop, if Father would let me. Ice we could probably get from E.B. Tuthill at his new dock on Fort Pond Bay, around the Point, and we could ship the fish to market through him, too. We could handline, and use one of Father's gillnets, and maybe even borrow his haulseine. We'd need a smaller boat, a sharpie, and other gear.

We were past the first hill at Montauk, Nominicks, in short order. This was the old boundary of Montauk, and once the easterly limit of East Hampton Town. The four-rail cattle fence followed the line north from Nominicks to the bay at Waterfence, east of Goff Point and Napeague Harbor. It turned east below the hill to angle across to the ocean past First House, Conklin's. In the yard there, a woman was hanging wash on the line, chickens moving around her feet. We eased a bit offshore, the rising bluffs indicating bad bottom. Four or five miles east, just visible as we passed the seaward opening of a long swale, was Stratton's, Third House, with the highest hill in Indian Field behind it. Finally we passed Turtle Hill, what Mr. Homidy called Wamponamon, the great easy upswelling of earth bearing on its back Montauk Light, and rounded up under the Point, to sail north-northeast, still on the port tack. A mile or so past the Light and inside Block Island Sound, we came about for the first time and headed back, close-hauled on the starboard tack.

It was dusk by the time we came up to Coal Bins, just past North Bar and a quarter-mile from the Light. We made fast to the little Government dock, a line to a stake on the beach to hold the sloop off and stop her from grinding against the spiles in the surge. We were around Montauk, snug enough as long as it didn't blow. Behind us, along the

South Shore, there wasn't a place to be as safe until you got to some of the inlets through Great South Beach, fifty or sixty miles west, and they were only safe entrances in the right weather for those with local knowledge, which we didn't have. We sat on deck and smoked our pipes, feeling a good deal less anxious than we had in a while, before going ashore to bag a late supper from Keeper Jim Scott's wife at the Light.

I woke up late the next morning, seven o'clock or so; we'd stayed at the Light until near midnight. It was foggy, what little air there was moving from the east; the steam hooter was sounding every thirty seconds, mournful and low. Fuel for it was the reason Coal Bins was named what it was. Nat slept on. I lay there a few minutes, getting more comfortable on the hard wooden bunk and pulling my blanket around me against the damp, and thought about the sloop. Who'd built her? Who'd lost her? Was he still alive? Likely not. I shivered. We'd found some soggy clothing jammed behind the cabin sheathing, and thrown it overboard, and there were a few letters and papers in the bilge after we'd pumped her dry. They'd been too wet to handle; with this weather, it was a question when they would dry. I wondered what the papers would tell us.

I rolled out, got bacon and a potato, and juggled them, the frying pan, a mug, and the coffeepot over to the dock; made a fire on the beach, and had breakfast. The loom of the sun could be seen through the fog; it would burn off. Sunday morning, the first in a long time when I would not have gone to church, barring when I was sick. Even bunker fishing last summer, we didn't fish Sundays of course, but came in to Promised Land and walked home for church and dinner, if we were close enough, or went into Providence or Whitestone or wherever we happened to be near and tied up so whoever wanted to could go to church. If there wasn't a Presbyterian one handy, Father and I stayed, quiet, on the vessel. He'd read in the Bible he kept alongside the tide tables and Coast Pilot in the wheelhouse. It was strange to be sitting on the beach and knowing you weren't going to church, couldn't, considering the closest one was close to twenty miles away unless you counted the Baptists' on Block Island, and could do just about anything you wanted to. I'd have to go over to Third House, a walk of two miles, and let the Strattons know what I was up to, but that was the only obligation I was under. I scrubbed out the frying pan with sand, rinsed it and the mug, and left them and the coffeepot on a timber next to my fire, ready for Nat to use, before starting.

Some of Mr. Benson's fifteen hundred sheep were grazing back of Money Pond, looming up suddenly in the mist. They were fresh-sheared and more foolish-looking than ever. Nat had told me shepherds performed with their animals, but looking at these beasts, all be-shat, I couldn't believe it. Strange he'd spread such stories, his father tending sheep and all. I'd gone about a mile when I came around a bend and saw up ahead, at the turn-off for Oyster Pond, Charles Puff Homidy, back-to, off his horse and closing the gate. He'd swung back up into the saddle and around before he saw me, and looked surprised.

"Ah, good morning, Jeremiah Huntting Dimon. You are, I see, on your way to Third House to make your explanations to our mutual friends and relatives, the Strattons; I am on root to George Washington's noblest local monument, the Montauk Light, built during the Administration of the Father of His Country. I am also, you see, taking the long way around." This was true; he must have come through Indian Field, a mile or two out of his way. He never was one for the direct. I hadn't known we were related, through the Strattons, either, but we all were, if you looked hard enough, and sometimes it didn't pay to look, and find you had kin you didn't want to claim.

He reined in, and I climbed up on the fence. It was a treat to hear him talk, no matter what you thought of him, and he looked to be primed this morning. There were clayey stains on the knees of his britches; maybe he'd been praying back in there.

"Would you like a Sunday sermon? You need not feel embarrassed; the Reverend Charles Stuart Pufferson Homidy -- yes, I know you call me that -- will preach on the mote in thy neighbor's eye, and the beam in thine. Now, you know what a mote is, do you not? A speck, not something around a castle. Good. Now, there are differences about the beam, and having no Greek, no Latin, and less Hebrew, I will assume that the Good Lord meant a large piece of wood, perhaps a chip, presumably not from the True Cross.

"If it were not so, he would have told you. What we are getting at, young man, is a certain look of superiority I have often detected in the eyes of those of your tender years, looking upon their ravaged elders, like myself; a look of superiority half-buried beneath a veritable logjam of beams in their own innocent orbs. To get down to specifics, when you saw me coming through that fence, you, with all the wisdom gained whilst dallying in the Groves of Academe at Bridgehampton -- yes, I know all about you -- decided that there was something wrong, it having occurred to you that going around through Indian Field was not the fastest way to get from Third House to the Point.

"It has not yet dawned upon you, young man, that a straight line is always the shortest but not necessarily the best way of getting between two points, in this case Stratton's and the Point itself. It has not yet dawned upon you neither that no two people upon the face of God's earth think alike, or act alike, and that it is God's design that this be so. It is His design, too, that we be pretty much what other people think we are, or fear we are."

"I am what I am," said Charles Stuart Pufferson Homidy, "because that is what people expect me to be, and you are what you are because people expect you to be your father's son, quiet, know-it-all, big enough to pull an oar but not so big as to get in fights over your size; high cheekbones like an Indian -- ever wonder where they came from? -- but pale blue eyes and light hair; half-educated, hard-driving, like enough a Good Templar of a member of the Band of Hope; a bit of a prig in any case. You will be what people expect you to be, a farmer and a fisherman with investments, an elder of the Presbyterian Church, just as I am what people expect me to be, that is, another Homidy, a Falstaff if you like. Thus endeth the sermon for today. Let us raise our voices in Hymn Number Three Hundred and Forty-One, 'How Beauteous Are Their Feet, Who Stand on Zion's Hill, Who Bring Salvation on Their Tongues, and Words of Peace Reveal.' " Mr. Homidy shook his reins, kicked his mare in the ribs, and rode off into the fog. I sat for a bit on the fence; he'd taken the wind out of my sails in a way nobody ever had before. Then I climbed down and headed for Third House.

There were guests, city people, sitting in rockers on the porch running around the ground floor of the old two-story-and-a-half building, so I went around to the kitchen door. Inside, the cooks were hard at it, making Sunday dinner. Mrs. Stratton, Aunt Glo, said she was pleased to see me, and in time for dinner too.

A girl I hadn't seen before, my age, appeared in the doorway and threw a basinful of dishwater out into the yard, square across my bow. She turned and went back in without a smile, tall, straight-backed, long brown hair gathered at the nape of her neck, dark-complected, brown eyes, full lips. Mrs. Stratton saw me staring at her and laughed. "That's Diana. Our huntress. Look out she doesn't tommy-hawk you." Diana turned and looked levelly out through the doorway at her mistress, then went back to her scrubbing.

"Shouldn't tell you this," Aunt Glo said, puffing a bit as we walked through the house looking for her husband, for she was stout, "but Jim Hall's boys nailed her in the necessary last week. Kicked her way out through the west wall;

she'd have killed them if she could have caught them. Sam thrashed 'em both, but he couldn't very well do anything to her. Indian she is, or mostly, a Fisher and a niece of the Occums. Born in Indian Field, but raised over in Connecticut after her mother died. She's like a lot of them; they think they're going to win their case against Mr. Benson, and all come back here to live." Aunt Glo sighed. "She's a worker, though, for all her peevishness."

I ate at the table nearest the kitchen, with the Strattons, and was introduced around. I felt shabby. There were the de Rhams and the Jefferyses, from New York and with a lot of money, and some others whose names I didn't catch. Two dozen guests in all, counting another girl about my age, this one small, fair-skinned, with dark hair and round face. Diana the Huntress waited on table, silent and quick. My face got hot when she leaned across with a platter and her arm brushed mine. As we ate, Mr. Stratton answered questions from the men about his duties. They were overseeing the cattle, anywhere from two to six thousand a season, sent on Montauk each spring by farmers from as far west as Good Ground; Tuesdays and Fridays riding among them, tending the Fatting Field, Bull Pasture, and Calf Pasture fences; making sure the Montauk Indians, such of them as were in residence illegally, did not improve upon their ancient right of gathering and selling the wool caught on twigs and branches, by pulling it off the sheep, now owned by Mr. Benson, who indeed owned most of Montauk and was the Strattons' landlord and employer. The talk turned to his purchase of most of Montauk at the partition sale in '79, of the Indians' suits against him, and of Austin Corbin's plans for a great port at Fort Pond Bay.

The white men who'd settled East Hampton had, in 1660, twelve years after their arrival, bought the best part of Montauk for a hundred English pounds, payable at ten pounds a year for ten years, in corn, four shillings a bushel, which was about twice what we were getting a bushel now in 1887, and perhaps an indication of trimming on the part of our ancestors, or in wampum, six beads to a penny, no glass allowed. As the Proprietors of Montauk, the purchasers and their heirs had, with the East Hampton Town Trustees acting as their agents for a good deal of the time, owned Montauk for more than two centuries. About the time I was born, put up to it by Mr. Benson, though Mr. Stratton didn't mention that, a few of the heirs -- there were hundreds by this time, their shares all reckoned up in shillings and pence the old way -- had gone to law to force a sale. A judge had been found who ruled, finally, that such an arrangement was contrary to progress, foreign to the American way of doing business, and unthinkable in this day and age, and Montauk was auctioned to Mr. Benson, all ten thousand acres for $151,000. The heirs went off, some of them, happy with their cash. Father wasn't; he got around three hundred dollars, and wouldn't have taken that except it wouldn't have done any good not to, and still figured he owned a share of Montauk, and nobody was going to tell him he couldn't gun there. But the Indians, who had been allowed to stay in Indian Field under the old arrangement with the Proprietors, soon found out about progress and this day and age.

"Indians don't think the way we do," Mr. Stratton observed, leaning back in his chair and unbuttoning his vest. "They've signed all sorts of papers and don't have a leg to stand on. They keep coming back, and expect to settle in again just like nothing had happened. Indian givers, pure and simple. You feel sorry for them but when you get down to it they are not exactly the noble red men their ancestors were. Most of these Montauks so-called are no more Indian than I am, or at least not much more, and some of them is real tarbabies." Diana was bringing the coffeepot around, and for a moment I figured she'd pour some down the back of Mr. Stratton's fat neck. I remembered what Mr. Homidy had said about my cheekbones.

Mr. Stratton went on: "You go to that Shinnecock Reservation over at Southampton. There's not a one of them can speak any more Injun than mux or wampum or firewater, and one of those Geronimo Apaches would have them all for breakfast."

"Do you think Austin Corbin is going to let people like that stand in the way of the Long Island Rail Road, and the American Steamship Company, and the New York, Montauk & European Railway and Steamship Company, and a Port of Entry here?" he went on, getting a little wrought up. "Not in a million years! He's in with the Duke of Sutherland, and John Starin, men like that, A.P. Blake even, and inside of a couple of years we'll have the railroads and docks and you'll be able to get on the cars in London, ride to Milford Haven in Wales, get aboard a liner, charge across the ocean, get off here, climb back on a train, and be in New York all inside a week. You figure a day's steaming saved, and all that coal, and the time that's money for the kind of man who'll be traveling on those ships, important people, and the freight and all, and you can see that a bunch of mangy quarterbreed Indians is not going to stand in the way." His audience nodded; his point about important men had registered with the important men at the table. Someone in the kitchen snorted; Diana, most likely.

The important men sat on the verandah later smoking, and the women rocked. The fog was mostly gone, and the wind had gone around southwest and picked up. The Strattons had heard about the sloop from Mr. Homidy, of course. "We'd have been glad to have you with us, not that we really need any help, but if you'd rather go off on the water that's all right, too," Mr. Stratton said. "One less mouth to feed." I told him about meeting Mr. Homidy that morning, and he looked thoughtful: "Coming out by Oyster Pond, eh? He left here early, while I was at chores in the horse barn. Strange he'd go that way."

I headed back to the Point to walk off my dinner. The Strattons, and the girl from dinner, waved goodbye from the porch. Diana Fisher was nowhere in sight. A killdeer ran ahead as I cut across the home pasture toward the road, dragging one wing and going kill-dee, kill-dee to toll me away from her nest in the short grass.

Nat had traded an hour's chopping and splitting driftwood for the Block Island fishermen at their shanty down the beach for a pair of lobsters -- Sabbath-breaking, he observed with satisfaction -- and we had them for supper, roasted on the beach. We turned in early, figuring on a start first thing in the morning.

While we were getting breakfast Monday, we saw the people from the Light all hurrying over the crest of Turtle Hill, toward the beach at Turtle Bend. We took the skillet and coffeepot off the fire and went after them. The Block Islanders, who had been about to leave, saw something was wrong and came with us.

We could see, from the hill, a pair of heavy trap sharpies anchored under the bluff, deep-laden with stakes. The pound-net crews were doing what they did each summer, rebuilding the fishing stands, flimsy piers really, for the city sports to cast from for bluefish and bass later in the season. It fit in with their own stake-driving for the big bay fish traps; the stands went in just after their own stakes. Men from the pound-net crews were standing with the Scotts around two shapes on the cobble beach.

As we got closer, I could see the shapes were bodies, as I'd guessed from the way the watchers stood, still and stiff on the windward side, hands together in front in awkward fashion. The bodies were twenty feet or so apart, dressed in shirts and trousers, no shoes and what flesh was in sight a coffee-with-a-lot-of-milk shade. Getting closer, they looked puffed and sort of pitted. I couldn't tell if they were face down or face up. One had light hair and the other's was kinky. A Negro. Nat walked up the beach and threw up. I knew without thinking that these were the previous owners, or at least the crew, of the sloop. Their sloop. Captain Scott had sent back for a horse and cart, and the bodies were roll-ed onto an old sail and bundled into the cart. The white man had had an empty knife-sheath hanging from his belt at the small of his back, sailor-fashion.

"I suppose," Captain Scott said, "that we had just as well send them off to Amagansett or East Hampton as send a message to the minister to come all the way on Montauk to bury them. I don't want them in the icehouse for two days, I know that." He decided to take them himself, and arrange for their burial. The pound-net crews told how they'd found the two when their sharpies came around the Point in tow of Grimshaw's steam launch.

Nat was apologizing for having been sick as we climbed back aboard the sloop: "Not that I'd never seen a body be-fore," he made sure to tell me. I'd felt less repulsed than in-terested, having seen a man's carcass before but none that had been in the water for a week or more in warm weather, as these probably had. It was hard to look at without im-agining it happening to yourself. Though if I'd drowned back there in Hook Pond in May, they would have dragged and got me up before I began to spoil; there'd have been a good many tears shed over what would have been a fairly handsome corpse. I choked up a little at the thought. In this case, when Nat and I were probably the heirs of two people we'd never seen alive and would never see again, unless we met in the Great Beyond, the sight had been disturbing. But not sickening; even the smell, sort of sweetish. I'd never been bothered much by gutting deer and dressing ducks and skinning muskrats, or butchering hogs and grinding sausage meat or killing an old horse. I got it, I suppose, from Mother, who'd as soon drown a bagful of kittens as not -- just a job that had to be done, not for pleasure like the wicked Land brothers who'd hung a mealsack full of live kittens off the clothesline and let go at it with their duckguns from thir-ty paces; and from Father, with his ship's doctoring and tooth-pulling. Not to speak of cutting-in on a whale, with guts big enough to crawl around in and blood enough to float a vessel, running through arteries a foot across.

We caught the last of the flood and headed north-north-west toward Shagwong Point. A pair of Noank sloops and a small schooner passed close aboard as we came up inside Shagwong Shoal. A mile or more south, away up on the hill back of Big Reed Pond, a man was digging, gravel showing gold-yellow against the green spring grass of Indian Field. His horse was tethered to a crabapple tree on the skyline, black against the morning light. Too far to tell, for sure, but he looked like Mr. Homidy, thigh-deep and going at it fast. "Six feet long and six feet deep and three foot across, maybe?" Nat joked. "More likely some of that Amistad silver he's after." The Amistad had anchored off Culloden Point about fifty years back, the cook and captain killed by her cargo of slaves and the rest of the crew set adrift. A Revenue cutter took her and sent the blacks back to Africa, but we still heard of buried treasure. That was why they called it Money Pond, below the Light; there was supposed to be some in it. The Pond was supposed to be bottomless, too, and I'd never been able to figure out how the two things jibed.

We left Montauk behind and headed toward Gardiner's Island, full of talk about pirates and treasure. Nat, his father working on the Island, knew its stories -- Kidd and Bradish; the Spanish and French and mulattoes who'd tied John Gardiner, who cared for young squaws and the bottle and precious little else, to a mulberry tree, and Paul Williams, the pirate Block Islander. Nat, like a good many others, was sure that the Gardiners hadn't turned in to the law all Kidd had left in their keeping.

"Stands to reason. They admit they've got some rings from him, and some cloth-of-gold," Nat said. "You'd have to be a pluperfect fool to believe they wouldn't have hung on to more than that. Money talks, and they'd get away with it where a poor man wouldn't. Look at them. Top of the pile for two or three hundred years and there's some of us been on the bottom all that time, and some of us on the bottom are as much Gardiner as the Gardiners.'' Taking into account Lord John's squaws, and human nature, and marriages, there were no doubt Long Islanders of a good many shades who could claim, if they knew, Lion, the first Gardiner, who'd been a solider in the Low Country wars and come to America to build a fort at Saybrook, as an ancestor. Nat, though, probably didn't have Gardiner in him. His mother was a Long Swamp Lester, red-headed and handsome and recognizable as one as far as you could see her. Nat was light-haired, almost white, like a good many in his father's tribe. Mother said he did not have a strong jaw. He was lighter-built than me, sloping in the shoulders and his face showed marks from the smallpox epidemic of '80. He'd lost a sister in that. He was bright and handy, though, for all that Mother claimed a phrenologist would have a deal to say about him, and not much of it good. It wasn't the bumps on the head she objected to, though; it was his family.

The east side of Gardiner's Island, rocky beach and clay bank, slid by. There was no one in sight, the Manor house and outbuildings being across the Island on the sunny south slope facing Springs. We could see cattle, horses, and sheep in the pastures the other side of Tobaccolot Pond. Fish hawk nests showed in some of the trees, and there were more of them down on the sand on the long low spit of Gardiner's Point, piles of branches and grass, some of them high as a man's chest and, at this time of year, all with eggs or fresh-hatched young, no doubt. We rounded the north end of the Island and its Lighthouse in mid-afternoon, coming about and heading down toward Fireplace Point at Springs. We tacked again at Lion Head Rock and made for Cedar Island. We fetched the Northwest Harbor entrance there late in the afternoon, in time for the first of the flood again, and beat in close to the granite Lighthouse. We began to see oyster-ground stakes. A schooner was working the grounds between Major's Cove and the Hog Neck side, over by the old anchorage of whaling days, what they called Indian Jail. They'd anchor there, outward bound, until the Indians in the crew sobered up. The schooner's crew was using coffee-mill winches to bring the heavy dredges to the rail.

"Oysters R not in season," Nat remarked. "They must be going to move them somewhere." Oystering, on a big scale, was new on the bays, and we didn't know much about it, except that it was a complicated sort of farming operation, and we weren't crazy about farming, even on the water. "Lots of money in that, and in those grants of oysterland," Nat said. "But it's all going to them that has it already, and the politicians." Since '84, the Suffolk County Oyster Commissioners had been granting underwater lots at a dollar an acre and four acres per person. "They got the cooks on the dredges and their wives and the deckhands and the president's mother and all her cousins signed up at four acres a head," Nat growled. "A Chimborazo steal." Sometimes he talked like an Anarchist.

We worked her in to Sag Harbor and tied up at Uriah Gordon's boatshop on Conkling's Point, off Bay Street. The sun had set by the time things were shipshape, and we were hungry, having missed breakfast in the excitement and not having felt much like eating for a spell afterward. Nat said we ought to go ashore and eat a real meal, and led the way to Mrs. Hetty Mack's Fort on West Water Street, a resort I'd seen from the street but never would have dared enter alone. He was greeted with a pat on the back and a wink, from Mrs. Mack; my introduction was met with a head-back laugh and a "From Amagansett, I presume?" I tried to figure out what was funny about being from Amagansett as she led us to a table. That "I presume" was from Stanley meeting Livingstone in Africa; it had been a joke since the year I was born, and about time to turn it in for a new one.

Grocery stores in East Hampton and Bridgehampton sold whiskey by the drink sometimes when the Town of East Hampton or Southampton had voted wet, and out the back door when they hadn't, by the bottle. The Fort stocked some groceries, canned stuff mostly and the sort of thing would raise a thirst on a drowning man, herring and hard-boiled eggs, but that end of it came second to the whiskey business. The restaurant part of the Fort was a half-dozen round tables, across the room from the bar, served from a kitchen at the back of the building. The stairway to the top floor was next to the kitchen door: "Rooms upstairs!" Nat whispered and smirked, and I leered back at him.

We had steak and potatoes and a schooner of lager beer each. Nat invested twenty cents in a fistful of cigars, and we leaned back and smoked after supper, feeling man-sized. There were two silent men standing at the bar, being served when they'd push their glasses at her by Mrs. Mack, but otherwise the place was empty. "You should see it on a Saturday night," said Nat, a bit sheepish, afraid the Fort had not lived up to his stories. "It's worth a trip. Like they say, if you could be an Irishman just one Saturday night you'd never want to be a white man again."

Uriah hailed us from his shop on our return. "Where in thunderation did you get that?" he shouted, waving his arm toward the dock and the sloop. "Never seen one north of Charleston. Saw you from the house, when you come in, and had to toddle down and have a look. Where you been?" We mumbled, embarrassed at having to tell, and he said, "You're young Bennett, Nat; who's that with you?" Nat told him and Mr. Gordon laughed, the second time I'd been laughed at in the Harbor inside of two hours.

"When you see your father, tell him old Gordon still wants to know why he had that whaleboat built in New London, and not in the Harbor. 'Twould have been the last I built." Father had wanted something different from the usual Gordon model whaleboat -- more sheer -- and had taken his trade to New London. The boatbuilder didn't mind, you could tell, and he asked us inside: "Come on in, and see what's left of the boatbuilding trade in Sag Harbor."

We told him about salvaging the sloop, and the bodies, and Nat fetched the papers we'd found in the wreck. Mr. Gordon cleared a space on his desk at one end of the cluttered shop, and laid the papers, dry now and stuck together, in the light of an oil lamp. "You'll want me to make up spars, and help you rig her, I suppose?" he clucked as his stubby fingers fumbled with the sheets. Mr. Gordon was short and pop-eyed, a bit womanish save he was bald and good-natured. "And on credit, too. Well, there isn't much going in my line these days."

Seeing he wasn't getting anywhere, I reached across and unfolded one of the papers, peeling it off from the rest. It was a letter, pencil on ruled paper, a single sheet:

Mathewtown, Gt. Inagua
January 13th, 1887

Flag Fish Company
Gloucester, Massachusetts
United States of America

Gentlemen:

I am in receipt of yours of the 14th of November last and, in response to your inquiry, please be advised that we will be pleased to offer you salt at the previous price per quintal on our pier here, any lighterage and other loading charges to be bourne by you, payment through our New York office subject to terms as per previous arrangements . . .

The letter was signed James D. MacPherson, Agent, Brodie & Bruce Salt Works. The writing was careless. "That's a draft, for a clerk to copy out in ink," Mr. Gordon said. He turned the sheet over. There, so faint and water-washed we had not noticed it, was a sketch map. "Montauk," I said.

"Now you know where they were coming from, most likely, and where they were going. This might tell you why," the old man said, peeling apart two more sheets. These were smaller, and had not been folded. One was covered with ciphering. "Somebody aboard that sloop knew navigation," Mr. Gordon said. The other was blank.

One piece of paper remained. It was part of a letter, ink on both sides of the sheet:

> but on the west side of the Wnd. pass. things remain pretty much status quo ante. Cane industry continues to expand with much land being cleared but until Madrid learns to accept facts and leaves off arbitrary decisions there will be nothing but continual trouble although it is doubtful if matters will get completely out of hand for some time. Economic policy can only cause discontent. Almost ten years now since El Zanjon agreement but the promises have not been kept. End of actual servitude made very little practical difference in the situation. Careful watching may be in order but don't put much trust in what you may hear from H.M. Consul in Habana or Santiago. The Don is getting hardening of the arteries and his heirs will be those who are there with their wits about them when the day comes, and there may be ways to hasten that day. In this regard respectfully suggest inquiries at Vienna might . . .

"Cuba, that's what that's all about," Mr. Gordon said. "Inagua is just across, up from the Windward Passage; you can see Baracoa Mountain from Mathewtown when it's real clear. I was there forty, forty-five years ago, in a salt schooner."

We read on, Nat putting one hand out when I went to turn the sheet over, to make me wait so he could catch up.

> Hayti, on the other hand, is peaceful and in not much worse shape than at any time since the death of the late lamented Faustin I. The govt. has been borrowing, as you know, in Europe; I cannot imagine any Rothschild in his right mind extending credit that direction but there it is. Ulises Heureaux appears doing well across the line in Santo Domingo and talk of annexation by the U. States diminishes. Heureaux borrows too. As it stands, everything in sight here is dicey save the salt at

Gt. Inagua and ordinary investments in these parts might be looked upon with a jaundiced eye, particularly if Cleveland manages to scuttle the tariff and make dealings in the North more interesting from your point of view. These are my opinions; take them for what you will.

Your Obt. Servant,
Franklin Pierce Thompson

"Well, boys, what do ye make of it?"

I looked blank, I guess, but Nat piped up: "He was a business agent, something like that, American, thirty or thirty-five years old if I've got my Presidents straight, and he was writing to his employer, a foreigner, most likely an Englishman."

"Assuming you're right," Mr. Gordon went on, "and that this letter was never delivered, or received, what's left to wonder is how it got off Montauk, and why it didn't go by mail, up from Key West or Nassau by steamer. And who it was going to, that's another question. And why he never got it. Were there any yachts in Fort Pond Bay or thereabouts when you came up today?"

We hadn't seen any yachts, excepting Mr. Gallatin's Bertie, anchored outside Three Mile Harbor as she generally was in summer. We turned in no wiser, Nat and I on the sloop and Mr. Gordon in his house the other side of Bay Street.

In the morning, we commenced refitting. Mr. Gordon found an old mainsail and he dickered with the Rysam sailloft to re-work it for us. We would end up with a shorter boom than what she'd been built for, the foot of the sail laced to it Yankee-style. We'd use the jib from the Napeague Station, and leave the bowsprit a stub. It was a taller rig, but Mr. Gordon said it would do well enough. The job took a week, with all three of us sawing and splicing and fitting. Mr. Gordon had agreed to let us pay for his work and materials after we got to fishing. The last job was the biggest, building a bulkhead, enlarging the hatchway, and splitting the hold fore and aft with another bulkhead and drilling holes through the bottom into half of it, to make a live-well. The weather held clear and cool, and we had a pleasant time.

Chapter
III

Fishing For A Living

It was the 28th of June before we left Sag Harbor, full of hope and armed with the latest Fulton Market quotations. Bluefish were bringing fifteen to seventeen cents a pound, and weakfish eight or ten. We worked the sloop around to Barnes' Hole, north of Fresh Pond, to return the whaleboat gear, load our fishing traps, and say hello to our families.

Father'd just gone east, to get the New Bedford mackerel schooner as he'd planned. As usual, he'd let out a good deal of the farm, keeping the home lot, in corn and potatoes, and some pasturage, to be worked by a hired hand and my brothers. John Chatfield and Elias Osborn Dimon, the youngsters, were in the kitchen with Mother and me; Samuel H., my older brother, was already married, and living down on Atlantic Avenue. My sisters Esther and Anna Elizabeth were in the front room sewing. Or supposed to be.

We talked, and then I headed up Main Street for Mrs. Theodore Conklin's new ice cream saloon and a discussion of fishing prospects with Nat. It was good to be back home, in Amagansett. There were differences between Amagansett, any of the South Shore villages -- East Hampton, Bridgehampton, even little Wainscott and Sagaponack --and the ports, Sag Harbor and Greenport. Here, on toward dark, I could just see the two dusty tracks either side of the long strip of grass down the middle of Main Street, a highway almost as wide as I could throw a baseball. The villages were laid out that way in the beginning. There were ducks and geese and tethered milking cows, by day, on the grass in the middle. There were no streetlamps, as there were in the Harbor. Here, each houselot was a hundred feet or more wide, the big square or saltbox houses set back behind picket fences, barns back of them, plenty of room. In the fall, there'd be giant piles of stove and fireplace wood neatly stacked in the front and side yards. Now, in warm weather, you only needed enough for cooking. In the Harbor, Main Street was only a spit and a stride across, and the houses were jammed in like bunkers in a seine. Most of them didn't have room enough behind for a stable, let alone a proper barn. A good many people over there burned coal for heat, even for cooking, the railroad and the steamers making it easy for them to get. The stores were all pretty much in a bunch, and when you got to the edge of town you knew it. In Amagansett, the village just sort of petered out; it was hard to tell where Amagansett left off, things were strung out so, and our three stores were far apart.

Nat was sitting on the porch of the ice cream saloon. We'd take three gillnets, we figured, with buoys and anchors; Father's two-hundred fathom haulseine; my own thirteen-foot sharpie, what you might call a skiff; handlines for bottom fishing and trolling; my muzzleloader; and a clamrake. Most of the gear was Dimon; Nat and his folks didn't have it to lend, never had. Some of the younger boys listened and made suggestions, which we ignored.

After the first trip down to the sloop the next morning with Ranger and the wagon, I went back for the sharpie while Nat worked the sloop down to Albert's Landing, to be closer to home. We still had no name for her, although we were thinking of calling her the "Discovery." On the last trip home, I unharnessed Ranger, turned him out to pasture, and said good-bye to Mother and my sisters. The boys were out hoeing, sulky at me for going off and leaving them to do it, and I got no more than a wave from them, nor them from me, as I stepped off for a season's fishing. My step was lighter than I felt as I was uncertain about the venture.

The summer passed quickly and we did make some money, even with having to make payments to Mr. Gordon and George Eldredge. Nat and I had some disagreements, neither being captain ("a bad arrangement," Father sent word through Mother), but we never fought. We stuck in the Bay with a few trips around the Point in good weather, and shipped mostly through Ed Tuthill at Fort Pond Bay. He iced and boxed the fish, and sent them over to East Marion in his smack to be picked up by the steamer Shinnecock; she took them to Peck Slip in the East River. Prices held up through the season, although bluefish naturally brought less as more of them arrived from wherever it is they spend the winter. We had some pleasant times, the first being Fourth of July evening, when we anchored in Cherry Harbor off the Gardiner's Island mill, and could see fireworks away up at Greenport and, over the high ground by Green River Road, in the summer colony at East Hampton. Another was in August, when we went back to Coal Bins and spent a day picking blackberries on the hills. Mrs. Scott made some up into pies for us, and put up the rest in quart jars with sugar, pound for pound the old way, for us to enjoy later.

We both fell overboard at different times, and though we both could swim, it was no fun. I had on my usual when I went in, boots, wool trousers and shirt, and a heavy flannel wampus, long-sleeved and hanging down past my boot-tops. The clothes and boots dragged me down, and I swallowed a good deal of water before Nat managed to bring the sloop around and come up on my lee side. As it was, I lost my hat. Nat slipped between the sharpie and the sloop his time, coming alongside, and was bruised up some before I fished him out. Another time, running west past Culloden Point in the dark with the wind over our quarter and the tide with us, we got royally snarled in one of Everett Tuthill's, from over at East Marion's, pound nets. We had to lay out the anchor with the sharpie and haul ourselves clear on it. Everett didn't have his lantern on the offshore end, the way he was supposed to, so we didn't feel too bad about his torn netting.

Some of it was bluefishing with the gillnets in Cherry Harbor or east of Goff Point, or up off Flaggy Hole, setting them and coming back later to lift them, taking out the blue-fish, throwing away the sea robins and bottlefish and once in a while what they called a Democrat, a horned sculpin, ugly critter would give you blood poisoning with his prick-ers if you weren't careful; shaking out the weed and sticks and crabs; and if the weather was right for it, mending the twine as we went along where it had got torn. In between, we would anchor and bottom fish, or troll if it looked right for that.

There was some serious hook-and-line fishing, for por-gies and blackfish and cod, working a couple of handlines apiece and cutting bait. Once or twice, we trolled off the Point for pollock. For three days, we took out parties, sports staying at Third House who'd come over to Tuthill's dock looking for someone to show them how to fish or to fish for them. This was a nuisance, nurse-maiding them and some of them seasick from the time we left the dock, but there was money in it if you could keep your patience. About all we didn't try was swordfishing -- we didn't have an iron along, was our excuse, but we were really shy of going off-shore and staying out there any length of time -- and lobster-ing -- because we had no traps and there wasn't money enough in lobsters to make it worthwhile -- and clamming -- except for food and bait. I like clams but not clamming; you might as well be chopping weeds in a cornfield.

The best of the fishing was hauling the big seine for bluefish and sometimes a few striped bass. We'd pick our weather, and our spot -- off the beach at Cedar Bush, southwest of the fishworks, was a good one -- in the evenings sometimes. First we had to get the seine off the deck of the sloop and into the sharpie, just so, handing it neat and even. We'd row ashore, and make one end of the seine fast to an anchor on the beach. It was waiting, then, with just enough of the sharpie's stern on the beach to hold her. We'd sit and smoke, not saying much, hoping that the terns would come along, diving and screeching to show a bunch of bluefish was moving along. It happened that way a few times, bait driven to the top, jumping to get away from the feeding bluefish, only to be gobbled up by the terns, diving over and over again, so excited they killed and left more bait-fish than they'd ever eat, Nat and I excited too, rowing as hard as we could, the seine lengthening out behind us, to run around the bunch. More often, there'd only be a few terns, and nothing more than a slick on the water, if it were a still evening and calm, to mark the fish below.

Other times, there'd be no sign at all, but we would finally set the seine and haul it just the same, fifteen minutes or so to run it out and around to the beach again and maybe an hour for the two of us to work it ashore, each handling an end, never knowing until the bunt, the bag, in the middle was almost in the wash whether or not we had anything. We got a sharpie-load once; usually we had six or eight fish for our trouble. After the seine had been hauled, it would take us another half an hour to get it back into the sharpie, and, if we weren't going to use it again for a while, another ten minutes to hand it back up on deck from the rowboat. It gave you an appetite.

Nat and I got back to Amagansett for three Sundays; the others we loafed, not from being religious but more because we didn't really need to work seven days a week, and because if we did other fishermen would think less of us. Most of them, the older men, treated us kindly, helping with advice and lending us tools or a hand when we needed it. The only disagreeable times we had were a few with people who had rented Horace Bennett, a second or third cousin of Nat, and his sloop Edith, for the day, or W.L. Talmage and his catboat Millenium, from Springs. They would want to troll right on top of us, when we were lifting a gillnet; they were jealous of anyone catching more than them, and would holler.

For a good deal of the summer, there was cannon-thunder in the distance. The North Atlantic Squadron arrived in Gardiner's Bay, as usual, around the first of July, and practiced with its big guns. The cruiser Atlanta was there, testing a giant eight-inch gun and some smaller ones. She'd run a red flag up at the dip; we'd watch and pretty soon the flag would be two-blocked, hauled up to the yardarm, and there'd be a flash and a cloud of smoke, and pretty soon a rumble. It made you proud to be an American, and didn't seem to hurt the fishing. They did this three or four times a day, until something gave way in the big gun's mechanism and the Altanta went off to have it fixed.

In mid-August, the Grand Army of the Republic, Edwin Rose Post, held a Giant Patriotic Campfire at Fresh Pond. A thousand veterans were expected, and we were hired to ferry people ashore from the steamer, bringing them around from Sag Harbor, and generally lend a hand. They ate and drank beer and sang "Tenting Tonight" and some of them cried, and they had three bands and a high old time all the way around. There were speeches, too, lots of them. One old goat from Hay Ground got going on the Future of the Republic and its Destiny. "The Eagle of the North must spread its wings over the ignorant and afflicted to the South" and so forth. I wasn't listening very careful, and it was a while before I realized he wasn't talking about the War of the Rebellion, but South America. We were a bigger, wiser brother, he said; we'd had to straighten out Mexico once, and no doubt would have to again, and, as for Cuba, that was a relic of the cruelist Papist Empire that ever lived, and if the Cubans couldn't shake off their oppressors, well, then we'd have to do it for them, and we were the boys for the job. I remembered the papers on the sloop, and what the letter'd said about Cuba.

Then he shifted over to Grover Cleveland and the Rebel Flag Order. Back in June out in Wheeling, West Virginia, what the old goat called "Our Loyal Comerades" had refused to march beneath a banner strung over the street that said, "God Bless Our President, Commander in Chief of Our Army and Navy," they were so peeved at him.

His whiskers shook and he waved his arms. "This is what it means, the 'Return of the Democracy.' The flags we bled and died for to win are returned to the Confederates! That and Snivel Service! It's the Grand Old Party for me, the Republicanism of the Republic we fought for." He was more worked up over President Cleveland's pension vetoes than he was over Rebel Flags, though, when you got right down to it. He didn't get much of a hand; a lot of that crowd were Democrats, even if they had fought in the war. A lot of everybody around were Democrats, for all the local joke about the sculpin. The Dimons had belonged to that persuasion, for a long time. They hadn't thought much of the war, and Father had spent most of it in the Pacific, whaling. The speaker wound up with "Maw, Maw, Where's My Paw," about Cleveland's bastard child.

Nat and I got even later. With some of the Springs boys, we rolled a quarter-keg of beer off into the bushes when no one was looking and woke up the next morning feeling muzzy. We had to work, part of the agreement, picking up around the picnic grounds and searching for strayed lambs among the Loyal Comerades. Some of them had gone off into the woods to sleep and missed the steamer. It wasn't much like the Sunday School picnic back there in June.

At the end of August, Father and I had a talk. His fishing was over for the season, and he'd agreed to go temporary keeper of the Georgica Station, Old Captain Forrest wanting to take the winter off and go to California on the cars, to see if he felt like spending his old age out there with his daughters and sons-in-law. They'd been writing, puffing up California, all about oranges and sunshine and no winter. People are like that, they move someplace or do something and nothing will do but everybody else has to do the same; they get like missionaries or Millerites. The Life Saving Crews went on at midnight, September 1st, and naturally enough Father wanted to know what I was going to do. The Institute's fall term was to begin in a month. Father'd liked to have seen me go, but he wouldn't order me.

"Jerry, you're pretty near full-grown now, and you can make up your own mind. You say you want to keep on fishing through the fall with the sloop, and go back to school after Christmas. I say, and I would wager if I was a betting man, that if you don't go back now you'll never go back. You've already got four more years of school than I ever had, though, so I suppose we should be thankful for what we've got. Go a-fishing, if you want." He wasn't one to ramble on, nor argue.

The Discovery -- we'd finally painted the name on her transom -- had been left at Long Wharf, and I went over Monday. There were yellowleg and willet on the big salt meadow back of Goff Point at Napeague, and we were to take a party of Harbor notables over the next morning for a day's shooting. That evening, waiting for Nat to come over from Amagansett, I walked up to Uriah Gordon's house on Bay Street.

"Goff Point, eh?" he said, sliding out a chair for me at his kitchen table. "You know where the name comes from?

Didn't think so, for all you're so smart you're not going back to the Institute." At least, then, I knew who Charles First was, Charles Stuart as in Charles Stuart Homidy? Well, William Goff was one of the Regicide Judges, who'd condemned Charles to be beheaded. Goff had had to run, or lose his own, at the time of the Restoration, in the spring of 1660, and that summer he'd come ashore there. But East Hampton would not hide him, though neither would it hand him over to the government, which was Connecticut then and would be for another four years. Off Goff went, to appear, a generation later and a greybeard, from an attic up in Hadley, Massachusetts, to lead the farmers against King Philip's Indians. "As old as I am now, he was," Gordon said.

"While I'm thinking of Montauk, here's something might catch your fancy. Saved it for you. He handed me a month-old copy of the Sag Harbor Corrector, folded, an inside page out and doubled over:

Fort Pond Bay

Mr. Perry Belmont, the member of Congress from the Suffolk-Queens-Richmond district, says he is at present overrun with missives urging the claims of various points on Long Island for Government largesse. The Peconic River and Brown's Creek waterway improvements are two of the most urgently pressed schemes. East Rockaway and Glen Cove in Queens County want an appropriation for river and harbor work, and are not at all backward about letting the fact be known.

Mr. Belmont speaks of a government breakwater at Fort Pond Bay, near Montauk Point, as one of the most likely of the public works to be brought to the attention of the Congress. The bay in question opens to the north. From northwesterly Boreal attentions it is protected in a measure by the islands in Peconic Bay, but a breakwater is needed to fend off the northeasterly storms. At present, Fort Pond Bay has no commerce whatever and no inhabitants line its shores. Its importance is in the future wholly. It is the proposed terminus of Mr. Corbin's

ocean steamship line which is sure some day to be es-
tablished, bringing England and America one day nearer together, binding closer the Anglo-Saxon cousins.

It is perhaps the most important single scheme af-
fecting the future of Seawanhaka. The scheme would be
from the first a tremendous success. To go all the way to
New York by steamer is as unnecessary as to go from
this side all the way to London Bridge, instead of Liverpool or Queenstown. And the building of a railroad
terminus on the sands of Montauk Point and the vast in-
crease in passenger traffic which would surely result
would benefit the Island greatly.

But Mr. Corbin must abandon all idea of being per-
mitted to buy his steamers in England. His Fort Pond
Bay idea is a good one, and we hope it will go through,
but he must run his ocean ferry with Yankee boats.

I laughed. "That don't sound much like Editor Sleight,
that bit about buying at home; it's generally low tariff, no
tariff with him. And the Tuthills won't like hearing that 'no
commerce whatever and no inhabitants.' A measure of protection from the islands in Peconic Bay, ha. Put Mr. Perry
Belmont and Sleight out there in a dory some day blowing
hard northwest and they'd sing a different song. Mr. Stratton was talking about all this back the end of June, at Third
House."

"Yes, yes, right after you found the sloop," Mr. Gordon
mused. "Did you ever find out any more about those two, on
the beach?" We hadn't, though I'd wondered, in my bunk at
nights. It was as if the Discovery didn't really belong to us,
and it made me uneasy thinking about somebody having
slept in that bunk, and him gone now. Nat had said that
maybe they'd been running away, maybe from the sheriff or
whatever it was they had down at Nassau. Maybe Franklin
Pierce Thompson, if the white man on the beach at Turtle
Bend had been him and not just his messenger, had embez-
zled. There wasn't any money on board, that we knew.
We'd searched her stem to stern one Sunday afternoon, and

had turned up nothing more than rusty fishhooks and odd bits of metal. We'd even shifted the ballast, heavy dark rocks, some kind of broken-up coral I guessed, something I'd heard about but never seen, until we'd looked beneath and through it all.

Chapter IV

A Mishap At Goff Point

Before dawn Tuesday, Nat having come aboard sometime during the night, we took on the shooting party. There were five, a man who kept a drygoods store in the Harbor, the manager of the watchcase factory, his son, who was beginning his third year at Yale that fall, a banker, and Dr. Jermain Fordham. I was impressed by the Doctor. Everybody knew he'd crowned a long career two winters previous by caning Dr. Ludwig Hoff in the Main Street of the Harbor, frightening horses and giving the village enough to talk about for a long time. The German had earned his thrashing by a slander, a double-bore, breech-loading one so to speak, aimed at Dr. Fordham's private and professional life. He'd been telling men in the saloons, which is where he waited for summonses from the afflicted, that Dr. Fordham had violated his Hippocratic oath by inducing an abortion in a young woman whom he had violated in quite another way. To ornament his libel, Dr. Hoff had been saying that the victim was "schwarz, but comely, like in der Solomon-Lieder." He took his beating like a man for all he was a foreigner, and left town as quick as he could.

While we loaded the shooting party's shellboxes, hampers, and patent folding-metal snipe stool, Nat let me know where he'd been the night before. "Do you a world of good, Jerry," he snickered. "You've been getting peckish. A man needs to get his ashes hauled, ever so often." I pretended to pay no attention. Any time I felt like it in the Harbor and had a couple of dollars Nat would do what he called "fix you up with one of Hetty's girls," but it didn't do to think about it.

We were halfway to Cedar Island by sunrise, a lively one with bright ruddy skies to the eastward over Gardiner's Island and Montauk. Yesterday had been clear and cool; now there were thin high clouds, with mare's tails. The wind was southwest, fair for Napeague. "Red sky in the morning," Mr. Masters, the factory manager, observed, "Sailor take warning." We were getting close to the equinox, when the sun crosses the line; line-storm time was drawing nigh, but I wasn't much worried.

It was a pleasant easy sail. The sports, all members of Sag Harbor's Century Gun Club, ladled out yarns about lively doings aboard their houseboat Pastime, moored over in Noyac Creek. She'd been a floating gin mill, used those rare years when both Southampton and East Hampton Towns had voted dry, and there was no place for the bar in French's rum palace on Division Street. French's was split down the middle by the Town line, and ordinarily French would just slide the bar across the room, east when Southampton had climbed aboard the water wagon, and west when East Hampton had. If they were both dry, the Pastime would be anchored out in Shelter Island Sound beyond either Town's jurisdiction, and the rum-hounds would row out, and be rowed in. Gradually the occasions for the Pastime to be navigated into battle against the teetotallers had become rare and she was sold to the Gun Club. The members ripped out her bar, although they did their share of swilling, and put in bunks and a cookstove. I'd never been aboard her, and enjoyed the tales of triples on black duck, retrievers who knew more than their masters about gunning, hornification, and poker hands, although I could make head nor tail of the latter. My folks wouldn't have them in the house, playing cards.

Off Hicks Island we fined up for the Napeague Harbor entrance and tacked in slowly, anchoring in Skunk's Hole, behind Goff Point, in two fathom of water close to the beach. Nat and I stayed aboard, I not caring much for that kind of shooting and Nat ready for some sleep after his night's labors. Three of the men set up little blinds of driftwood and brush a gunshot apart on the beach, sticking the folding decoys up in front, and two of them walked in around the small ponds and marshy spots, putting up birds for the others to stool, and getting some shooting themselves. The first kill, greeted with cheers from the rest the way it always is, was made within a few minutes, by the banker. I baited a handline, to pass half the morning catching a few bottlefish. Nat slept on until eleven o'clock or so, when I was frying up the fish, skinned and rolled in flour, for dinner. He'd never hear you, sleeping when there was work to be done, but his nose would wake him up when there was something good cooking.

We were sitting on deck, next to the firebox, eating the bottlefish like chicken drumsticks in our fingers, that's what they look like cooked that way, when the Phillips steamed in, headed for the Orient Guano Company dock up in the east corner of the harbor, where they'd been driving the pilings the day we met Mr. Homidy at the Life Saving Station.

"Better house your topmasts, call the watch below, and batten down all hatches, boys," her captain shouted as the Phillips passed. "It's going to blow before long."

He was teasing about the topmasts and the hatches and the watch below, knowing we had nothing but the hatches and they not the battening kind, but he meant it about the weather. The wind had dropped out, and the

clouds had taken on an unhealthy copper color, like somebody who's got liver trouble. We had no barometer, but I
guessed the glass would be falling if we had one. We were
rinsing the pan and coffeepot over the side when Nat looked up and jerked his thumb to the southard. The sky there
was darkening considerably; overhead it was bronzish, the
mares' tails having thickened into a solid bank of reddish
cloud. A breath of wind became a gentle breeze, and we
swung to it, bow east. If it was going to storm, there was no
use moving; we were in as safe an anchorage for something
as small as the Discovery as there was around. We took the
sharpie and towed the sloop a bit off the beach, though,
and doubled up on our anchor warp. It commenced to rain
big drops raising a splatter, and our party came down to
the beach lugging their gear and two sacks full of birds.

They grumbled as they came aboard, the first boat-
load, but they knew as well as we did that the weather was
going to act up. The birds had stopped flying altogether
when the wind had dropped; they'd rather run than flush.
It was raining harder when Nat rowed alongside with the
rest of them, Dr. Fordham and Charlie Masters, the college
boy. He passed up two hampers, two shellboxes, and Dr.
Fordham's English ten-bore from the boat. Young Masters
clambered up, and reached back into the sharpie to pull up
his gun, a twelve-gauge Winchester lever action, the new
model. I remember I was thinking that there wouldn't be
room for all of us below and that Nat and I would be left out
in the rain. Masters was leaning over the side when there
was a sharp report and he lurched forward. I was right behind him, and felt my face all damp on one side. Dr. Fordham caught the young man and pushed him toward me,
and I grabbed him, my right palm already bloody where I'd
wiped the side of my face; his blood, not mine. There was a
hole, an inch and a half or two inches wide, in the back of
his coat, below the right shoulder. The opening smoked a
bit, and so did the front of his coat, around a smaller hole,

as I laid him back on the deck. The charge had passed
clean through his shoulder, just below the collarbone. I
guessed what had happened; he'd levered, he'd thought,
all the shells in the magazine out through the shotgun's action, and had miscounted; one remained in the breech, and
had fired when the weapon's hammer caught on the gunwhale of the sharpie.

"I didn't bring my bag, God damn it, We'll have to get
him someplace I can get tools and work on him as quick as
we can, boys," the Doctor said. "Wrap him up, and get me
something I can stop him up with." Nat brought up our
blankets. The drygoods man stripped off his coat, shirt,
and undervest, and tore the vest into strips. Nat and I hurried to make sail, and as we did saw Dr. Fordham rip some
of the undervest-strips into smaller bits, and douse them
with whiskey from a bottle in one of the hampers. There
was less blood than you'd have expected. The boy was conscious, moaning gently and regularly, his face white and
his eyes wide. His father held his hand.

As we got under way, they handed Charlie down
through the hatch, and Dr. Fordham crawled into the cuddy
with him. It was raining harder, blowing marlin-spikes now,
still from the east. There was no use in trying to beat up to
the Guano Company dock; we'd be half-way across the bay
in the time that'd take. The sloop tore out through the entrance, dead before the wind. We took in the jib, and went
just as fast. The wind was backing gradually to the northeast, and Nat began to bring her all the way around to port,
to get the sloop on the other tack. The sea had built up, and
tide being on the ebb and bucking against the wind, and the
boom-end dragged as we slewed around. My heart was in
my mouth; I was fearful we'd be tripped, and capsize. Nat
caught her, though, and we flew along. The three passengers on deck sat between the fishhatch and the cockpit,
drenched regularly by the water we took on deck going up
over a short steep sea and nosing into the back of the next.

At the Three Mile Harbor channel, Mr. Masters crawled forward, and stuck his head into the cuddy. He backed out,
and shouted, "He's begun to pump blood, and Dr.
Fordham's got his fingers in there for a clamp. He says, take
her up to the Head of the Harbor and we'll get him ashore
and under cover." I had the tiller now, and nodded. There
were houses closer, but the Head of the Harbor was nearer
to East Hampton, and Dr. Osborne's medical instruments.
The Doctor shouted up instructions for a litter made from a
pair of oars and two coats, oars through the sleeves.

We reached the dock and carted Charlie up the bank
and across the road to the Miller house, Dr. Fordham alongside all the way, walking sideways with his right thumb and
forefinger in the hole in the boy's shoulder, pinching shut
the blood vessel that had been nicked and burst nearly an
hour before, when we were halfway across the bay. Charlie
had long since passed out.

The drygoods man borrowed a horse next door and
made off toward the village. Nat and I ran back down to the
sloop, for it was blowing a full gale now and we had had time
to do no more than throw a pair of lines around the dock's
pilings. We ran the anchor warp over to a tree stump down
the bank, to hold her off the dock, lashed the tiller over to
spare the rudder's thrashing about, and doubled up on the
sail lashings. I got hammer and nails from below and tacked
the fishhatch down. We were shivering, for all it was early
September, as we trotted back across the road to the Miller
house. The Millers lent us dry clothes, and my trousers fell
to the floor with a thump when I changed; I'd forgotten the
hammer in the hip pocket.

Charlie'd been laid catty-cornered across the kitchen
table. The fire on the wide hearth had been stoked with logs;
the Millers still cooked the old way, crane and trivets and
spiders, on the open fire. Dr. Fordham sat alongside the
table, right hand still at the wound, thumb and now the second finger inside, still clamping. Dry blankets had been

wrapped all around the boy, turned down at the shoulder. The Doctor's wet canvas gunning jacket was unbuttoned in front. It was close in the kitchen, but he couldn't get it off without letting go with his hand. Mr. Masters stood by, holding the Millers' one kerosene lamp. The wind roared over the chimney, and the fire kept up a steady sizzle as rain dripped down through the flue.

A good two hours passed, Charlie half-conscious part of the time, before Dr. Osborne, a short, stout man getting along in years, arrived. He'd ridden the drygoods man's borrowed horse back, and he'd had to lead him half the way, around fallen trees and branches. He put his black satchel on a chair and opened it, barely looking at the patient. He brought out a sort of scissors affair, forceps I found out later, and Dr. Fordham grunted, "Can't be dirtier than my hand, go ahead."

His colleague leaned across young Masters's body, dripping rain from his overcoat, and slid the forceps down alongside Dr. Fordham's finger and thumb. Bringing the ends together as you would cut with a pair of shears, he said, "There." Both doctors pulled their hands away, Fordham clenching and unclenching his fingers and the pair of them finally taking off their coats. The forceps remained clamped in place, latched by ridges between their handle parts.

The boy's father swayed, and I took the lamp. Dr. Fordham put two wash basins on the table, and half filled them with water. Dr. Osborne reached into his satchel and poured something from a bottle into the basins. Two instruments, like little table knives, were laid in one basin, with another pair of forceps, some needles, and a couple of lengths of what looked like waxed thread. Mrs. Miller brought in towels, her best by the embroidery, and Dr. Fordham added them to the collection in the basin. Dr. Osborne took out two sponges and another bottle. With one sponge, he soaked up some of the solution, and washed carefully around the wound, where Dr. Fordham had cut away the clothing with

Mrs. Miller's sewing scissors. He squeezed the sponge over the wound, and the mixture ran in. Charlie opened his eyes and tried to sit up.

"Keep him down," Dr. Osborne said to the father. "If you can't you do it, Miller. Your patient, Doctor." He waved Dr. Fordham toward the youth, picked up the other sponge, and poured onto it from another bottle. I knew the smell, chloroform. He pressed it against the boy's nose and mouth, forcing him to breathe through it for a minute or two. Charlie relaxed.

"Hold the light over here," Dr. Fordham ordered me. "If you're going to puke or faint say so now and let Mrs. Miller do it. Otherwise, steady." He had his sleeves rolled up, and he'd washed his hands in the basin. He kept on talking.

"That's five per cent carbolic acid. If we had it, a three point three carbolized vapor from a steam-maker would be good. We haven't, but he's young and tough. As it is, this is ten times better than what we had in the War. No anaesthesia, no antisepsis. We've got to clean things up some, now."

He was picking around the edge of the hole with the little knife, flicking bloody bits onto the table and the floor. "This is a scalpel, my boy. Wool shirt and wadding and God knows what else here, and inside too." He worked fast. "Roll him over onto his side, Doctor, and we'll have a look at the exit." He picked away rapidly again. They rolled Charlie over on his back once more, and Dr. Osborne threaded one of the needles.

"Catgut," Dr. Fordham said to me, and took the needle. He bent, and grunted, "Light, damn it." I moved the lamp. He held the forceps with his left hand, pulling up, and made tiny stitching motions with his right. Finally, letting the needle dangle down Charlie's armpit, he cut the catgut with the scalpel, the way I might cut thread with my Barlow knife after sewing a button back on my coat. He threw the needle back into the acid solution, put his right thumb and forefinger into the loops of the forceps-handles, and pressed

them together gently, slipping free the latches. "She's ooz-
ing," he said, peering in, "but she's holding." Dr. Osborne
handed him, clamped in another pair of forceps, a length of
red India-rubber tubing. Dr. Fordham slid it into the wound
until only an inch or so stuck out. Then he packed pads ripped from Mrs. Miller's towels around it, soaked with the carbolic acid solution. A long length of towel, around under the
armpit and over the shoulder, held the pads in place. They
rolled Charlie onto his side and repeated the placing of the
drain and the packing on the exit wound, using another
towel-strap, diagonally around the left side of the neck and
under the armpit, to hold the arrangement.

"He's lost a lot of blood but he'll make it if septicaemia
don't set in," Dr. Fordham predicted as he washed his
hands once more. "Jerry, you can shut your mouth now.
Don't know if he'll ever get much use out of that arm,
though." We eased Charlie onto an old door down from the
attic, to move him to the Millers' bed, still drugged. "He
might vomit some when he comes to," Dr. Fordham warned, "don't let him choke on it." We returned to the kitchen,
leaving his father and Mrs. Miller to watch him.

By the light of the fire, flickering as the wind roaring
overhead varied the draught of the chimney, we cleaned up
and had coffee and pie on the operating table. "You set Uncle Zebulon's leg there, remember, Doc?" Mr. Miller said to
Dr. Osborne, who laughed at the recollection. A broken leg
generally seems as funny as a crutch to those who don't
have one. Zebulon was half-witted Uncle Zeb, Tweet Thissaly for the way he said Sweet Cecily, peddling from his basket of herbs.

I went to the front room, but could make out nothing
but the swaying mast of the sloop, a hundred yards away
through the rain-smeared pane and lowering dusk. Back in
the kitchen, Mr. Miller was talking about ghosts. The house
was supposed to be haunted, although I didn't believe in
that. Not much anyway. " 'Way back before the Millers had

this place," he said, "some crazy woman, one of the Princes, great-great grandmother to Prince Licorice she was, had a baby and smothered it and buried it under the hearth." Prince Licorice chewed all the time, Hard-a-Port or Brown's Mule, and let the juice drip down his chin, like a child with a licorice stick. So he was Prince Licorice, the way Arthur King was King Arthur.

"Well, they missed the child, as she might have known they would, even in a household with a dozen more on deck," Mr. Miller went on, looking at the funereal hearth, "but she wouldn't tell them where it was. No corpus, no delicti, they said. Finally, one day when her husband was clamming and the children were playing in the woods, she slit her throat, upstairs, and jumped out the window. How she got it open I don't know, let alone how she got through it, just a little thing, painted shut, and only two fathom from the ground. She died, anyway, and a long time later when the bricks on the hearth began to settle away and they went to put new sand under 'em, they found the infant, all dried out like a 'Gyptian mummy. You can hear it crying sometimes, in the night." The doctors looked skeptical, but Dr. Osborne agreed that the female kind, post-partum, was liable to almost any kind of mischief.

Time passed, and Mr. Masters came out of the bedroom and said, "He's waking up." The doctors rose from the table, and Nat and I pulled on our oilers and headed out to the sloop. It was dark, and the rain had stopped, although the wind was blowing hard as ever, from the northwest. There was a good deal of surge in the little basin, and the sloop rose and fell in the grip of her lines. All around her, hard to see in the murk, was a porridge of leaves and bits of cattail and branch, all fetched up against what was now a lee shore. The tide, three or four feet above its usual peak earlier, had fallen rapidly, the northwest wind undoing the work of the east and pushing the water out of the bays and harbors back into the ocean. We were fearful the Discovery would take ground, perhaps to heel over and fill, but there was nothing much we could do. We ran back to the house, pushed by the wind strong on our backs. After dosing young Masters with laudanum, Dr. Osborne had headed back to the village afoot. Dr. Fordham was listening to Mr. Miller's account of the time one of the Pinkeye Fullers had been hoeing, barefoot in the August dust, and mistook her left big toe for a hoptoad, and chopped it off. The Doctor agreed that this was amusing and instructive, indicative of the instinctive dread of reptiles shared by all daughters of Eve, and turned to me. "What's it like out there, Jerry?"

I told him that the wind had backed to northwest and was blowing hard as ever, although the rain had slacked off, three things he ought to have been able to figure out for himself without moving from the kitchen, just by listening, although I didn't say that part of course. He pulled his whiskers and pursed his mouth.

"Ever hear of Buys Ballott?" None of us had.

"A Hollander. Thirty years ago, back before the war, he figured out something about these storms, hurricanes, and this is what this is, a West Indian hurricane, the edge of one at least. If you're going to follow the water, Jerry, you might live longer if you'd learn what Mr. Ballott figured out."

Half an hour later, with the help of a pie plate, my recollection of a Catherine wheel, and the hole in a seine cork, I'd learnt. I guessed I'd always figured a northeast storm came out of the northeast, northwest out of the northwest, and so forth. There were sometimes calms in the midst of great storms, but I thought of the middle as something in time, not in space or place. All of us there knew the sailor's rules of thumb about backing and veering winds, but what the Doctor was trying to tell us, the idea of a storm as a sort of giant thing, trundling along like the Hindoos' Juggernaut I'd heard described in a missionary sermon, was new.

"Laws, laws, everything in the world can be described by scientific laws," Dr. Fordham continued, his brow furrowed. "There isn't anything in the world that can't, or won't sooner or later, be explained by simple logic. Don't look at me as if I was Bob Ingersoll preaching No Hell, either. They'll figure it all out someday." He looked grouchy they hadn't already.

"You boys may live to see it all made clear," he said. "I won't. The railroad is in Sag Harbor, and pretty soon it'll run through East Hampton and Amagansett to Montauk and you'll be able to go aboard a steamer there for Europe, and your lives won't ever be the same. We've got gas light in the Harbor, and before you know it we'll have electricity, like in New York. They're talking up a waterworks, and inside of four or five years there'll be flush commodes in a good many of the houses. No more trips through the snow, like enough no more typhoid, no more slops and chamberpots, in time no more thinking a bodily function is something dirty and sinful, because it will be clean."

"Things are speeding up," he concluded, "and life is never going to be the same around here. The change isn't all going to be for the better, either, but it's coming and you'd better make the most of it."

In the morning, Nat and I, brushing hay from our clothes, for we'd slept in the Miller's barn, a small one and draughty, went over to look at the sloop first thing. We had to bail some, but she was all right, a few scratches along the waterline from driftwood was all. The Millers fed us breakfast and we got ready to sail Dr. Fordham back to Sag Harbor. The banker had already left. Dr. Fordham hung back, giving last-minute instructions to the Millers on the care of the patient -- he and his father were to stay until it was safe to move the boy, a week or so; his mother and sister would be over from the Harbor by nightfall to nurse him, probably -- and I saw the Doctor take Mr. Miller's hand and put what must have been banknotes in it, despite Mr. Miller's headshake no.

Sailing down Three Mile Harbor, the only sign of the

storm we could see, aside from our mainsail and jib, wet but drying fast and steaming a bit in the sun, was a fishing shanty washed out of the banks on Sammis Beach and listing on the clamflat on the Harbor side. The air was clear and crisp, the way it usually is after a line storm, and I felt a little excited without knowing why. Out in the bay, there were great floating mats of kelp and eelgrass, big enough to stop the sloop if we hadn't taken care. We tacked up the bay and the Doctor took up where he had left off the night before. I began to wish he would leave off something else, improving us.

"Knowledge, of everything and anything," he said, like a preacher lining out the text for the day. I got that church feeling in the back of my neck. "In a way, you boys know less of the world than you might have had you been born a generation back, and already have made a voyage or two, to the Pacific perhaps. This sloop's been more places and seen more than either one of you. Don't you ever wonder about things, your sloop for instance? Not curious enough to really try to find out where she came from, and how?"

Nat and I protested; we'd tried as hard as we knew how to find out where from, where bound, about the sloop, and I added that I figured I was as curious as the next person, and maybe more so. He had no call to keep hectoring us. Dr. Fordham ignored my grumbling, and looked around as if he had never seen the Discovery before.

"You rigged her, didn't you? I mean, this isn't the original rig? She had that firebox when you found her? Just the cleats?" He kept asking random questions, pausing now and then. After a bit, he filled his pipe, and stuck his head into the cuddy to light it out of the wind.

"What's that ballast down there?" he asked, after he'd backed out and crawled aft to the cockpit well. I told him I thought it was coral rock, presumed it was. I knew as soon as I'd said it, presumed, that the word sounded high and mighty, and felt my face go red.

"Presumed? You'd better learn not to presume, or assume, much of anything in this world. I've seen coral, have some home, and limestone rock I guess was coral once, and it don't look anything like that." He crawled up and through the companionway, to reappear in a minute with one of the ballast rocks in his hand. He brought it aft, a stone the size and shape of a small ham, but sharp-angled. It must have weighed six or eight pounds, and being wet from the bilge-water it shined black. Dr. Fordham turned the rock over. Holding it against his leg with his left hand, he reached into his trousers pocket, pulled out a jackknife, opened it with his teeth, and scratched at the rock. "It's all like this?" he asked. "How much?" Three-quarter ton, we guessed.

"This, gentlemen, is not coral rock; it isn't even limestone rock. Unless I am very much mistaken, it is pyrolusite." Nat and I must have looked blank. "Manganese dioxide to you." We looked blanker, at least Nat did.

"Manganese, gentlemen, is what you put into steel so you can make a bank vault tough enough that the cracksman will not be able, with his blowpipe, to draw the temper of the steel, drill a hole, and introduce his Nobelite. Manganese, say twelve per cent, and a little carbon, in your steel, is what they use for mine-car wheels and rock-crushing machinery and armor for the dreadnaught. It's hard, and it's malleable, and when Robert Hadfield patented austenitic, what some call gamma nonmagnetic, manganese steel, four or five years ago, you didn't have to own a bank or a mine, or a rock-crusher, or be a safe-cracker, or an admiral, to foresee the usefulness of his invention. A remarkable thing, manganese steel, and it will be a good many years before all of its uses will be discovered."

He paused, and Nat and I started to ask what we were thinking: "How much is what we've got worth?" The Doctor laughed. "You haven't got any treasure here, if that's what you mean. Your Discovery is not ballasted down with fossil ambergris or Kidd's gold, and you can't set up as the Manganese Trust. I don't know what the market price for manganese ore is, but I'd be surprised if what you had was worth more than fifteen or twenty dollars. You'd be a damned sight better off with a three-quarter ton of bluefish."

He invited us up to his house for dinner, after we had docked at Gordon's once more. We unloaded the gunning gear and birds into his phaeton, and went up to the big house on the north side of Turkey Hill. In the study was a brass telescope, pulled all the way out and mounted on a tripod. "I use it for star-gazing," the Doctor said, "and when the leaves are off the trees, and they mostly are after yesterday, for looking at the harbor and out on the bay and keeping track of what my neighbors are up to. Here."

He took caps off either end of the telescope and aimed it down toward the foot of Main Street. "Look." I bent over, not touching the instrument, and peered through, with my left eye. Dr. Fordham remarked it: "Squaw-handed in your optics, too, eh?" I could see an oyster sloop alongside Long Wharf, through the shadowy branches in between. The oystermen were sitting on deck, mending a sail. Nat elbowed me aside to look for himself.

There were shelves upon shelves of books here; a whole wall of medical texts. There must have been a dozen small plaster busts between the books or above the bookcases; I recognized one, Socrates; we had him in marble at the Institute. In a corner, on a stand, was something like a great brass globe, except that it was hollow, and made up of geared ring upon geared ring, running at angles to each other, with clockwork and weights within.

"That's Ephraim Byram's Universe," the Doctor said. "He made two of them, years ago, right here in the Harbor, and I got this one for a bad bill. A pretty piece of work."

He took a small crank from a bracket on the stand holding the contraption, which was nearly three feet across and must have weighed a hundred pounds, and gave a few turns to the works, lifting one of the weights an inch. The machine came alive, rings turning in orbit with no more noise than a quiet ticking and the hum of oiled gear teeth.

"It had been done before, of course," the Doctor said, waving a hand over the Universe. "Kepler wanted Frederick of Wuerttemberg to give him the funds to build one, almost three hundred years ago, in silver, with cups instead of rings for the orbits. Each sphere would hold something, he thought; aqua vita for the Sun; brandy for Mercury; and so on. They never built it, but Kepler made a paper model. Frederick of Wuerttemberg couldn't have one, but Byram made himself a Universe up in the old Oakland works on South Street. He was a clockmaker, really, but he was a genius. Self-educated, and hard to get along with. This is part his theory, part others, but his execution, the whole thing. Born, and died, fifty years too soon."

We went in to dinner, presided over by Mrs. Fordham, a tall woman with a handsome face, a pleasant smile, and little to say. The food was good, served around by a colored cook. Nat and I kept quiet as the Doctor told his wife, briefly, of the events of the day before. "She's a touch senile," he said matter-of-factly after we had returned to the study. "All in the arteries."

The Doctor opened a low glass-fronted cabinet and pulled out a heavy book, which I recognized from the Institute as one of a set of the Encyclopedia Britannica.

"Great Inagua: Most southerly of the Bahamas Islands," Dr. Fordham said. "Yes, I was up at the Dry Tortugas at the end of the War, where they had the Assassin Mudd later on, but I never got that far south. If it's like those other islands down that way, it'll be low, and coral and limestone, and no such thing as manganese. Yes, yes, look: 'lowland surrounding large salt lake.' "

He put the book back and hauled down a large cotton-backed map of the Western Hemisphere, the school kind on a roller. "Here 'tis," he said, pointing. "And right here's Hispaniola, that is the Hayti end of it, and here's Cuba. They were both mentioned in the letter you found?" He went back to the Encyclopedia, and looked up Hayti. He grunted a few times, and traded that volume for the CON to EDW one, with Cuba in it.

"Yes. Santiago Province. Cabo Maysi on the Windward Passage. Baracoa excellent port." I broke in. "Uriah Gordon was at Inagua once, and he says you can see Baracoa Mountain from there when the weather's clear."

"Baracoa. 'The Anvil de Baracoa is somewhat below 3,300 feet in elevation.' Baracoa is a pouch-shaped harbor, a drowned valley. Your mountain is part of the Sierra de Cobre, part of the Sierra Maestra system. 'Extremely wild and broken.' The north coast there, northwest of Cabo Maysi, is high bluffs and terraces. Around by Santiago, copper deposits. Iron too. Rich hematite near Daiquiri running above sixty per cent iron. Copper mainly in well-marked fracture planes in serpentine; ore is pyrrhotite, with or without chalcopyrite. The Cobre mines once the greatest in the world, worked for two hundred years after 1524, unused for another hundred, revived fifty or sixty years ago.

"Ah, here it is: 'There is manganese ore along the coast between Santiago and Manzillo to the west.' Nothing more than that, but this set is twenty years old, and nobody gave a damn about manganese until Hadfield. That, it'd be my guess, is where your ballast came from. The southeast coast of Cuba. And they didn't gather it along the beach like cobblestones, either. It's been mined, you could see the pick marks."

We stood like dunces, but getting the general drift between the hotites and the pyrites. "That's enough of this," the Doctor said, and put the Encyclopedia in the cabinet and jiggled the map back up on its roller. He sat at the desk and took out paper and an envelope. He scribbled out a note, put it in the envelope, sealed it, and wrote something on the front. "Here," he said, handing it to Nat, "the two of you deliver this to Mrs. Hetty Mack. You're good boys."

Chapter
V

---❦---

Not Quite
What I'd Expected

On the street and out of sight around the corner, Nat handed the envelope on to me. "Madame Hetty McNamara, The Fort, By Hand" was written on it, in a hen-scratch hard to make out. That's who Hetty Mack was. She laughed when she read it, and passed it back to me:

> My Dear Het,
>
> The bearers of this missive are two young men to whom I am indebted for cool service under fire, that is at Goff's Point yesterday and latterly at Three Mile Harbor, and on behalf of myself and other members of the Century Gun Club, I wish to provide them with the best that your house has to offer in the line of food, drink, if they want it, and the company of your Columbines. Please provide them with the above, charge it to my account, and oblige.
>
> With my respects, your
> Faithful Admirer,
> Jermain Fordham, A.B., M.D.

I handed the note back to Nat, who surprised me by having nothing to say for himself, on reading it. "Let's go upstairs," said Mrs. Mack, leading us through the saloon, empty at mid-afternoon. "You might like to converse with some of our young ladies for a while, and then come down for a supper on the good Doctor.''

The stairway opened into a large parlor on the Main Street end of the building. The piano had commenced to play at the sound of our tread on the stairs. A woman of at least thirty was pounding on it gracefully, her bustle in our direction, ''Over the Waves,'' or something like that. Two younger women were sitting on a horsehair sofa, very straight, and crocheting. I realized the one nearest the front windows, her face in shadow against the light, was Diana, Mrs. Stratton's Huntress, from Third House. She looked different, all pulled in with stays at the waist in a fancy white dress and with her hair up, but she was Diana, no mistaking that. She kept her eyes on her handiwork.

Mrs. Mack introduced us around. ''Nat, I think you know the girls, Lucy over there at the piano and Prudence and Diana here. Girls, this is Jerry Dimon from Amagansett. You know each other?'' she added, jerking her head toward Diana and then toward me. She was quick, Mrs. Mack, and caught it right off, our being acquainted. ''Good. That's settled, then.'' Nat settled down on the sofa, next to Prudence, who began to ask him about Charlie's shooting himself. They knew him from his vacations from Yale. He liked to drink beer and sing songs, they said, like all the college boys. I sat by the window, hands between my knees, not feeling much like a college boy. Before long, Nat and Prudence disappeared down the hallway at the back of the parlor, and Lucy, who'd been looking sort of sorry for herself for being old and not having company of her own, left off piano-thumping to go downstairs. Diana walked over and took me by the hand, not saying anything. She led me down the hall, past a folding clothes-rack from which she picked a small towel, and into a small room, with nothing in it but a bed, a straight-backed chair, and a commode with a washbasin above and a chamberpot below. She sat at the edge of the bed and pulled me down beside her. Still without saying anything, she reached up, grabbed my ears, and pulled me around to kiss her.

I put my right arm around her waist before breaking off the closed-mouth kiss. I finally remembered something appropriate for the occasion: "What in Gehenna is a nice girl like you doing in a place like this?" She laughed, the first time I'd heard her. "I could ask you pretty much the same, but I'll tell you later, Jerry." She did things to the back of her dress and then pulled it over her head. "Help me with the stays," she ordered. I got to thinking about the stays just then, as I fumbled, just as hard as I could. Whalebone and springy. The price of whalebone had held pretty good, was even up, a dollar and a half a pound; oil had gone all to blazes, two bits a gallon. It was coal oil was doing it. Father scrimshawed up busks of baleen for Mother's stays, his last voyage. She kept them hid, but I'd seen them. Mermaids they had on them. And cocoanut trees. If she knew. I was looking at the worn carpet and thinking about baleen when Diana, from the waist down, hove into my line of sight. She was as naked as the day she was born. She had more hair on her nether parts than I'd have expected, and by the looks of her upper works she belonged with the milking herd.

She walked over to the commode, wet the towel, and worked up a lather on it with a cake of Pears soap. She hoisted her left foot up onto the top of the commode and washed between her legs. My mind was blank until the advertisement worked its way through, like I was reading it on the inside of her thigh, which was white as a sheet of paper:

> HENRY WARD BEECHER wrote: "If CLEANLINESS is next to GODLINESS, soap must be considered as a means of GRACE, and a clergyman who recommends MORAL things should be willing to recommend soap. I am told that my commendation of PEARS soap has opened for it a large sale in the UNITED STATES. I am willing to stand by every word in favor of it I ever uttered. A man must be fastidious indeed who is not SATISFIED with it."

Mr. Beecher had preached in East Hampton; his father'd been minister there in Grandfather's time. Diana said, "Get your clothes off," a little impatient. I did, holding off as long as I could for fear of letting out into the light of day what I could feel rising. She began to wash me where she had washed herself, and I could feel what had been about at half-mast being peaked up. I could feel it, but 'twas as if it belonged to someone else. This wasn't happening to me. She gently pulled and rubbed, wiping off the soap, and threw the towel over onto the commode. She lay back, grabbing my hands as she did, and pulled me onto her.

We kissed open-mouthed when it was over, and I rolled back by Diana's side. It had been not quite what I'd expected. I'd heard someone say it amounted to no more than a sort of between-the-legs sneeze. You might as well take snuff, he'd said. That wasn't quite right, either. Still, I felt good, and affectionate enough toward Diana, who surprised me by seeming cheerful. We lay there a minute, and she laughed.

"You asked me how I came to be in a place like this. Remember the day you were at Third House? And that old goat Homidy had been there the night before? Well, he kept coming back, and hanging around, and he'd go back to East Hampton and come back on some excuse or other three or four days later, spending his days up in Indian Field digging fool holes for gold and the evenings and mornings pestering me, until finally one night after supper he got me alone and backed me into the barn and cornered me. He come at me tongue hanging out and a line of gab a mile a minute and grabbing, and I was up against the box stall. I reached up and there was a whiffletree hanging off a peg and I fetched him one over the top of his head would have killed him if he hadn't had on his plug hat. He fell down and I would have thought he was dead, except he bled so."

"When he come to he told Mr. Stratton, private, that I'd seduced him and had tried to blackmail him and that when he wouldn't pay I'd tried to kill him. I don't think your Uncle Stratton nor his wife neither believed a word of it, but it was his word against an Indian's, and they threw me out. I fetched up in Sag Harbor waiting for the steamer back to Connecticut; figured at least I knew some people over there. Mrs. Hetty Mack heard about me and offered me a position, so to speak, and here I am."

I raised up with my head resting on my hand and my elbow on the bed. I could see across her moving lips and her face, and out through the window. We were at the back of the building, and I could look down and over the fence into the yard of a house facing on the next street over. A woman was hanging out wash close by a man, her husband I guessed, who was splitting stovewood, coat off and suspenders fire-engine red against his collarless white shirt. It seemed strange to be looking out, from that room and that company, on a man and a woman engaged in such workaday pursuits.

"The next thing is, you're going to ask me why I don't get out of this, and you don't have to ask, I'll tell you." I hadn't been going to, but I had been wondering. "First of all, I wasn't no rose when I got into this; I had a baby over by New London before I went to Montauk. He died, two months old. Two months and a week. Secondly, I had enough of scrubbing pots and milking cows and handling other people's slops. The hours are short enough, the food is good, I get nice clothes, there's a woman comes in to clean for us, and to tell you the truth I sort of enjoy my work sometimes. Mrs. Mack runs a good house, everybody knows that, and she keeps an eye out for us with the customers, and won't have none that would mistreat us. Do you know anything I'd be better off at, and half-Indian to boot?"

We got dressed and went out to the parlor, where we spent the rest of the afternoon drinking beer and listening to the piano, no college-boy singing. We had a big supper in the restaurant, the two girls and Mrs. Mack at the table with us, all very genteel, like a family. After supper, and cigars, Nat and I went back upstairs with the girls. It was a good deal better this time; it took a good deal longer, too, and I was beginning to get on to it all. I was dressed and saying goodbye at the side entrance, feeling pretty big for my britches, before I realized the time was only early evening, and that Diana had a night's work ahead of her. A week night, though, and maybe there would be no customers. For her anyhow.

We headed back down the Bay in the morning, after loading our fishing gear, left behind when we took the gunning party aboard. There were striped bass backside, off the ocean beach, and Father wanted the haul-seine brought back, and us, if we wanted to take a crack at bass-seining with his crew. He had to stay at the Georgica Station, of course. We'd run down to Cranberry Hole and unload the seine, and walk up and get the beach wagon to haul it over to the ocean side, but we hadn't made up our minds about going bass-fishing. There wasn't much time left, if I was to go back to school that fall, to enjoy independence.

Outside of Cedar Point, I was relieving myself over the lee rail, examining my privates with some apprehension, when my mind was taken off guilt-filled thoughts by the sight of long lines of coots, scoters really, not the freshwater mudhens some people call coots. They flew low over the water, not yet settled in on the grounds they'd spend the next few months on, diving for small clams and mussels and whatever else they might find on the bottom, before flying on to the southard. We put up a few small bunches close under our bow. They hadn't been shot at much, you could see that.

Nat went below and brought up my duckgun, wrapped in an old oil-soaked woolen pants-leg. Nat handled her carefully, watching where she swung; the accident was fresh in our minds. He went over her, measuring with the ramrod before putting a charge in to make sure he wasn't loading a new one on top of an old. Gun loaded, he put the box of caps in his left coat pocket, with the cotton shotbag, and slung the powderhorn around his neck. "Don't lose her overboard," I called as he went forward.

The duck gun had been mine for three years; it had been Father's when he was thirteen -- his father had had one of the Homidy's, Charles Stuart's uncle Nathaniel, probably, he was good with guns, change her over from flint to percussion lock. When she was still a flintlock, she had been Grandfather's as a boy, and his father's too, I guessed. She was a King's Arm, a Brown Bess, this one an officer's musket probably, Father said, brought home by a Dimon from the French and Indian Wars or the Revolution, he didn't know which. She was finer in the stock than most of the old muskets, and had no bayonet lug. On the left side, opposite the lock, a copper snake four or five inches long was set into the walnut. On the lock side, the wood was charred from the flash of nobody knows how many firings. Except for the lock and the ramrod -- the original long since fired off at a duck or a Redcoat by mistake, as happens with muzzleloaders when you get excited, and don't they kick when it does -- she was the same gun as she was when made, though by now accustomed to shot rather than ball. It was odd that people thought a boy was old enough to have a gun at just about the age he was able to fornicate, though few did at thirteen.

A half-dozen coots flew up under our bow and made off down our lee, our larboard, side. Nat was perched just forward of the mast and had to twist ahead and down to shoot under the jib. He knocked one down, and I brought the sloop about and we ran over to the dead coot, Nat picking him up with the crabnet. He reloaded and gave the gun to me. I missed the first shot, but got two coots the second try. We took turns, and had a half dozen birds by the time we anchored off Cranberry Hole late in the afternoon.

I dressed them, slitting them through the skin and

feathers asshole to appetite, Nat's observation, although it was really the other way around, and I've never cared much for that expression, and peeling the skin back either side from the line of the breastbone, to slice the breast meat clean away from the bone, giving us two small steaks about an inch thick from each bird. The rest we threw away; we wouldn't have been able to, had Father been there. He was a coot stew man, legs and gizzards and all, but we had neither time nor inclination nor ingredients for that, and the long cooking seems to bring out the fish in the bird. I like my fish with scales on it, maybe because of all our pork at home tasting sort of codfishy, from the gurry the pigs got.

Nat had a good wood fire going in the cook-box, and put seacoal on top of it, big lumps rounded by the sand and surf. After we'd anchored and things were steady, we put the big sheet-iron skillet on the fire and let it get good and hot, with no cooking fat at all. When it looked right, I threw a handful of salt in and the salt sort of hopped around the way it does, with a haze over it. I took the coot breasts from the bucket of seawater in which they'd been soaking since I'd trimmed all the yellow fat off -- you don't, you might as well be eating that coot stew -- and threw them on the skillet. After about two minutes each side they were ready, bloody red inside like good beefsteak and almost charred and salty outside. We had bread to soak up the juice, and coffee, and I headed up home.

Mother and the girls were in the kitchen wing at the back of the house, cleaning up after supper. I'd seen the boys still playing ball in the half-light on the Main Street. Mother put me to drying dishes, and I told them my adventures, those that bore repeating, and I felt like I was lying, not telling the most important. I slept in my old room that night, the first time in a while. It was strange, being up there in the southeast end of the attic, hearing the steady roar of the after-storm surf, breaking on the bar like a long line of toppling cliff. It must have been a sight Wednesday, I thought before I fell asleep, with the northwest breeze peaking it up and blowing the white spray back off the tops of the plunging green breakers.

The room was almost half the attic. The floor in the other half of the attic, the other side of the chimney, was piled high with old trunks and such lumber. Hams hung from its rafters, and strings of onions, and broken chairs were jammed up in the eaves. There was a stand like a wooden horse-block just back of the line of the rooftree. Mother spent a good deal of time standing on it, looking out the open scuttlehole south over the peak of the roof toward the ocean, when Father was winter codfishing.

The house had been built by her grandfather, when he was a young man eighty or ninety years before, in the square style of that time, not like one of the old saltboxes, although Mother said he'd used some of the timbers of the tumbledown saltbox that had been on the lot before, and all of its chimney, with its four fireplaces and great domed oven and hearth in the cellar, which had been there before too. That cellar was the first thing they lived in, in the settlement days; they'd dig it and roof it over, and live in it until they got around to raising the house over it. Using the old timbers and chimney over again was more than economy; people said we were, on the East End, as bad as the Chinese for worshipping our ancestors, and they were right. We'd lived there, straight through, two and a half centuries, on the same ground. There were people in the city who didn't know their grandparents' names, let alone where they'd lived.

Mother was raised there after her parents died by her uncle and aunt. They'd had no children, and left their farm to her. On the second floor were three bedrooms, two one side of the stair and chimney and one big one the other, and a few closets stuck in the angles around the chimney and staircase. The ground floor had the dining room, the kitchen and eating place before Father built the flat-roofed two-story kitchen wing, back in the days when they still cooked in the fireplace, like the Millers; the sitting-room, with a little bulge of wall with three windows built only two years before, it was supposed to hold Father when he was home, with his big chair and pipe and newspaper, only he was home precious little and when he was he was generally working, eating, or sleeping; and the parlor, with the glass-fronted cabinet with bird and hawk eggs, blown by Mother, arrowheads turned up plowing, the old Indian pepperidge-wood mortar and stone pestle, and the bookcases. The parlor was for entertaining company, the Minister, say, or for such female events as a quilting-bee.

We had a picket-fence out front, a couple of locust hitching-posts, and a horse-block. The well was close behind the house, next to the side kitchen door, and the privy was, just then, off toward the barn. Moving it around, digging new privy holes and filling up old ones, was one of my chores when I was home, and a reason I was home as little as I could. Most people left their privies be a decent time, but Father had read something in the papers and ours traveled around like the circus. Beyond the privy and the icehouse, just a roof showing above the ground, was a fence that marked the back boundary of what we still called a pightle, the kitchen garden, which had a little fence of its own the other three sides. Through the big gate was the corncrib, high on four locust foundation-posts, each one topped with a big tin pieplate upside down, to keep the rats off, and the long line of outbuildings, each built against the next, leading to the barn. First, a closed shed, full of fishing gear. The beach-boat was bottom-up alongside that one. Next, the long open-faced shed for the wagons, stoneboat, sledge for hauling wood in the winter, and the pung, on runners, for the winter too. Next the stables, three of them, for the two plowhorses we generally kept and old Ranger. The doors faced the barnyard proper, with its high board fence, gate, and manure-pile. The fence continued around to enclose the pigpen, up against the front of the barn alongside the barn-yard. Looking at the barn, the doorway on the right, with the swinging doors, led to the cow end, and the doorway on the left opened on the harness room, with pegs along the wall studs holding all sorts of gear, even yokes from when we kept oxen.

The barn had been built at the same time as the house, and like the house it incorporated parts of its smaller prede-cessor in its timbers, pegged together; you could see holes in them where the assembling had been different from the ori-ginal, peg-holes empty and no longer needed. Some of the board sheathing under the shingles -- they were unpainted, never had been, in contrast to those on the house, which were white -- probably came from the first barn; some of it, Father said, was flooring from the old house, foot-worn side in, flat underside out, against the backs of the cedar shing-les. These boards were close to three feet across, laid up on the rafters to nail the shingles to, with three or four inches between for the air to get in, so the shingles could breathe, and not rot. The rest of the sheathing was driftwood, planks picked up on the beach, some of them still tree-shaped in cross-section, with bits of bark hanging off at the edges. In the gaps between the sheathing and the shingles, on a sun-ny day, light came in to make long streaks across the barn's dusk, motes of dust dancing in them, and it was hard to un-derstand why the rain never seemed to leak through. The shingles swelled, first drop, was why, but you'd never be-lieve it, to see the holes.

There were always cats in and around the barn, to keep down the rats and mice, and an old blacksnake lived some-where underneath. When we went down to drag out some oars or the old duckboat or beanpoles, slithering along on our bellies, we worried about running into him, for all we knew he would not harm us. We were not, by Father's order, to harm him, either. Our hens ran loose, and we lost some eggs and chicks to the snake, but reckoned he was worth it for killing mice. Rats, too, they said, but big as he was, maybe six feet long and three inches through, I doubted he was quick enough. He drove the hogs near wild when he came into sight; they would kill him, for what he'd done in the Garden, people said, if they could.

Father's shop was well clear of the other outbuildings, off to one side for fear of fire, the rest being attached to the barn, all but the corncrib. The shop was a great clutter inside, a long low one-story building with a dirt floor, double doors at one end, and windows, which the other sheds didn't have. The shop had a small forge, which he fired up from time to time to do some blacksmithing, mostly fixing tools and simple work. He could make shoes, and shoe a horse, but he'd rather a real smith like Mulligan did it, so much being at stake in shoeing a horse just right.

Behind the barn was the little home pasture, a small field of two acres. Through the gate in the hedgerow, all scrub cherry and weeds and old gnarled oak lop-fencing grown up so thick you'd have to chop your way through it almost, and raised up like a dirt wall above the land either side, what with the dust blowing in a dry winter and catching in the brush, to raise the hedgerow, and the dirt washing and blowing away from the fields, to lower them, was the home lot, corn and potatoes, some of the latter already dug and the corn about ready to be cut. Beyond that, through another hedge, was the big home pasture, and our hay field, stubble now and set off from the pasture by a barbed-wire fence. The hay was long since in the lofts either side of the barn.

The big lots up north of Main Street had been let out this year, and were in wheat. Father had other land, the woodlot, up back of Stony Hill, part of one of the allotments still in the Dimon family from twenty years after the Town was settled; a piece of salt-hay meadow at Accabonac Creek; beach-banks land west of Promised Land he had bought from the Town Trustees once when he'd taken two years off from being a Trustee himself, so he could buy without being criti-cized, and one of the old twelve-acre pinelots at Lazy Point. Not so much land as some, but a lot more than others. Still, cash was scarce, and Father sometimes worked off his high-way tax on the road, rather than pay it out in money, for all he'd been a Trustee.

Father and Mother worked hard, and expected every-body else to. Not much time for play; work was pleasure to them, or so they said. I didn't have to wonder what Father'd say, if he knew what I'd been up to, in the Harbor. There was that story about him on a whaling trip finding a Kanaka girl in his bunk, anchored one night at Honolulu. He'd pick-ed her up without a word and carried her up the ladder out of the forecastle and across the deck, and dumped her over the side into the harbor. I hadn't heard it from him and never would. He read the Bible every night, at home, aloud and with his small glasses far down his nose, just above his beard really, his cold blue eyes bright in the lamplight as he read about some battle of the old Kings of the Jews. He look-ed like one of those old Hebrew warriors or prophets, those great men of the Old Testament we were brought up to ad-mire and fear, hard and righteous, those men for whom we were named, me and a good many of us. People of the Book. We were, too, of the Old Book. We read in the New Testa-ment, and believed it, or said we did, but the Old Testament was ours. Father's anyway.

We went bassing the next morning, on the beach with the seine in its cart before sunup. We worked east to Dutch Ship Hill, the second wagon carrying the beach-boat, six-teen feet long, before Clint Edwards saw signs of fish and de-cided to make a set. There were a dozen of us, and we had the seine into the boat and the boat out through the surf in short order, though the sea was still riled up from the storm. We ran out in a great half-circle from west to east. It was hard work, pulling against the set. We ran in on the back of a sea, and the rest of the gang dragged the boat up clear.

Then the seine came in, six men at either end tugging in rhythm. As the half-circle grew small, we could see the water roil; we had fish. And a good deal of trash, from the storm. We picked it out of the twine as we brought it in.

We had a good load for the cart, and sent it up to the village, my brother John, the youngest there, leading Ranger, for the fish to be boxed and iced, and got ready for another set. With luck, we'd have ten or fifteen shadboxes, all the big Studebaker wagon could hold, to take to Sag Harbor to be shipped in the morning.

Chapter
VI

——◆——

Sunday Mediations

We bassed again Saturday on the morning tide, with good luck, and I got home that afternoon in time to pound samp for Sunday dinner. Mother was old-fashioned, and served the old long-cooking Indian dish of cracked corn simmered with a bit of salt pork, with boiled potatoes and pie, after church. Services were shorter than they had been when she was young, and it had been years since there was regular Sunday-afternoon church too. There was time to cook, and eat, a big dinner, but she held with as little work as possible on the Sabbath. That left me to do the work on Saturday afternoon, pounding samp.

We were going to the East Hampton church, to hear the Reverend T. DeWitt Talmage preach his last sermon before returning to his Brooklyn tabernacle for the winter, and to meet Father, who would not leave the Station long enough to come to Amagansett for church. Mother took the reins; we had the team hitched to the big wagon, with planks laid across the box in back to hold my brothers and sisters and sister-in-law, eight of us in all. The boys were furthest back, looking unnatural in their best clothes, with round-brimmed hats, and shoes; Sam and his bride ahead of them, still newlyweds and solemn; Esther and Anna Elizabeth just behind the seat, whispering and giggling; and Mother and I were in front. Father was waiting for us, in his Life Saving Service uniform and cap, looking like Admiral Porter up in the shrouds in a picture of the Battle of Mobile or Vicksburg or one of those places.

We jammed into the East Hampton Dimons' pew, with three of Father's cousins. It was two-thirds of the way down front, behind the Hunttings and Daytons and Osbornes but ahead of the Bennetts and Millers and Clewises and, naturally, the colored, who sat in the last two rows at back-center, under the balcony, just as they had in the 1717 church. This one had been built in 1860 and they'd torn the old one down as a public improvement. There was one good thing in sitting up there; they were first out the door.

We rose for the first hymn, Number Sixty-Six, "Lord, we come before thee now; at thy feet we humbly bow." Mr. Homidy had recited from that one, about feet, how beauteous they are, that day on Montauk. You could hear the wheezing of leather in the organ, and you knew that there was a boy somewhere inside, hidden away like the soul in the body, laboring away on the pump. I tried to stand straight, conscious of the people behind me. The Reverend John D. Stokes stood in front of his chair to the right of the pulpit, a scrawny man with glasses and chinwhiskers. He looked uneasy. He always did when someone else was going to preach in his pulpit, especially a divine of such heavy gauge as the Reverend T. DeWitt Talmage. We sat down again for the prayer. After ten minutes or so, I raised my head a bit, and looked around. The big wen on the neck of one of the Lesters, two rows ahead, stuck right up, with his head hanging down on his chest like that. As with most of the men, bending forward to pray, beside putting the wen on display, had exposed a band of white hide below the red at the back of his neck. Another hymn, Number Six Hundred and Fifty-Seven, the one about golden fields, and the Scripture lesson. Finally, the Reverend Talmage put his hands out to either edge of the pulpit and looked out and down at the congregation:

"And she went and came, and gleaned in the field after the reapers; and her hap was to light on a part of the field belonging unto Boaz, who was of the kindred of Elimelech. Ruth, Chapter Two, Verse Three."

His words were clear and round, the "gleaned" and the "unto" stretched out. He was clean-shaven, a big man with staring eyes under bushy eyebrows, and with fluffs of hair above either ear, like a Cochin China rooster.

"A Case of Love at First Sight." He stopped. You could tell this was the name of the sermon. "The time that Ruth and Naomi arrive at Bethlehem is harvest-time. It was the custom" -- he stretched this out, like "unto," and sort of blew it up, like a football -- "when a sheaf fell from a load in the harvest-field for the reapers to refuse to gather it up: That was to be left for the poor who might happen to come along that way." The farmers in the congregation leaned a bit forward; nobody did any such thing around East Hampton or Amagansett, let alone Wainscott.

". . . Can you expect that Ruth, the young and the beautiful, should tan her cheeks and blister her hands in the harvest field?" Somebody off to the right swatted gently at a fly. Tan cheeks. I thought of Diana.

"Boaz owns a large farm, and he goes out to see the reapers gather in the grain. Coming there, right behind the swarthy, sun-browned reapers, he beholds a beautiful woman gleaning -- a woman more fit to bend a harp or sit upon a throne than to stoop among among the sheaves. Ah, that was an eventful day!"

He leaned over the pulpit and looked us all in the eye. He had a bit of a cast in his left. "It was Love at First Sight." I'd read a good many of his sermons in the Star, after having heard them, and knew where he put the capital letters.

Preachers generally have a habit of salting their writing pretty liberal with capitals, like the Germans.

"Boaz forms an attachment for the womanly gleaner -- an attachment full of interest to the Church of God in all ages; while Ruth, with an epah, or nearly a bushel, of barley, goes home to Naomi to tell her of the day. . . ."

An epah, more than a peck and less than a bushel. Suppose I told Father we'd got about an epah and a half of flounders in the fyke? Love at First Sight. Tan cheeks. I could see one of the Dunton girls up there in the alto section of the choir. She wasn't tanned, or sunburned, or blistered. She was pale with washed-out blue eyes. Her hair was up; a year or two older than me, in stays I guessed under the choir robe, narrow waist, I could see where her bosoms pushed up the robe; she saw me staring at her and looked down. I wondered if she'd ever done it, what she'd look like without those robes and the rest, what she'd feel like, imagined her arms around me, felt myself rising, and listened to the sermon.

". . . Into a sick room where there is a dying child. Perhaps he is very rough in his prescription, and very rough in his manner, and rough in the feeling of the pulse, and rough in his answer to the mother's anxious question; but years roll on, and there has been one dead in his own house, and now he comes into the sickroom, and with a tearful eye he looks at the dying child, and he says, 'Oh, how this reminds me of my Charlie.' Trouble, the great educator." Somebody behind me sniffled. He was talking about a doctor. Charlie Masters hadn't died. Hard to picture Dr. Fordham with tearful eye.

"Sorrow, I see its touch in the grandest painting; I hear its tremor in the sweetest song; I feel its power in the mightiest argument. Grecian mythology said that the Fountain of Hippocene was struck out by the foot of the winged horse Pegasus." Struck out? "I have often noticed in life that the brightest and most beautiful fountains of Christian comfort and spiritual life. . . ." Pegasus was Chris Schenck's best trotter. Fountains. Washing. Soap. Pears. She soaped and rinsed herself, and then me. Stiff.

My neck was getting stiff, and I moved my head slowly. Father cleared his throat. He'd do more than that if he knew what I was thinking. God knew what I was thinking. What would He do? Without moving my head again I rolled my eyes up and looked at the ceiling over the choir, where it met the wall above the organ. There was fine molding-work there, and all around the top of the four walls, in a sort of ledge. When pigeons got into the church they'd perch up there, until they were chased out by one of the elders with a long bamboo pole, through an opened window. "Oh, these beautiful sunflowers that spread out their color in the morning hour! But are always asleep when the sun is going down! Job had plenty of friends when he was the richest man in Uz. . . ."

I rolled my eyes right, toward the high clear-glass windows on the south side of the building. I could see the roof and chimneys on Reverend Stokes's house next door. The second time, we'd kissed a long time before we did anything. I licked my lips and looked up toward the choir. The Dunton girl had dark circles under those pale eyes. That was a sign of what old Stokes up there had told the East Hampton Sunday School boys once was the Sin of Onan. Was it the Sin of Onan in girls? How could they do it? On their backs, I supposed, and tried to imagine the alto throwing her seed on the ground from flat on her back. And where was Uz? If you said U.S. fast that would be Uz.

"When Ruth started from Moab toward Jerusalem, to go along with her mother-in-law, I suppose the people said: 'Oh, what a foolish creature to go away from her father's house, to go off with a poor old woman toward the land of Judah.' They won't live to get across the desert. . . ." Deseret. The Mormons had a dozen or more wives, and the Army had to go across the desert, and take the wives, all but one I suppose, away from them. They were mighty men, Father'd joked once, and Mother'd shushed him, in front of the children. It didn't sound like him, but he'd said it. I remembered some dirty story Nat had told me, something about once a night being enough for anyone. I snorted, and Father turned a hard look on me.

"Jubal . . . rude instruments of music . . . very bad man by the name of Richard Baxter . . . illustration of the beauty of female industry . . . languishing over a new pattern or bursting into tears . . . persons under indulgent parentage . . . Madame de Stael . . . I learn from my subject the virtue of gleaning . . . Elihu Burrit learned many things while toiling in a blacksmith's shop. . . ."

I stared straight ahead at the far wall over the Reverend Talmage's head, thinking of nothing at all, until I could feel a tightening around from one jaw to the other, across my neck and the back of my head. I realized my mouth was open and I was breathing through it. Hard to keep it closed. "Fragment left that is not worth gleaning. Ah, my friends . . . sheaf for the Lord's garner . . . a few moments left worth the gleaning. . . ." I came to with a jerk at this hint of imminent conclusion.

"Now, 'Ruth, to the field!' May each one have a measure full and running over! Oh, you gleaners to the field! And if there be in your household an aged one or a sick relative that is not strong enough to come forth and toil in this field, then let Ruth take home to feeble Naomi this sheaf of gleaning: 'He that goeth forth and weepeth, bearing precious seed, shall doubtless come again with rejoicing, bringing his sheaves with him! May the Lord God of Ruth and Naomi be our portion forever."

A sort of sighing rustle came from the congregation, as they stirred and swallowed and coughed as quietly as they could the coughs they had been holding back all during the sermon, only about an hour but long enough. It was dry and dusty in the church, and I'd had a tickle in my throat too, relieved now with a closed-mouth ump-umph. Another hymn, the collection, and the benediction, and we filed out behind the ministers and the choir.

Chapter
VII

———✤———

A Berth
For A Likely Boy

It was back to the Bay then, until the middle of October, when fishing began to peter out. I came home the night of the 21st, a Saturday; the weather was getting chilly for living on the boat, and I was wondering how long we could keep on. Mother gave me Friday's paper. The Star had an interesting account of the steamer George W. Beale, out of Greenport, being cut in half in the East River the Tuesday previous. A man I'd never heard of had been drowned. "I forgot to tell you," Mother said. "A letter for you." I don't know as I'd ever had a letter before, postcards from relatives gone to Hartford or Niagara Falls excepted. "It came yesterday, on the stage from the Harbor."

I recognized Dr. Fordham's medical scrawl. Some members of the Century Gun Club, he wrote, were thinking about moving the Pastime over to one of the ponds off Major's Cove at Shelter Island; they'd engaged the gunning rights for the latter part of the season, and would need a boat as tender. Were Nat and I interested? There'd be work up into mid-December, unless there was a general freeze before then, and that not likely.

We started Monday bright and early. They'd arranged to have the steamer Sunshine tow the houseboat over to Shelter Island on her way up to Greenport, and Nat and I sailed over astern. It was only a couple of miles. We poled and pulled the houseboat up the narrow creek into the pond at high tide, but had to anchor the sloop outside. By nightfall, we'd driven stakes to hold the Pastime to the bank, off enough so she'd rise and fall with the tide; rigged a gangplank onto the meadow; and filled the woodbox with stovelengths cut from fallen trees and branches in the woods.

We built blinds for the gunners in a half a dozen spots the next morning, as Dr. Fordham had told us to before we left Sag Harbor. It was easy work, cutting a little brush and weaving it in, finding and sawing driftwood planks to make seats in the blinds, shoveling out the sunken hogsheads on the low beach between the ponds and the cove, big ones with seats nailed into them, half-filled with sand blown in over the summer. They were a gun-club sort of rig, a little fancy-Dan. On Thursday, the Doctor set us to fixing up the Club's stool, the biggest rig of decoys I'd ever seen, black duck, brant, geese, broadbill, and the Lord knows what else, even sheldrake and shelhen. We made up new anchor lines for all of them; cast new lead anchors and balance-weights, and put them on where they'd been lost; doctored up shotholes; and put loose heads back on, matching up broken-off heads with headless bodies. The stool were a great porridge of styles, some bodies just chopped out of cedar fenceposts by Shinnecock Indians, with heads carved by hand, and others beautiful factory-turned ones, with all the feathers painted in.

Their live decoys, mallards and Canada geese, were boarding out with a farmer over by Ligonee Brook, and on Friday we went there with a wagon to help round them up, whooping like a bunch of cowboys to herd them into a pen -- their wings were clipped -- and finally into crates. We made three round trips that day, with the stool, food, dogs, shells, groceries, and finally six members of the club. They drank a lot of whiskey that night, and stayed up playing cards, and Nat and I turned in aboard the sloop. They were a good deal solemner at breakfast, which we cooked for them before dawn. They cut cards for choice of blinds, and the shooting started at first light. I hadn't expected them to do much, it being clear and still, but they did all right, for sports. We'd been baiting the ponds with shelled corn all week, and the ducks hadn't forgotten. Nat and I did most of the retrieving, just picking up the birds when they drifted over to the banks of the ponds. There wasn't much for the dogs, two Chesapeakes and a big brown and white spaniel, to do, except fetch the few ducks, shot from the hogsheads, which fell in the bay. We had sixty or seventy birds inside an hour and a half.

Nat and I strung them on a line down the shady side of the Pastime, and the club members turned in to catch up on their sleep. We routed them out for a big dinner, and they wandered back to the blinds smoking cheroots for the dusking. This was not as lively as the morning shooting -- they'd already made quite a dent in the regular population, black ducks mostly that had spent the summer there, nesting, and those they hadn't shot caught on fast, as black duck will -- and it was more trouble for us, finding the dead and crippled birds after it got dark.

They didn't shoot Sunday, didn't dare, being well within earshot of their families, and fellow church-members, Presbyterian most of them, in Sag Harbor, and that afternoon we took them home, ducks draped in long ranks down either side of the Discovery, a pair of geese dangling off the boom by their big webbed feet. Nat and I had to dress and pick them for all it was the Sabbath. We threw guts and gizzards into the harbor and sold the feathers the next day to the rags-and-bones man out in Eastville.

Dr. Fordham and some other members planned to take the next Friday off, and try some battery-shooting Friday and Saturday. We were to get the battery ready, repainted and rigged. He'd tell us where to set it Thursday, when he'd have a better idea what the weather was going to be. The battery was in his barn, and we spent the next two days scraping and painting the whole affair. It was a box, really, shaped like one of those cardboard boxes they sell penny candy or roasted nuts in, small at the bottom, just room enough for your two feet, and a little wider than your shoulders at the top, with a little seat across one corner. Sitting in it, your chin was just about level with the water. It had four wooden wings sticking out, one from each side, and beyond them canvas wings, to keep the chop from slopping over and sinking the whole rig, the battery having a freeboard of about three inches and weighted down with pig iron below and cast-iron decoy ducks just outside the little gunwhale. If you were a duck, flying along and looking down on things, you'd see a big square of wood and canvas, about twenty-five feet across and painted gray like the water, with a square hole right at the middle, with a man sitting in it worrying that you would see him or that the whole thing would all of a sudden sink out from under him thirty feet or so to the bottom of Shelter Island Sound, leaving Mr. Gunner trying to swim home in a heavy canvas coat, with a pocket full of shells, rubber boots, three pair of socks, two sets of underwear, iron-clad North Woods trousers, and two wool shirts, the whole soaking up eight hundred pounds of cold water.

They did sink, sometimes, but they were more likely just to fill and leave you sitting up to your nose in salt water wondering about why mankind is damned fool enough to risk his neck for sport. But help would be nearby. A boat would be anchored down to leeward until the shooting commenced, and then you'd leave your anchor on a buoy and work back and forth picking up the dead birds and shooting over the cripples, towing a rowboat the while so you could switch gunners, if the shooting was good, and it usually was, the battery being about the best way, if the most complicated, of killing ducks around.

We worked Wednesday reloading shells, taking our time and doing it right as the Doctor told us to. We slept in his attic, ate with the family, and stayed away from Mrs. Hetty Mack's. I thought about Diana a lot, though, lecherous notions all snarled up with remorseful ones, and sentimental ones. On Thursday, we anchored the battery in the fairway between the south end of Shelter Island and the old salt-works on Hog Neck, out in the middle a pistol-shot from either shore. We hung a lantern on a pole stuck down inside, so no one would come along and run the battery down in the dark, and so we could find her before daylight.

The Doctor took first turn in the battery Friday, and we dropped down with the tide -- there wasn't much wind --to wait for the shooting to begin. We anchored and cooked a pot of coffee. There were three in the party beside the Doctor. One of them was a ship owner from Boston, a friend of the Doctor's from the War. He got to talking about Habana; his firm shipped ice down there, and brought rum north.

"It's hard on a vessel," Mr. Seavey said, "but there's a dollar to be made. Ice is about the only product I know of makes itself, and you can go right on mining it year after year, north of Boston any rate." Maine and New Hampshire, with all that logging, had sawdust for packing between the cakes, too. Ice rotted out a vessel in a hurry, but what Mr. Seavey and his partners lost in that respect, he continued, they had made up to them by Almighty Providence in another cargo carried by some of their other vessels, namely salt, which was such a preservative that some of the older whaleships had it packed in between the frames, behind the ceiling, the whole vessel pickled so to speak.

"Codfish and flour and the rest down to the salt islands, even fresh water in casks sometimes, and salt back," Mr. Seavey said. "Turk's and Caicos and Inagua; there's nothing much there except niggers and salt, no soil to grow anything, just brush and salt pans, and they'll pay a price for fresh water." I wished he'd keep talking about Inagua, but he got onto how much smarter the colored were in the British Islands than up here, and that turned into a general discussion of the colored. It was light by now, and the Doctor got off to a good start with a double on broadbill, bang-bang, two of them floating down toward us. I rowed off in the sharpie to pick them up, and thought about the sloop, and the papers we'd found below.

Dr. Fordham, at cards that afternoon on the Pastime, brought the island of Inagua up again. He hadn't heard the talk that morning, but he knew Mr. Seavey had interests down that way, and told him about our finding the sloop, and about the two dead men. "What were those names, Jerry?" he asked. "MacPherson of Brodie & Bruce Salt Company, or some such, and Franklin Pierce Johnson or Thompson?" Mr. Seavey said he knew who MacPherson was, but the only Thompson of his acquaintance was a connection of the Gardiners, in East Hampton, and the only Johnson our late lamented President. Dr. Fordham snorted at the word "lamented."

"There was an El Zanjon and the Don, too," I said. "That's Cuban politics and the Spanish," Mr. Seavey responded. "Not Inagua at all. If you're that interested in the lower latitudes, a likely boy like you could do worse than to go to sea with us."

He was sort of teasing, but, without really knowing why, I took him up on it, my heart pounding. I was at the Sag Harbor depot Monday morning to catch the 7:19 toward New York.

It had been easy enough to arrange. Nat could handle the Discovery as well as I could, about. Father, when I told him, thought some deepwater sailing would do me good, particularly since this would only be a two months' voyage or so. Mother didn't seem to think too much of the idea, but didn't take on; she'd said goodbye a good many times in her married life. Mr. Seavey, when I'd taken him up on his offer, had back-watered a bit about having a berth for me, but he'd written me a letter to carry to Captain Elmer Shelton of the schooner Lavolta. "She's small, two hundred tons, but stout," he said. "Built about the time you were born, down in Ellsworth, Maine, for us, Whitcomb, Haynes, & Seavey. I guess he'll take you on, able seaman I suppose, but that's up to him. She'll be somewhere along South Street early in the week, loading flour."

I'd been on the cars before, as far as Riverhead, so I wasn't nervous when the conductor came to punch my ticket "in the presence of the passenjare," the way the song goes. I was in the last car, the safest in a train disaster. The engine coupled with a bump and we were off, up into Bridgehampton in ten minutes and over the Butter Lane bridge and out through Scuttle Hole. The car I was in was a humdinger, gold leaf lettering on the varnish outside and red plush seats, mantle lamps, and window shades with adjustable wood slats inside. I was hungry by the time we switched onto the Main Line west of Riverhead, and I bought a ham sandwich, coffee, and a big round doughnut, the store kind with a hole, from the candy butcher, a Paddy. I'd sat on the south side of the car, and it was hot in the sun as we rattled along through the pine barrens. I didn't know how to work the blinds, and I was ashamed to draw attention to myself by moving to the shady side, although the car was almost empty. I was near the back, with only a drummer or two and an old couple behind me.

I drowsed, smelling coal dust and the plush on the seats and the cigar smoke coming back through when the doors up ahead, between the cars, were opened. The next car was the smoker and the conductor would come out of it to call the stops. I'd open my eyes when I heard a rush of air. Somewhere between "Lakelandddddd," on Lake Ronkonkoma, and "Brenwahhh," Brentwood, I woke up all excited and put my hands in my lap so nobody would notice. It didn't go away, and the steady thumping as the car hit the joints between rails didn't help. I looked at the back of the neck of a girl with her mother, about half-way to the front of the car. She was old enough to have her hair up, and had a pretty neck, and wore a sort of velvet collar around it, and a floppy hat, sort of a cowboy thing with a big loose brim and a high crown. They got off at Farmingdale.

It was on toward noon by the time we got to Long Island City, and I got aboard the railroad ferry Southampton, it was odd to see a name from home, a double-ender with a pilot house at either end and a rudder for each one. I tried to figure out which was the bow and which was the stern, or if it changed each trip, and forgot about home, and girls' necks. If I'd known, I could have taken one of the Annex boats clear down to Wall Street; the Southampton ran to 34th Street, and I had to get down to Fulton Street. I stood on deck on the way across, hanging on to my bag.

To the south was the Brooklyn Bridge. We'd come up under it last summer in the Narragansett, the first time I'd seen it or for that matter the city. It was new to a good many of the crew, too, and Father leaned on the rail in front of the wheelhouse and grinned down at us. "You must look like a bunch of hatchlings in a nest from up there," he said, "your mouths all gaping up like that. Mind someone don't drop a worm in." I knew enough not to gape this time, but, dressed as I was in an old coat of Father's, and wearing a peaked wool winter cap, people would know well enough I was a country boy without me having to gape at all. They couldn't sell me the Bridge, though; I was on to that.

The horse car driver on the other side waited until there were people hanging off the steps, more people than you'd think the team could haul, before he started off. It was uphill, and I'd have been better off walking. I had a seat and put my bag down between my ankles and looked around. The man came for my fare and I heard people talking about "transfers," but I didn't know what that was all about until after I'd climbed up to the elevated railroad and gone through the gate and paid again. It cost you money in New York City every time you turned around.

You'd never believe, from the water, how many buildings there were, and how big. Three, four, five stories --every one of brick or stone, and bigger than Clinton Hall or the church at home. There were even taller ones, some so many stories I'd lose count, distracted by all the people. Men with whiskers in the latest styles, like I'd seen in Harper's New Monthly Magazine, clothes that seemed to be too tight, and small hats. All sorts of foreigners -- white, black, brown, and yellow. And women, in new clothes and old clothes, fat and thin, tall and short. Children, lots of them, playing in the cross streets. Horses, more in one block than you'd see tethered along Main Street in East Hampton for Town Meeting Day. The city smelled, too, of horses, of people, and smoke, and coal, and food, and beer and whiskey, and cigars, steam irons, and grease. Either side, up level with the tracks, there were wires, so thick between the poles that if you fell off the roof of one of those buildings you'd just bounce on the wires and go right back up to where you came from. Telephone wires and electric-light wires, dense enough in some places to almost cut off the sunlight to the second-story windows. Windows, with people hanging out of them, even on a November day with a damp easterly breeze. You could see right into some of them where the wires weren't too thick. There was a man sitting at a table in one place, suspenders over his underwear, unbuttoned down the front, a big spoon up to his mouth, paying no more heed to the people rattling past on the elevated railway twenty feet from him than if they'd been in China. It made me think of that afternoon in the Harbor, looking out the back window of the Fort from Diana's bed, and I got a funny feeling in my chest, like when you've been eating too much. I got off at Fulton Street to head east for the river.

I started looking for the Lavolta at the Market. There were schooners there all right, two-masted most of them, some three, and about the right size, but mainly fishermen, dories in deck. I kept on down South Street, dodging teams and wagons and stevedores with wheelbarrows and drays. Some of the jibbooms of the larger vessels came clear across the street, close to poking holes in the fronts of the buildings above the chandlers' and commission merchants' and saloon keepers' signs.

I found her between Old Slip and Coenties Slip, halfway out on the south side of a wharf and inboard of another schooner about the same size, a hundred feet or so on deck. The Lavolta -- her name in gilt -- had the usual dark green topsides, with a red and white band all the way around her, about a foot wide, on the outside of the bulwarks. The inboard side of the bulwarks was white, and her topmasts, deckhouse, and hatches were white, too. Her decks, what you could see of them between the neatly strapped stacks of pine lumber, were bare teak, grey, and her masts, booms, and gaffs were linseeded, oiled. She looked a handy vessel. There was no one in sight, so I stepped over onto the rail and thumped down to the deck.

"Ye'll go right through the garboards;" the voice came from the deckhouse. The garboards are the bottommost planks of a hull; an old joke. Out stepped a small man in a derby hat, linen duster, and carpet slippers. He had long mustaches, drooping down either side of his mouth. "Who are you, boy?"

I figured he must be Captain Shelton, nobody but the Captain being likely to be dressed like that, sirred him, and gave him my name and Mr. Seavey's letter. He read it quickly. "Can you hand? Reef? Steer? Good. We can use you." I signed on as A.B., twenty dollars a month. The Captain made me read the Articles before I signed them.

There were eight of us -- the Captain; the Mate, a younger New Englander and agreeable enough looking; the Cook, a small leathery man named Downes with H*O*L*D tattooed across the first finger-joints of his left hand and

T*I*T*E across his right; four other seamen, and me. The Captain and the Mate shared quarters aft, the Cook slept in the deckhouse, right in the galley, and we were in the forecastle. My mates were all older than me -- a Portugee from New Bedford, an Old Englishman, and two State-of-Mainers. These two had shipped in the Lavolta before; the Portugee and the Englishman had come aboard with the salt cod at Gloucester. I guess they could tell I'd been around the water before; they didn't bother me any.

We spent the next day loading flour, using a whip rigged in the shrouds. The Mate supervised, and between drays we would all go below and stow barrels. There wasn't a bit of play between them when we had finished, nothing to go adrift and smash and make us a thousand gallons of cake batter mixed with salt cod in a seaway. We finished late in the afternoon and closed the hatch. All the while, the Captain sat in a kitchen chair on the poop in his duster, back to us, smoking or paring his fingernails with a knife, and watching what was doing on South Street. When we'd finished, he called the Mate, who came back to tell us that the Captain said no one was to go ashore, that we'd sail on the slack tide in the morning. The Englishman said "shit" and got a sharp look from the Mate, but no more. Soon after supper -- pea soup, fresh pork, biscuits, coffee, not bad -- the Englishman disappeared, snuck ashore. We said nothing but the Mate missed him along toward nine o'clock. "Dimon," he said, "come along. We're going to fetch him back."

We'd been to a dozen or more gin mills, beer saloons, and groggeries before we found him, belly up against the bar in a German place away up by Peck Slip. He saw us behind him in the mirror -- they had a clock on the wall across from the bar that ran backward, and had backwards figures on it so you could tell the time without turning around and wasting drinking time -- and swivelled, having trouble getting his left foot down off the brass rail as he did and stumbling, sloshing half a schooner of beer on the Mate. "Come along," said the Mate patiently. "Won't," said the English- man, as much of his face as you could see between the whiskers that dirty reddish color some men get when they're drinking. He started to turn back toward the bar, and the Mate stepped closer and hooked his right fist into the man's belly. The Englishman doubled up, and we haul- ed him out to the gutter, where he puked. The barkeep hadn't paid any particular attention; the Englishman must have been paying by the drink and hadn't had to settle up before leaving. We set off down South Street, me half-drag- ging my shipmate, and embarrassed that people on the street wouldn't have been able to tell which of us was the drunk; we had been sort of tacking. I was winded when we got back to the Lavolta and climbed aboard, observed by the silent Captain Shelton from his chair on the poop.

We were up before sunrise, and warped the schooner out from inside the other vessel, her crew helping, and out to the end of the slip. The Captain was looking out for the owners' interests as usual, one of the Maine men observed: "He don't never like to pay for a tug unless he has to." We waited a bit for slack water. Then the Captain had us swing the Lavolta, turning on the knuckle of the wharf, and we horsed up the fore and main sails. "Peak 'em," the Captain said quietly, and walked to the wheel. He put the helm over to starboard. "Let go and sheet in," he ordered, and we dropped back. The stern went slowly to port, and the sails filled. We stopped, and then gathered steerageway on the port tack, bow up the East River toward the bridge. The Captain waited for a break in the traffic of tugs, ferries, and other vessels. When it came, he put the helm hard over, and we gybed, swinging quickly as the strengthening ebb tide caught our bow. We were off the Battery before we had all sail set. The Captain knew what he was doing, and he took her past Governor's Island before calling the Portugee to the wheel and dragging his chair over to the aftermost pile of lumber. He stood on it; from the wheel, small as he was, he'd had to stand on tiptoes to see ahead over the deck cargo, and you could tell he didn't trust anybody else to keep such a careful watch, so he got up where he could have a good view of things. We all gawped at the new statue of "Liberty Enlightening the World" as tall as a mountain on Bedloe's Island, but we didn't have much time to sight-see. The Mate had us busy, making ready for sea. We took turns eating breakfast down off Sandy Hook, and by noon had passed a pair of pilot schooners and were well offshore, running before a fresh northwest breeze and coming up on the blue water of the Gulf Stream.

Chapter
VIII

——◦——

Good Weather All The Way

I had my first trick at the wheel that afternoon, taking the helm from the Englishman. He was shaky and hangdog. The Mate watched me carefully the first few minutes, stepping over to look over my shoulder at the compass inside the big wooden binnacle to see if I could keep her on course. It wasn't easy; the Lavolta was running free, dancing off southeast, booms way out over the port side, their ends almost dipping as we rolled. We were into the Gulf Stream the next day, and saw a sea turtle paddling along headed for Newfoundland and points east. The Captain ironed him with a swordfish lily, standing on the footrope on the starboard side of the jibboom, in his linen duster and hanging on with his left hand, a sight to behold. The Mate took the helm, and the Captain conned him after the beast went out of the Mate's sight under our bows: "Starboard . . . Steady . . . Port your helm . . . Steady as she goes . . . Easy now . . . There, you bastard."

He said it the New England way, baastid, and flung the iron as he spoke. The lily went clean through, we found after we'd let the turtle tire himself, and bleed himself, out, towing around the little nail keg, and hoisted him aboard, three of us hauling; he must have weighed two hundred pounds. The Cook did the butchering, using a hatchet to hack his head off, jaws still working and tears in the poor turtle's eyes. We rolled him over on his back then and the Cook cut all around to separate the top and bottom shells. He cut in with a butcher knife and lifted off the bottom shell, using the top like a big basin to do the job in. It was bloody work, with the heart still beating now and again; he saved the best pieces for the Captain and the Mate and himself.

Seeing I was watching when he performed his celestial rites -- at noon, when he and the Mate would use the sextant and the chronometer, a big clock really they kept in a box below, and again in the evening -- the Captain told the Mate to try and explain it all to me, to see if I might be made into something more valuable than just another able-bodied seaman: "The four Ls, my boy, lead, lookout, latitude, and longitude." We'd sit at the table in the cabin for an hour or so, each forenoon I wasn't on watch, and he'd explain to me from Bowditch, while the Captain was on deck, generally sitting in the kitchen chair with his feet up on the rail, aft of whoever was on the helm, staring off across the water.

We'd go on deck, and I'd practice with the sextant on the sun, trying to bring the mirror image down to the horizon. They'd take the noon sun themselves, turn and turn on the sextant and the calculations. The Mate did all the teaching. Navigating wasn't so much of a puzzle as I'd expected, but you had to keep at it. We'd stream the log, a three-cornered board at the end of a long length of light line, each watch, and count the knots in the line as they ran out for a minute by the sandglass. That gave us our speed, in knots; we kept track of it on a slate, with the courses as they changed and the time. The Captain, or the Mate, would figure out each morning where we ought to be, taking into account time, speed, leeway, and anything else he had, like the set of the Gulf Stream or the way his piles, the Captain's, from sitting in the chair the men said, felt that day, to get what he called a dead-reckoning position. Ded, for deduced, the Mate whispered it was really.

Anyhow, then we'd take whatever we could catch from the stars, sun, or moon, a lunar that was, altitude and some-times azimuth and time, to get what the Captain called a Sumner line and the Mate called a line of position. This we'd pencil in on the chart, and maybe advance the last line of position by however much we deduced we'd run since we'd got it, and work in the dead reckoning position to get what the Captain called a cut but what was usually a triangle or some other geometric figure four or five miles on a side. The Mate would prick a hole right in the middle with his divid-ers, and the Captain would say "As good a place as any."

It was interesting, but it wasn't as easy to sort out the sines and cosines and haversines you had to use to make the sextant readings into lines of position and the Green-wich Hour Angle, really no more than the difference be-tween your time and the time in Greenwich, England, which they'd settled on to be the navel of the Universe, you'd have thought they would have picked Washington or Jerusalem, which was longitude, and declination, which was latitude. There was only that one fifty-year-old hogyoke of a sextant aboard, too, and the Captain kept fretting that I'd drop it, on the deck to bend it out of shape, or overboard, and then where would we be?

There were a few words from my bunkmates about this being some sort of a school-ship, and a few jokes played on me when they found my seafaring had been all fishing, not deep-water, but nobody seemed to mind the Captain and Mate teaching me to navigate. They were a placid lot; they ate, they slept, they went on watch, and they didn't seem to think about much of anything. They weren't much for sea stories, and the only music I heard out of them was later, working the bars on the capstan, "Away Rio" and others like that, and that isn't really music, it's part of the job. You don't have to sing to be a sailor, though, any more than you have to be a dancer to be a soldier, and march.

We were east of Bermuda inside of a week, good weather all the way. We creaked along, the spars and deck cargo all working up a regular concert. Nights when there was no moon we'd leave a trail of lights in the water, on either bow and astern, like lightning bugs. Phosphorescence, the Mate said. You'd go to the lee rail forward to pee and that would leave its own little flash when it hit. Southeast of Bermuda, we began to get a few flying fish aboard, usually after dark. In the daylight, they'd fly up and away from us. The Cook would fry up the ones we found on deck for breakfast, and they were good, like frost fish, or whiting, at home. There were always seabirds astern, waiting for our garbage, and once we saw a whale far off, a finback by his blow. There were sails in sight a good deal of the time, and the Mate cautioned us to keep a careful watch at night, and pay close attention to the running lights.

By day, there'd be smoke on the horizon in one direction or another as often as there'd be a sail. One small steamer crossed our bow close aboard one day, headed northeast from Habana for Europe, we guessed, and light, in ballast probably, so that her wheel would come clean out of the water as she climbed up over a swell and started down the far side. Thump, thump, thump it went, a beat about as fast as a man's heart, throwing spray from the blades before it dug in again. We overhauled another small steamer, an Englishman, deep and headed south like we were. He must have been making four or five knots but we passed him just the same, the Captain saying nothing but sitting there in his kitchen chair looking as close to pleased as he ever looked, with his piles.

South-southeast of Bermuda, the wind gradually hauled ahead and picked up, and we came about and ran for the Bahamas on the port tack. We made our landfall ten days later, a long, low island, yellow sand and some trees, with a lighthouse on the north end. "San Salvador," the Mate told me. "Old Christopher himself had his first sight of the New World here." We changed course and ran southeast for another day then, passing Samana Cay in the night, before heading southwest again through the Mayaguana Passage. We were less than a day out of Mathewtown, on Inagua, when we passed west of Hogsty Reef. All we could see from the masthead were two sandbars, no bigger than Cartwright Shoal in Gardiner's Bay, on the near end of the reef, and some breakers on the east end, five miles off, where big rollers from the Altantic, coming in through the Caicos Passage, were breaking.

The northerly sandbar had a cairn on it, a cistern arrangement for stranded mariners, the Captain said. Drawing closer, we could see a figure on top of it, waving a flag or shirt. The Captain had us luff up and run in toward the land. We hove to a half-mile off, and the Mate and the two Downeasters rowed ashore in the yawlboat. They came back towing another small boat, the yawlboat being rowed by the man who'd been on the cairn, a husky black. They clambered aboard over the stern, and we hoisted out our boat, letting the other fall aft on its painter to be towed.

"All he speaks is Spanish, a Cuban I guess," the Mate told the Captain. "Wouldn't let us row, he was that pleased to get off of there." The darkie grinned and nodded as if he understood. He had his shirt back on, and a pair of short dirty white trousers, nothing else. The Captain waved over the Portugee: "Let's let old Vasco de Gama here try him on for size." The Portugee jabbered at the black man for a bit, and got back more than he gave. It was a treat to hear a Negro talking a foreign tongue.

"Say, he from Guantanamo, back t'other side Cabo Maysi, out fishing, his how-you-say scull oar break, he's got nothing left but the loom of it, too far to swim, drifts up here, slow, slow, long time, wind go sou'west push him this way, trade push him back, back and forth, now he want to go home." The black man smiled and nodded, and when we began to trim sheets to get under way again he elbowed right in and latched onto the line as if the faster we got the Lavolta moving the faster he'd get home. Wherever Guantanamo was; I remembered Cabo Maysi, the west side of the Windward Passage, across from Hayti and where the manganese mines were, or near them.

We anchored off Mathewtown the next morning, in about five fathom, the Mate said, but the water was so clear you could see the rocks and seaweed on the bottom. The black was sorry it wasn't Cuba, you could tell; I supposed he'd hoped we'd take him right home.

Ashore, there was rock running right down into the water, with small sandy beaches in between. There was a stone pier up by the town, and a larger one just abreast of us. A big lighthouse stood on the point down to the southeast, and there were palm trees all along the shore. Three buildings caught your eye, two bright pink houses down by the Light and an eight-sided building north of the town the Mate said was the jail. The bright sunlight glinted on the top of the wall around it; broken bottles set in the masonry. The town itself was laid out in blocks like a little city, the way Sag Harbor was. The buildings down by the water were some of them two and a half story, in stone; behind them were a lot of smaller houses on a gentle slope, stone by the look with wooden roofs and porches. There were four or five church towers, thirty or forty people crowded in the shade alongside a small building on the waterfront watching us, a hundred children lobtailing about in the sun, two hundred dogs and chickens in the streets, and six sloops anchored inshore of us. Twenty-five or thirty small boats like the one we'd towed in, but most of them with mast stepped and sails brailed up around them, were pulled out on the short stretch of sand in front of the town.

Two Customs men rowed out and were met at the rail by the Captain, who led them to his cabin. They came out a half-hour later, laughing at some joke and the two of them smoking the Captain's cigars. He saw them to the side, and ordered the yawlboat away. The Hogsty Reef black, so eager to please you couldn't have stopped him, jumped in and rowed the Captain ashore. Captain Shelton stepped onto the stone steps at the landing, and shook hands with a waiting white man, in a white suit and wearing a broad-brimmed hat. The Captain waved the yawlboat off, sending it back to the schooner, and disappeared into a large building near the landing, one with a bit of grass and a flagpole flying the Union Jack.

"The Commissioner," the Mate said. "Dimon, keep an eye out for the Captain; I want the boat back there for him before he reaches the end of the landing." That was going to be hard to arrange, there being a good hundred yards of water between us and the landing, and less than that distance for the Captain to walk. I waved the black up out of the yawlboat and got in; the Mate didn't want me going ashore, I figured, but he hadn't said the yawlboat had to be fast to the schooner.

I rowed around the anchorage, keeping a weather eye out for the Captain. The sloops each had at least one female aboard, with shiny black faces below bright kerchiefs. Men were sculling back and forth in dinghies, taking boatloads of green things the size and shape of bananas in to the landing. The women and men shouted back and forth, voices high and musical, and joked between the passing dinghies. Another sloop came in, rounded up, and dropped anchor, the great mainsail thrashing above a boom a good deal longer than the sloop herself, and she must have been a fifty-footer. The sail was like nothing on heaven or earth, patch on patch, so worn in spots it looked like fishnet. Yet she moved; the sloop, Droits d'Homme, it said across her stern, had come in at a good clip, and pointing too. These sloops weren't much like the Discovery. Later I found the anchorage was full of Haytians, up with truck from their rich mountain fields to sell the Inaguans, who had no more land fit to till than they had mountains.

I saw the Captain halfway down the landing, strolling along in conversation with the Commissioner and made the yawlboat jump, but he was still at the steps before I got there. He didn't seem to mind, and talked for a minute more. They shook hands, and the Captain stepped in across the transom; I'd backwatered in as smartly as I could for him, stern first.

He motioned the Mate aft when he'd boarded the Lavolta. The Mate gave the orders, and we weighed anchor and worked in under short sail until we could anchor again, close to the stone pier south of town. After the Captain was satisfied the anchor would hold another cable was flaked down in the stern of the yawlboat. The two Downeasters ran it in to the pier and made it fast to a bollard, an old cannon-barrel planted muzzle down. They rowed back out and joined us on the capstan. The cable had been rove through blocks at the stern and up to the forecastle, and we heaved around on the capstan until the schooner's stern was in toward the pier, maybe three rods off. Then the Mate paid out on the anchor cable and we took up on the other until the stern was square to the face of the pier and about eight feet from it. "Nigh enough," the Captain shouted from the poop. "Mediterranean style," the Mate told us, "all very well if it don't come in blowing southwest." A bunch of blacks on the pier dragged out a sort of heavy gangplank, and we made one end fast on the poop. The other end kept sliding up and down the end of the pier as we rose and fell to the slight swell, but the blacks came trotting down it as if it were steady as a rock. We took off the straps for them and they began unloading the lumber, four or five boards at a whack on one shoulder and as spry as goats on the heaving gangplank. They loaded the boards on two-wheel donkey carts.

"Horses don't do very well around here," the Mate observed, taking off his cap and wiping the sweat from his brow with his red bandanna, "and you might not do so well doing what those Quashees are doing in this climate neither but there are a plenty of them and they're anxious to work, so you can take easy. Just don't let them get below or start to fighting amongst themselves." So we rigged an old jib as an awning up forward and soldiered in the shade, all of us, the Hogsty Reef Cuban too, and watched the stevedores work.

They'd about finished with the lumber toward dark, and the Mate told us we could go ashore, with the understanding that we were to stick handy by in case the wind shifted or the swell picked up. There wasn't far to go anyhow, I soon found out. Mathewtown petered out about four blocks in from the water, nothing but thick grayish brush and some sickly-looking ponds, gray too and buzzing with mosquitoes. There were two burying-grounds back of town, across the road from each other and walled in. There was a dead dog in the gateway of one of them, an empty rum bottle jammed down his throat. In the gloom I could make out jugs and bottles on a good many of the mounds. The coral rock was right on the surface in the road, and you could tell by the smell nobody in there was planted much below the frost line.

I hurried back toward the waterfront, followed by three solemn pickaninnies. My shipmates were in a small building at the foot of the main street, around a table with candles on it. I went in; the place was sort of a store, with canned salmon and the like on shelves, and wizened vegetables hanging from the rafters. A stout woman of color was ladling out rum from behind the counter. The air was close and still, and after I'd bought a cupful of rum, the white kind, and joined the rest of the crew, the landlady went outside and swung up big shutters on the south wall, so the building was opened up like a booth at a fair. The sky far to the south over Hayti was lit by lightning and after a while we heard a low rumble. You could see the clouds, big anvil-shapes, light up red and pink in the flashes. None of us had much money;

the Captain was too shrewd for that, and would pay us off at the end of the voyage. I bought one round, fifty cents American for five noggins, and we headed back to the schooner, scrawny curs with rat-tails running out at us and barking, lightning flashes giving us enough light to see them and to make our way.

The next morning, we had to turn to, hoisting out the flour barrels, last in, first out, for the Inaguans to roll down the deck, up a pair of oak rails onto the poop, and across the gangway onto the pier. It took three of them on a barrel, and when they got ashore they rolled them up onto the same kind of two-wheel dray they used in Sag Harbor for barrels of whale oil, and they were dragged off by a team of those sorrowful donkeys. The flour unloaded, we went through the same performance with a hundred and fifty fifty-five gallon casks of water. We were glad when we got to the salt cod, stowed fore and aft of the hatch, below the deck. The stevedores brought out a ladder and ran it down into the hold. They'd climb out, holding a bundle on one shoulder with one hand and hanging onto the ladder with the other, and stack it on the landing. Coming back, they'd swing down into the hold, hanging from the combing and dropping, so as not to interfere with the traffic up the ladder. It was so hot you'd catch your breath when you stepped out into the sun -- all of us had big woven straw hats on by now, bought from a peddler woman -- and those blacks worked up a mighty sweat. What with that, being soaked up in the salt cod, and the flies, and piling it right there on the landing in the donkey dung, I didn't know if I'd ever be able to look salt cod in the eye again.

That night, the Captain didn't much like the looks of the weather, and we worked the Lavolta out into the anchorage again. He said he'd let three of us go ashore, and we drew straws. The Englishman -- Captain Shelton made a face when he saw it -- one of the State of Mainers, and I drew long, and rowed in. The Englishman headed off to promote a drunk for himself; Downeast loped up toward the Methodist Church, where they were committing hymns loud enough to be heard clear down the beach; and I decided to walk out to the Light.

The Keeper, an Englishman, and his family were sitting on the verandah of one of the two pink houses at the base of the Light when I got there, and seemed pleased to have some company to show their Lighthouse off to. The Keeper took me up to the top, and pointed out specks of reddish-yellow light far to the westward. "Burning cane fields over in Cuba," he said, his face lighting up and fading out as the beacon rotated, "and there's your vessel, down there." The surf at the base of the cliff below the light sloshed back and forth like suds in a washbasin, and I got dizzy looking down.

Halfway back to Mathewtown, I walked out on a smooth lump of rock above the surf and sat down to watch it again, closer-to. There were hermit crabs everywhere, clattering along on the rocks and in the cracks, dragging their shell-houses with them. I heard a different noise behind me, steps; I swiveled on my backside and saw a figure next to a tree maybe eight yards off. The beam from the Light swept around and I saw it was a girl, black. "What you doin, mon?" she asked, and came toward me. "You wan make jig-jig?" She marched up bold as brass and sat down alongside me, swinging a long rustling skirt, and put her left arm on my shoulder and her right hand on the front of my trousers. I couldn't say anything. "A shillin, mon, we screw all night," she whispered, and got up. She led me by the hand down a gully to the beach. I don't know if I said anything, but she pulled her dress up over her head, laid it on the sand, and dropped down, coaxing me down with her hand. She unbuttoned my shirt and ran her fingers over my chest, going "um, um." Pretty soon she had my pants and drawers off, and was kissing me hard, her mouth open and sweet. Her nipples pressed on my chest, and she swung her leg over me and pretty soon we were going at it hot and heavy, she on top. I hadn't known you could. We rested for a minute, later, with our arms around each other before she took my hand again and walked me to the water. We paddled around for a while, and she began splashing at me. This foolery got us hugging and kissing again, and before long we were back on the sand, she on all fours this time and me behind, reaching around to pull on her nipples. She hadn't any extra meat; I could see the bumps along her backbone when the Lighthouse beam swung around, and her waist was small. She was broad in the sternsheets, though.

This being the second time around, my thoughts strayed a bit and I craned around to look at her heels. Sure enough, they stuck out behind, or up, in this case, with her toes wriggling in the soft sand, sand like flour. I'd been told they were all like that, as sure a sign of black blood as little crescents of white under a fingernail, the white under my nails was little specks like clouds, fuzzy, no black blood, though Indian maybe, and I'd noticed a good many of them back home, where you were pretty much obliged to wear shoes a good part of the time, would slit the heel open for comfort. But then some of them would cut away the uppers, a little hole outside of both little toes and both big toes, and I'd always thought that was for bunions from walking around barefoot back down South and not being used to shoes. There was a buck shod that way in gum boots once at Promised Land, pitchforking bunkers, a buck shod a buck shad, gurry sucking in and out of the holes at every step. In and out, in and out, in and out. I moved my hands back around the inside of her hips, smooth there, and she looked back around her left shoulder and smiled: "Go it, big mon." I did. Then we slept for a while.

Maria was her name. She'd been born and bred in Mathewtown, never been off the island; her father was a straw boss at the saltworks. She'd been to school some and said she could read but you had to pay to go and money was scarce, and what was the use of school in a place like Inagua anyhow? Nassau, that's where she wanted to go, she said. I watched her put her bandanna back on, thinking I'd never before touched hair we called wool at home. "You been Nassau?" I told her about New York. "You foolin," she said, when I told her about the elevated railroad. Did she know of Franklin Pierce Thompson?

"He that Yankee work for Brodie & Bruce, go off last spring in the sloop with two niggers, some say to Cuba. We never see him no more. My sister sleep with him one time, she pine for him."

I told her about the sloop. "No mind about boats," she said, "but that sound like the one. How she ever get way up there?" I tried to explain about the ore, the manganese. "Hore me no ores," she said, and began to haul on me again. As we walked back up the beach to lay on her skirt again, there was giggling and two small figures ran screeching from behind some rocks. "Little buggahs!" Maria howled, "git you home 'fore I mortify you asses!" I laughed and she turned snappish. "You pay now." I gave her two shillings, fifty cents really, the other half of the dollar I'd had when we'd anchored at Inagua, that and a ten-cent piece. She headed for home, swinging her hips and sniffing the air, and I went back to the landing. The yawlboat was still there, but there was no sign of my shipmates. I sat down and leaned back against the palm. The Captain had been right; the breeze had hauled southwest, and the surge in the roadstand was stronger. I snoozed, as limp as last week's lettuce after all that loving.

Chapter
IX

Another Headstone
With Nobody Under It

I came to with a jerk and a bump of my head against the trunk of the palm I was leaning on. A hand was over my mouth and something pricked at my throat. "Up," someone behind me said. I slid up, back on the trunk and the hand, and the knife, rose with me. Another pair of hands tied mine behind my back, and I was gagged and blindfolded. Nothing more was said, and I was dragged off, staggering between the two men -- they had a pretty good hold on my arms -- for two or three hundred yards. We went over a threshold; I tripped but they caught me; and up a steep run of stairs. Someone kicked my legs out from under me and I went down hard on my back. An attic, I guessed when I had hold of myself enough to commence guessing. Somebody rolled me on my side, tied my ankles together, and drew them back and made a line fast between them and my wrists, close together now. There was a creak and a thump, a trap-door most likely. A snap; a padlock? Steps going down the stairs, and silence. There'd been talk, in the forecastle, of vaudoux ceremonies in the islands, sacrificial infants, "goat with no 'orn," the Englishman said they called it. Maybe I was going to have my throat slit on some altar by a bunch of Hottentot Church of Englanders, not even Catholics. Captain Shelton would have to write Father and Mother, and there'd be another headstone up by the schoolhouse with nobody under it. Tears came to my eyes at the thought, and I felt bad I hadn't been to church more regular lately.

A dog barked, just outside. Another mongrel answered, and from way across Mathewtown came a third howl. In a minute, every dog in town had taken up the chorus. It died out, and a cock crowed. Before long all the roosters in Mathewtown were at it. The crowing died out, and the floorboards squeaked.

A hand pressed my arm, and I went stiff. There was a shush close to my ear, and I felt the back of a knife-blade against me, under the lashings. There was a tug, and my hands came free, followed by my feet. "Maria," she whispered, and slipped the blade under my blindfold at the back of my head. She got it off, and unknotted the gag. We tiptoed down the stairs and out, ducking between the next two buildings. She led me to the edge of Mathewtown, and inside of a long two minutes we were dogtrotting down a narrow track, brush slapping at my face every few steps. We'd gone a mile or more when all of a sudden the brush opened ahead. The moon was up, and a great spread of water was shining in its light, water marked off by dikes into squares two or three hundred yards on a side. The salt pans; a quarter-mile to the right was a great white mound, a mountain of salt, waiting to be taken away by donkey cart to the schooners.

We caught our breath, and then set off across one of the dikes, walking and running by turns. On the far side, we headed down a track in the brush once more. There were crashes off to the side. "Wild hogs," Maria muttered. Finally, I could feel a slope underfoot and we soon burst into a clearing on top of a hill, fifty feet high perhaps, but a mountain for Inagua, the brush trimmed low by the northeast breeze, the trades. Ahead of us, as far as we could see, more shining water, undivided by dikes. "Great Lake," Maria said. "Mathewtown," she added, pointing back. You could see the roofs of the buildings in the moonlight. "This where those oldtime Indians lived, before the Spaniards. Caves down below, come on."

She led me down the lake side of the hill and into a cut in the rock that turned into a sort of low doorway. I fished a match out of my tobacco pouch and struck it. We walked in twenty feet and were in a high-ceilinged chamber, bats hanging all about. The match went out. Maria went back, feeling along the walls, and brought in dry grass and branches for a fire. As it flared, the walls showed, where they were too steep and smooth for the bat dung to stick, scratchings, pictures of men and birds, and designs I could make head nor tail of. There were half a dozen straw dolls on the cave floor. "Voodoo traps," Maria said. "People come out here to make magic; law say you can't, so they do it in here and get magic from the oldtime men, the duffies, the ones made those pictures."

We sat facing across the fire, and Maria told me why I'd been put in that attic. "Them boys hear you asking about Franklin Pierce Thompson. They go to Glass-Bottom Bucket and tell them loafers there I romancing you out on the beach and that all you can think about is man missing from The Salt, Brodie & Bruce. Somebody hears them and thinks you too interested, and takes you away for a little private conversation about that topic. Those little buggahs looking for you to torment, they see what happen and tell me. You up under eaves of Brodie & Bruce office. They don't do me nor my fathuh no favors, The Salt, so I not afraid to take you away. I think they slit you throat and throw you in the sea like Jonah I not do that. They going to be after you right smart now."

Before long we were all tied up in a granny knot on my coat and her skirt above the packed-down bat dung. The last thing I thought of, falling asleep, was how it smelled in there like the church belfry back home. We were on top of the hill before sunup, watching back toward Mathewtown for any sign of pursuit. As the sun rose, quick it does in that latitude, Maria pointed east. Far out on the lake was a long pink line.

"Fillymingoes," she said. All at once, they rose, thousands and thousands of flamingos, each a shape now, pink and white against the red sky. The great flock settled in a minute, and it was daylight. Starting from the east, a low puff of cloud came blowing over the lake. The water looked grayish from the hill, but as the cloud crossed over the line of the far shore, its cottony round underside turned pink. "It gets that color like it was a mirror," Maria told me. "That's the little shrimps colors the water, that's why them fillymingoes is pink, too. From eating 'em." We looked toward Mathewtown again, over four or five miles of scrub and salt pan. I could make out the topmasts of the Lavolta; she'd been warped in to the pier again. "Nobody come now, in the heat of the day," Maria said, and we climbed down to the cool of the cave. At dusk, she headed back to town to fetch food and water.

"Everybody miss you, your Captain he storming up and down, but nobody miss me," she giggled on her return after dark. "I try to get a musket for you but all I get is Fathuh's cutlass," and she waved a sort of big knife, not a real cutlass. She had food, and another straw hat. Mine was still back on the beach under the palm tree.

I was to wade across the lake, about due north, to a clump of trees on the horizon. The lake was up to my waist mostly, she said, less than that where the flamingos fed, save for a few holes I could swim if I happened to strike them, and the distance was four or five miles. Three or four hours, she said, if I got under way at first light and missed the worst of the heat of the day. On the far side I'd find the end of a track, "a dom rough one," bearing off northeast toward Union Creek. I should be able to reach the Creek by the end of the second day, if I didn't get lost, or caught, or bit by something or other, or drownded. I had fresh water and I could get more by finding hollows in the rock and scraping away the leaves. At the Creek, I was to wait on the south-west bank until someone appeared on the other side and waved me across. That was important, because if I "come on them sudden, they likely slay you dead." Mistuh Walker would take care of me. She would say no more, except that Mistuh Walker was a Yankee too. The end of the shore road that went half-way around Inagua from east of the Light was at Union Creek, where the track came out, and I was to study things pretty carefully before I stepped out onto the beach there.

I set off as soon as there was light enough in the morning, awake enough to be scared and achey in the groin from the carryings-on of the night; it had been the first I'd known that that sort of thing could be comforting, sort of like two children telling each other not to be afraid. After a few hundred yards I stopped, but Maria was out of sight in the gloom. The going was easy, across a flat plain with short dry grass sloping gently a half mile to the lake. Snail shells no bigger than a grain of rice crunched underfoot, and there were small fish, stranded after the last flood and pickled by the salt in the water and sand, every foot or so. I reached the water, and hitched my load of provisions up around my neck, the cutlass hanging down the middle of my back. It was a long wade out to where the water was knee-deep, and the bottom was hard sand with a few rocks, easy going underfoot with shoes on despite the thousands of snails, live ones this time. It was broad daylight by now, and starting to get hot.

I'd splashed two miles when I heard what sounded like a pistol shot behind. I turned, but could see no one, just a bunch of big pink spoonbills, pelicans, and gulls rising from the shore of the lake back by the hill. I kept on, going as fast as I could, looking behind every minute or so. On the fourth or fifth look, there were three people standing on the hill --men, easy to see against the whitish haze to the south. They'd caught Maria heading back to town, I guessed, and maybe shot her. I felt numb, but it didn't slow me down any. I tried to convince myself the shot had been meant only to stop or frighten her.

I made the far shore before noon, wading along until I sighted the end of the trail coming out of the brush. I had to cross a flat stretch of sand to get to it, leaving tracks no matter how carefully I trod. The track was shoulder-wide and shoulder-high, so you had to go along all stooped over. I walked inland a mile or so and sneaked off to one side to rest and eat. There were little doves, and some chunky green birds that flew like ducks, parrots I guessed. There weren't many hermit crabs, back in here, but there were lizards, curious little fellows ducking in and out of holes in the rock.

Even if someone had started off across the lake after me, and I was pretty sure they hadn't, not having seen anyone, and I'd taken a careful look behind before ducking into the brush, I was at least two hours ahead of them. Coming around by road, through the little settlement Maria had said there was at Man o' War Bay, would take a full day or better, even if they had one of Inagua's few horses, taking into account having to double back to Mathewtown from the hill where I'd last seen them. More likely whoever was after me figured I'd die out here, which might not suit them exactly because if they'd wanted they could have slit my throat easy enough, but which probably wouldn't bother them much either; or that I'd come back with my tail between my legs, and that all they had to do was take me up when I appeared. Either that, or they knew I was headed for Walker and were content with that. I wished I knew more about Walker, and what I was getting into, not fancying the fire after a couple of days in the frying pan.

I started off again, and rounding a bend in the trail roused something large and dusty. It smashed off through the brush. Cow, wild donkey, or pig I could not tell; I'd seen the leavings of all three. The bugs were as bad as Napeague Beach at home, small flies and mosquitoes mostly, and it was hot as an oven. Some creatures like infant lobsters I recognized from stories as scorpions; I was glad to be shod ankle-high.

I slept that night on a big bare patch of smooth rock, Maria's little sack of beans for a pillow, and woke up not knowing where I was for a bit. Her cocoanut was noonday dinner the next day, with beans soaked in the milk. Late in the afternoon, I saw blue water through the bushes ahead, and crawled off to the side of the path to listen. Surf, a long way off, drummed over the steady whistling of the trade wind in the brush. There were no human sounds. I stepped off carefully down the track. After two or three hundred feet, I saw the road, two ruts in the rock, full of sand where they were deep. There was no sign of a creek, and I backed into the bushes to think things over. Union Creek had to be off to the right somewhere. I'd have to go on the road, because if I tried to follow it along in the brush, I'd make as much noise as an elephant, and if I tried to follow along on the beach just through the palms and bushes to the left of the road, I could be seen for miles from either direction.

I took a deep breath and set off down the road, pleased to see that there were no fresh tracks, wheel, hoof, or foot, in the sandy places. It opened up ahead. On the ocean side, there was a wide bay, surf breaking on a reef a mile or more away, and on the other side was a big pond, mangroves along the far side, roots running down into the water. To the right of the end of the road was a rough, shuttered, stone building. I eased up to it, and sat pretty much out of sight for ten minutes, heart thumping away, eyes peeled, before I dared walk out to the bank of the creek between the salt pond and the bay.

The tide was running out strong. The channel was a

hundred yards wide, but it didn't look deep. I saw a big dog-fish, or a small shark, in the shallows. "Hellooo," I shouted, and the echoes helloooed up the creek, putting up some ducks. I looked back at the building and the road, half expecting a shot or a shout behind me. Nothing happened; I helloooed again, and sat.

Pretty soon the bushes moved three hundred yards away, back from the grassy bar on the far side of the creek. A man walked out, telescoping shut a spyglass. He waved his hat in a big half-circle: Come across. I waded in, shark or no shark, making a good splash and not wasting any time. The water was up to my thighs, and warm. The man moved back out of sight as I picked my way between the turk's head cactus on the bar. The pond to my right was quiet again; the ducks had settled back to their feeding. I felt between my shoulderblades as if someone was drawing a bead on me, and I thought that the dust and salt caked in my whiskers -- more than I'd ever had before, not having shaved for a week anyhow before coming ashore -- must make me look pretty sorry. My pants and coat were torn, and the new straw hat had snaggles in it.

The man stood up in the edge of the scrub as I got closer. "Keep to the beach," he said, and waggled me on. He was white, whiskery, and dirty-looking, wearing a waterproof like he was expecting a northeast storm, and a straw hat the same as mine. He had a repeating rifle, lever-action. On the beach, I took off my shoes, and slung them around my neck with my other belongings. The walking wasn't easy. Every so often there'd be mangroves right down to the water and I'd have to wade for a spell. Going along, Inagua's brush and a few palms on my right, I thought of walking away from the picnic grounds at Fresh Pond and began to wish I'd never left that picnic.

I'd gone two miles and about reached the point where the offshore reef branched out from the shore when another man stepped from the brush ahead. He carried a gun, too, and said nothing as I approached, but watched me carefully. "C'mere," he said finally, as if I wasn't. I came up to him and stopped, and he pointed to a path up from the beach. It led to an open meadow, about half an acre, on higher ground with a prospect both ways along the shore. There were a few trees like cedars. And five little palm-thatched huts stood back out of view from the beach. Four dinghies were pulled up on the far side of the point, only their masts showing, and a dozen men were sitting around small fires, having their supper, meat roasted on sticks. Some were black and some were white, but they were all rough-looking, and most of them had pistols in their belts or sticking out of their hip pockets. One man was off by himself, eating out of a tin plate, the only such instrument in sight. I was motioned over. "I'm Walker," he said. "You'd be Dimon, I take it." I nodded yes. "Bring your ass to an anchor," Walker said, waving his spoon toward the ground. I sat and watched him eat canned pork and beans. The men opposite finished their meal, and as they walked off toward the beach I saw that one of them was the Hogsty Reef Cuban. He waved.

"We figured you'd show up here; we heard from Mathewtown you'd put up leg bail," Walker said. "Never fear; they can't get at you. Don't dare." He yelled for coffee and one of the men brought a potful and two tin cups, and rinsed Walker's spoon and plate for me to use. I'd never been much for pork and beans, too much gas, but I gobbled it now. "You're a lucky young man," Walker said. "I don't see eye to eye with Brodie & Bruce about a lot of things; they think they own this island, but they know better'n to monkey with me. I don't know what happened to Thompson, except I guess he's been put to bed with a spade, and maybe they don't either, but they wanted to find out what you knew, and once they'd got it out that would be the end of the line for you."

He stood up, a tall man dressed for a Wild West show, except that he had on a big-brimmed straw hat instead of a felt one and wore leather boots up to the knees in front and cut way low in the back. "Your schooner's loaded her salt and sailed without you, yesterday. We'll be going over into Cuba in a day or two, and you can come along." He hitched his pistol belt up -- he wore a single revolver, a big heavy one butt forward on his left hip -- and walked away, leaving me to finish my beans. Later, I lay down on the shady side of one of the huts and slept until dark.

We got to talking that night, at a small fire away from the rest. "I'm a surveyor by profession," Walker said. "Might as well tell you what we're up to; you'll find out soon enough anyway, it's not much of a secret. I'm the representative, so to speak, of certain North American interests in these parts, like Thompson was of British for all he was from Philadelphia. We got along well enough, by the way, even if you might say we was rivals.

"You've heard of what's going on over in Panama? The canal scheme? It'll be built, that's certain, no matter what a mess old Dellysoups and his Campagnie Universelle du Canal Interoceanique make of it. You know they've lost maybe sixteen thousand men on it already, most of them French, because these West Indian bucks who've been doing the digging is immune to yellow fever, most of them? And that's not counting the railroad, either, with a dead John Chinaman for every tie. Well, for every man, white man, that is, they've lost a thousand dollars or so, and it's plain as the nose on my face that de Lesseps and his gang are broke, flat busted, cleaned out.

"I was on hand, at the mouth of the Rio Grande over at the Bay of Panama, seven years ago, when they broke ground, it didn't take a genius to tell from that little fandango what was going to happen. The Frog in charge of the steamer forgot about the tide -- there's a hell of a rise and fall, maybe twenty feet -- and they got stranded a half mile off shore, all ethered up on iced champagne and the Bishop of Panama the soggiest of the lot. When it came time for de

Lesseps's '*premier coup de pioche,*' that's the first whack with the pickaxe -- they had a little gold one -- they couldn't get to the beach to strike the blow. They made some darkie wade ashore with a box and bring them out a peck of Panama dirt, and they fell to striking that with the pickaxe, everybody having his photograph taken doing it.

"They've pissed away seven years now, and killed God knows how many coolies, and they haven't got their Canal half-built. Part of the trouble is that de Lesseps, soft in the head, must be eighty now, thinks he can build a sea-level canal. You don't have to be a surveyor to see it can't be done, at least not where old Simon Senile's working, you've got to have locks. The only person's going to build that canal is Uncle Sam, and that's where we come in, and why the people I work for don't want the British poking.

"To get to Panama from the East Coast, or from Europe, you've got, pretty much, to come through the Windward Passage, that is, between Cabo Maysi and Hayti, unless you want to go God knows how many miles out of your way. Now the people I work for are interested, to say the least, in shipping. Whether or not the canal is going to be open to all on an equal basis, as the goody-goods keep preaching, makes little difference to my employers. They'll be using it, regular. They're going to need the Navy to keep an eye on the canal and their interest, and they're going to need places to take on coal. It's a hellish long haul from San Francisco to New York, even if you can cut across the Isthmus and don't have to go all the hell and gone down to the Straits of Magellan, and that means coal.

"And protection. Once the canal is opened, the United States is going to have to guard it like you would your balls in a saloon brawl. That's why I'm being paid to take an interest in Cuba, that is, east Cuba mainly. It's not much of a secret; the Spaniards know we're prying around. They're going to lose Cuba, and I get the feeling sometimes that they don't, some of them anyway, worry too much about my little poking and peeking because they think they are going to sell the property to the highest bidder, and what I'm doing, even though they'd be pretty much obliged to shoot me if I was caught at it in a public way, is not much more than an inspection before auction. Sixty years ago, old John Quincy Adams had it put to him by his Ambassador to Madrid: The Don is too proud to sell outright, and too proud to let rebels take the island away from him, yet he needs cash. Why not make him a big no-interest loan, and have him put up Cuba for collateral, for fifty or a hundred years? Pawn it; it'd satisfy his pride and his pocketbook, and at the end of a hundred years he'd never have the cash to redeem it, so you'd just renew the loan and be in a position, like any banker, to tighten the screws a bit. It was too big an idea, and it wouldn't go."

Walker got up and came back with a bottle of rum. He took a pull and handed it to me. It was Jamaica rum, the dark molasses kind, and I had trouble keeping it down, on top of those beans.

"To get back to Cuba. There's a place, Guantanamo, a bay and a town, inland, both the same name, between Santiago and Cabo Maysi. You could anchor the Royal Navy and the Czar's and the American, all of them, in there, room to spare. A tight entrance, easily defended. Guantanamo will be straddle the best track to and from the canal. What I've been up to, off and on and depending on the situation over there, is spying out the land, like in the Bible. It's easy enough to get in and out, but I have to watch my step, between the Spanish and, what's more to worry about, the Cuba Libra gang. They're smart enough to know that when the time comes a lot of our talk about freedom may not mean so much, when it comes to American interests down there in the long haul. So I'm careful, and I haven't lost a man yet but one to the fever, and he wouldn't keep his bowels open, but I probably will before I'm through. I've made some pretty good chain men out of a couple of these monkeys, but there's not a one of them can read or write

English, and that's one of the reasons I'm willing to take you on. That Cuban your schooner picked up tells me you can read and cipher."

We had another drink, and I told him about the Discovery and the bodies. "That sounds like Frank," Walker said. "Where'd they plant him?" In the South End Cemetery at East Hampton -- he'd heard of the Town -- I answered, Thompson up near the monument for the John Milton's crew and the black man down at the bottom of the hill in the fence corner, where the drainage wasn't as good. I described the papers as best I could recollect, and then remembered the ballast. "Manganese," Walker said. "Sure, it's over there, but I don't know if it's worth mining, although that much ore would be enough for a good assay. It wouldn't surprise me none if some day I got orders to do the same thing, gather up some samples."

I got onto Fort Pond Bay, and the Port of Entry plan. "More or less what I'm up to down here at Guantanamo," he said, and paused to belch. "You've got to be able to see ahead, ten, twenty years from now, that's what counts in the money game. That and luck, and having the sense to hire people like me to do your foresighting for you." He stood and headed for his thatched shanty, swaying a bit.

I slept under an old sail slung between two palms. Walker had given me some netting and warned me to use it: "Keep the mosquitoes off." He had a notion mosquitoes aggravated fevers, and was given to taking quinine, Jesuit bark, too, and made me take it, in a draught with rum; bitter.

We spent two days lazing around, the men sleeping in the shade or playing cards. The second day, the Hogsty Reef castaway and a white Bahamian took me out turtling. We got one, dropping a round weighted net, a bullen, on him. One of the men butchered out the turtle, and that night we had a feed. The Bahamians had rounded up a bunch of conches, like what we called winkles at home but three or four times the size, and put them in a kind of corral of sticks stuck down into the sand, in shallow water. If you didn't do that they'd crawl off. They had to open them by bashing a hole through the heavy shell, up near the head, right at the spot where Mr. Conch was anchored to his shell. That was why the Bahamians, the white ones, called themselves Conches. Conks was the way they said it. They ate an awful lot of it, and also they were pretty hard to pry anything out of.

The Conks took the conches and made up a big pot of slumgullion, chopping the meat up pretty good with their cutlasses and pounding it with the backs of the blades, and putting in a lot of pepper and spices and odds and ends of vegetables. They cooked the turtle in chunks over their little fires, and Walker broke out the rum. We were sailing for Cuba the next morning, he said, and a little party was in order.

It turned out to be a pretty big party, and before it was finished Walker had to shoot one of the Cubans, in the leg. We'd done eating, just about everybody was drunk, some of them dancing, except me and Walker. I was scared, and sort of hung back and cut my rum with water. Just after dark, one of the Conks got into a disagreement with this Cuban, a little fellow in dirty white, his shirttail out and tied in front like the rest, and they were going at it, something about a watch, in a crazy mess of Spanish and Bahamas English. All of a sudden the Cuban pulled a knife from inside his shirt, and started after the Conk, who proceeded to run away. Both of them had pistols in their waistbands, but I guess the Cuban didn't want to kill him, only cut him up.

Walker yelled at the man to stop but he headed for Walker, blood in his eye. Walker yanked out his Smith and Wesson, and stuck it out in front of him in both hands. He was holding low. The Cuban came on, and Walker let go, hitting him in the left leg and knocking him over backwards. The Cuban started to scream, all the same high note, for a minute or so. Walker took his knife and pistol away, and cut his pants leg open with the knife. The slug had gone right through, above the knee, and Walker said it didn't seem to have hit the bone, in a satisfied sort of voice. He dribbled some rum from his tin cup on the hole -- it seeped through, and ran out the bottom onto the dust, mixed with blood -- and bandaged him up with strips from the trouser-leg, squinting against the light of the fire.

We were half a day late getting started the next morning, because four men had to cart the Cuban back to Man 'o War Bay, with some money to board him with a family until he got well, or died. The little steamer that was to take us across showed up just as the men were getting ready to set off, and Walker rowed out to tell the Captain to wait. We spent the rest of the morning tidying up the camp. Walker had all the dinghies but one hauled up away from the water, where they'd be safe until we got back. Then we went out, the dinghy making two trips and then going back to wait for the sanitary corps detail.

Chapter
X

Keeping Our Ebony General In Business

The steamer was really just an old diving bell of an over-sized launch, about seventy-foot long and with one single cabin stretching most of her length, the wheelhouse no more than the forward part of the cabin, which had benches down both sides and in the middle like the East River ferry. Her nameboards read "Spanish Wells Mail," but the men called her the Spoonbill, because she was long and drooping in the bow, like the bird. While we waited, I toured the engine room. The Chief Engineer -- only engineer, really -- was a white Bahamian, like the Captain. He took Copenhagen snuff, packing it under his upper lip, and wore a shirt with no collar and a bandanna tied around his neck to keep the sweat from running down from the top of his bald head onto his back and chest, and making gullies in the good topsoil there. He was a little man, with no teeth to speak of, and told me he had been Chief on the Great Eastern. "The Great Iron Ship," he said, "biggest wessel in de world." He looked at me out of the corner of his rheumy eye to see if I had swallowed that. "Yis, mon, fifty-five men to de watch, in de black gang." The Chief's black gang on the Spoonbill was a sad-eyed Abaco buck, black enough for anybody, who fussed with the fire like Mother with her kitchen range, dribbling chunks of coal from his shovel here and there, just so, and shaking his head mournfully at what the Chief was telling me.

The Chief walked over to the bulkhead. A small strip of lath had been tacked to one of the frames, about shoulder-high and sticking out toward the side of the boiler, which was one of the up-and-down kind, riveted wrought iron. He stuck his hand flat between the boiler and the end of the stick, quick, because the plating was good and hot. "Three finger. Hunned-fift' pound, don't want much more 'n at, Sam." "Aye, aye, Chief," Sam replied, and I got out of the engine room and aft, wanting to be as far from the boiler as I could get, with that style pressure gauge and that man clerk of the works. Pretty soon the stretcher-bearers appeared on the beach, and we soon got under way, towing the dinghy behind.

I slept on deck that night, looking up at the stars and wishing I was home. By morning we were coming around Cabo Maysi, great mountains rising up steep from a mill-pond ocean on our starboard bow, different from anything I'd ever seen before. We chuffed along steadily, and late in the day the Captain had his Deck Gang, a younger and more cheerful edition of the Black Gang, bring the Spoonbill onto a new course, northwest, straight for the mountains. We were within a mile or so of the shore, rocky cliffs, before I made out the channel entrance.

"Guantanamo," Walker said, and shooed us all into the cabin out of sight. I polished up the glass of a porthole and watched. We made the entrance and slowed, coming around to starboard. "Caimanera is away down there, around the bend," Walker told me, gesturing toward the portholes across the cabin. We went up a creek, cliffs to the left and lower ground to the right, and made fast to a little dock. Walker said we could go on deck. Half a dozen barefoot Cubans stood silently watching us, not helping Deck Gang with the lines. After a while, a team, led by an outrider in high-fronted boots like Walker's and pulling a carriage contraption, two wheels at the after end of a pair of long shafts that held up a buggy with a top, pulled up. A big, fat man in white, clean linen for a change, wearing a red sash, got out and talked with Walker. Then off they went in the carriage. The Spanish-speaking members of Walker's gang climbed over to the dock and talked with the Cubans, or tried to talk to them, because they were awfully solemn-choly. I sat with my legs over the side and stared at the water. It was blue-green, like no water I'd ever seen. By the way the banks, soft limestone like at Inagua but browner, dropped off, I figured the little basin we were in was very deep. You'd have to be right on top of us to see the Spoonbill, closed in by little hills and the bluff, which made it close and hot. Birds were tweet-tweeting back in the shade of the trees at the top of the cliff. I got up and went into the cabin to get out of the sun.

There was a clatter ashore finally, and Walker reappeared with a string of ratty ponies; he was astride the likeliest of the lot. We got our gear and we were off, me aboard the smallest pony, being the youngest though far from the smallest. We went east at a good clip, away from the water and uphill. Walker brought up the rear, and kept looking back. The men seemed to know where we were going, and showed no concern. We passed the fat man's house -- he was standing in the gateway to a courtyard -- and the road entered thick woods. In an hour or so we came out on a high bare ridge, and could see back to the bay. The ocean was three or four miles south and far below. I was on higher ground by far than I'd ever been.

We commenced our surveying, a different camp each night and a picket posted. There were troops out looking for us, Walker said, Spanish regulars, but he doubted if they'd look very hard or bother us if they found us by some mischance. He was more worried about some of the political bandidos, strays left over from the 1868-78 war, or the little one in 1880, or some of the newer ones. Each morning bright and early, we'd be out with the theodolite and Gunter's chain, devil's guts Walker called it, me taking it all down in the field book for him and the men taking turns with the offset pole and being out as pickets. As a survey, Walker said, it wouldn't pass muster in the States, even out where they had Indians to contend with, but he didn't dare take much time nor pains. We worked mostly by triangulation, going up on top of one mountain or hill and taking bearings on all the other peaks in sight, and then going to another and repeating the process. We worked right on around inland of Guantanamo Bay, trying to keep out of sight of the cutters working in the canefields below, until we were close to the sea again. Walker said it was a good country to be a surveyor in, all up and down like that. You'd think the work would be easier in flat country but I learned quickly how they used the hills to sight from. If they had to work on a flat plain, they'd have to build little towers to get the height.

This was Santiago Province, and about half the people we saw -- we couldn't dodge them all -- were Negroes of one shade or another. We also saw indentured laborers, Chinese, although they'd pretend we weren't there. Crossing a valley to get to another hill, we'd wait by the road that follows the bottom of most of the valleys before we ran the traverse across, trying to keep from being seen by the drivers of the big two-wheeled ox-carts. You could hear them coming a mile off, big wooden wheels screeching under five or six tons of cane. They raised half a dozen crops a year, Walker told me, the soil was that good. Walker had timed it so we were working just after the end of the rainy season. There was a lot of traveling on the roads, which I guessed even an ox-cart would get bogged down in the wet months. I was amazed to find out a good many of the people in Santiago Province had leprosy, and you'd seen some poor devil walking along with a face as flat as a biscuit, no nose nor ears, he afraid of us and we not wanting to look at him but not being able not to. A lot of them had consumption, too, and you could hear them coughing and hawking like an old man getting out of bed in the morning as they came down the path.

We ate pineapples and goat mostly. The men shot a few hutias, big things like land muskrats, but I can't say as I enjoyed eating them. There were turkey buzzards in the sky always, circling high above the ridges, and a good many hawks. Down in the swamps by the sea, Walker said, there were crocodiles and caymans, but we never saw any. The worst trouble we had was with chiggers, little burrowing bugs would drive you mad with itching. I'd sprouted the good beginnings of a beard, so between scratching at that and harrowing out the chiggers I was between Job and Lamentations a good deal of the time.

Walker seemed to have more than the usual interest in innards: "Your bowels, Dimon, keep them open, key to health in the tropics. That and keeping your feet dry." The feet was second fiddle to the bowel, though. Each morning he'd go off behind a tree and squat down and you could hear him grunt and groan and then there'd be a quiet spell while he inspected what he'd brung forth and then generally a tsk, tsk. He never seemed satisfied; I had an idea his everlasting quinine had soured his digestion, and given what he seemed to turn out each morning regular enough some sort of imperfection. He'd come out from behind his tree though with his big jaw stuck out as if he wasn't going to let the bad news he'd just heard from his droppings faze him, tugging that gunbelt back into position just right below his belly, which was of a proportion to match the rest of him. He'd be all right except when we'd come across, alongside the trail, a pile of somebody else's shit, and that would set him off again. He'd look at it and draw his conclusions and go tsk,

tsk, and say something like "Poor Devil!" or "Wormy." In the morning, he'd say first thing, "A fine day, Dimon. How's your lower intestine?" I hadn't been brought up for that kind of talk, at least from a grown man.

We'd been there better than a week, working every day and sleeping out in the open, when Walker led us to a big house, at the back of a valley. Like most houses in those parts, it was royal palm top to bottom -- beams, rafters, thatch, everything. The furniture was royal palm, and the dishes, too. They even concocted liniments from royal palm, and healing broths. The place had a big porch along the south side, and we rested there while Walker talked in Spanish with the man of the house, who kept his wife and what sounded like daughters inside. "We'll wait," Walker said, and the Cuban disappeared behind of the house. He returned in an hour, and whispered to Walker, who got up and sauntered out into the middle of the clearing. Pretty soon, twenty or thirty men walked out from the trees, led by a small man in a grimy white uniform, on a pony. He was hung with a sword and a pistol, and wore a solar topee. He was coal black, although most of his men looked about white to me.

The man swung down and shook Walker's hand. "An honor, as always," we heard Walker say, wiping his palm on the seat of his trousers, and the man answered something you couldn't catch. They went to the far end of the clearing and sat facing on the ground. The other band sat in the shade and smoked, paying no attention to us. Walker and their leader talked for ten minutes, and Walker gave him an envelope, which the man put into an inside pocket unopened. They rose, shook hands again, and parted. Walker came up on the verandah with us and his visitor led his pony away from where it had been grazing, reins on the ground, his men falling in behind as he walked into the woods. Walker winked at me. "A little Christmas present. That'll keep our ebony General there in business for another year or so." The white Bahamians snickered.

The General's main occupation, it turned out. was burning canefields. We often saw his pillars of smoke by day and bright patches of fire on far-off slopes at night. His band, and others, lived by blackmail; the planters anted up or had their crop burnt. Twice we came on what was left from another kind of fire, small patches of ashes, once still smoking, where houses had been burned by Spanish troops. There was a pile of just-turned dirt in one dooryard, a grave for the family probably, Walker said. "That's the way they hang on," he told me. "They kill just to make an impression, sometimes. There's money in Cuba, for the Spanish, and they won't give it up until they have to. I don't blame the Cubans for wanting to get rid of them. Though they're not wild for trading Spain for Uncle Sam, even knowing we'd do better by them."

I thought a white man wouldn't put up with living that way, the burning and the killing, but it didn't seem to make much difference to these Cubans. They just kept on chopping cane and planting their fields where anybody else would either have started a revolution or quit the country. The way they wouldn't look at us, pretend we weren't there, was part of it too. I guess they'd do the same to the Dons, and maybe it didn't make much difference, as poor as they were.

We managed to stay well clear of the troops; there weren't that many of them down in this end of the Province anyway, Walker said. It was almost a month before he was satisfied with what we'd accomplished, and he began to talk about heading back to Inagua. One day I asked him what the date was. It was the 27th of December, two days past Christmas and I hadn't even known. "You're welcome to come back with us, Dimon," he said, "but I don't know as there's much percentage in it for you. I guess you'll want to get on home, and you can't go back to Mathewtown very well. We'll just be squatting up at Union Creek for a month or so while I work up the field notes into something presentable to send on. If I was in your shoes I'd get over to the American Consul in Santiago de Cuba and see about passage north. We can ease you into Caimanera, and my friends there'll get you over to Santiago."

The Hogsty Reef Cuban and I were paid off on New Year's Day, 1888, and the last I saw of Walker and the others they were loafing in the woods east of Caimanera, waiting for the Spoonbill, Walker fretting over his bowels. He'd had a bad report that morning. Hogsty's real name was Jesus Jose Maria Balmaseda, the first colored Catholic I'd run across, although they all were down there. He led the way toward his birthplace. By this time I could understand a little of what the Cubans said, and Hogsty had picked up a little English. He was agreeable and pulled his weight, and I'd gotten fond of him. I had a letter and a twenty-dollar gold piece from Walker; he'd given Jesus Jose Maria ten, in silver.

Caimanera wasn't much of a place, but the streets were cobbled, a few of them, and there were some fine buildings, one a big church with bells we could hear up in the hills. Hogsty took me where Walker had directed, to a house down by the water. I pounded on the courtyard gate and the black man left me with an "adios." Without thinking, I ran after him, and shook his hand. We were both surprised. Then I heard the gate rasp open, and turned. A hatless man in sandals stood in the entrance, the chief servant I found out later. He made a face like he'd smelt frowy butter and I knew how I must look. I poked the letter toward him. He looked at the address upside down, waved me in, shut the gate behind me, barred it, and disappeared into the house.

There was a pool in the center of the court, with plants in pots around it. I looked at myself in the water. There wasn't much you could see, under the big hat and whiskers. The wrinkles around my eyes showed whiter than the rest, from squinting in the sun, and what little hide was in sight looked pretty dirty. It didn't look like me, but then I never much recognized myself in a mirror. My coat and pants had small rips and were stiff with dirt and salt from my sweat. I'd grown an inch or so, too, or my clothes had shrunk, and my ankles and wrists stuck out. The man returned and led me in to see his master, whose name I never really got -- it was Fuentes y de la Huerta, or thereabouts -- who told me in passable English that any friend of Walker's was a friend of his. They gave me a room, and servants filled a tub and a barber was fetched while I had a wash. The head servant brought me a suit of clothes, tight trousers in Cuban fashion, underlinen, a white shirt, a dark waistcoat, and a coat with buttons from Genesis to Revelations. He took away my own clothes like he was carrying a dead cat, and I never saw them again. The barber tackled the top of my head first and then gave me a shave, leaving me a pretty good mustache and long burnsides.

I stayed three days, and they were kind to me. We got up late, maybe nine o'clock, and had a little strong coffee and a roll. Around noon, we'd have dinner, *almuerzo* they called it, and along toward ten o'clock in the night they'd have supper, all of us. The Mrs. was an agreeable lady running a bit toward fat in her late twenties. Her husband, a quiet man who had a business of some kind, never told me how he knew Walker, nor did I ask. They had three daughters, the oldest young enough so I guessed they figured she was safe around me, ten or eleven. The girls, who reminded me of my sisters far away, would point at one of their eyes, and tee-hee, and say *azul*, on account of mine being blue, though blue eyes weren't all that uncommon in Cuba. There were also two stout old girls in the household, who were aunts. Supper would be a big meal, bits of cold meat and sausage, soup, fish, crabs, sweet potatoes, rice, and with wine. They drank maybe a bottle and a half among them each night, although the girls' wine was watered and they never seemed to get tipsy. Mr. Fuentas told me it would be better if I didn't go out of the house, so I stayed there in the evenings, when they'd all go down to the square in the middle of town and walk around. I could hear the military band playing there, mostly a Spanish sort of music, though they had an Iberian rendering of old "Hurrah, Hurrah, we'll sing the song we sung. As we went marching through Georgia."

On the third day, I went to Santiago in an underslung buggy, a volante, with the Fuentes' groom riding alongside to lead the team. It was an all-day excursion, even in good weather, they said, so we left at dawn. Mr. Fuentes got up early to see me off, and I knew better than to offer to pay him for the lodging, clothes, and buggy ride. We shook hands, American style. I'd been afraid he'd try that hugging business they call *abrazo*, and I gave him my thanks as best I could.

It was a long day, hot and dusty, and I'd doze until a wheel would drop into a pothole or hit a rock and wake me up. We reached Santiago after dark, and the groom took me to a hotel down by the water, where I took a room. I signed the register Jeremiah Huntting Dimon, United States Citizen, and put down Seaman in the blank for occupation. The clerk told me where I could find the Consul in the morning. The room was neat and clean, and after sloshing off the dust of the road I went down to get supper. There was a door in the side of the hotel, opening onto a yard walled off from the street and lit by lanterns. I sat at a table in back, under a big palm. It was the first time I'd ever eaten alone in a restaurant in my whole life, and even though there weren't many people in the place, I felt as though they were all looking at me, and was uncertain about how to go about getting some grub. A man brought me a card with what they had in the place written on it, but since I couldn't decipher it, I asked for a beefsteak, potatoes, and beer, which he understood.

Chapter
XI

The Bad Penny Turns Up

I was halfway through the steak when I felt someone standing behind me, and craned around to see a belly as big as a pillow under a black vest traversed by a gold chain bearing an elk's tooth. A left hand was hooked in the watch pocket, and a right hand was swinging a beaver-tail. I looked up into the smiling face of Charles Stuart Pufferson Homidy.

"The bad penny turns up," he said. I knew he meant me, but I thought he could have said it of himself. "Are you going to ask me to join you, or am I going to have to wend my way back to Amagansett to tell the good people that a son of their fair village fell aboard of poor old yours truly amongst the heathen Caribbees, and then condemned him to his last supper alone?"

"Yes, yes," I mumbled, trying not to show my surprise, and he eased down into the chair across the table and went on. "I will not ask what brings you to these parts, or observe that it is indeed a small world, but proceed to what is without a doubt uppermost in your inquiring mind, viz., what in the name of all that is good and holy is Puff Homidy doing in

Santiago de Cuba? Rest your mind at ease; I am here, if not on the Lord's work, at least upon good works, what might well be termed a missionary endeavor. Some of the local capitalists engaged me some time ago to build them a wind saw-mill, to be assembled here, in the hopes of transforming the bounteous forests of this lesser but blessed isle into an honest dollar. They were mightily impressed with what I sent them, but they couldn't figure out how to put the works back together in running order. They cabled north for the author of the machine; I took the first steamer south and assembled the mill upon an elevation back of the town. They were so taken with the cunning thing -- they can get five thousand board feet out of it in a long day with a decent breeze, and with no more than two agile Celestials on the helm -- that they asked me to sojourn for a time, to build them a few more mills out of local timber, and teach them to build their own, the better to alchemize their cedar and mahogany into gold. Between you and me, Jerry my boy, I think they'd be better off with steam mills, but it is not my wont to argue with a customer, particularly one beguiled by the notion of all that free energy going to waste to leeward.''

"You've grown,'' he said abruptly, and snapped his fingers for the waiter. "The usual for me, and a pair of the cup that cheers for the two of us.'' I finished the steak while he was waiting for his provender, and telling me about trying to explain the mill to the Cubans. The waiter came back with a tray with bottles, glasses, ice, and a pitcher. He put ice, rum, brandy, and some odds and ends in the pitcher and shook it around and stirred it with a long spoon. Then he poured into the two glasses; all he'd used to measure with had been his eye, but he had just enough to fill both glasses right to the brim. That ice might have been some of Whitcomb, Haynes & Seavey's, down from Maine by schooner. The drink was smooth as milk. "Your first cock-tail?'' Mr. Homidy asked, and I nodded. "A *refresco*, with *ron*. That's rum.'' The waiter came back with a plate of sliced dried meat. "Try some," Mr. Homidy said. "Smoked wild pig; it'd raise a thirst on a fish."

His grilled chops arrived. He attacked the four of them, and rattled on. His mother had never rapped him alongside the head with a spoon for talking with his mouth full, you could see that. He went through his trip down and into a jumble of tales about mills, full of spur wheels and wind-shafting and people getting struck on the head by the arms. He snapped his fingers and the waiter came back and mixed another pair of *refrescoes*. I had some more smoked pork, and listened. Pufferson could almost put you under, like Professor Mesmer, who'd lectured at Clinton Hall when I was fourteen. He'd had the Electric Girl along; they'd stretched her between two chairs on the stage and the men went up and stood on her belly, foolish grins on their faces. If he'd taken his great turnip of a watch out and swung it, the way the Professor had, I believe I'd have gone into a trance fit for belly-walking too. Great market for cedar in the States . . . letter of introduction. . . . A lot of them are Masons, have Rid the Goat . . . question of decent steel for the blades. . . . The trades are steady, but as I said steam might be better . . . need railroads here . . . big on duelling, watch your step my boy. . . . used to work with oak or pine, not this tropic stuff. . . . You'll have another alleviator, won't you?

I started to shake my head no, but by the time I got it in motion it was too late. The waiter poured again, and I ad-mired the way his hand swooped down with the pitcher and came back up, just enough for the two glasses again.

"And what have you been up to, young man?"

I took a long sip before answering, and then launched into a recitation of my adventures. Mr. Homidy let me run on; the next morning I could remember him sitting across the table, and asking some questions, I couldn't remember what. I couldn't remember what I'd told him, either, but I could remember it was important, and that I was quite some shakes. We'd had more drinks, too, but I couldn't remember how many. In fact, I couldn't remember when, or how, I'd got to bed, but there I was, church bells jangling outside. Who but a Cuban, I thought, would make church bells out of iron and cracked at that? My head was pounding, and my tongue feeling as if a troop of ox-carts had trundled across it. My clothes were on the floor beside the bedstead and the sun was high, by the shadow on the floor. There were pigeons cooing loudly on the ledge below the window. I got up and took a long drink of water from the spout of the pitcher on the commode. I went to use the chamber pot and saw there was puke in it, and had a vague recollection of being sick. There seemed to be something very wrong but I couldn't exactly put my finger on what it was; the sky over the roofs of Santiago looked bluer than it should.

I felt better after some coffee, a couple of rolls, and some fruit down in the restaurant. Then I set out for the Consulate. I had some trouble getting past the clerk, a Cuban, but I finally got in to see the Consul, a dry little man in glasses and a very high collar. His name was Hughes. I told him I'd been left behind by my ship at Inagua and had gotten over to Santiago to catch another. He frowned. That posed a problem of regulations, he said. Pausing every few words to suck in some air and smack his lips on top of it, he went on about entry, passports even, suck, smack, and said it might be better to just consider me an American seaman stranded in Santiago, suck, smack, and, if I couldn't get a berth on an American vessel bound north, suck, smack, he'd consider advancing me my passage, steerage, on the next steamer, suck, smack, suck, smack. I told him I had a little money, trying hard not to mimic his breathing nor his bottlefish grimace. And, trying not to sound as young as I suddenly felt, I added my parents would probably be worried. He'd arrange to cable them, he said, suck, smack, but I'd have to reimburse him, suck, smack. I was willing, and we left it that I'd try for a berth on my own and check in at the Consulate each day. He ended up with a general warning about houses of assignation, suck, smack, rum palaces, and cockfights. He stood up -- I hadn't sat down, he had the only chair in the room -- and I left, wondering how he breathed when he didn't have somebody to talk to.

There were coasting sloops and small schooners two and three deep alongside the seawall, but they wouldn't do. An English brig swung at her anchor, and there was only one steamer, the Dee of Cardiff, at the pier. I walked out past her, a five or six hundred ton vessel loading bagged coffee, and sat on the end of the pier. There couldn't be much ebb and flow of tide in Santiago Harbor. The water was brown, thick as chowder, and as aromatic, though not in the way would make you want to crumble pilot biscuit in it and taste. There were fish in the Harbor all the same. Big brown pelicans were gliding along and folding themselves of a sudden and dropping straight into the water, almost always coming up with something. A pulling boat went past, headed for the brig, and its oars stirred a smell like a last-year's dead horse. The wind was southerly, dropping out.

"A norther coming." It was Puff Homidy, tip-toeing up behind again without my knowing. "And how is your pate this morning? No offense intended, but you had a few taken last night, as our Hibernian dynamitard friends say." I was all right, I answered, wondering again what I'd said the evening previous. He grunted and groaned, sitting down beside me.

I told him what had passed with Mr. Hughes. He sat quiet for a few minutes, fingering the beaver-tail. "Tell you what, Jerry," he said after a while. "I'm about to embark for the Colossus of the North. The Dee back there is headed for Baltimore, with a stop or two along the way. I am considering seeking passage aboard of her; you have a little money; if you would care to accompany me on the voyage, as a passenger, there being little question of your working your passage as a redemptioner aboard a steamer, most especially one of British registry and with a crew of East Indian Ganymedes, I would advance what you might need to make up your tariff, upon your signing of a promissory note, say ninety days, at a reasonable rate of interest, seven and a half per cent per moon? What say you, Jerry?"

I was a long way from home, and I'd made my mind up before he finished. I sat without saying anything for a while, though, too, so's not to give him the satisfaction. "That's kind of you, Mr. Homidy. I accept your offer," I told him finally.

We walked back up the pier and found the Captain of the Dee, a Scotchman from the Clyde like his ship, which had been, we found out later, registered in what he called Leekshire, Wales, for some business reason. He didna carry passengers as a rule, he said, dragging out rule rrrulle, but he could fit us into the mates' stateroom. Price. Weel, that could be reckoned later, no rrrush about that. Mr. Homidy tried to pin him down, and it was something to hear, the two of them going around and around over their bargaining like two dogs over something slipt from the butcher's wagon. They settled it finally, twenty-eight dollars each, and then it dawned on Mr. Homidy that Captain Strathmiglo meant that our meals would be figured separately. So they went at it again, and finally hit upon thirty-three cents per mouth per day, the duration of our voyage being impossible to calculate. Then we were shown to the stateroom, which started another dogfight.

The stateroom was right over the engine room, with one porthole and no air. The iron plates underfoot were hot enough to cook on, and the cabin was about six feet wide and seven deep, with two bunks either side. The only furniture was a basin on a stand. "A bargain is a barrrgain," purred the Captain, and Mr. Homidy gave up. There was no sign of the First and Second Mates, who would share the cabin with us, save their spare clothes, heaped in our bunks.

We'd sail in the morning, Captain Strathmiglo an-

nounced, and he asked for half our passage money, as surr-
rety that if we missed sailing he would not be in the position
of having such valuable accommodations going begging.
The heat had got to Mr. Homidy; he folded, though not without one last feeble struggle. He counted out twenty-eight
dollars Cuban, in paper, but gave in without a whimper
when the Captain insisted on Cuban silver, or United States
dollars. The Cuban shinplasters were worth maybe forty
cents American just then, and were so dirty you stood a
good chance of getting scabies from having them in your
pocket. I was borrowing the whole twenty-eight dollars; I'd
use what I had left of Walker's twenty dollars for food and
spending money.

"That man is tight enough to hold kerosene," Mr. Homidy remarked, and we went ashore, figuring to come aboard
first thing in the morning, to save us at least one night in
that oven. We had dinner at the same place. "Strike a blow
for liberty?" Mr. Homidy offered. I refused, and bought a
bottle of beer to go with the meal. There was to be a bullfight
late that afternoon, he said, in honor of some saint's birthday, and he was going, and he thought I'd find it education-
al. I was still angry with myself, and him, for the night before, and said I'd stick to the hotel.

We got under way at sunrise, the norther beginning to
blow just as Mr. Homidy had predicted. It was smooth
enough in the lee of Cuba as we steamed east through the
day. Along toward dark, though, after we passed the entrance to Guantanamo Bay, the distance between us and
the shelter of the hills to windward began to grow as the
shore bore away more to the northard, and the Dee commenced to roll.

For thirty-three cents a day, Mr. Homidy maintained we
should dine with the Captain, and won his argument. I
thought I had a pretty good stomach, on the water, but
when the First Mate came up from below, where the mates
and licensed engineers ate at their own table in the crew's

mess, I had to stop eating. He was waving a big chunk of gray meat, impaled on a fork, and complaining bitterly about maggots. The Captain said he couldn't see any maggots, and chased him below with a curse. It wasn't bad enough he had a Hindoo crew on deck, the Captain remarked, but he had two Englishmen as mates. His engine room was all Scots or Welsh, though. He looked over at my plate, observed how little I had eaten, and smiled, no doubt reflecting that at the rate I was going thirty-three cents a day was going to make him some money. I turned in.

The next couple of days were uneventful, although it got as hot as ever it was at home in July or August. It was pleasant all the same. One afternoon, a little bored, I sneaked a look at the chart in the cabin behind the wheelhouse and saw that Captain Strathmiglo had laid out a course up through the Windward Passage and the Mayaguana Passage, the same way we'd come in through the Bahamas in the Lavolta. From the far end of Hispaniola, it was almost a straight line to Baltimore, through the Windward Passage, past Inagua, Hogsty Reef, San Salvador, and up outside of Cape Hatteras to the Virginia Capes and Chesapeake Bay. He could have got more of the Gulf Stream behind him by running up between the Bahamas and Cuba to the Straits of Florida, but then Captain Strathmiglo had a steamer and didn't have to worry so much about the Gulf Stream, and you could see by the chart that going up through the Old Bahama Channel you'd have to watch what you were doing every minute.

Captain Strathmiglo stepped in and caught me in his chartroom. He didn't seem to mind. He reached up and took down one volume of the Admiralty Sailing Directions from the shelf over the chart table. "Isle de la Gonave, laddie," he said. "We're passing her down our larboard side, and I'm fond of reading about these places as I see them. Good as a university education, and farrr less expense." He showed his tea-stained teeth; the Captain liked to play-act the miser

Scotchman. He stepped out on the port wind of the bridge and read what the Lords of the Admiralty had to say about La Gonave, looking down at the words and then up at what they described.

I had slept an hour or two the second night out, fitful in the heat, when the air turned cooler. It had come on blowing half a gale out of the north, and I went on deck and climbed the ladder to the bridge. The binnacle light was enough to show the Hindoo helmsman's face, his mouth working as he concentrated on keeping course. The masthead lights swung in wide arcs aloft, and the glow of the red and green running lights could be seen above the bulwarks at either wing. The wheelhouse doors were open, and I walked through onto the windward wing. There were lights, fires, off in the distance, on our quarter now, high up. Cabo Maysi, I guessed, canefields burning again, the General at work most likely. I returned to the starboard wing, and studied the blackness off the Dee's beam. There it was, the pulsing loom of Mathewtown Light, looking as if it flared up and down, instead of sweeping around as I knew it did. I'd first seen Maria by the beam from that Lighthouse, I thought, and swallowed hard.

Chapter
XII

What Every Traveler Has To Learn

Captain Strathmiglo gave Hogsty Reef where we'd found the Cuban a wide berth the next morning, and we couldn't even see the cairn. I slept a lot every day after that, and walked around and around on deck. Sometimes Mr. Homidy and I'd find a place in the lee and the sun, if there was any, and sit on deck. One afternoon when we were up off South Carolina, Mr. Homidy stopped in the middle of a long story about a bucketful of live eels, spilled by mistake down a well in Freetown, and how Old Man Banks went a-spearing from the top of the well curb to retrieve them, to say he'd talked too much that night back in Santiago. I didn't say anything.

"Wine is a mocker, strong drink is raging, Jerry, and the chiefest of them that rage is rum, especially when it's mixed with fruit juice and sugar and the rest. I'd appreciate it if you didn't let anybody know I was acquainted with the late lamented Franklin Pierce Thompson, nor anything about who he worked for. As for my own business connections in that line, the less said the better too."

I nodded, and thought hard. The harder I thought the

less sure I was about anything that had passed that night in the restaurant. It seemed to me I'd done all the talking, but then came a sudden recollection of Mr. Homidy's leaning across the table, his face like an owl in a rosebush with his eyes big above his whiskers, telling me something about Thompson. Same line of work but for London . . . Iron and Steel Association . . . Walker . . . Protective Tariff League . . . Walker's employers more or less the same crowd, except he was keeping an eye on Guantanamo, east Cuba, and he was mainly engaged in some researches involving Fort Pond Bay. It was indeed sad about ole Frank P. but then he'd known what the risks were, been paid accordingly, and now you know, too, Jerry though there was no call for them to try to wipe your slate just because your natural boyish curiosity led you to ask about him. . . . My head began to ache again, and I tasted bile.

"I hadn't known you'd known Walker, that's all," I said, not sure why.

"I don't know him, exactly," Mr. Homidy said hurriedly. "I'd hoisted in a good deal too much benzine that evening and would just as soon you forgot all about that, and considered yourself well out of it." He looked uneasy, the first time I'd seen him so. We sat silent.

Homidy and Walker and Thompson. Homidy and Walker working for American investors Homidy had called them. Even A.P. Blake, he'd said. Thompson working for British capital. Both syndicates interested in east Cuba, and in the port of entry scheme at Montauk. "You might say we were rivals," Walker had said. Brodie & Bruce was a British firm; you wouldn't have expected the British to perform that way, like greasers.

Maria was dead probably, but what for? Thompson, and at least one of his two companions, was dead too. Who'd done it? Why hadn't whoever killed Thompson taken the ballast in the sloop? Maybe they hadn't known it was Cuban manganese. Around and around, things were meshing, though I couldn't tell why, like Byram's brass universe in Dr. Fordham's study. I looked at Mr. Homidy. He was lighting a big Habana.

"Your Father ever tell you about the time we rang the bell on the Session House at Halloween, the bell off the wreck John Milton? Well, he and I got about thirty fathom of codline. . . ." He was off, and I half-listened as I tried to figure things out, unable to remember more of that night at Santiago. Thompson was buried near the John Milton's crew's grave, in the South End Cemetery. Homidy knew that; maybe that had made him remember the Halloween story.

We had good weather until we got to Cape Hatteras, where it was bound to be bad in the winter, according to the Captain. It was blowing fresh out of the northwest as we came up on Diamond Shoals, and the sea was a sight to behold. The Gulf Stream comes in close down there, and what we were in was like the tide rip at the Race, only a hundred times as big, the current setting against the wind and peaking the seas up. It was bad enough wind northwest; what it would be like blowing hard northeast I didn't want to think. I didn't feel very good, not that I was sick. You'd think the pitching would be more or less the same, sail or steam, but it isn't. The Dee would dig her bow right under, a bloody bathing-machine the Captain called her. The next sea, she'd just as likely ride way up on it, bow high, until the sea passed amidships. Then the bow would slam down into the trough, her broad flat bottom sending great clots of white spray out port and starboard. It was a pretty sight, it being clear weather and blue skies, but the Lascars didn't appreciate it. They were shivering most of the time now.

We came in past Cape Henry at mid-day January 19th, Mr. Homidy eager for sights he remembered from the War; he'd been on the Peninsula with McClellan's Army, in one of the three-month regiments. He kept one hand inside his coat, like Napoleon, and pointed out the terrain with the other. We spent the rest of the day, that night, and half the

next day going up the Chesapeake, Captain Strathmiglo on
the bridge the while, trying to keep her off the mudflats. We
had cleared Quarantine at the Capes and were moored at
Bowley's Wharf, Baltimore, before mid-afternoon of the
20th. I'd packed what little I carried -- a cocoanut still in the
husk and some oranges for the family, from Hayti, mostly --
in a straw bag long before the first line was on the dock, and
Mr. Homidy and I were the first down the gangway, me carrying my big straw sombrero, feeling funny about wearing it.
I knew I must look odd, sunburned in the middle of the winter and with Cuban-style whiskers and Spanish clothes. We
took a hack to the railroad depot. Baltimore is almost as big
a city as New York, and the houses have white marble door-
steps. We hadn't long to wait, being on the main line between Jersey City and Washington. We got to Jersey City
around midnight, took the ferry over to Manhattan and the
horse-cars across to the East River Ferry, the Southampton
again, and ended up in the Long Island City depot between
three and four in the morning, with a long wait for the 8:32
east. I slept on a bench for a while, and at seven we went to
the lunch room in the terminal for breakfast.

We got to Sag Harbor and caught Jerry Baker's noon
stage. Mr. Homidy got out at East Hampton, and reached
back in and shook my hand. "You won't forget our little understanding, now will you Jerry?" I didn't know whether he
meant the promissory note or how he'd asked me to be silent about what he'd told me that night, but I nodded no.
Jerry dropped me by the Schoolhouse in Amagansett a half-
hour later, and I walked down toward our place feeling the
cold, the lane all frozen ruts, pot-holes, and washboarded. I
managed to come around back and walk right into the kitchen and surprise Mother. She kissed and hugged me,
which wasn't like her -- none of us being brought up to show
emotion -- and she admired the cocoanut. I was sorry I
hadn't thought to get off the stage in East Hampton to go
down to the Georgica Station to see Father first. I could have

walked or borrowed a horse to ride home. I'd go over the next morning, I told Mother, and meet him after church.

All the way north, I'd tried to decide what to tell Father. When it came to the telling, though, it was easier than I'd thought. First of all, the cable from the Consul in Santiago had come as a surprise. The cable reached the family a few days before the Lavolta got to Gloucester -- they'd had a slow passage -- and Captain Shelton sent his own wire. So they got it backwards, that I was safe and in Santiago, Cuba, and then afterward, that I'd missed sailing at Inagua and had been logged as run. I told Father pretty much what had happened, walking together back to the Station after church, leaving out Maria and counting Walker and his work as plain surveying, which was close enough. You could see he wanted to mull it over, that being his way. He'd known all along I wouldn't have jumped ship, and he knew well enough about waterfront ruffians and being Shanghaied.

I'd been full of stories the night before at home, but I learnt pretty quick what I guess every traveler has to learn, that is, we are all full of ourselves and that folks are as interested in telling you what they've been up to while you were away, even if it was only wearing a track in the yard feeding the hens, as you are in spinning your own yarns. Pretty soon I just stopped talking about where I'd been unless asked a question.

Father told me Nat was codfishing with Chase Filer, so I stopped by the Filer shanty on the banks east of Hook Pond Gut on my way back to Amagansett. Nat and a Swede were baiting trawls in the lee on the southwest side of the building, for all it was the Sabbath. I sat down and lent a hand, opening clams and cutting bait for them. The Discovery, Nat said, was laid up for the winter way back up in a dreen, or ditch, at Accabonac Creek. He'd dragged her up on a high tide the first week in December, planting deadmen, timbers, in the meadow either side to make her fast to. "She's safe enough up there," Nat told me, "but we'll need a tide and a half to get her out."

There was another thing, he remembered. About two weeks previous, a man had come over on the stage from Sag Harbor and looked him up; he said he'd heard that we had some unusual ballast on our sloop, and he was a miner of locusts, a rock fancier. Nat remembered what Dr. Fordham had said about our being better off with that weight in bluefish, and sold the lot for ten cents a pound, bluefish having brought fifteen or sixteen cents early the season before, and eight later on. Nat sort of struck an average, and figured he'd driven a pretty good bargain. They agreed that the ballast amounted to around three-quarters of a ton, after Nat had taken him down to look at it, and they shook on a hundred and fifty dollars. The man came over the next day with a hired wagon and team and two helpers, drove right out on the frozen salt meadow alongside the sloop, and took off the rock. Nat heard later that the ballast had been crated in the Harbor and shipped to New York on the cars. Homidy had sent a cable from Santiago, too, then.

I couldn't be mad at Nat; we had no use for the stuff, manganese or not, and I'd have done the same thing. A hundred-fifty dollars was a lot of money. We could replace the ballast easy enough in the spring.

I came back over to the shanty Monday afternoon, and found them baiting up again. As we talked, I kept half an eye on Chase and two boys, cutting ice on the pond a quarter-mile to the northwest. Mr. Filer's Morgans, Damon and Pythias, stood on the shore, hitched to the wagon. You needed eight inches or better to work them on the ice; there couldn't be much more than three-inch ice, and they were dragging the scoring plow by hand, sawing off slabs, and pushing them in toward the wagon in a channel of open water they'd cut. They were shoving the ice up a sort of gangway onto the wagon. The air was still, and you could see the steam come out of Damon's nostrils a second before you heard him snort. The Mate on the Lavolta had told me, what was it, a sound traveled a mile in five seconds? That seemed about right, a second to hear the snort. It seemed as if I'd sat here before, thinking about sound and watching the puffs of steam, but I was remembering last summer at Napeague, listening to Charles Stuart Pufferson Homidy and watching the pile driver across the harbor.

By this time Nat and the Swede had finished the last tub of trawls, and slung it into the beach wagon, ready for going off in the morning again. We went inside to wash the clam off our hands; there was a pump on the sink along the west wall. Nat and I got coffee and sat at the table beneath the window on the ocean side. The Swede lay in his bunk, reading a newspaper.

"That's in Scandahoovian, from New York," Nat observed. "He don't have any English, or pretends not to. Peaks flukes and crawls in there every chance he gets." The Swede knew we were talking about him, though, and stuck out his tongue without shifting his eyes from his paper. There was an 1886 calendar on the wall in by his bunk, for Longmans & Martinez Absolutely Pure Prepared Paint. The girl on it was all pink, cheeks and arms and lips, with tight pink stockings from her toes right on up into what looked like a black set of stays, but with ruffles around the bottom. She sort of tapered upwards, like a porpoise, a fine figure of a woman well put together all through her hips, with her bosoms swelling over on top so's you'd want to give them a pinch. Her shoulders and arms were bare. She had a little smile, and a twinkle in her eye. Underneath it said "Time for a Little Touching Up -- One Merchant in every Town in the United States."

"Chase keeps after him to take that down," Nat said. "He claims Scabby Necks all have dirty minds, it comes from too much bathing when they're young." The Swede said something we couldn't catch and kept right on reading.

Nat had forgot to tell me the day before that Dr. Fordham wanted to hire the Discovery again in March, for the spring shooting. If the ice cleared away early enough, we ought to be able to get in some fyke fishing ahead of time, between the second week of February and early March. Father wanted me to do some chopping in our woodlot, and between that and getting the fykes ready there'd be enough to keep out of mischief. Nat would keep on with the Filer crew for another week or so.

The next day I was up in the woodlot on Stony Hill with an axe and a bucksaw, felling and trimming for a while and then sawing into stovelengths for a change. I wasn't feeling too ambitious -- I'd spent a good deal of the morning daydreaming about the Longmans & Martinez paint girl, in fact -- and started out for home around noon, having cut maybe half a cord and had my sandwich. It was warm for January, and when I came down out of the woods I sat on the lop fence at the north end of the Gardell pasture and looked out over the village toward the ocean. There was a little snow on the ground on the shady side of the hedgerows. It was a sleepy place, Amagansett; the houses all looked small from up on the hill. I remembered one time I had a fever, and stood at the top of the stairs as the family was going off to church, and felt dizzy, looking down; it was as if I was thirty feet tall and they were midgets ten stories below, not one. As if I was outside my family looking in. Coming back after being so far away sort of made me feel the same way.

Our National Emblem flapped well clear of the Liberty Pole to the southwest breeze, a red, white, and blue handkerchief at this distance. There was something else flapping, down on the beachbanks; I stared at it for a long minute before it came to me the weft was up. My heart started to pound; maybe I'd get a chance at a whale.

I started out as fast as I could go down through the fields. The quickest way was over gates and through hedges, across the Main Street and down the lane past home. I tossed the axe and saw in over the fence as I passed, jogging now for want of breath. Somebody was blowing a fish horn from a scuttle behind me, and I could see men and boys headed for the beach hell bent for election in front. I'd be too late. At the foot of the lane, though, a good many of them were standing off to one side looking the other way as Great-uncle Sylvester directed four or five men hauling our whale-boat out of Father's boathouse. I looked in it, panting, and saw that the bow-oar's thwart had not been taken, and threw my coat on it. "We've got a crew; let's go sardinin'," Sylvester boomed, and some of the men and boys came over and helped pull the boat the rest of the way to the water; there was no chance now they'd have to go, with a full crew.

Chapter
XIII

A Forty-Five Barrel Bull

One of the Miller boys was straddle the boathouse roof. "Just back of the bar," he hollered, pointing east, "and coming like a house afire." I was too busy to look. The gear was out of the boat, it being stored bottomside up, and that had to be carried down the beach. "The time to get ready is before you go," Uncle intoned, Father's old admonition, and he carefully watched the rigging of the boat, paying no attention to the yelling. The West End crew had two boats on the beach, and another in the water, already headed in our direction at a good clip. The Lesters, handy by, were getting their boat ready too. Finally it was done, and we eased her down into the wash, each man standing by his oar. I realized I didn't have my boots on at the first slosh of icy water around my ankles. From the remarks, I wasn't the only one.

There we were, Sylvester, boat-header, at the stern; Dan Loper, leading-oar; Tom Rose, tub-oar; Frank Barnes, midship-oar; me, bow-oar; and Gabe Edwards, boat-steerer, at the harpooneer oar forward. Our oars were peaked up and out. "Now," Sylvester said, and we ran her forward on a little tumbling sea and jumped in. "Pull . . . Pull . . . Pulllll . . .," he grunted, still outside the boat and pushing, right arm along the gunwhale and left back, hand cupped around the sternpost. Our bow rose on another breaker and Uncle threw himself over the stern and unshipped the steering-oar. We evened up our ragged stroke to Dan Loper's pace as Sylvester turned the boat east. He was peering ahead, and I craned around to look too. "Eyes in the boat," Sylvester call-ed, an edge to his voice. I felt my face go red; I knew better than that. Without raising my eyes, though, I could see that we were well ahead of the others. Four boats were strung out astern, the green and white hull of one of the West End boats the closest but still a cable, two or three hundred yards, behind. Even though we were running pretty much dead before the wind, none of the boats had sail set; we'd be on the whale quick enough without that, him headed west and us east, and both carrying the mail.

"He's sounded. Let 'er run," Sylvester ordered. We stopped rowing, our way carrying us along. Sylvester kept on steering as we coasted, heading offshore a bit. I wished I'd worn mittens, and I had a tight feeling just below my breastbone. "Let's go," Sylvester said quietly, and we began pulling again. The whale had showed, and not far off, from Sylvester's tone. We began to turn, slowly and to starboard. There was a great whooshing, and another; the whale was blowing. "Settlin'," Sylvester murmured. By this time, the boat had swept clean around, and we were headed west. Out of the corner of my eye I could see swirls, offshore two rods, and a slick, what was called the glip. We were waking him, trailing along just to one side of the creature's wake and maybe a hundred feet astern. In this close to the beach he couldn't go down too far, and the swirls were from his flukes; they'd be half the length of our boat, tip to tip, pump-ing up and down. We followed along; the other crews, seeing what we were doing, would respect our right to a first crack at him, and hang off to one side until the ball was opened.

"Easy now," Sylvester whispered, and the stroke slowed. There was a splash, and another whoosh, and Sylvester roared, "Spring ahead!" We bent to the oars for five or six strokes, and Sylvester roared again: "Give it to him, Gabe! Back water, all." There was a thump just behind my back; I saw the shaft of the harpoon rise up from its crotch to my left and the butt of the hickory jerk aft and pause as Gabe got set to iron him. The harpoon shot forward out of my sight and Gabe said quietly, "We're fast." Then three things happened at once: A great rock of black whale-hide rose and pushed the blade of my oar out of the water, that was the beast humping his back as he sounded; Gabe swung himself around me, hand on my left shoulder, and skipped aft along the thwarts; and the line began to run out, whipping along out of the tub back aft and under my left elbow. Then Sylvester danced forward, shouting "peak oars" as he came, and I could see lance-butt come out of the crotch. Gabe snubbed the line, and sheered us off to one side a bit with the steering oar. Not much line was out; the animal couldn't settle far in shallow water, and we'd be that much closer to him on his rising.

We were making a passage, no doubt of it, but we didn't seem to be having the sleighride I'd always heard it was, mile a minute, fast to a rank right whale. We weren't going a great deal faster than we could row. I was still scared, though, for he'd come up again soon enough, bound to be out of sorts having a couple of feet of Swedish iron harpoon in him, and I was out of breath from being scared. The command came: "Stand by your oars." We got the looms out of the sockets again. "Pull . . . Pull . . . Pulll." A soft splashing, and a great whoosh ahead. Then a giant whack, and we were soaked with spray; thrashing his flukes, he was, trying to get at us. "Hold water!" and we braked the boat with our oars. I heard Sylvester grunt; he'd darted the lance: "There, dum ye." The lance-warp came swinging back within my eyeshot as he hauled the barbless iron out of the whale and got it into his hands for another jab. Three times he did it, and then there was a great smudder of foam and blood.

I sneaked a quick look over my shoulder as the whale sounded the second time. He arched his back and then the giant flukes came high up out of the water as he settled away. We peaked oars again, and the creature started offshore, more rapidly now. He rose after a couple of minutes. We were closer this time, and when he blew the spray came drifting back like pinkish rain. We pulled up close to him, at right angles to his body and close to his head I guessed, and held the boat there for a minute. Sylvester was grunting and shuffling his feet, churning the lance-head deep inside the animal. "Back water, back water," he shouted, and the whale went into his final flurry. We lay-to six rods off. This time we all had a look as he thrashed and puffed water, blood, and air all together out his blowhole. He gave two big slaps with his flukes, bringing them down flat on the water so hard it sounded like a cannon going off, before he turned up his toes and died, sort of shivering at the end. The slaps were something like the way a man'll slap his thigh when he's made a bad mistake. We sat and watched him for ten minutes before Sylvester, who'd been standing in the bow the while with his arms hanging straight down and the lance in his hands, flat, the way you hold a pitchfork along toward dark, and chewing on his mustache, decided it was safe to go in and cut a hole in the creature's lip for the towing warp. The other boats came up and joined us, kicking up a white-ash breeze on the way home, all hitched to the whale.

The sun was down when we landed; they'd built a bonfire on the beach to show us the way. We worked the whale in as far as we could, making the hawser fast to wooden deadmen set in the sand, and leaving boys to gradually take the slack out of the hawser as the tide came in, to work the whale as far up the beach as we could. Father was there, and looked at me some when they passed a jug of rum around amongst the crew, but he didn't say anything when

I took a pull. It was damned cold. After the boat was put away and the gear straightened out, we walked back to the house, and I told him how the rally had gone as Mother made us a late supper. He'd have gone boat-header, instead of Sylvester, had he been there. He'd tried to pace out the length of the animal before we left the beach; it was hard to judge in the dark, but he guessed fifty feet, a forty-five barrel bull perhaps. Maybe twelve hundred dollars worth of whale, with bone to six feet in his jaws, and all for one crew, or most of it, because we'd have to share some for the towing, and trying-out. Not a bad day's work.

John and Elias woke me before dawn, rank to get down to the beach. It was blowing out of the northeast, and snowing. Father had already set out for Georgica, afoot -- he couldn't stay away long, being Keeper of the Station, least of all in a northeast blow -- and had left word for us to take the wagon down, it would be needed to cart blubber up to the tryworks, loaded with a jag of wood. We'd need a fire on the beach, he said, and what driftwood there was wouldn't last long. We were at the whale by daybreak. So was just about everybody else, weather or no weather.

He lay there on his belly, flukes east, one raised up where they'd made fast another hawser and taken a strain, to coax him in. His lips had curled down in a kind of sneer and his nigh eye was open, a little one for his size, kind of piggish. Some boys had run out between breakers, for there was six inches of water around him most of the time, and were parading up and down on his back. People didn't stay long in this weather, once they'd had a look, but more would come for those who left. We were all busy laying out the gear. Some of the younger boys had already cut small squares out of his hide with their jackknives, as keepsakes, before we were ready to start our cutting-in. Sylvester put a stop to that, though, when they lay down on the beast's forehead and reached around under his lip to saw off lengths of baleen. There was maybe five hundred dollars worth of whalebone in that mouth, he said, and those limbs of Satan weren't going to run off with it a shilling at a time. He chased them back up the beach to tend the fire.

We were ready to commence operating, had made the first cut and placed the big hook, when Mudd, the druggist from East Hampton, showed up with his camera. We lost a good half-hour while he posed us in front of our whale, his wife holding his hat to windward of the lens to keep the snowflakes off and him with his head under the big black hood and his plump bottom sticking out astern and us trying not to wiggle or shiver. It was no weather for working on the beach but we had to do it, for fear it would come on blowing hard and we'd lose the whale, or have him buried in the sand. As soon as we had our picture taken, the peeling-off of the blubber began, back of his head, two of the older men with sharp spades hacking down to start the process which would finally strip the animal of his inch-thick skin and five-inch layer of fat, in sections as big as we could heave into wagons. As soon as one was loaded, one of the youngsters would lead the team up to the tryworks in the right-of-way up on the west end of Dog's Hole Highway, what some people call Bluff Road. He'd slide the blanket-pieces off there onto a pile outside; the trying-out could wait; the cutting-in had to be done quick. I sent Elias back home for another jag of wood.

While we were starting on his hide, the others had cut off the whale's lips, working with spades, axes, and hatchets, and carefully prised the whalebone out of his jaws, using the same tools. This made up a good wagon-load, and was taken up to our barn to be cleaned, sorted by length, and bundled. Part of the crew engaged in cutting off his head, to make him the less to roll over at high tide. This didn't take as long as you'd think; the oldtimers knew just where to find the joints. One boy or another was cranking the grindstone most of the time, the tools lost their edge that quick with the sand and bone.

It was airish, blowing harder now, and we began to take turns warming ourselves at the fire. When I went up for the second time I found Mr. Homidy, in a buffalo-skin coat with a muffler under his chin and over his head, clamping down a visored cap with ear-lappers, in conversation with Dr. Fordham. The Doctor wore the black winter Prince Albert I'd seen him in last fall, and a stylish sealskin hat. They looked like a pair of Grizzlies getting ready to fight, swinging their arms as they were to keep warm, heads forward as if they were about to bite chunks out of each other.

"You are an ignorant man, Homidy. Hullo, Jerry. This fossil maintains yonder beast is a fish."

"Of course it's a fish, Fordham. It don't fly, like a bird, nor walk like an animal, nor has it the power of reason, or speech, like humankind. It swims in the vasty deep, and what swims in the vasty deep is a fish."

"Listen to the man. I swim; am I a fish? A dog swims, and so will a cat, as anyone who has tried to drown a litter without a sack and a stone can testify. Are they fish? Is a frog a fish? Is a sheldrake a fish? The whale, Homidy, is an animal, a mammal. He breathes air, the same as you do, and he has warm blood, and he suckles his young."

"Suckles his young? Is he some kind of morphydyke? Your learning has softened your brain, Doctor, for the whale is a fish, and the Bible tells us so, unless you are so far gone down the path toward Ingersollism that you would reject the Word of God. Where was Jonah for three days? Inside the belly of a whale, we all know that. What does the Good Book call the beast? A great fish."

They wrangled on. After looking at the crowd that had gathered close around to hear the dispute, and seeing that no girls or women were within earshot, the Doctor offered his clinching argument:

"Did you ever in your travels, Friend Homidy, come across a fish equipped with a penis?"

"You mean a fish with a cock," said Mr. Homidy, the

Defender of the Faith, "I'd have to say no."

"All right, then; don't you know the whale has one?"

Mr. Homidy looked trapped, but he shook his head no. He couldn't be telling the truth, for all his Christianity; you couldn't very well grow up on the South Fork of the East End of Long Island without knowing that a gentleman whale, even a small one, was pretty well outfitted in that regard. The evidence was a hundred feet away, but it was on the underside of forty or fifty ton of whale, and wouldn't be admissible until high tide, eight or nine hours off, when and if we could roll him over. Homidy was staving off losing the argument until then, figuring that it'd be forgotten by that time, or that he would have managed to turn it around until it was Dr. Fordham who was arguing that the whale was a fish, and he that the whale came hung like a bad woman's dream.

Nobody said anything, and the Doctor began to look foolish, as if he'd remembered it wasn't any use wrangling with Mr. Homidy, and that he shouldn't have lost his temper. He turned to me: "You've grown. Homidy here says you got into some scrape or other down at Turks Island?"

Inagua it was, I told him, and not my doing. He'd heard, he said, that I'd jumped ship down there and that Mr. Seavey had been disappointed, as I'd seemed a likely young man. He'd have to write him, the Doctor added. I didn't much want to talk about it with Mr. Homidy eavesdropping, and to change the subject asked Dr. Fordham what brought him to Amagansett.

"The same thing that brought our disputatious friend Homidy here, Jerry, a look at Leviathan. The word of your capture had been carried yea unto the Harbor ere bedtime last night, and the Port is green with envy, not having had a whale of its own this decade."

He began to sound just like Mr. Homidy, from talking to him. I'd noticed that before, even with me. It was catching, like the itch. It was time to get back to work, and I made my excuses. The next time I looked the two of them were gone, replaced by a flock of females and children. Along about supper time, at the top of the flood tide, we managed to roll the whale over onto his back. He had a penis all right, two or three feet long and shaped like a carrot, showing white in the light of the big fire. Someone hung a hat on it, and we took a strain one last time on the hawsers and went home.

We had a day and a half more work before the carcass was left to the gulls, and then we fired up the tryworks, using a wood fire under the first batch through the two trykettles until we had enough scraps skimmed off to feed the fire and let Mr. Whale cook himself. We blubber-boilers worked four shifts around the clock, using his flukes as a pad under the blanket-pieces while we cut them into horse-pieces, stirring, feeding the fire, testing the oil with a gobbet of spit, bailing into the cooling kettle, and barreling. It kept on easterly weather, snowing off and on, but it was snug inside the rough-boarded potworks, although a trifle close.

I'd done it all before, of course, except for the whaling proper, but I worked harder at it this time. My lay, having been on the boat, would be around one-twelfth, and I was that much more interested; the other times it had just been part of the chores and no money for me. The trying-out was only half done Saturday afternoon, but we were ready to quit for the week, done in. All hands under thirty planned to attend the dance that night at Clinton Hall in East Hampton, and we had more than the usual Saturday scrubbing ahead of us. Mother said Elias and I could go with Sam and his wife in the pung, there being plenty of snow. Sam didn't much want to take us, but he was more or less obliged to, to get the pung. Mother outfitted me with an old shirt of Father's, very fancy, and other odds and ends. My Cuba coat was the best I had now, and I felt awkward as we paid our two bits at the door of the Hall. Professor van Houten's Orchestra was already playing. There were chairs down either wall, but Elias stood at the far end of the room, opposite the Orchestra, with the boys.

Mary Cooper, the English girl whose father ran the farm on Gardiner's Island, was dancing with Charley Bob Rackett, the wall-eyed one from Springs. I was warm, next to the fireplace. Jimmy Homan came along and poked me with his elbow: "Out on the porch." Nat was there, back in the corner with some others, half out of sight in the coats. He had a pint of whiskey, and we passed it around and around, hiding it when couples passed through the porch, until it was empty. Nat had the last swallow, and carried on the way I'd seen him do before. He puffed out hoo and rolled his eyes, thumped his stomach with his free hand, made a big aahh, and whispered, like he'd lost his voice, "Who been cutting my whiskey?" Jimmy passed around cloves, and we pulled our shoulders back and marched into the Hall.

It wasn't a card dance, but I never did get around to asking anyone. I'd of liked to dance with Mary, though it was pleasant tapping my foot and watching the others. Before long the Professor struck them up in "Good Night, Ladies." Sam let me have the reins on the way home; he and Lydia were cuddling and spooning with the buffalo robe up all around them, just as if I weren't there and they weren't married and as if they wouldn't be home alone to do whatever they wanted decent and private; it was sort of disgusting. Elias was asleep. The highway was smooth-packed snow, and the runners sang.

Monday morning, it was back to the tryworks. Uncle Sylvester rode over to the Harbor and took the morning train to New York with Elias -- he'd never been -- carrying samples of the oil and bone, to dicker with the merchants down on South Street. I'd liked to have gone, but I'd already been there twice since November. We found out the next day he'd made a good market, bone at a dollar sixty-five a pound and oil thirty cents a gallon, and my share would be around eighty-five dollars, which, with what I had coming to me from the Lavolta, if I ever got it, and my share in the Discovery's account, gave me quite a nest egg.

It was the first of February before we'd finished with the whale, and the Filer crew had quit for the season. I hunted up Nat; he was eeling through the ice over at the Head of the Harbor. A half dozen of them were at it, each at his own hole in the ice, working the grains at the ends of the long shafts up and down in the mud like churning butter, only off at an angle, to cover as much territory as they could. There were four eels wiggling on the ice around Nat, cooling off until they weren't so spry and hard to handle, and half a bucketful already quieted down. Nat picked up the eels, his pail, and the grains and moved.

We talked as he chopped a new hole, and agreed to go fyke-fishing. We had one fyke in the barn, in tolerable shape, and Nat thought that for seventy-five dollars we could get Billy Banjo Lester's whole rig, six fykes, barrels, tubs, anchors, and the rest, from his widow. We'd take the money out of the Discovery account.

The weather was mild the first part of February, and we dragged the sloop out of the meadows and put her on an anchor inside of Louse Point. We brought cobbles for ballast over from the beach in the wagon. There was a lot to do; Billy Banjo'd been failing the last year, consumption, and had let his gear run down more than we'd figured. His wife was a good deal younger than he'd been, and a good deal smarter, Nat said. He had designs that direction, though he'd never say so, the widow being fifteen years older.

A fyke, if you're not acquainted with one, is shaped like a big wire rat trap, only twine. The flounder comes swimming along the bottom, nosing for something to eat, and he runs up against the leader. He heads offshore, toward the business end of the whole affair, and there's a short set of wings to coax him if he starts to stray. He goes through one cone and then another, and he can't find his way out, just like the rat in the trap or the miserable sinner enmeshed in vice. The bunt end is buoyed, and all you have to do is lift it and open it up and dump your fish right out into a barrel. You don't even need any ice, that time of year.

That's all there is to it, except for ice sometimes taking off the whole rig, or uprooted New Hampshire pines coming down with the tide from the Connecticut River and fetching up in your fyke and tearing it all apart, and four or five days of hard blowing out of the northwest when you can't get off to tend your gear, and then you can't find it when it moderates because the gear's been carried off, and getting your ears froze. My hands got so cold and stiff, one day lifting the fyke off Barnes Hole, I had to pound them hard on the gunwhale to get the blood going again, and broke my little finger. Mother set it for me that night, and made a cunning little splint out of the handle of a broken spoon that fit just right. I could work the next day, but it was tender for a couple of weeks, and hard to pull a mitten over. We did all right, four or five barrels on good days, working out of Springs and selling through Miller at the store there.

It set in bitter cold March 7. We could tell we were due for a spell of it, and put the Discovery on two anchors in Accabonac Creek and set off for home. I was reading that night when Mother raised her eyes from her darning, my socks, and I could tell she was going to say something weighty. Anna Elizabeth and Esther had gone to bed and John and Elias were doing lessons in the kitchen. "Jeremiah, have you finished with school?"

She returned her eyes to the work in her lap. The fringe on the shade of the big kerosene lamp between us hid the bun of hair high on the back of her head. She'd worn her hair that way as long as I could remember; gave her something to pin her hat to, she said. Not that she wore a hat very often, even feeding the chickens or hoeing under the summer sun. In the winter, though, she'd wrap a muffler over her head, going out in the yard for wood or to the necessary. Father maintained that if you didn't wear something to protect the top of your head, you'd go soft on top, like a rotting spile. He never set foot out of doors without a hat; that was why he still had a full head of hair, I guessed.

Mother had an apron on, as usual. She, or her apron, smelled like fresh bread. That was usual, too. As women went, she really wasn't very tidy. There was flour on the sleeves of her black dress, away up by her shoulders. She was strong; she'd whaled me often enough, and not so long ago at that. She could hitch up a team as fast as Father, although he'd had to help her the few times I'd seen her ride a horse. Give her a leg up, he called it, and she didn't like it, that word leg. 'Twas a limb, to her. She didn't ride straddle, of course. I'd seen women do so, wild girls really, but it was hard to figure how they could without hurting themselves.

"You hard of hearing?"

I came to with a start. School, she'd said. I didn't know. The fishing was going good. "Well," she corrected. Maybe Nat and I could keep on with that, get a bigger boat, hire a crew. Anyhow, I had plenty of time to decide, until the end of summer.

"It'll be fall before you know it, Jerry, and unless you make up your mind before long you'll just dilly-dally along until you're too old for school, and then you'll wish you'd stayed on, and it will be too late. I know your father's worried about it, and I am too." She looked across at me. "There's your brothers, too. You don't know it, but what you do, they'll likely do."

I nodded, and she went back to knitting and I to the paper. Father could make me go back to school if he wanted to, but I didn't think he would. I didn't know what I wanted to do, and it came to me that I'd been putting off thinking about it. I felt tired, but resolved to think about where I was headed soon.

Sunday was warmer, and it commenced to rain half way through the service, beating down hard on the high windows of the church. The men stirred; many of them had teams hitched outside, and for all it had moderated it was still near freezing. The Rev. Porter paused and looked at the northeast windows too, and went back to his sermon. We were mud to our knees by the time we'd walked home, into the wind. The rain came down fit to float the Ark the rest of the day, and into the night.

Chapter
XIV

—◆—

Jake Hopping
Floats The Teunis A. King

The rain turned to snow about noon on Monday, and Mother had us load up the back pantry with stove wood. The wind was blowing hard, still out of the northeast. It gradually picked up during the afternoon, and when the boys and I went out to the barn to tend the stock along toward three o'clock we had to break the ice in the inside water tub with the butt end of a pitchfork. The hens were all under the barn, in there with the black snake, who'd probably been sleeping down a hole since the first frost. We carried out a big basin of heated corn and slid it under for the chickens; they'd make out all right, pecking snow for water.

Mother led us in prayers that night before bed, with special words for those in peril on the sea, and for Father and all the others in the Life Saving crews, on such a night, Amen. She loaded up the old warming-pan with coals for me; it'd be cold up in the attic room under the eaves. Cold it was, even under three quilts and the covers hot from where the pan had been down by my feet. The house shuddered and creaked under the gusts, and I remember the way the Lavolta sounded in a seaway, everything working, and the anchorage at Mathewtown, the water clear and blue and the seaweed waving on the bottom, like dead men's fingers cocking a snook at you for being alive.

In the morning, the wind had backed around a bit to the northard, but it was blowing a pluperfect hurricane, and the snow was pelting along parallel to the ground, so thick we could see the barn only once in a while, and then only when we wiped the steam off the kitchen windows. The snow was fine, and blew in around the sash until we thought to pack some of it back in the cracks as caulking. Doing chores, we could wade through the drifts, but had to shovel hard to get one side of the big barn doors open enough to squeeze through. We got into the horse stalls through the top half of the Dutch doors. Back in the house, Mother set the girls to sewing, and me to straightening out the cellar and tending the fireplaces and stoves. The boys made up a big batch of doughnuts, and did some quilting, though they didn't care much for that.

Late in the morning, Sam came up from his place to see how we were faring. It was rugged on the road, he said, but he'd have the wind at his back going home. After the noon meal, Mother sent me across the road to see if the Appletons were all right. They were, and had plenty of wood and grub. The snow had slacked off some, I saw coming back to the house, but it was still blowing great guns. I was worried about the sloop; the wind northeast so long would have pushed the tides in the bay away up, and with Louse Point underwater almost anything could happen in the creek. I'd never be able to get over to Springs to see till it stopped snowing, though.

The morning was still and sunny, and I rounded up Nat and we set off afoot, the drifts too deep for a horse. Up on Main Street, the elms were all ice, shining like rock candy, and we came on people shoveling out, and heard the telegraph line was down and no one knew much about anything outside their own dooryards. The last stage through from Sag Harbor had been Saturday, and the train had stopped even before the great blizzard, on Sunday, when the track washed out over at Hay Ground. Deep Lane, north of the village, was full of snow up even with the fields either side, maybe twelve foot of snow in it, but the fields were almost bare, swept by the wind. The going was easy as far as Stony Hill, but in the beech woods there the snow lay deep. It took us two hours to make East Side, where one of the Green River Road Smiths was headed in the other direction and told us there was a schooner ashore at the north end of Gardiner's Island. "Ye can see her from the bluff," he said, all excited, "and there's barrel shooks all along the beach, a million of them I guess." When we came out of the trees onto Louse Point, her two masts were in sight; the vessel was laying over on her port side, about half way between Bostwick's Creek and the Lighthouse on the low, sandy north tip of Gardiner's Island. We were more interested in the Discovery, though. She'd dragged, and gone onto the meadow, but didn't seem to have been damaged. She was full of water, and we pried out one of the plugs in her bilge and drained her so the water wouldn't freeze solid and spring her planking. As it ran out we leaned against her on the sunny side and figured how to get the sloop afloat again, with tackles and pry-bars probably. We fetched the sharpie from where she'd washed up in the bushes, and set off to round up help. Nat thought some of his cousins could lend a hand.

They would, and they told us the wrecked schooner was the Teunis A. King, out of Rockport for New Haven with a cargo of barrel shooks. The deckload of staves was what Smith had seen along the beach, and her mate had already come off the Island trying to find a telegraph office so he could let her owners know what had transpired. They'd been coming up on the Race when the gale began, and had tried to work offshore, clear of Montauk and Block Island, so they could run before it, but the rigging had iced up, what canvas they had on had blown out, and the vessel had just scudded off to leeward until she'd struck. They'd been lucky and gone on at high water, which with the storm was maybe six feet above the usual, and instead of her breaking up on the pebbly bottom running way out in the shallows east of Gardiner's Point, and like enough the whole lot drowning, the King had fetched up on the low sand hills almost in the middle of the Point, and lay right over until they could swing down from the shrouds into a foot or so of water. The Captain guessed where they were, and led them down the Point into the woods, and then went on and found the Manor. Mr. Cooper and the Island people went out with lanterns and blankets and brought them to shelter.

We stayed the night with Nat's cousins, a sorry lot, and went to work on the Discovery in the morning. There wasn't even any use looking for our fykes. A man came along and watched us doing the last of skidding the sloop back into the water, using her anchors and a luff on luff purchase, one tackle clapped on the hauling part of the other, a rig you might remember for heavy work. Nat's cousin whispered he was Mate of the King. We finally got her afloat, and the Mate said, "Handsomely done, boys, but you forgot to mouse the hook." He hadn't lifted a finger, and could have told us, but he was right. We'd forgot to put a preventer across the hook of the block doing most of the work.

He spoke again. He'd given up on the telegraph, he said; everybody thought it would be a week or more before it was back in order. He'd hired a Springs man to take his message over to the Harbor, to be wired on when the line was open. In the meanwhile, it was his opinion that the schooner could be floated, and there'd be a lot of trotting back and forth across the Bay involved. Were we interested in a charter for a fortnight, say twenty dollars a week? We were, and in the morning ran the Captain and the Mate up from Cherry Harbor and anchored inside the Point close to the beach, opposite the schooner. There were barrel staves and heads all over the Bay, going to and fro with the tide like slops in a bucket, it seemed like enough to make barrels for the whole world. The Captain looked sour enough to curdle milk when we passed through one extra-thick patch of shooks thump-thump-thump.

After looking things over, we went back to Cherry Harbor. The Captain though it was worth trying to float her, and Mr. Cooper recommended Hopping & Topping, the house movers, who'd cut their teeth on nautical problems by taking the boiler out of the Narragansett the year before. Squire Gardiner wasn't on the Island, he added, but he imagined it would be all right if he, Cooper, hired out horses and oxen to help.

We fetched Jake Hopping over on Saturday, and he peered and figured and paced and finally said it could be done. She'd have to be unloaded; they could hire one of the fishing steamers laid up for the winter at Greenport to take off what was left of her cargo. Then the teams, big twelve-hundred-pound plowhorses, would be used, with drag-scoops, to gouge a sort of channel from where she lay across the Point to the steep-to west side, where there was deep water. They'd never get her off the way she came on, from the eastward, any more than you'd get a fishhook out of your hide the way it went in. She'd have her bottom ground off by those little rocks, even if you could. Her own anchor capstan could be used to help pull, and Hopping would lay greased timbers as ways to slide her along on.

And so we got started, to move two hundred ton of schooner maybe three hundred feet. Nat and I had been employed to run the Discovery and nothing else, so we had a lot of time for spectating between trips to Cherry Harbor, Fireplace, or Greenport. The King's Captain and Mate took charge of getting the cargo out, a crew of wharf rats from Greenport lugging the bundles of shooks across the beach and over a gangway and a little scow they hauled over behind the bunker steamer Stephen F. Wilcox to use as a floating dock.

The teamsters started back and forth, tipping the big

iron scoops up and over at the end of each crossing, dumping sand to build a bank either side of the ditch they were digging. The plan was to slope the ditch some, leave the water end dammed off until last, and then dig it out on a spring tide. You couldn't dig down below the tide level anyway without hitting water. Between the greased ways, a crew of men heaving around on her capstan against her anchors laid off, the Wilcox and a steam tug pulling, and a couple of feet of water in the ditch lifting, Hopping figured he'd get her off.

There were two yoke of oxen helping in the digging, smarter at it than the horses. They went better in the soft footing, too. It was funny, how gelding what was going to be a bull would make him so smart, and patient, and strong; made you think. They wouldn't pull a hearse, though. It was hard to imagine who'd been the first to hitch a yoke to a hearse to find that out, but it was a fact.

The tug, a little thing named the Tenacity out of New London, steamed in on Wednesday, looking busy before it even got on the job. There was a familiar figure standing in the bow like a figurehead, the great rope fender a continuation of his corporation. Mr. Homidy, it developed, was bearing instructions from the owners, J.G. & S.T. Bowman, of Boston, and had been engaged as their agent in the business. What he'd done, we heard later, was to buy for ten dollars the message the Mate had paid the Springs man five dollars to take to the telegraph office, and enlarge and improve upon it while waiting for the line to open, which it did Saturday, and sign it himself. He hadn't offered his services, exactly, but just seemed so helpful and right-spirited that the owners had asked him to represent them. This didn't sit too well with the Captain, for under usual circumstances the master is the owner's agent in all matters relating to his vessel, but since she was really their vessel and he'd put her ashore for them, he didn't have much room to argue.

They had her cargo out by this time, and Mr. Homidy

set the gang from the Wilcox to scouring the beach on Gardiner's Island for what barrel shooks had washed up. There wasn't even any use looking over on the other shore. From Sag Harbor around to Promised Land, the shooks were gone. Mr. Homidy sent us over with word to Wreck Master Parsons in East Hampton to get them back, but Mr. Parsons said it was no use, he'd need an army all with search warrants to retrieve them, even if he had the time to follow the tracks back from the beach in the snow, and was willing to make enemies out of friends and relatives, two departments which just about everybody on the East End fit in, one or the other. Unless you could nail it right on the beach as it came ashore, he told us sadly, the Wreck Master was well advised to let it go, at least on Long Island.

Hopping was ready to give it a try the morning of the 22nd. Mary Cooper and her mother drove out with the noon meal for the men ashore, and Nat and I rowed in to say hello. The spectators, Nat's father among them, he having left his sheep down by Tobaccolot Pond long enough to come watch, were perched along the crest of the low sandhills north and south of the schooner, a few of the men squatting on the fish hawk nests built on the sand, great heaps of twigs and driftwood three feet high and six or eight feet across. They looked like giant fish hawks, in their dark clothes with white faces, except it was far too early for nesting. The gang was still laying out the schooner's anchors on a bridle, so we knew it would be a while, and swung around in the Teunis King's rigging with an eye on Mary. I went up the mainmast ratlines and shrouds on her starboard side, the King's I mean, and down the other hand-over-hand, hanging free as she was laying away over to port. Mary pretended not to notice.

The crew and some of the Gardiner's Island men took up the slack on the chain cable with the capstan, and the tug and the Wilcox took a strain on their cables, big manila hawsers. The tug had a hundred-twenty fathom out, the

Wilcox a hundred, and the bight of both hawsers stayed submerged. Nothing happened, though the schooner's timbers sort of groaned. Jake was directing the performance from top of a dune. He shouted to the men on the forecastle, and they strained at the capstan. He waved his hat in circles at the Wilcox and the Tenacity, and the tug stopped her engines; the air was still enough you could hear the bells. "He's dropping back, going to jump on it," Nat observed.

The tug drifted backwards, pulled by the weight of the sinking hawser, for perhaps two hundred feet. Then we heard three bells and a jingle, there was a big cloud of black smoke out of her stack and a flurry of foam at her stern, and the tug forged ahead. She fetched up at the end of the hawser, and it snapped out of the water, taut as a bowstring and squirting water its whole length. Then it parted, about a third of the way out, one strand snapping first and spinning off at an angle, and then the other two.

We were well to the side, but we still ducked as the heavy cable came curling back like a colossal buggy whip. The cable curled up onto the schooner's forecastle, catching on the jibstay, the frayed end snapping around and catching a man just inside the starboard bulwark on his side. He dropped out of sight and we heard a scream. Jake was cursing and waving his arms criss-cross in front of his face at the tug and the Wilcox. Everybody ran to the edge of the ditch opposite the schooner's bows, keeping a weather eye on the Wilcox's hawser, still taut. The Captain's bearded face appeared over the rail. "It's that god-damned Henery. His arm's broke above the elbow and he's got a couple of stove-in ribs," he shouted. The Gardiner's Island people looked pleased it was one of the schooner's crew, not one of theirs.

The Captain, Hopping, Mr. Homidy, and Mr. Cooper settled on sending us with Henery to Dr. Sweet, the bonesetter, in New London, and trying again in the morning. They'd need time to splice the hawser, and Saturday's tide would be better, if anything. Sending the tug would be quicker but more expensive, and besides they had the outboard two-thirds of the hawser to retrieve, and so forth. What they didn't want to say was, Henery wasn't all that important when you got right down to it. He came to, and the Gardiner's Island women wrapped his chest in strips of canvas, and slung his arm across his chest and wrapped it in tight to his body, the Captain dosing him the while with rum and reading him the Riot Act for not looking lively and getting out of the way of the hawser. He was pretty drowsy and didn't argue, being as short on words as he was long on rum, and by the time we had him stowed below and were headed for Plum Gut he was asleep, snoring and puffing fumes would wither flowers.

The tide was falling and we had slow going. We finally picked our way up the Thames, the Thaymes, the Nutmeggers call it, and tied up at the coal dock early in the morning. The watchman directed us to Dr. Sweet's place, an easy walk but not for poor Henery, who was sober now and whose ribs pained him every step. The Doctor's wife let us in. This Sweet, like his father and grandfather, had been a blacksmith as well as a bonesetter, but now he did nothing but set bones, all up and down Connecticut, Rhode Island, and Long Island.

He set Henery on a stool, stripped him of his coat and the bindings, took his shirt off, and peeled him out of the top half of his union suit. Henery complained about undressing. His woolens were none too clean, but what really bothered him was having Mrs. Sweet see his tattoos. He had "SWEET" under his right nipple and "SOUR" under the other. Dr. Sweet paid no more attention to the coincidence than his wife, and felt all around the ribs, fast, with both hands. He gave little pushes here and there and Henery caught his breath. Mrs. Sweet brought in a basin, and the Doctor sponged Henery off. Then he went to work with a big roll of cotton bandage, around and around, with loops up over Henery's left shoulder. Finally, he tore and split the bandage, and tied it end to end. Henery was mummified from his waistband to his dirty neck by this time. ''Now the arm,'' Dr. Sweet said with determination, and passed his hands around and down it from the shoulder. It hung limp, black and blue most of its upper part, a darker color than his side had been. The bone hadn't poked through the skin.

Dr. Sweet's hands came up again, right one inside the arm at the pit and the left on the outside just above the elbow. He didn't seem to strain, but there was a little noise, something like a person bringing his teeth together with his mouth shut, and dribbles of sweat ran down Henery's brow. The arm was set, and Mrs. Sweet helped the Doctor splint it before starting breakfast. At the table, I explained that J.G. & S.T. Bowman would foot the bill for their seaman, and the Sweets agreed to put him up until the owners could send money down for the bill and a ticket on the cars up to Boston. Henery began to doze; his head would slump, and he'd come to with a jerk when his muscles would pull against the bad ribs. Mrs. Sweet led him off to the spare room, and the Doctor volunteered a ride in his carryall down to the river.

The day didn't look too promising, gray with a damp brisk breeze out of the northeast. We had a cold, wet time of it over to the Gut, passing through in mid-morning. We had to beat to fetch Gardiner's Point. As we got closer, we could see the Tenacity and the Wilcox in position, ready to try again. We got the jib off, for the wind was half a gale by this time. We tacked under Crow Head and ran back along the beach, headed for the schooner. A long plume of smoke was blowing out from the tug's stack, aimed like a feather on a Red Indian. We were close enough to hear the cheering when the schooner began to slide, and it was not even high water yet. She eased right off into the deep water on the west side of the Point, her masts swinging to the vertical as she did. The men on her forecastle cast off the bunker steamer's hawser, but the Tenacity kept right on, headed for Greenport with her. They dassn't tarry, for although they'd caulked as best they could, the King was bound to leak like an eelpot after all the straining and wracking. They'd put what pumps Hopping and the Mate had been able to borrow aboard of her, to help out her own pumps. At Greenport, they could call on the Niagara Fire Company pumper cart if they needed, and if she made water too fast for that they could beach her.

It was raining cats and dogs by the time we'd anchored. Hopping had the wharf rats picking up the greased timbers and other gear, and Mr. Cooper and his gang had already started back toward the Manor House, with the horses and oxen. We rowed ashore and found Mr. Homidy talking with a short, clean-shaven, dark-complected man. The Mate, who'd engaged us, was off to Greenport, and we were wondering how we'd be paid, and hoping it wasn't up to Mr. Homidy. The two of them were almost shouting, for the wind had continued to pick up. They weren't arguing, just calculating the pay for the horses, oxen, and men. The short man was the Squire. Mr. Homidy turned toward us: "You'd better get out of here with your sloop while you can; Old Boreas will be hard at it in a while. Take her up in Bostwick Creek, boys; there's water enough for that, though you'll play hell getting her out again."

We ran down to the Creek under jib alone. The Wilcox had left, towing the float, and we could see Mr. Homidy and Squire Gardiner coming down the Point in the Squire's buggy. We ran the sloop just inside; Mr. Homidy had been right, there was five or six foot of water. The buggy was at the north bank of the Creek by the time we'd anchored, and we took the sharpie and ferried the two of them across, leaving the buggy and swimming the mare. Otherwise they'd have had to swing all the way around the Creek and its marsh, into the gale most of it. Ordinarily, you could ford the Creek easy enough.

Mr. Homidy and the Squire headed up toward higher ground and the path toward the Manor. Straightening up from making the sharpie fast to the sloop's quarter cleat, I saw Mr. Homidy look back, stop, and point up the beach. Squire Gardiner turned, and the two of them stood stock-still a moment, staring over our heads back to where the schooner had been. Squire Gardiner snatched his bowler from his head and flung it on the ground. He began to wave his arms, and advance on Mr. Homidy, who backed away. They stopped, and stared some more. We looked, but could see nothing out of the way. Something was happening, we couldn't see what. Nat and I jumped into the sharpie again, rowed ashore, and loped up the little hill.

There it was, almost a mile away out on the beach, Block Island Sound running into Gardiner's Bay, smack across Squire Gardiner's Point. The beach had busted through; the Sound, pushed high by the storm tide and the northeast gale, had slopped over into the ditch cut for the Teunis King, and begun to run through like a mill-race, melting the sand like butter. The scene was pretty much the same as Hook or Georgica Pond being let out, across their Guts, but they'd shut themselves up again, given time, and this wouldn't, not by the look of it. The cut was opening fast as a man could walk. When the tide began to ebb the water would run back through the other way, cutting even more of the beach. There wasn't any stopping it, now.

Squire Gardiner, eyes bulging, addressed Mr. Homidy: "You, Sir, will hear from my attorneys about this." He turn-ed and stumped off towards the woods, stooping and pick-ing up his bowler without breaking his stride. Mr. Homidy stood silent. "I'll be dipt in shit," he murmured finally, and headed off toward the Manor himself, the wind and the rain whipping his coattails. Nat and I went up to the shelter of the trees and watched. Soaked as we were, this wasn't the sort of thing you'd see every day, one island turning into two. The opening was two or three hundred yards inside half an hour, but the rate of cutting seemed to be slowing. The water didn't look very deep; seas were tumbling and breaking all the way through. The foam and smudder on the lee side opened up in a great trumpet shape as it spread out on the Bay. By the time we'd started for the sloop, I figured the Gardiners had lost eight or ten acres of their precious Island, and it looked like they'd lose a lot more before things balanced themselves. 'Twas only sand, of course, but people could get all worked up over a piece of beach, and seaweed rights. And then there was the Light. The Keeper, Sam Ellis, and his son George had been down to watch the King being hauled off; they were on another island now, but I guessed that was the Government's worry. They had a dory if worse came to worst.

The weather moderated during the night, and at first light we could see the ebb tide running through the gutway, half a mile or so wide by this time and cutting away mostly on the north side, making the new island with the Light smaller and smaller. We went over to the Manor and found that Squire Gardiner had already ordered Mr. Homidy off the Island, the big one, and had had him rowed over to Fireplace. The Squire was generally raising Hades around the outbuildings, his face shiny-dark like the underside of a thundercloud, and he didn't look too happy to see us, two reminders of what had happened. We kept out of his way, and had breakfast up at T'other House, with the Coopers.

"Nobody thought," Mr. Cooper said, mouth full of fried fresh ham. "Don't tell the Lord and Mahster, though. My fault as much as anyone's." He didn't have much use for the Squire, nor the sort of respect for quality you'd expect in a Britisher. He kept his job because he knew more about scientific farming than anybody else around. The Squire was too busy breeding Arabian race horses, and wagering on them, to pay much attention to the crops, and Percy W. MacIver, the railroad magnate who leased the Island's gunning, had more to do with Farmer Cooper than the Squire did. You couldn't serve two masters, but he seemed to well enough. "They'll go to law about it, right enough," Mr.

Cooper observed, and passed wind, pleased at the prospect of a suit. "Manners, John," Mrs. Cooper reminded, and Mary got up to take the pie from the oven, embarrassed.

Squire Gardiner was waiting for us down at the dock, impatient. "You, Dimon, are you still working for that miserable son of a bitch hypocrite Homidy and his accomplices? I thought not," he said, voice high-pitched in his agitation. "Go to East Hampton, and fetch the Latitat Sutphen. Tell him Gardiner has work for him." He was Lawyer Sutphen to everybody else; that was the way it was with the Squire. Nobody paid him much mind, though, even when he maintained that, under the old patents, he could hold court leet and court baron, whatever they were, and hang anybody he felt like on his Island. He was a Democrat, for all of that, and some said he might be named an Ambassador when Cleveland had taken office, but it hadn't happened.

Chapter
XV

―❦―

Not For Something
He Did Or Didn't Do

I sent Nat looking for Mr. Sutphen the next morning, after coming off Gardiner's Island. I'd seen the Lawyer engaged in disputation, besides, at Town Meeting on Local Option, and was a little shy of what he might say, hearing the
Squire's command. I went after Mr. Homidy instead, for our
pay, and tracked him down in his brother's shop, alongside
the Homidy homestead north of East Hampton, at Hard-
scrabble. He saw me through the window, but the only door
was on my side of the shop, and he couldn't slip away without moving all sorts of gear off the benches on the far side,
prising open a window, and squeezing through, which was
doubtful, his middle by all appearances being bigger around
than the sash.

"Come in, Jerry my boy," Mr. Homidy said, opening the
door and bowing. It was hot inside, a small stove going full
blast with pots of glue bubbling on the back lid. His brother
Elnathan was turning chairlegs on the lathe, pumping its
long springpole with his right foot. He straightened up to
nod to me and returned to his work, long spirals of white
pine curling off the point of his chisel to break and flutter to

the floor. Mr. Homidy pulled down a chair from among a dozen unpainted ones slung over the rafters, and offered it to me. "You may speak freely, Jeremiah. I have no secrets from brother Nate here, nor he from me, for all that our paths have diverged, and that he still thinks he will make his fortune forging chairs by hand to sell against chairs made by machinery in manufactories worked by Bohemians straight off the boat at three dollars a week, and that he cannot see that America, and the world, belongs to those who will progress with the times. Speak, Jerry, and utter unto us why we are honored with your presence. Can it be that you are in search of the Grail, certain monies due you from J.G. & S.T. Bowman and Company of the Hub of the Universe? Rest assured that I shall communicate the news of your quest to my former employers, for the truth is that I am no longer in their service, nor any longer their agent in these parts ipsos factor in no way concerned with their obligations. You might impart that fact to our mutual friend the Squire, in the event he has not reconsidered his rash threat, made in the heat of inflamed sensibilities, to haul me before the bar of justice as if I were responsible for what was so demonstrably an act of Our Maker."

A small man with a big head shuffled in, dragging a broom. He didn't swing his arms when he walked, and his trousers were unbuttoned in front. "My nephew, Solomon, Jerry, do you know him? Aptly named, for wisdom is his concern, for in lack of it he has few equals." Solomon paid no mind, and swept the shavings from the lathe into a pile, unlatched the firebox door of the stove with the butt of the broom, and threw in the trash. "I warned Elnathan," Mr. Homidy continued. "Did I not, Nate?" His brother pumped the springpole a bit faster and said nothing. "He married his cousin, as who around here does not. Only Sarah was his second cousin, not his third or fourth once removed, and Homidy both sides of her family to boot. Observe and profit, Jeremiah; yonder half-wit is the product of over-breeding, a species of Homidy Hapsburg. Don't worry, he don't know what we're saying, at least it don't register."

Solomon didn't seem to have heard, but his father was frowning, and gave his brother a sad look when he turned to look for a template on the wall behind the bench. He fitted it to the chairleg, and took off a bit here and a bit there until they matched, and you could see the turned leg spinning against the edge of the pattern without a gap its whole length. Mr. Homidy leaned back in his chair and crossed his legs. They tapered pretty much all one way, from fat thigh to slippery heel, where the leg on the lathe had a pleasing double taper, and a groove in the middle, like the girl on the paint calendar.

"If this goes on long enough, Jerry, we'll have a town where all hands go around with their flies unbuttoned, and their jaws hanging down, and points to the domes of their cavernous heads." Solomon snuffled, and a long drip of snot that had been sliding down his upper lip receded back into that particular cavernous head. "Looking at him, I tend to believe Charles Darwin was right, and we are descended from the Borneo orang-utang. For the sake of your offspring, Jerry, be wise, and find yourself a spouse in Bridgehampton, at the least," Mr. Homidy concluded. I cleared my throat and raised the money issue again.

We'd kept our part of the bargain, I said, and expected him and his employers to keep theirs. "Not my bargain, Dimon," he said, squinting at me. "I didn't engage you. This does not become you, my young friend, this change from son of nature to money-grubber; what would your friend Walker say? Was it for this that I snatched you from a life of riot and dissipation in. Santiago de Cuba, a brand from the burning? Ingratitude, thy name is youth! And, Jeremiah, whilst we are in pursuit of this grossest of topics, need I remind you that my advance to you of passage money is an open item, and that a certain note will become due and payable with interest in not a great many days?"

That cut me down to size. Mr. Homidy smiled. "No, no, I know you're good for it; as investments go it's golden, and if you wish to renew for another three months you are welcome to do so, upon payment of the interest it goes without saying. I shan't press you, nor shall you press me. Agreed? I will take up your charter with the owners, and perhaps we can simply deduct your debt, plus interest and a small commission for my advocacy, from that sum when it heaves over the horizon."

There wasn't much for me to say and I left, heading back to the village afoot. I hadn't got to the Gould place when I heard a horse behind me. It was Mr. Homidy; there was no place to duck him, out in the bare fields. "Let not your heart be troubled, Jerry," he trumpeted. "Your Redeemer liveth, or is he your Old Pretender?" That was his idea of a joke, something to do with the Stuarts and his name.

He wouldn't leave me be. Seeing him there on the horse, looking down on me, made me think of the day I'd looked up from the sloop toward the high ground behind Shagwong Point at Montauk and his horse had been grazing, tethered to a tree, and he'd been digging. I spoke: "What were you doing that day up in Indian Field, shoveling?"

He drew rein. "A good question, Jerry, a good question indeed." He licked his lips and looked at his hands, crossed on the pommel of his saddle, an old McClellan, one of the Army ones he'd peddled one year. "Enjoying the prospect, you might say." He was punning. "Where every prospect pleases, and none but man is vile. Prospecting for a mine, so to speak. Looking for Indian pots. Captain Kidd's treasure. For your one good question, a good many answers." The horse broke wind and dropped a pile of dung, heaped and steaming on the stubble.

"It won't hurt none, I suppose," Mr. Homidy went on after a pause. "You know who I've been working for. They're nothing if they're not thorough. They didn't need a survey, the way they did from Walker at Guantanamo, because they can buy a map of Montauk right from Washington, heights and all, the new Government topographic one. What they did need is what they call the geo-logy, the soil and the drainage and the rest. They sent me a list of what they needed. Those holes in Indian Field, now; they ask, 'How thick is the topsoil? What's at one foot? Two foot? Send us samples. How much rock? Sand suitable for making concrete? Boulders for breakwaters?' All this on top of what the railroad's surveys had already found; they bought those, on the sly.''

He swung down and we started off again, him leading his horse. "Talk about your Amistad treasure, Jerry; that vessel wouldn't float the money there is in this, no not even if it was in diamonds. Imagine being in on buying Manhattan Island for twenty-four dollars, or all Liverpool for a few thousand. That's what it's all about, and that's why I have to play my cards pretty close to my chest. People talk about this; it's been in the papers a hundred times; but they don't believe it yet enough to bet their money on it. If they knew how close it was to happening, if they knew what I'd been up to, they'd think different, the smart ones anyhow, and start to run the price up. Quiet is the name of the game, Jerry, and don't you forget it. Stay out and keep quiet and you'll have no trouble; play it the right way and I'll see that there's something in it for you, all legal and aboveboard. There's two kinds of people around here, Jerry, the Indians selling for twenty-four dollars and the Dutchmen buying for twenty-four. You might as well join the Dutchmen, and I won't tell the Indians.''

We spoke no more of it, and Mr. Homidy turned off at the Hook, below the Mill, headed for Pantigo. Lawyer Sutphen's bay was in front of the Cuffee house, down Freetown on the road to Three Mile Harbor. He and Nat were with the Cuffees in the kitchen, talking about Indian Field and the Benson purchase as if they'd been eavesdropping on Mr. Homidy. I listened, and thought. Run the price up, he'd said; he must have been talking about the small bits and pieces Mr. Benson hadn't gobbled up, or the right-of-way for the railroad line to Montauk. Or had he been talking about the Benson land? Benson was supposed to be in on the scheme. Maybe something was going on unbeknownst to him; a double-cross being worked on Mr. Benson? He'd bought this house lot for the Cuffees, part of the settlement of the Indian Field disputation, but they'd hired Lawyer Sutphen, to try and get Indian Field back. At least, that was what they claimed they wanted; people said they and the other Montauks who'd gone to law again were just trying to get more out of Mr. Benson.

The Cuffees were an old couple with children grown and moved away, pleasant and well-spoken for all they were as black as red. Cuffee was an Ivory Coast name, Father said. The Overseer of the Poor paid them to board Aunt Sadie Fletcher, and people talked about that, because she was white, and for all the old catamaran was up in her nineties, some thought it wasn't right she'd be under the Cuffees' roof. Aunt Sadie hovered around the table while Mrs. Cuffee made us sandwiches and her husband talked with the Lawyer. The gist of Mr. Sutphen's report was that there wasn't much hope, but that he'd keep trying, and that he expected something on his retainer. That was the way it went when you got snarled up with the lawyers; talk, talk, talk, and pay, pay, pay.

Nat introduced me to Aunt Sadie. I'd met her before, but she didn't recollect. He shouted: "Jeremiah Dimon -- Dimon -- 'Gansett!" She nodded, quick like a bird, and made sucking motions with her cheeks and lips. She hadn't a tooth in her head. "Ask about the British," she croaked, "confound their knavish tricks, confound their politics. 'Fraid of the British, not I, said the little red hen." She cackled until she commenced to cough, and sat down hard on her bed in the corner. "Don't rile the old girl, Nat," Mrs. Cuffee said. "She get started, she'll drive us all out of the house." Aunt Sadie paid no attention, and fished a fried long clam from her apron pocket. "Look at the old fool," Mr. Cuffee said. "She can't chew butter, but she sure can gum them clams."

"About the Pope in Rome," she whispered, swallowing her clam, "never would of happened if they'd elected Mc-Clellan." Aunt Sadie drew breath and began to quaver "Lilli Bolero." Mr. Sutphen rolled his eyes and pushed his chair away from the table. "If I'm to get to the Island by dark, we'd better go, Mrs. Cuffee. Thank you for the sandwiches. Come, boys."

He had a way of speaking to us I didn't much care for, but then I guess he was just making up for being summoned by the Squire, like he was a mechanic to fix the Manor clock. Doctors were used to being called for, but the other professions, lawyers most of all, generally expected you to come to them. The flood tide made up a pretty good chop going across. Lawyer Sutphen lost Mrs. Cuffee's sandwiches to leeward not an hour after he'd packed them in, and Nat and I looked the other way. It was night by the time we'd made the Discovery fast and we went up to T'other House. The Coopers put us in the attic and I had impure thoughts about Mary, sleeping just below.

We were summoned to take Lawyer Sutphen back to Fireplace at noon the next day. Mr. Cooper whispered, as he was settling up with us on behalf of the Squire, that he'd heard Mr. Sutphen had told his employer there was a cause for action, and was on his way to Riverhead to commence a suit against J.G. & S.T. Bowman and Company for damages to the tune of ten thousand dollars, for the loss of land and the inconvenience of having his Island divided. "Better ask him while he's about it to see if he can get your hire-money out of them," Mr. Cooper added. "You'll never get it out of Homidy."

We didn't want to get involved with Mr. Sutphen, though, and neither of us said anything to him about the matter. I went ashore at Fireplace, too, and Nat took the sloop down to Accabonac Creek as I headed off toward Sag Harbor to find out if Dr. Fordham still wanted us for the spring gunning.

Dr. Fordham wasn't home; the cook said he'd gone out to a Lodge meeting. I found him toward nine o'clock, alone at a back table at Mrs. Hetty Mack's. He'd been drinking. His face looked sort of polished, and he was sitting up very straight in his usual doctoring outfit, black broadcloth coat buttoned up high over a standing collar.

"The Prodigal returneth," he said carefully, and motioned me into a chair. "Behold a healer displaced by one of the Home-Taught School, a Doctor Draw-Fart who drains abscesses with cow-flop poultices. I have missed my calling. Had I been a simple shit-shoveler among medicos, might I not now be a man of wealth?" He looked at his glass. "I am embarked upon a Gaudeamus."

I didn't know what he was talking about, but I didn't want to start an argument with him in that shape. He could tell I didn't understand, though, and tried to explain: "Patients, Jerry, are low, vile, miserable, and ungrateful wretches . . ." He raised his tumbler and sighted across it at the far wall, drawing a bead on them. "You can get yourself by mail, not even setting foot outside the Corporation limits, a degree in medicine, Eclectic, Botanic, Homeopathic, Thompsonian, whatever cut and style you want, and set up shop, just like you were a carpenter, only with more chance of success with less training, for most people are a damned sight more particular about who puts their houses together than who patches them up. Who shingles their roofs than who roots their shingles. Not bad." He sipped his whiskey.

"Set yourself up, no worries at all, unless you really intend to practice medicine, the way I was when I started. Made no matter this was my birthplace, they didn't want me, the four old frauds who was our medical ornaments those days. Told me so -- just enough work to go around, they said, no room for any more doctors here, for all they

told the public they were short-handed and over-worked --
and formed a combination against me. Not a one of them
would help me, even if it meant the patient dying, and some
of them did. I beat 'em, finally, but only because they'd got
lazy, and wouldn't get their fingers out of their ass when a
patient needed them. Doctors, not fingers. I'd be on deck,
night or day, and this is the thanks I get for it, after three
decades. Cow-flop poultices, at a dollar an application. Het!
Het! Some lager for Mr. Dimon here and another charge for
me!'' There was no sign of Diana, nor of any of the girls, just
a few men at the bar. I had to help him home finally and the
cook gave me rats, as if it'd been my doing, him getting
drunk and tangled in the boxwood by the front door, swear-
ing in Latin after he slipped off the stoop.

The Gun Club wouldn't want us until after Town Meeting, he said in the morning when he had his thoughts sorted
out. A lot of them were involved in the politicking. There
was, besides, the annual Corporation Meeting in Sag Harbor
Village. ''The members will be laboring in the vineyard,
Jerry,'' Dr. Fordham remarked, rolling his eyes at the word
vineyard as if it made his head hurt, ''and so will I. The Village Fathers, in their wisdom, are about to establish a Board
of Health, about twenty years after the rest of the world, and
there is fifty dollars a year in it for me if I can corner the ap-
pointment. As you may recall from our conversation last
night,'' he went on, rubbing the palm of his left hand over
his temple to refresh his memory or perhaps wipe some of it
away, ''medical economics have an importance not always
appreciated fully by the layman. In other words, we follow-
ers of Aesculapius cannot live on air.''

We agreed that Nat and I would be on deck and ready
for work the next Wednesday, the fourth of April. I went up
to East Hampton early Town Meeting day, alone. Nat stayed
to work on the boat; he'd got into trouble enough the year
before, when Selah Hooper and his brother, the hare-lip one,
had beat him up for something he said. By late forenoon

Main Street was lined either side with teams and wagons, carryalls, buggies, Rockaways, and buckboards. There wasn't a woman on the street, if you didn't count a Shinnecock squaw peddling baskets, she all done up in bright colors, scarves a-flying like pennants on a man-o-war, nor a child under fourteen either. For all the Town was dry, and had been for two years, the Republicans had set up a wagon just down the street from Clinton Hall and were ladling out Stone Fence to all comers. Across the highway the Democrats had their wagon, with rum for those who didn't like the Grand Old Party's whiskey mixed with cider, nor their politics, and gin and beer mixed, what you call Strip and Go Naked, for the serious drinkers. There were some ticket-splitters sure enough of themselves to mix Stone Fence and Strip.

Captain Ananias Phillips was trying to get the Boys' Republican Eagle Drill Company to step left foot to the thump of the big drum. I'd have been jealous of their uniforms if they hadn't made such a spectacle of themselves, stumbling in the ruts in front of the Stone Fence wagon and trying to sort out their feet. The band was Haffen's, from the Harbor, hired at great expense. They had four or five good tunes down pretty well, but the high parts of "John Brown's Body" seemed to buffalo them. A big fat Dutchman with a beer belly played their helicon bass, its polished copper bell about three feet across, oom-pah, oom-pah. He was good, but the military band at Santiago would've wiped their eye.

Men were drifting in and out of the Hall in little knots engaged in private conversations. You saw men smile who hadn't since last Town Meeting; Justice Fuller, with the old slit eyes, hardly stopped flashing his lone gold tooth long enough to suck on his cigar. Somebody trundled a hogshead out into the street, and a gang of boys pestered simple Uncle Zebulon, old Tweet Thissaly, into climbing up on the barrelhead and lisping through four verses of "Rock of Ages." They wouldn't let him down until he'd perpetrated the Gettysburg Address and "how many slices of bread in a barrel of flour." He understood one no more than the other, but he had the words just right, save for his sissing on the S's and C's.

The meeting commenced just after noontime, the Hall so packed that the windows were opened, a half-circle of men and boys around each. Moses Tiffany had the chair, and rapped for quiet: "Clinton Hall is full today," he said, after looking around the long room to silence the crowd. "And so is Stratton Leggett!" somebody shouted from the back, and there was general laughter. Then the Cold Water Army made temperance speeches for an hour; nobody spoke up for the Beerocracy, but everybody knew it would be a close thing, the Option this year. Elijah Thompson made a speech for high license. Having the whiskey-sellers pay five hundred dollars a year for the privilege, he said, might cut down consumption by discouraging them, and since liquor was being sold in any event, why should not the Town make some money from it, enough perhaps to pay the Constables and make up some of the poor-money spent feeding the families of victims of alcohol?

There was a to-do at the back of the Hall at this point, and I wormed my way through to see what was going on. Constable Baker had Jimmy Brady, from the Harbor, by the collar, dragging him out the south window, the press being too thick to get through the door. An old man was being boosted through behind them. "He picked my pocket! He pocked my picket!" the man was saying, all excited. The Constable hauled Brady around to the other end of the building, where word was passed in through the window that Squire Sherry was needed. The Squire appeared at the back door, out of breath and upset at being called from the Hall just when things were beginning to liven up. He looked more cheerful when he saw he had a case to try, as anybody would, working on commission that way. The Constable, Brady, the pickpocketed man, Theron Mapes was his name, and the Squire set off across Main Street toward the Sherry farm, a bunch of us boys following.

We went right in. The Squire paid no attention, and we watched from the parlor doorway. Squire Sherry fussed a bit, and placed a big Bible and another book on a table at the end of the room. He sat in a chair behind the table, hands clasped in front of him, and you could hear him breathe heavy.

"Well, Constable, what is it?"

"Your Honor, Brady here picked Mr. Mapes's pocket."

"You seen him do it?"

"No, but Mapes felt him, and hollered."

"What do you say, Brady?"

"Guilty, Yer Honor."

"Brady, this is not the first time I have had you before me. Tell me, why is it we get the scum of Sag Harbor over here, instead of what decent people there is? Eh, Brady?"

Brady hung his head and the Squire continued.

"If you're going to thieve, you scoundrel, why don't you do it home, eh? And if you're going to go to the trouble of coming all the way up here from the Port, did you ever think of using that much steam to get an honest job? Now did you, heh?"

Brady mumbled something, and the Squire looked at him thoughtfully.

"I'm going to fine you ten dollars, young man, and if ever I see you in this Court again it'll be the House of Correction for you, throw the key away, no mistake."

Brady looked up. "All I got is two dollars and some coin, Squire."

The Squire leaned back in his chair, brow furrowed above bloodshot eyes.

"Constable, take him back to the Hall."

The Squire sighed and smiled, and we boys poked each other. Take him back to the Hall! That meant . . . yes, it did. The Squire hiccupped, and it dawned on me he was a good deal drunker than he looked. The Constable marched out with Brady by the arm, and Mr. Mapes, looking puzzled, tottered after them. We left, anxious to find out exactly how long it took Brady to float his private pocket loan for the rest of the fine.

I squeezed back into the Hall through a window. Mr. Homidy was making a speech. I hadn't known he was there, and he was hard to miss even in a crowd. He was aiming his speech at the Supervisor, George Asa Miller from Springs, for all they were both Democrats. He was supporting Nathan Babcox, the Republican, and I could only figure there was some sort of conniving going on.

"This puts me in mind of the time the illustrious Phineas Taylor Barnum was caught upon his uppers, far from friends and family, long before fame and success had settled upon his shoulders," Mr. Homidy was saying. "His entertainers had deserted him, his exhibition animals had died of the Persian mange. All he had left was his tent, and one strong-lung-ged and faithful retainer. Together, they pitched the ragged pleasure pavilion, and inscribed upon it a legend: 'See the Gyascutus: 25¢'

"Soon the Reubens flocked, and Barnum told them of the fabulous Gyascutus, nineteen hands high at the shoulder; eats nothing save warm human flesh. Claws six inches long, teeth like a miner's pick. Can leap thirty feet from a crouch.

"There was a roaring and a fearsome yowling from somewhere at the back of the tent.

"Barnum peered behind the drapery and commenced to scream: 'The Gyascutus has broke loose! Run for your lives! Women and children first!' The yokels departed, trampling each other at the entry. All, that is, but one man. He stood his ground alone where hundreds had been seconds before, arms folded, looking straight at Phineas T.

" 'The Gyascutus is loose,' Barnum repeated, a little lower this time. 'Ain't you going to save your hide, friend?'

The man looked at him for a minute, and then spoke, slow.

" 'I have seen the Gyascutus. I have been around back and looked. I have seen the Gyascutus.' " Mr. Homidy paused, and gazed around the Hall.

" 'I have seen the Gyascutus, and HE AIN'T NOTHING BUT A MAN!' That, friends and fellow Townsmen, is George Asa Miller. He may have been Supervisor for a long time, but he ain't nothing but a man, and Nathan Howell Babcox is a better one."

Mr. Miller smiled, as if he knew he'd get reelected, Homidy or no Homidy, which he did about half an hour later. The vote was a hundred seventeen to eighty-six, with twelve spoiled ballots. The Town said no to Local Option again, by about the same margin, and the Meeting adjourned, the budget meanwhile having been adopted by voice vote. Haffen's Band struck up again, this time all eight of them standing in the G.O.P. wagon.

Father came out, looking tired, and spoke to me, the first chance he'd had. He was going back to the Station for a bit and would be heading home for the night in an hour or so, on a borrowed buckboard. I could watch for him, and ride back to Amagansett. "Observe and take profit, Jeremiah," Father said, looking oddly at the two lurching masses of men at the booze-wagons. " 'Twill do you no harm to see what rum can do." He headed off toward Georgica.

George H. Burling, Editor & Proprietor of the Star, was ambling through the crowd. He nodded; he knew me from coming in to pay the subscription. "A fine afternoon, Master Dimon. Over to watch the jollity?"

I allowed as I was, and he said he despaired of putting it all down on paper. "A mere word-painter could never do justice to this," the Editor said, indicating with a sweep of his arm the scene on the street. "A Hogarth is required." I didn't know what a Hogarth was, but didn't let on. "Care to observe my feeble attempt to capture the event for posterity? Accompany me to the Temple of Journalism."

I was glad enough to leave; what fighting there was wasn't worth watching, the combatants being too drunk generally to do much more than shove and blaspheme. Some of them had been sick, too, leaving small muddy cesspits in the dust of the street.

Mr. Burling's printer's devil, Uly Grant Davis, caught up with us near the shop. It was one big room, with a trestle counter dividing the front from the work space behind. The press was at the back. It had a big flywheel with a crank for Uly. There were racks all down the south wall, and stone-topped tables in the middle. By the north wall was a neat pile of great sheets of paper, three or four feet to a side. "This week's supply," the ink-stained Uly said, and turned over the top sheet. The underside was all printed, pages four and five, with long stories and column of jokes and patent-medicine advertisements facing me, and page one, with the world and United States news, and what I guessed was page eight, upside down on the other half of the sheet. Uly laughed at my puzzlement, and explained.

"It comes printed one side, you see. They give Mr. Burling the paper, and print the news on half of it, and his masthead on the top of the front page, in return for that advertising. Patent insides, they call it, even though half of it's outsides. The advertising, you see, that's what it is. The people who sell the medicine pay the people who give us the paper, to get their advertisements circulated. Then we set the type and print the other four pages."

The story went that Mr. Burling had just two engravings of people, one Mrs. Lydia E. Pinkham whose Compound revived the drooping spirits, invigorated and harmonized the organic functions, gave elasticity and firmness to the step, restored the natural lustre of the eye, and planted on the pale cheek the beauty of fresh roses of life's spring and early summertime; and one Dr. Sage, whose proprietors would pay five hundred dollars for a case of catarrh in the head which they could not cure. Both faces appeared in his advertisements. Mother claimed the Pinkham Compound had more alcohol than gin, and wouldn't have it in the house; I'd found an empty bottle, and memorized the label, being interested in female organic functions. People said that Mr. Burling used Mrs. Pinkham when the story was about a woman and Dr. Sage when it was about a man. It wasn't so; he didn't even print the only pages that ever had any pictures himself; the only reason for people thinking that was that his pictures were sort of smudgy, and older people looked pretty much all the same anyhow.

The Editor & Proprietor poked up the stove, rolled up his sleeves, and stood at one of the type cabinets. "He's setting the Town Meeting story straight in type from his notes," Uly said. "I can set type, but I sure couldn't do that." He showed me around as Mr. Burling continued his type-setting.

Finally, Mr. Burling put some ink, thick like tar, on the type he'd set with a little roller and Uly laid a small sheet of paper on. Mr. Burling placed a block of wood above the type and whanged it twice with a mallet. He handed the paper to me: "Here, you've been to the Institute. You can be our proof-reader."

> Supervisor George Asa Miller of Springs won yet another term at Town Meeting Tuesday last. When the smoke had lifted o'er the field of battle it developed that the outcome was 117 to 86, with 12 votes disqualified, Nathan Howell Babcox, the Republican, having come out on the short end of the string. Temperance triumphed by a vote of 120 to 83, again with 12 spoiled and nullified ballots.
>
> Temperance was not much in evidence on the street, however, and the Triumph of Democracy was again marred by scenes of rowdiness, with the Harbor element much in evidence. One young man from the Port, of Hibernian persuasion, was indeed apprehended in the act of removing a pocketbook from someone else's trowsers, and was speedily hauled before the bench, which imposed a novel sentence.

All the Town would have heard "Constable, take him back to the Hall" by the time the paper appeared, but that would make no one the less anxious to read how much Editor Burling dared print of it.

> A budget of $2,316.19 for Town expenses in the next twelve-month was ratified by a voice vote, the yeas exceeding in volume the nays by a degree that made the pigeons fly as far east as Van Scoy & Dayton, which laid in a good supply of spring garden seed this week, and as far west as Town Pond.

Mr. Burling was hard to beat when it came to working in a plug for a steady advertiser. I hadn't seen any pigeons fly.

> The scene upon the Main Street of this fair village following was worthy of the brush of a Hogarth, and buggers description.

I felt my face flush. "Shouldn't that be 'beggars,' Mr. Burling?" He laughed. "I figured an educated man like you would catch that, Jerry. I stuck that in" -- he laughed again -- "to see how sharp-eyed you were, or if you could spell."

There was a clatter of wheels, hooves, and harness from the street, but it wasn't Father. He'd had time enough, and I left, thinking to walk up toward the Station and meet him on his way. There was a brace of drunks coming out of hibernation on the steps of the Hall. The two rum-wagons had gone on home, as had the musicians. Mrs. Hedges, the first woman I'd seen since morning, was at her gate up by Mill Hill looking around like after the storm. I asked if she'd seen Father. Not since he'd gone south on foot a good two hours back, she said. I began to figure that there was something doing at the Station, not that it was weather for a vessel to come ashore.

The summer cottages up toward Divinity Hill and Jericho were empty, set back from the lane behind wide yards. Some of them would play at tennis there, in the summer, or croquet, part of another world, best ignored. Now, it was just lonely, trees bare, flower gardens empty except for weeds, not a carriage in sight, the footmen and cooks and maids and bankers and their wives and sons and nose-in-the-air daughters all back in Manhattan or Pittsburgh. There were half a dozen geese just settling in to Lily Pond for the night when I came along, and they swung up quick and flapped off honking in protest at the sight of me.

As I neared the Station, Sylvanus Hills, the seventh man, stepped out and walked toward me. "It's your father," he said slowly when I was nigh enough to hear. "He was taken tired all of a sudden when he got back and lay down. Right hand was stiff, couldn't make it work right. Now . . ." He stopped.

"What happened?" I asked.

"I think he's gone, Jerry. Rolled right out of the bunk onto the floor, that was it. He was breathing for a spell, heavy, and we could feel his heart beat, but then it stopped. Don't go in, Jerry. Don't."

But I did. They'd put him back in the bunk, and closed his eyes. His hand was cold; I touched it with my fingertips. The crew had all been standing there when I entered, and they walked out without saying anything. I sat down at the table and cried as quiet as I could, and wondered why I hadn't said more to him when he'd left me at the Hall. Sylvanus came in and told me they'd sent for Dr. Osborne. The Doctor took a long while getting there; they'd lit the coal oil lamps before he told us what we all knew. "A stroke," he pronounced, "and if any of you is fool enough to take that as meaning the Almighty has struck this man dead for something he did or didn't do, you have another think coming." He turned. "Your father died, Jerry, of a cerebral haemorrhage, in plain English a blood vessel burst in his brain, and it's a mercy he didn't live, all crippled up like enough and no more able to take care of himself than a baby. It can happen to anybody, any time, some of your tubing letting go, though in my experience it's more to be expected with men like him, at their prime or past it. You'll want him took to

Amagansett, I expect?"

I was numb. I felt nothing, and could think of nothing either until I realized it was up to me to say what was to be done, and to tell Mother, too. They said I was the man of the family now, over and over until I reminded them of my elder brother. I felt more like a boy than I had in quite a while. Father was buried the next day in the Corner Cemetery across from the Schoolhouse, in a driving northeast rainstorm, close to freezing.

Chapter
XVI

---◆◆◆---

A Patient Lost
And A Patient Saved

The place was Mother's, of course, but there hadn't been any question, even before the Will was read, but that Samuel would take over the farm, and inherit it when the time came, he being the first-born. He'd already started the plowing. You had to get the potatoes in early, to get a running start on the Colorado beetles. Mother soon went aboard of me again about my plans. I put her off with the obligation, for the time being, I had to meet, having promised the Century Nat and I would work the sloop for them. That would be a month, maybe; we were already late starting.

There were brant, brent geese Nat called them, in the Bay, and the spring flight of the Canada geese was beginning. The Pastime was the headquarters again, in the little pond off Major's Cove at the south end of Shelter Island. It was strange, being back there again as if the calendar had run backwards and it was the end of October, and Father's death and everything in between hadn't happened, or was a dream. They were the same gang, the Gun Club, mostly, with but one face strange to me, Sineas Tooker, raised in Sag Harbor and now back, after forty years up in Hartford in the clothing line. He'd made a mort of money, they said, and was building a twenty-room summer cottage on the Bay east of Gordon's boat shop.

Mr. Tooker was quite a talker, more a city man now than an old Harbor boy. They were all yarning one night aboard the Pastime, tired but pleased with themselves after a good day's shooting, sixty-three brant, a dozen geese, and some widgeon, and working on their second bottle of whiskey between them. Mr. Homidy's name came up, about the Town Meeting. "Puff Homidy?" Mr. Tooker said. "He's back down here again? Last I saw of him was five years ago, he was working up around the Wethersfield Bow, selling patent stump-puller to the rustics. That man could learn iron to swim." The Banker wanted to know what patent stump-puller was; I suppose he figured he could use it to extract interest from widows and orphans.

"A paper of white powder, two nails, and a length of brass wire. You pour the powder top of the stump in a little pile, drive a nail through it, and the other down in the side toward the roots, and connect the two with the wire. It's the electrical action does it; you might call it the arboreal equivalent of Dr. Dye's Voltaic Belt, at least that's what Homidy tells the farmer. 'Slow but sure,' he says, 'don't expect results in less than two weeks, but all in a rush then. Don't tinker with it neither, at your peril.' Of course by the time the fortnight's up Mr. Homidy is two counties away in an unknown direction, and the granger is out five dollars and a half for his twenty-five doses of stump-puller, and all that's happened to his stumps is that they've seasoned a bit tougher and sunk more root."

Mr. Tooker paused and lit his pipe again, one of those deep-bowled German kind with a tassel. "I tell you, boys," he was speaking to the members, not me nor Nat; once they'd got away from their wives and families they liked to pretend they were young again. "I tell you, boys, they talk about the Connecticutters selling wooden nutmegs to the rest of the Union, but there's more humbugs afoot across the Sound than you could shake a stick at. You'd think the whole State was a dame school, they're wool-pulled that easy. There's the Louisville Lottery, still going strong, and the Royal Dominion. There's drummers going up and down the country peddling agencies for the Right Speedy Corn-Sheller, and for chemical fertilizer, in return for a little cash and notes 'not transferable,' and they just add an 'e' to 'not,' and have 'em; the mails are full of Wall Street circulars; and the old Yankees drop like flies before the next-of-kin dodge and 'estates in Australia.'

"Right in my store, one of the clerks fell for the Silver Mountain Mining Company swindle, and up in the hills they're still buying eggs from King Dagobert's Fowl. Never heard of King Dagobert? He reigned about the same time as Old King Cole, I guess, in France. The good Abbe Whosis went to build a cathedral where the King's castle stood a thousand years back, and what does he find while he's clearing off the ruins? A setting of eggs, left there by mistake when Dagobert was served his eviction notice by the Sheriff of Nottingham. The Abbe is a saving sort, and sets 'em, and in twenty-one days old King Dag's special breed of hens and cocks pecks out through those thousand-year shells, and the Abbe sees he owes it to humanity to keep the breed going, so he's organized a special sale of second-generation eggs, to help out with the mortgage on his new church, and for a modest sum certain select yokels of the hillier part of Connecticut may purchase some of the Dagobert eggs, to be set 21 days, which gives the egg agent time enough to be three jurisdictions away.

"There's nothing like a religious hook to make a sale, and with Dagobert's eggs there's a chance to take advantage of the Catholics, too. Every one of my clerks was a Sunday-School teacher, one a Superintendent, and I'd have to be a bigger man than Grant to say it didn't help. That was honest trade, of course; in a good chouse, a diddling of your country-folk, it works even better.''

"We've got 'em, too; I was telling Jerry here just the other day," the Doctor said. "Ever come across any of the Travelling Eye Doctors up around Hartford? From the Manhattan Optical Hospital, all armed with diplomas? Steal the eyes right out of your head, and the spoons off the table afterward. Then there's the newspapers: Professor Hayden's Love Powder, Adee's Free Prescription for Visceral Gurgescence, Mountain Herb Pills, they're for youthful indiscretions, Jerry, Dr. Morse's Indian Root Pills, Osgood's India Collahouga, Samaritan Nervine, Jones' Fever Cure, Chills and Fever Specific, that one works, some quinine in it, Clark's Aromatic Tablets, and God alone knows what else. About all mercantile hornswoggle has that medical quackery don't is mock auctions and chromos, and you can bet that some Doctor Crocus is working nights to adapt them to the healing art.''

I could guess the banker had a tale or two, if he felt so inclined, but he was not going to give away any trade secrets. I'd inherited my opinion about money-lenders from Father. He wouldn't have approved of sitting listening to idle men drinking whiskey and gamming when they weren't at cards. I liked hearing them; and felt guilty about that, because of Father.

Cards was what they cut, for the morning blinds, before they went to bed. They sometimes liked to stretch the suspense out that way. George Brinley, who ran the drygoods store, and Dr. Fordham got the goose blinds, two coffin-shaped boxes sunk side by side above a little pond at the edge of a cornfield. At first light, though, we made out a white flag hanging off the arm of Beebe's mill behind Suffolk Street, the signal that Dr. Fordham was needed back in the Harbor. He offered me the blind; Nat could take him over. The sloop went off double-reefed to a blustery wind out of the north. Mr. Brinley and I went down to the blinds with a wagon, eight live goose stool in two crates behind. Being the hired man, so to speak, I set them out, tethered by the leg in shallow water, and led the horse back up into the woods out of sight. Mr. Brinley sat smoking in his pit, hunched down back to the wind.

There was one old Judas of a gander in the bunch, as pleased at the prospect of some shooting as we were. He gabbled away, and I lay down in my blind and Mr. Brinley in his, about six feet away. He stubbed out his cigar; the geese would come in to leeward and smell us otherwise. Pretty soon the stool commenced talking about themselves and turning and looking off to the south. The old gander began to honk, and before long we made out a long line of black specks against the sky. "Coming up from the fields at Wainscott," Mr. Brinley said, quiet, as if they would hear us. "Lie low." They approached slowly, beating their wings steadily as they worked to windward. They began talking back and forth with our stool. The tethered geese, led by the gander, Benedict Arnold, the Club members had named him, were doing their best to persuade them. The flock passed overhead, and I held my breath and rolled my eyes back, to see them without moving my head.

Suddenly, as one bird, the flock swung to starboard and dropped, coming in toward our stool in a long slide, wingtips down. I eased back both hammers of my gun, an eight-gauge borrowed from Mr. Tooker. He's waiting too long, I thought, they'll hang on and go right over our heads. The leading birds set their wings to brake themselves, and dropped out of sight behind the grass. "Now!" Mr. Brinley grunted. I swung up to sitting, legs straight out in front and stomach muscles straining, and looked down the gunbarrels at the Canadas, coming straight in with their wings out bat-shaped and their webbed feet braced to hit the water. I picked one and let fly with the right barrel, and swung to another and touched off the left. When the smoke cleared, there were five birds down, my two, one dead and the other trying to paddle away dragging a wing, and there were three dead off to the right, in front of Mr. Brinley. I hadn't even heard him fire. The rest of the flock was already out of gun-shot, protesting with every wing-beat. I killed the cripple, laid the geese behind the blind, and threw cornstalks on them to hide them. No more came, though, and we went back to the houseboat in late morning. The stool were as glad to leave as Benedict Arnold had been to come; they were hungry and anxious to get back to their pen alongside the Pastime.

As we neared the houseboat, coming out of the trees, I saw the sloop's sail come out from behind the steamboat Shinnecock, which lay to the lee side of Long Wharf. The Doctor hadn't been long on his call.

Nat and Dr. Fordham rowed in from the sloop half an hour later. The Doctor looked upset, and gave me a peculiar look. He stepped into the deckhouse without saying anything. All Nat knew was that it had been a confinement.

The members took turns cooking, a day at a time, and the banker soon set Nat to shucking oysters for the noon meal, to go with beefsteaks, and me to picking black duck for supper. I was picking away, easy work on birds that were still warm, getting up an appetite for dinner beefsteaks by thinking about supper duck, when Dr. Fordham came out and sat between us, legs hanging over the side of the house-boat.

"Two things to tell you, Jerry. Stay, Nat, you might as well hear too. First of all, I just lost a patient. You both knew her, I think, Diana Fisher, over at Hetty Mack's. *Placenta previa*, they call it; infant jammed across the canal. Not much I could do; they called me too late. I might have been able to do something yesterday, but the damned fools were trying to save money and called in the Widow Musgrave and she was pretty near gone before I got there."

He went on but I didn't hear. I was listening to my pulse pounding in my ears, and trying to think. Diana. What was this, the middle of April? I counted back. One, two, three, four, five, six, seven, eight. August. It couldn't have been mine; she must have been a month pregnant then, when I was with her.

Dr. Fordham droned on. "Seven or eight months, I'd guess. Only way would've been a Caesarian section. No fetal heartbeat that I could make out. Never performed one and don't know if I'd dare; man delivered a paper at the Medical Congress in Washington last fall said there'd been a hundred-fifty-three Caesarians attempted up to now in the United States, and that fifty-six of the women had pulled through. Not bad odds but the shape she was in by that time, nobody tending her but that Goddamned old baby-puller and her Madam, not a chance."

Diana. My God!

"That's the first thing," he continued. Now, the second is that I'll need you and the sloop both, for a couple of days. Pack a hamper with grub for three days. I've made arrangements for a boat to tend the Club."

I set to work getting ready to leave in the Discovery, but I wasn't much help. Nat knew I was upset if the Doctor didn't, though, and did most of the work. Father's death was awful, but it didn't do to be anything but tough-minded about it. This was different. When I could believe Father was gone, which most of the time I couldn't, I felt as if it'd been my fault. I could think it out and know it wasn't, but the feeling was still there. Now, Diana; it WAS my fault. I felt like I was going to puke, and couldn't eat. The other two gobbled an early dinner and we set sail at noon. After we'd rounded the Point and turned northeast, toward Plum Gut and parallel to the Shelter Island shore, we could see, through the bare trees, the roof of the houseboat and its flag-pole, and anyone who looked across could see which way we were headed. The Doctor hadn't answered the other members' questions.

He directed us up against the Plum Island shore and we anchored under the lee of the land before dark. We drew straws to see who'd have the first watch, there being only two bunks. Even if there'd been three, I'd have wanted someone on deck, this being no anchorage at all really. I drew short, and Dr. Fordham told me to wake him up if a steam vessel of any size showed up. They went below.

I was hungry at last, and sat with my back against the cabin trunk and had two ham sandwiches. It was cold and overcast, although the air was clear enough. I saw the lights of plenty of steamers, running up and down the Sound and ducking in and out of the Connecticut River across the way, and what must have been the Fall River boat, all lit up stem to stern and going like a house afire, but none of the steamers turned off into the Gut. I sat huddled in my old gunning coat, shivering, thinking about dying. Poor Diana. I wondered what the baby would have looked like, and felt sick again. The Saybrook Light's loop pulsed up and down, and Plum Gut Light across at Orient glowed steady, a red eye in the dark. I struck a match and looked at the Doctor's watch; he'd left it with me. Nine o'clock, four hours were up, time to wake Nat. We traded bunks. I was exhausted, and asleep as soon as my head hit the bunk.

I didn't wake until well past dawn. I smelled pork and coffee, and poked my head out the companionway. There was a steam yacht, ship-rigged, the biggest I'd ever seen close to, anchored not a hundred yards away. Uniformed sailors were swabbing down her decks, just their shoulders and the back of their heads, pompomed hats on them French fashion, to be seen over her bulwarks. "Columbiad," her headboard read, in gold. Her hull was black, and a little plume of steam trailed from her stack.

Dr. Fordham was smoking and staring at the yacht. "Didn't tell you before," he said, "because there was no use the story's getting out if she wasn't going to show up and if it wasn't going to come off, but that's A.P. Blake's own yacht." We knew who he was; everybody in the world did, I guess. The richest man in America, perhaps on the globe.

I'd seen his picture times enough; fierce eyes, full-face always, with a heavy black mustache and white or gray hair. He wasn't a railroad millionaire, or a steel one, or a great manufacturer. He was a money man, the one the others went to when they needed money. Mr. Hominy had mentioned him back in Santiago. I could remember, barely: "Blake might even be involved. . . . They've got to have him on their side even if he isn't." I coughed in the cold morning air, and thought I could taste rum and pineapple juice and bile the way I had waking up the morning after that night in Cuba. I poured a mug of coffee, and Dr. Fordham continued.

"Amos Melville, I went to Medical School with him, is Blake's personal physician. Has no other patients at all, now. He sent one of Blake's men, a man from the Blake Bank, out day before yesterday with a letter for me. You'll find this all out sooner or later, so I'm going to tell you now but it will have to be between us, for ten or twenty years maybe. Understood?

"Good. Now, Blake's probably the biggest man in the United States, not barring the President. One of the reasons he is is because he doesn't delegate power; he keeps it all to himself. Likes it. If anything happened to him just now, we might have another Wall street panic, like twelve years ago. What's happened is, Melville's found he's got a cancer, of the jaw. Blake knows it, and Melville knows it. Now you know it, and me, and three other doctors, and no one else. Melville thinks he can excise it; my guess is that he can if anyone can. He's got an assistant with him, a young man but a good one, and he wants my help, too. Not that I'd be much use in surgery; the closest I've done in that line is a rodent wen off the left cheek of Elisha Wescott, in Sagaponack. But he needed someone with local connections, medical and otherwise, because he's going to do the operation here, aboard the yacht. Doesn't dare do it closer to New York; if word got out there's hundreds would be ruined, and hell to pay here to California. He needs someone like me on hand, too, in case something goes wrong, if you get my meaning. With cool heads, there's a great deal of salvaging could be done, before the news was generally known."

A pulling-boat headed our direction from the yacht. The boat came alongside and a petty officer in a blue jacket saluted Dr. Fordham. "Dr. Melville's respects, sir, and would you come over and confer?" He went, and Nat and I sat and admired the Columbiad. The pulling boat returned, and the petty officer said, no salute, "Mr. Dimon is to come with us, and Mr. Bennett is to follow along with the sloop. We're moving to Fort Pond Bay."

I was met at the gangway by the yacht's master, a tall man thin enough to hide behind a wire fence, in a blue wool uniform, gold braid on the cuffs of the sleeves where the petty officer had red embroidering, and gold on the bill of his cap. He led me forward. There was fancy-work everywhere, sword-matting in bleached cotton yacht-line, and sennit on the marlin-spikes in the pinrails. Deckhands were polishing the brass of the portholes; a big crew and they had to keep them busy. She was a good two hundred feet on deck, the Columbiad, and close to six hundred tons probably, three times the displacement of the Lavolta. She had all her sail bent on, fore, main, and mizzen, in a neat harbor furl, ready to sail, steam, or both. The Columbiad wasn't lofty, not one of those floating grain elevators like some yachts, but she'd show a fair turn of speed under sail. Her stack had a bronze monogram, A.P.B., like you'd see on the bow of a locomotive. The Captain led me in through a doorway in the forward deckhouse.

We entered a large cabin, tastefully appointed with animal heads, varnished mahogany, Turkey carpeting, and a tiled fireplace. Half a dozen men were sitting at a large table. One of them was Dr. Fordham, and he motioned me to a chair. A heavy man sat at the head of the table, leaning far enough back in his chair, arms crossed tight against his chest, for me to see a heavy gold watchchain across his waistcoat. The links were big enough to make an anchor chain for the sloop. He was Mr. Blake, and he was glowering and listening to a man who was probably Dr. Melville.

". . . On the left side of the hard palate, spreading to the upper jaw," he said. "I plan to avoid a visible scar, for reasons you'll appreciate, and work from inside. We'll have to take it all out, from the first bicuspid to the last molar. Hasleby here will make a prosthesis later, in vulcanized rubber; he'll supply dental advice, aboard. Mahon will handle the anaesthetic, and I don't need to tell any of you that's where the main risk, the immediate one at least, lies; Gibson is our man for advice on growths; and Fordham will back me up. The boy" -- Mr. Blake looked at me hard -- "The boy has assisted him before, and can stand by." There was a rumble. They were weighing anchor.

We came out of the lee of Plum Island and set off for Montauk, passing north of Gardiner's Point Light. Keeper Ellis came out and waved. The gutway looked better than a mile wide now, but the Light was safe enough. I could see white water on the shoal where there'd been sand and beach grass and a high and dry schooner a month before. I stood around, awkward and not knowing what to do, until Dr. Fordham asked me to help move the table in the saloon. Six of us lifted it out of its chocks and slid it aft. Then we rigged lines in a square against the overhead and slung sheets off them, making a sort of room about twelve feet on a side within the saloon. The foremast came up through the deck two-thirds of the way forward in the sheet-room. Basins of steaming water were brought from the galley and I was set to scrubbing within the sheets, first the varnished overhead, then the mast, and then the deck. A heavy chair was dragged in and I scrubbed that too. Dr. Fordham passed in a length of twelve-thread tarred manila, limp from a washing he'd given it, and I lashed the chair to the mast. A nickle-plated apparatus with an alcohol burner below -- a carbolic vapor-maker, they'd talked about one when they were working on Charlie Masters -- was brought in. Although I was worried now about what was coming, the work calmed me and I began to feel better.

All was ready, and I stepped out. The doctors were washing carefully, and had put on sort of butcher's aprons over their suits. The propeller's beat slowed and stopped; the anchor chain rattled out. I looked through a porthole and saw Rod's Valley a quarter-mile over the water. Mr. Blake appeared walking as calm as if he was in a barbershop, a bedsheet tight around his neck and over his shoulders and upper arms, trailing down toward the deck fore and aft. He looked like a Roman emperor in a toga except he was smoking a big Habana. "Enjoy that while you can," Dr. Melville told him cheerfully, "because it's going to be the last one you're ever going to smoke." He turned to the others. "Been after him for twenty years to give up cheroots, but he wouldn't listen. Now he's going to have to." Mr. Blake didn't appear to be listening any more than he had for the past ten years, and marched into the tent. He sat in the chair, and I could see through the gap between two sheets that he was still puffing his stogy as they strapped him down. Dr. Melville came out and pulled on rubber gloves. Dr. Fordham gave me an apron; I'd already traded my boots for carpet slippers. I was to sit against the bulkhead, ready to run errands. Two trays of instruments were brought in and placed on deck. I heard a cough. The vaporizer was at work. Ether was in the air, too. The coughing started up again, and there was a steady mumbling, most of it sounding like Dr. Melville. A good hour passed, and I was not called. Finally, four of them came out, sweat pouring down their faces. By this time, it was hard breathing even out in the saloon, the carbolic vapor was so thick. I felt uneasy in the stomach; a swell had built up and set the Columbiad to rolling.

"I think we got it," Dr. Melville said slowly to nobody in particular. He tossed his bloody gloves in a basin. The others slumped into chairs at the table and said nothing. "Jerry, get in there with Dr. Mahon," Dr. Fordham ordered. "He'll tell you what to do."

I didn't feel much like it, and fumbled at the sheets, trying to find my way in. Mr. Blake was sitting upright in the chair, his head strapped back against the mast with a thick band of cotton cloth, over his eyes like a blindfold. His mouth sagged open, with a little blood dribbling out of the left, lower, corner. He was breathing heavy, and there was a smell like burnt feathers in the air. They'd cauterized something. The instrument-basins were bloody. "Just stand by," Dr. Mahon said. He was at Mr. Blake's side, fingers on his wrist, taking his pulse. I looked down; there was a bloody mass in a pail alongside the chair. I fought against puking, focusing my eyes on the mast above the man's head. There'd been a half-smoked cigar in that pail, too, soaking up blood.

Mr. Blake stirred. "He's coming round," the Doctor said. "That basin there." I picked it up, and he motioned for me to hold it in front of Mr. Blake. We waited. Mr. Blake coughed and then was sick, vomiting blood at first, some of it sticking on the tips of his walrus mustache, and then plain puke. He was straining at the straps, and Dr. Mahon untied the one around his head and slid it off. As the cloth came off the patient's eyes, I was the only one in sight, and I was puking myself, square into the basin under Mr. Blake's chin. He opened his eyes wide. "Who in hell are you?" he gurgled. I straightened up, wiped my mouth on my sleeve, and told him. "Jeremiah Huntting Dimon." He puked again. The Columbiad took a long, slow roll, and he gagged. "Where in Christ's name are we?" he muttered. "Fort Pond Bay," I said.

"Fort Pond Bay? Fort Pond Bay? I never want to hear the name of the place again," Mr. Blake rumbled, hard to make out. "No, nor Homidy, neither," he added, slow and strange, and retched once more. He meant it. There it was in the basin like the cigar-stub in the pail. Corbin's dream, and Benson's, and John Starin's, and the Duke of Sutherland's. The New York, Montauk and European Railway & Steamship Company might as well give up right now, even though Mr. Blake, Dr. Mahon, and I were the only people in the world who knew it yet, and I didn't think Dr. Mahon was paying much attention. Mr. Blake was too busy being sick to dwell on it, but I knew he had made up his mind and would never change it. He'd remembered Mr. Homidy's working for him, even in the state he was in.

Chapter
XVII

—◆—

Homo Homini Lupus

Dr. Melville came in finally, cast off Mr. Blake's straps, and led him away slowly, holding him by the elbow. His sheet, no blood on the back of it, looked like a Millerite's Resurrection robe. I trailed along in their wake, still bearing the basin. The physicians and Mr. Blake were headed for the after deckhouse, and I went to the lee rail to empty the slopbasin. The Discovery was just rounding up astern. Poor Nat had been following orders, tagging along behind all day, and had just caught up. The sailors rigged the boat boom, and pretty soon the sloop was hanging aft from it.

We ate that night off fine china, each piece with a little A.P.B. monogram like the one on the stack. I watched Dr. Mahon, across the table, to see what spoon to use. We were served by stewards, grown men, and I was too flustered and tired to know much of what was going on, or listen to the talk. I turned in early, in a bunk with curtains like in pictures of the Pullman cars, one of four in a stateroom with carpet on the deck.

After breakfast, Captain Buckridge sent for me and Nat. It was still blowing and uncomfortable in Fort Pond Bay, and he was going to take the yacht up through south of Cartwright Shoal, to get in the lee the other side of Gardiner's Island. For all his brass and sternness, he was man enough not to be bashful about asking for advice, even from two boys. We had local knowledge, he said, and he'd appreciate it if we'd stick with him while he piloted the Columbiad up the channel. They'd tow the sloop. The chart showed a least depth of nineteen feet, he went on, and the yacht wasn't all that long-legged, only drew sixteen, but there was a spot west of Hicks Island he was concerned about, and was it buoyed according to the chart?

This time of year he'd find no buoys, I said, just spars, but they'd be in the right places. We knew the spot that worried him, and Nat thought it'd be all right if they took their time and had a man in the chains with a lead-line. The yacht got under way, and within a half hour we were coming up on Goff Point and the beginning of the shoal water. I could see clear across the low dunes and the meadow where we'd taken the party after yellow-leg to Napeague Harbor. None of the factories would be running for another month, and there was nothing doing inside the Harbor. The Captain rang up a slow bell, and unrolled his chart. We passed Waterfence, the west line of Montauk really, the rail fence running right out into the Bay to keep the stock where it belonged, on the east side. "Golf Point," he said, waving his hand toward the shore. "No, Goff," I corrected. Captain Buckridge stuck the chart under my nose. "Golf." There it was, printed right on it. I didn't argue, but thought about old Mr. Gordon's tale of the Englishman running from the Stuart's revenge. They played at golf at Southampton, the summer people. I'd seen their playing field, on the Shinnecock Hills, from the train last fall. It looked just like the rest of Shinnecock Hills, only mowed. They hit the little ball with a long stick; some of the Shinnecocks chased the ball for them when they felt ambitious. The East Hampton summer people stuck to tennis, or croquet.

"I'd hold her in a bit closer, Captain," Nat said politely. "Starboard your helm, steer sou-west a quarter west," Buckridge told the man on the helm. "Sou-west a quarter west, aye, Sir," he responded. The Captain rang for dead slow. "Steady on sou-west a quarter west, Sir," the helmsman said. "There's your first marks, Captain," Nat piped up. "The spar shows in the middle's for the branch channel down to the fish works; you'll have to leave it well to port." Nat was doing all right and I didn't horn in. The Mate went forward and set the leadsman to work. Nat proved a fine pilot; the man in the chains never sung out less than four fathom. We anchored in Cherry Harbor in late afternoon. There was no motion to the vessel here, and Mr. Blake was bundled into a steamer chair on the sunny side of the deck, pale and no more cheerful than the last time I'd seen him. You couldn't see his cheek; they had a muffler tied around the top of his head and under his chin like a boy with the mumps.

Supper that night was another meal in the grand style. I ate caviare for the first time; I'd had it as sturgeon spawn, fresh from the net and not as good as bottlefish roe in my estimation, too coarse entirely, but never transmogrified that way. The meal was heavy, with lots of spices, and wine. I woke in the midwatch all wet at the crotch. I'd been dreaming.

I'd been in church, at East Hampton, and Molly Dunton, the pale one, was up in the choir. All of a sudden everybody had disappeared, and she was looking at me with one eye shut over the rail behind where the Minister stands. She was singing, but I couldn't hear her, and after a time she stood up, and she didn't have a stitch on, save her Sunday School perfect-attendance pin with a lot of bars. Pretty soon she was rubbing up against me with her arms around my neck, and I felt the attendance pin scratching my chest, and then a gush down below, and I woke up. I tiptoed off and rounded up a damp towel, and cleaned up, me and the bunk, considerable embarrassed. The stewards made the bunks, and I guessed they'd notice the starchy spot. Even if I made the bunk up myself in the morning they'd have to strip it sooner or later. It was a sin, I knew, but I was blessed if I knew how you could avoid falling into it, unless it was by not eating fancy food. I remembered that Diana was dead, and Father, and my sense of sin was worse. I thought of Maria in Inagua, the first I had in a spell. It seemed like maybe if I hadn't had what Dr. Fordham called a nocturnal emission they'd all be alive. I thought about that and it didn't make any sense but I still felt bad.

It took a long time to fall back into a fitful slumber. I was dreaming I was aboard the Narragansett with Father, and he was ringing bells for the engine room, but they weren't answering them. Ding-ding, ding-ding; four bells in the morning watch, the first they struck each day aboard the yacht; six o'clock. I dressed; it was no use trying to sleep any longer. Crewmen were stepping out of the forecastle companionway, blowing and puffing in the cold morning air, clutching their first mugs of coffee. I pulled on my coat, and shuffled along in the carpet slippers. The Discovery was aft, swinging from the boat boom, and as I came closer I saw somebody was aboard her. He was wearing a blue uniform and cap; I thought at first he was the Captain. He knelt down on the sloop's foredeck, his left arm around the headstay; leaned outboard; and peered down at the planking on her starboard bow. He shifted his weight, and I saw he was the Mate, flat on his belly now and feeling down as far as he could with his right hand. He got up slowly and stepped toward the Jacob's ladder, dangling just ahead of the sloop. As he did, he caught sight of me looking down at him, and stopped, his face like he'd been caught with his fist in the jam pot. Then his face went blank again, and he swung about to grab the ladder, and I turned away.

I marched forward, climbed the two steps to the forecastle deck, and leaned over the rail on the port side. There was too much overhang to see anything, so I kicked off the slippers and climbed out onto the chains. Two sailors watched, faces as blank as the Mate's. I knelt, steadying myself with one hand against the yacht's side, and studied her planking down by the waterline. At first I saw nothing but the neat seams under the shiny black paint, but finally I made them out, two long dents, parallel, a foot apart, the lower beginning about even with where the upper left off, each an inch or so wide, making a shallow angle with the seams. They had been puttied, sanded, and painted over, but they were plain enough to see, dull streaks in the mirror finish. Neither matched the one long gash diagonally down the Discovery's side; that might have been made by the bobstay of the vessel that struck her. The upper of these great scratches down the yacht's side might have been made by a chainplate, and the lower by the end of a bowsprit -- a sloop carrying a chainplate and sprit, and laid well over to port. I swung back onto the Columbiad's deck. The Mate was leaning on the rail across the forward end of the poop, watching me with a tight smile, as I walked aft into the saloon. I took down a bound volume of Harper's Monthly and tried to read, to take my mind off believing what I now knew was so: The Columbiad had run down the sloop, and like enough on purpose.

The Harper's was the one for June to November, '76, and it had part of "Daniel Deronda" by George Eliot, with Gwendolyn and Mr. and Mrs. Gasciogne and Grandcourt and Mrs. Davilow. There'd been a lot of talk about Mr. Eliot, or was it Mrs., having a Jewess as a heroine. We had the set at home, and Mother had read it to the girls once. I leafed through the book for appearance's sake, thinking about the Mate and the sloop. There was a slip of paper toward the back, marking an article about "A Grand Business Man of the New School." The first page told about the business man, a Mr. Smith, and how he had been a beggar and some old maids took a shine to him and sent him to school; how he always ended up with all the money the other boys had; and how they "began by despising him a beggar, and ended in recognizing him as a capitalist." I turned the page, and saw two paragraphs marked in pencil along the margin:

"He had two grand qualifications for business; his mind was quick and his heart was hard. In all financial panics he enforced what was his due relentlessly, regardless of the woe it might bring upon nobler people than himself; but even though money was at three or four per cent a month, he paid punctually all his own notes as they matured. He would thus crush a debtor to the dust -- grind him to death; but still every dollar of his property, and every resource of his credit, were freely devoted to buy money, at any rates of interest, to meet his own obligations. To 'fail' was to him the worst ignominy. Mean in all minor matters, he was liberal in any sacrifices demanded by the mutations of trade. Almost every body detested him, yet every body knew that he might rely both on the skinflint's word and bond.

"Such a merchant, perhaps, should be judged by his own principles. He was essentially a bird of prey, with beak and talons somewhat ostentatiously and insolently displayed. He had no sympathy with the great body of the merchants of the country. Indeed, he laughed at all such sentimentality. 'Get the better of 'em,' was his motto. It may be said that he believed religiously in the maxim, *Homo homini lupus* -- 'Man to man is, and must be, a wolf.' "

Mr. Blake was stepping through the hatchway, on the arm of a steward. He was wearing a long robe with a velvet collar, and a Zouave cap of red felt. His left cheek was puffed out, and black and blue. I stood, the volume of Harper's in hand, finger marking my place. Mr. Blake squinted his right eye; the left was near shut from the swelling. It was gloomy in the saloon, coming in from the morning light on deck. He looked at me, and strode across the saloon, his step far surer than it had been the day before. He took the book from my hand, and opened it to the slip. He saw what I was reading and grunted, and returned the book. He looked me square in the eye, walked to the head of the table, and sat. The steward spread papers in front of him, and brought a pen, ink, and a box of cigars. He hadn't smoked his last, after all. The steward motioned "out" to me with his head, and I put the Harper's back on the shelf and left. Mr. Blake had put on glasses, and was peering at a document. He'd marked the passage; who else would have dared?

At breakfast, Dr. Fordham told Nat and me to have the sloop alongside the gangway in an hour; we'd be leaving. The Captain and the Mate escorted the Doctor to the top of the gangway when the time came, and the Mate grinned down at me. Dr. Fordham seemed upset. Nat cast off and gave the bow a long shove with his boot away from the Columbiad, and we squared away for Springs. "He don't want to pay you," Dr. Fordham said. "Claims he didn't ask for you and that if anybody's to pay for you and the sloop I should. Well, he'll pay, and pay double, it'll all be in my fee. You didn't say anything to rile the old bastard, did you? He seems to have taken a particular dislike to the two of you. I didn't know as he'd even noticed you, but he says you're sneaks and Paul-prys. Another thing that don't do his disposition much good is that he knows they started debate in the House on Mills's tariff bill on Tuesday but he hasn't heard what went on past the first day. Protection is that man's middle name, and when he gets going on Cleveland and free trade I wouldn't be surprised to see him keel over from apoplexy." Dr. Fordham paused. "Sorry, Jerry," he said, meaning for mentioning apoplexy. The Mate must have told Mr. Blake what I'd seen him up to, looking at the Discovery. I began to wonder how Cleveland must feel, everybody mad at him from the Old Comrades of the G.A.R. on up to Mr. Blake.

The yacht's anchor chain rattling in could be heard across the water. The Mate was on the forecastle, his figure hunched black against the sky, a bird of prey. His arm went up in signal to the man on the steam windlass. The Columbiad was under way in a few minutes, and half-way to Plum

Gut by the time we entered Accabonac Creek and lost sight of her black hull.

Springs people were all a-twitter over the Columbiad's having been in the Bay for three days. Yachts weren't that rare, but it wasn't the season, and until Jerry Baker came off Montauk in his stage and told people her name, most of them didn't know what she was. They asked a lot of questions, as we walked toward East Hampton; they'd seen the sloop alongside the yacht, and enough of them knew Dr. Fordham by sight to make some of the questions pretty much on the right track. Springs people may talk odd but they aren't all stupid. The Doctor put them off with cheerful remarks about just having been yachting, that was all. There was a story about it in the paper the next Saturday, the 29th of April:

> People living along the Bay were quite agitated the middle of last week to see a large black-hulled vessel proceed to Montauk, after heaving-to off Plum Island in rendezvous with a local sloop. There was speculation that she might be a cigar smuggler, but according to reports from Montauk she proved to be A.P. Blake's steam-yacht Columbia, believed to be the largest pleasure vessel afloat. Mr. Blake was not thought to be on board, rumor having it that he is inspecting railroad properties in Sunny California. A Sag Harbor physician is rumored to have visited the Columbia, giving rise to reports that there was some contagious disease among her crew. Mr. Blake is said to be the richest man on earth, and is reputed to be interested in the Fort Pond Bay Port of Entry scheme, although he is not known ever to have visited the place.

Nat and I engaged to spend a week helping Eldorus Smith put in his pound nets along Gin Beach, the gunning having played out. It was hard work, using the sloop as a platform to drive the stakes from with a maul, and Eldorus never quit worrying aloud over fish prices and prospects. I had another set-to with Mother Sunday, after church, about my plans, and it ended up with me promising to go talk to

Ora Wurmley about an opening he had in his store, first thing Monday. Nat and I had nothing lined up for the sloop, and if I hadn't agreed Ma would have set me to working for Sam on the farm. Ora was young enough for me to call him that, not Mr. Wurmley, and his store was up at the west end of the village, on the East Hampton road. We'd generally traded with the Edwardses, on our end, it being handier, but Ora didn't seem to mind. He wore a white apron, and was clean-shaven except for his burnsides, and had a sallow complexion and sort of wide-eyed open way of fraud with his customers. He sort of hovered, and was all yes-sir, yes-m'am, fine spell of weather we're having, not meaning it but people swallowed it.

He was alone when I arrived, and told him I'd heard he needed a clerk. He said he'd just lost a man, a Tabor, not cut out for the general-store business anyhow. "Do you think you are, Jerry?" he asked. I didn't know as I knew, but was still feeling so low that it had been easy for Mother to get me there. "Here, study a bit on this," Ora said, shoving a heavy ledger-book across the counter. I carried it up by the front where the light was better and sat on an empty shotgun-shell crate.

It didn't seem to make much sense, and I didn't see how you could make any money in the store business. Nobody ever seemed to pay cash. Here was Sam Loper, had bought "2 lbs. peaches part spoiled" back in January for ".20, and 26½ lbs. ham at .4 for 3.71," and settled up at the end of February, when he came in to buy two pencils and a pad of paper. Maybe he needed them to check Ora's ciphering. In the back of the ledger, he had Special Orders -- Overseer Poor. The poor got tea, sugar, molasses, besides necessities, and even some cocoanut once. They had Abram Holloman down for "pance" at 2.00, and I couldn't puzzle that out until I got down to the next entry, "shirt and drawers 1.00." There were a lot of entries all alike that puzzled me until I thought about it, although none under Overseer Poor: "Sept 17 to 1 qt Sundry Groceries 1.15." There were some pretty respectable people in Amagansett drank Sundry Groceries.

"Doesn't anybody ever buy for cash?" I asked. "Sure they do; we've got a cash book for that. I'd just as lib they put it on their account, though, most of 'em," Ora said. He came over and took the ledger.

"Here," he said, pointing. "Jim Leggett comes in and gets six papers of Hard-a-Port. He'd get more, but he's run up a pretty good bill. The six chews cost him 25¢; how much is that a paper?"

I thought a bit, and said four cents and a fraction, one-sixth I guessed. "All right," Ora said patiently, "now Ulysses Payne comes in; he's got plenty of money, although he charges. He can afford to buy his tobacco in quantity. He buys a box, that's four dozen papers, for $1.75. How much is that?"

"A shade less than three-and-a-half cents a paper," I announced after a pause. "And I pay three cents," Ora said. "You see? I'd rather be selling it six papers at a time. There's another thing, too; the rich man, he's done his slaughterin' in the fall, but when he runs out of meat along this time of year he comes in and buys a big ham or two; 'tisn't going to hurt him much to have to pay 14¢ a pound, though you'd never think it to hear him mourn. The poor man, he comes in and needs meat, he don't dare buy a dollar's worth of ham, he buys a twelve-ounce can of smoked Chicago beef at 28¢. It's the same with lard; the rich man will buy a full tub at 11¢ a pound, and the poor man can't get that much up, or doesn't dare ask for it on credit, and he buys Cotolene at 12¢, not half as good and a penny more. Give me the poor for customers every time; if they're good for it you've got 'em, on credit, and if they ain't good for it, they pay cash, or go hungry. Then too, if they owe you a bit they ain't likely to stray, and do business elsewhere. You got 'em again."

Ora chuckled and offered me a pickle from the barrel.

"Collect what's due ye when it's due," he intoned, "and pay what ye owe when that falls due. It's every man for himself, in business and in this life." *Homo homini lupus.*

Chapter
XVIII

Muxing Around

I told Ora as polite as I could I didn't think I had it in me to do very well in the store line, and excused myself. He sort of puffed up, but didn't try to change my mind. It was still early, and I didn't know what to do. If I went home, I'd have to face Mother. I dawdled on the road; the air was warm for the end of April, and sunny. Some of the fresh-plowed lots had wisps of fog, like smoke, rising from the damp earth.

When I finally got to the house, there was no sign of Mother. Her wash was on the line and I guessed she had gone down to see Sam's wife. I changed as quick as I could and headed off again. Nat was over in Sag Harbor, and having to make sure the sloop was all right at Springs was as good an excuse as I could think of to get away. She'd set me to work if she caught me hanging around.

I looked back over the village toward the ocean before entering the Stony Hill woods; no sign of weft or whale. Heading off through the big beeches, I found myself at the woodpink spot, down in a hollow on a slope facing north. You'd think the arbutus would like a southerly exposure, but they don't seem to. I fanned away some leaves, oak mixed with beech here, and there they were, the first, tiny whitish-pink blossoms on their little stems. I picked a good bunch and left them to get on my way home, on a slab of bark with some running pine and damp moss, saving one for my buttonhole. They'd make up to Mother for my dodging chores.

The sloop was swinging on her anchor right where we'd left her. I rowed out and muxed around, whipping some rope ends, splicing odd lengths of manila into something more useful, and tidying up. Pretty soon it was the middle of the afternoon, and it began to itch at me that I'd better be getting on home. I'd always been that way; start out to have a lazy day and between two or three it would start to gnaw at me and I'd have to give it up. The woodpinks helped smooth things over when I told Mother I'd talked the store business over with Ora, and what I'd decided. She just sighed and looked worried.

Tuesday was the first day of May, Cattle Drive Day, and I was glad to help the boys set up the pound, barring off Main Street from Rackett's Corner to by the Cemetery with lengths of rail fence. Then we drove our own cattle, except the two we were milking, up to the pound, each marked with the Dimon mark, ha'penny behind the right ear and a diamond over the left. There were only six; the Edwardses, three nicks under each ear, had fifteen; the Schellingers, ha'penny under each ear and a nick over the left, a dozen; and the Eldredges, an ell over the right ear and an ell under the left, twenty or more. The East Hampton stock arrived toward noon, four or five hundred lowing cattle trying to amble off into dooryards, and as many more sheep bleating and baaing. It was warm and still, and the dust settled on stock, trees, and herders, most of them horseback.

The cattle penned, the riders dismounted for a hasty meal. They were rank, anxious to get beyond the gate at First House by night. It was decided to work the herd along the beach. The fence was taken down by the Schoolhouse and the stock trooped through the land in front of our place. Mother shut all the doors and windows tight for the dust, and I followed along to the beach banks. Some of the stock tried to turn west instead of east when they got to the open beach, and it took a quarter-hour of unhandsome language and whip-snapping to get them onto the right track. They'd be harder to handle, not to speak of sorting them out by owners, when they came off Montauk in the fall, after a summer running wild. It was the way it always had been, for better than two hundred years, except that now everybody paid pasturage, not just those whose families didn't own shares in Montauk, or enough shares for their stock, and the payment was to Arthur Benson, instead of to the Proprietors. It was the way it always had been, but it was not the way it was always going to be. I could see that, if others couldn't.

Mother set me to spading the kitchen garden when I got back, and to planting it the next morning. We had pole beans, limas, in hills; and cucumbers, white spines, too; sweet corn, tomatoes, to be set out later from the hot-bed on the sunny side of the kitchen ell; carrots, Bliss's Improved Long Orange; turnips; cabbages, beets; cauliflower, and squash, Boston Marrow and Hubbard. I raked and staked and poked seeds in and never had a moment's peace; she could see me out the kitchen window and was on the back porch every five minutes telling me what to do. Mother liked her garden just so. On Wednesday, Sam and I took the Studebaker wagon over to Springs and loaded up with bunkers, seined by Eldorus, for the field corn, one in each hill, the way the Indians did. We were at that the rest of the week, and I began to feel like I'd turned farmer after all. Mother had taken to reading the American Agriculturist, I guess she figured she had to with Father gone, and they had something about turning the manure pile after a dry spell, so it didn't heat up for lack of rain, and I spent Saturday afternoon wrestling with that and wishing I had the man from the Agriculturist on the end of the pitchfork.

And so it went for the rest of the month, my seventeenth birthday and all; dressing the clover field with gypsum, working with the cultivator and hoeing, tinkering with the mowing machine, putting in sets of horse radish between the rows of cabbage in the kitchen garden, cutting poles for the beans and tomatoes, and tending Tulip, the old plowhorse, who was about to foal. It all had to be done, but I figured somebody else could do it as well as I could, or better, and enjoy it more, and leave me free to do something I liked, like fishing, and make some real money.

I thought about fishing a lot, chopping weeds those dusty May days. I'd made pretty good money at it, and was sure enough of myself to figure I always could, barring the times that were bound to come when there was nothing doing for a spell. Yet a good many fishermen never made much, never had, never would, but stuck to it even though they might have made a better living ashore for half the work and a third the discomfort. Working a farm, when you got down to it, wasn't all that hard. It was just plain dull.

Puff Homidy had that feeling about life; I could hear Father again: "He'd druther connive and gain half a dollar than do an honest man's work for half as long, and get five dollars." Except that not everything he did was conniving; some of it was gambling. That's what most fishermen were. Gamblers. Every time you made a set or dropped a hook or even scratched the bottom with a clam rake it was gambling. Father had once run his twine around a bunch of bunkers he thought was a middling-size school and pursed it and found he had so many he deck-loaded the steamer and still couldn't carry them all, even with boards up above the rail until the deck was awash, and he had to call Captain Josh alongside in his Hudson and dicker until they struck a bargain and bailed the rest of the fish into it. And how many other times had he made a set around nothing but water? Even digging clams; there were men who'd found a new spot and made a killing, working odd hours and careful until the others got wind of it. You never knew, and you always had hope. Like a miner; you always figured there was a chance for a strike.

The dust gave way to fog for Decoration Day, and I was working with the cultivator and Ranger in the home lot, in corn and potatoes again this year, when I heard the Bridge Hampton Cornet Band coming down the street, and the Edwin Rose Post 274, G.A.R., and the Phoenix Hose Company of Sag Harbor hove into view. We still did our fire-fighting catch-as-catch can, in Amagansett, and had to borrow somebody else's Company for an occasion like this. I pulled up Ranger, not that he took much pulling, the soil being damp from the fog and rain of the past twenty-four hours, and hard to work, and leaned on the cultivator handles to watch. Somebody opened the biggest cemetery gate, the one the hearse went through when we had that kind of a funeral, and the volunteers and old soldiers marched right in, followed by a troop of children carrying garlands. A man in black, too far to tell but it wasn't Reverend Mr. Porter, spoke for ten minutes; I couldn't make out the words. Then the children marched around, putting their flowers on the veterans' graves. I could see Father's, on the little slope at the southeast end, a mound of dirt, no headstone yet. Willis in the Harbor was still working on it. Father wouldn't get any flowers, not having been on hand for the Civil War. Nobody resented his having gone off whaling instead, but still he wouldn't get any flowers.

The band played something sad and slow, and a squad of six Old Comrades stepped forward. A man in blue off to the side shouted commands, loud enough to be heard easily but unintelligible. The squad fired, a bit ragged. They fired again. A third volley, and the procession left the graveyard. The Old Comrades, fifty of them maybe, had mostly been at the big beer picnic at Fresh Pond last summer, but they looked more serious now, more to be respected. They couldn't all keep in step, and their uniforms weren't very uniform. Most of them were Father's age, a few older, and Titus Mullins, who'd been in the Regulars long enough ago to have gone to Mexico with Zachary Taylor, the oldest of them all.

They were well clear of the graveyard now. The band struck up "The Girl I Left Behind Me," and I thought of how they must have felt, marching off to war before I was born, and got a lump in my throat. Then I remembered that Father had said half of them had been dragged off by the draft, or went as substitutes for somebody with money enough to hire them to do it. A tragic business, the war, he'd said. I'd seen General McClellan four or five summers before, sitting in a rocker on the Mulfords' front porch over in East Hampton, a boarder. He'd had his feet up on the rail, in slippers; he'd looked sad, and small, to be a General. He was as big as that colored General down in Cuba, though. What would the Edwin Rose Post have made of those Cubanos, with their shirttails out and their cartridges and bananas and cigars all jangling around in a big pocket on the front of the shirt? Bummers, they'd call them I supposed, but they wouldn't want to mix it up with them, not within arm's length of those knives. Or if they had a barn the General could burn. I got Ranger under way again and we followed the parade off down the field. The marchers were away ahead by the time we turned at the hedgerow, stepping lively to the rollicking "Garryowen." It was beginning to clear off, and the turned soil steamed when the sun struck it.

I walked over to Springs that afternoon. Nat had been going to run the Discovery in on the top of the morning tide to scrub and tar her bottom, and I'd give him a hand. We still didn't know what we'd do with her that summer; he wanted to try taking out day parties, sailing and fishing, but I didn't think I wanted any more of that, and felt like doing some real fishing again. Not that we were arguing.

Coming along on the Stone Road toward Eastside, I

could hear a clanging through the woods ahead, as if a giant
was trying to rivet a hole in a try kettle. Coming closer, there
were voices, and finally a steady mushy thumping like the
Cornet Band's bass drum would sound if it was full of water
and being pounded with a dishmop. Then that stopped, and
the clanging began again. The road led out of the woods into
the pasture around the Neck Path Fullers' Farm. You called
them that to keep them separate from the Hog Crick Fullers,
a different tribe altogether. The sound was coming from
alongside the barn; a steam thrashing machine with a knot
of men around it. There was a leather drive-belt running
from the big fly-wheel to a buzz-saw a good three feet across.
Taking into account the size of the pile of stove lengths as
against the pile of waiting timber, they hadn't had much
luck with the apparatus that day.

"A goddam catamite of a wrought-iron compounded
son of a bitch!" The voice came from the far side; I didn't
know it, but I knew the heavy legs in striped trousers showing below the boiler, and the answering voice: "A veritable
Jonah among agricultural engines, Mister Hull; were it
mine, I would waste not a moment in transforming it into
scrap for the junkman." There he was, elegantly outfitted
and topped with a new derby hat, Charles Stuart Pufferson
Homidy, a wrench in either hand. He went on, speaking to
Hull, the traveling steam-engine man, but as much for the
benefit of the crowd as for Hull.

"Steam you've got; better let off a little, too, hers, not
yours, before she goes off like an Anarchist bomb and hists
us all to Gehenna; steam we've got, but the question is, why
ain't it getting from there" -- he fetched the side of the boiler
a good whack with one wrench -- "to here, at the right
time?" The other wrench banged a cylinder opposite the
drive-wheel. "I am a windmill man, a wooden gears man, an
artisan not an engineer, myself, but it has been my experience," Mr. Homidy paused and looked around, "that the
damned fools designing machinery today generally
wouldn't know a hard-on from a hoe handle." The back

door of the Fuller house slammed; one of the women of the house had been listening up to that point. "It's all in the valves," he observed. "Ten cords for unraveling the Masonics of her, my wood your sawing, Mister Hull?" The machine's owner nodded miserably, and Mr. Homidy set to work.

I climbed the woodpile and squatted down to watch. The steam-engine man dragged out a box full of tools, and Mr. Homidy began rummaging. He made his selection, and laid the tools out in a neat line on a board: a couple of files, various wrenches, a ball-peen hammer, and a heavy screwdriver. Mr. Hull went around to the other side and did something and the steam began to vent, whistling steady like a teakettle. Mr. Homidy was silent for once, and commenced taking bits and pieces off the engine around what must have been the drive cylinder. He worked rapidly, still silent except for an "aha" as he looked into a cavity. He reached in and set about scraping with a turning motion. Beads of sweat sprung out on his forehead, and began to run down. That had happened to Dr. Fordham, working on the shotgun wound. Mr. Homidy tied his handkerchief around his head to keep the sweat out of his eyes, and went on. He fitted another part into the hole, and twisted it carefully, scraping and fitting until he had it right. Then he began to put the parts back together again. The crowd hadn't drifted away, but watched, giving him plenty of elbow-room. After a good three-quarters of an hour, he spoke. "Give her some steam, Mister Hull. I think we got it." That was what Dr. Melville had said.

Mister Hull twisted some knobs and climbed up on the seat at the stern of the thrashing machine and tugged a handle. There was a hiss, and the drive piston began to move, in and out, slowly building up speed, in and out, male into female and out. When it had settled into a regular chuff, chuff, chuff, he pulled another lever, and the big drive-wheel began to turn. The belt slipped, then caught; the chuffing slowed as the piston took the load, and then returned to its speed. The buzz-saw was spinning, the pitch of its hum gradually rising. Mr. Hull waved his hand to Farmer Fuller, who carried over a length of oak. Yyyunng went the saw, slowing as it bit into the wood, then gaining speed gnnuyyy as the blade passed through. Mr. Homidy wiped his hands and put his coat back on, looking pleased with himself.

There wasn't much mechanical he couldn't do, from setting up wind sawmills in Cuba to fixing a steam sawmill in Springs, and I was glad he was one of ours, and that somebody from away like Mr. Hull, with his fancy contraption, had to turn to Mr. Homidy when things went wrong. Though they were two of a kind, Yankee mechanics, nobody to beat them in any other nation, Hail Columbia Happy Land. Then I remembered the money Mr. Homidy owed us, and he must have been reading my mind without even looking at me, witchcat that he was, for he turned and smiled. "Ah, Jeremiah; about to embark upon a Jeremiad, I presume, regarding the whereabouts of certain small sums?" I told him as politely as I could that Nat and I would appreciate being paid, that J.G. & S.T. Bowman had made him their agent in the matter of the salvage of the Teunis King, and that even though he was no longer working for them we thought he had some responsibility to see that we got paid. He'd got back the twenty-eight dollars he'd lent me to get home plus interest two months back, I pointed out.

It didn't bother him any that the Fullers, father and two sons, and their hired man were listening. "See what I can do, my boy," he said. "Will you consider discounting your bill to me, say twenty per cent? A gamble on my part, that I might eventually collect, but one I am willing to undertake, considering our long friendship. Eh, Jerry?" I walked away; he'd been teasing, trying to euchre me in front of the Fullers.

I went to find Nat and the Discovery.

A fish hawk was screeching at Nat from her nest on Edwards's Hummock, while her mate circled slowly over Accabonac Creek. The tide was still on the fall, and the sloop was way over on her starboard side, with Nat wading bareshanks on the port, scraping off grass and barnacles with an old hoe. I got my shoes off and went to work. Nat had a bucket of tar over a low driftwood fire up on the beach. The air was still, and the fish hawk's splash when he went for his supper echoed against the trees clear across the meadow. The great bird rose from the water, an eel wriggling in his claws, and headed for a dead oak on the island, circling it to gain height. He lit, balancing on one foot, and went to work on the eel with his beak to quiet him down. He was still squirming, though, when the fish hawk flew over to the nest, the way they do after you cut them up and throw them in the frying-pan. We worked fast, to give the tar time to set before the tide came up again, and said little. Nat would do the starboard side the next day, Sunday; he didn't care.

I walked off Sunday dinner, east to the Highlands, restless again. Sitting on the grass there, you could see sails on the horizon, four or five schooners and a barkentine, and a tug with two barges. Below, Napeague Beach spread dusted-white toward Montauk; the shadblow was in blossom. You couldn't work, or whale, or fish, on Sunday, I thought, but you could work a vessel, as they were doing offshore. If a master let his vessel drift every seventh day there'd be a good deal more wrecks than there was. It was warm, and I lay back and puffed cigar-smoke at the blue June sky. There was one sandhill down there on Napeague I'd walked to a good many times. She was hollowed out on the southwest side by the wind, and I'd pick up bits of pottery, marked in little lightning lines by some old Indian with the edge of a scallop shell. Sharp chips of rock, too, quartz where they'd been making arrow heads. There were pieces of clamshell, the blue part gone off as wampum, too. They said when the white men came, and traded steel drills for furs, it turned the wampum market upside-down. Muxes, the Indians called the drills; to mux around was still to while away the time at some little chore like drilling holes in a clamshell, and not for white men really, especially Protestants. You couldn't mux around all your life, or you'd turn out to be the town drunk, or Take-Him-Back-to-The-Hall Brady, or Mr. Homidy if you were clever enough. I rolled up onto my elbow and looked around, as if I was worried somebody'd see me, loafing. It came to me it wasn't just anybody I was worried about, but Father. The flag was up at the Napeague Station, and a little white smoke curled from the stovepipe. George Eldredge was there, and I had half a mind to walk out and say hello, but I didn't.

I went back through the woods. My right foot fetched up on a rock in the leaves, and I brushed it off. A slab of slate a foot across; cornermarker for somebody's woodlot, the Parsonses' probably. They did that, the surveyors using stone not native, so the mark would not be mistook for just another rock. I turned it over: N.E.P., neat letters cut long ago. "Remove not the landmark." Dr. Talmage had preached on that text once. I put the stone back in the little pocket of soil it had made for itself over the years, lettering down, and wondered what Walker and his ragamuffin survey crew were up to. Over in Cuba again, likely, chasing up hill and down dale. It was still and warm in the Amagansett woods; Cuba in June would be a scorcher. I went on. A twig snapped against my cheek, and I stopped to look behind. Further on, a dry stick popped under my tread, and brought to mind the pop of a pistol back across the salt lake that day. I didn't know whether Maria'd done it for me, or because she hated Brodie & Bruce. I ached, thinking of her, and then was ashamed of what we'd done, on the beach and in the cave, with her maybe dead. It didn't seem right to be thinking of somebody that way, after they were gone, that is if it were ever right. Not on Sunday, anyway.

Chapter
XIX

Clamming Or
The Watchcase Factory?

The brush thinned ahead, and I came out onto the Abraham's Landing road. A phaeton was coming up the grade from the eastward. I recognized Dr. Fordham, and hallooed. He waved, and I sat on the bank for him to come up. *"Vox clamantis in deserto*, Jeremiah. A voice crying in the wilderness. Come aboard."

I climbed on, and we set off, the Doctor explaining that he was off the reservation to tend an ex-patient of Dr. Osborne's, who was in a bad way with an ulcerated leg. "She's living down there by Bellyache Swamp, hovedown in bed half the time and up playing Mrs. Hopkins the other half, with a couple of come-by-chance brats," he said. "The damned thing stinks to high heaven, and she shows it off to all comers, like it was a pet. I think she'd be disappointed if I did manage to work a cure on her, which is doubtful. It's a nice drive for a Sunday afternoon, though, and it gets me out of the Harbor."

We started between the fields down toward the village. "You know what *vox clamantis* comes from? Dartmouth College, my college, that's her motto. When old Eleazer Wheelock took Samson Occum out of Indian Field and went up to Hanover before the Revolution that's what it was, too, wilderness. 'A small school, but there are those who love it.' Remember? The great Daniel Webster; that was Dartmouth he was talking about. I don't know if I learnt much up there, except how to hold my liquor and argue with the clergy, but I had a good time at it. I could have gone straight off to the medical institute, in New York, for all the good college did me." It was the Dartmouth College Grant Mr. Homidy's beaver-tail had come from; Diana was kin to the Occums.

Dr. Fordham was quiet for a bit, then spoke again. "Ever tell you about anatomy class? Well, we all had to have our own cadaver, had to provide it ourselves, that was the first test really. There were sources of supply, but it still took some doing. The one I finally got was a floater, you know, hoisted out of the North River. Bought him from a policeman. We had a sort of icehouse to keep them in between sessions of cutting and slicing, but he was enough like Limburger to begin with. Had a hard time telling if he was white or black. Not that that makes any difference. They're all the same, once you get to working on them. Musculature, circulatory system, all the same except the color and the hair and maybe the heel-bone, and when they've been in the water long enough the color's pretty much equal too.

I swallowed hard, thinking of the bodies on the beach below the Light. Dr. Fordham continued: "Oh, we'd have rare old times. You'd as like as not come in one morning and find *labia majora*, *labia minora*, the whole damned hypogastric gateway, tacked up on the notice board so you'd have to read a note about a change in a lecture-time through the hole, or reach in your coat-pocket and find a pickled digit somebody'd tucked away with your pipe. The faculty don't do anything to discourage the foolery as long as it doesn't get out of hand, aha, encourages it in fact; seems hard, but for most men it's the only way. Otherwise they'd quit. What I mean is, they're not trying to breed cynics about the human body, they're just trying to get you past revulsion. Familiarity doesn't necessarily breed contempt; what they aim for is respect, in the long run. Doesn't always work that way, but that's the idea. Think you could take it?''

I said I didn't know, but thought to myself I could, and looked at my hands. I unclenched the right fist, and saw the tendons across the back move as I wiggled my fingers. There was a white scar behind the knuckle at the base of the second and third fingers, where Sam'd hit me with a hatchet once when we were chopping kindling. He'd looked at somebody passing in a buggy, and brought the blade down in the wrong place. If it'd come down any harder I'd have lost the use of those two fingers. Charlie Masters had partly lost the use of his arm from that shotgun charge last fall. Was it tendons, or blood vessels, or nerves had been severed? Father'd burst a blood vessel, they'd said. How did that happen, and why? You could learn about how. Maybe if you knew, death, like Father's and Diana's, wouldn't be so hard to understand. There were, or would be, explanations for everything in the world. Sooner or later, that was what the Doctor had said: "They'll figure it all out some day. What we don't know now is because of our own ignorance, not because there are any unfathomable mysteries.''

I knew what he was driving at, about my "taking it.'' "You don't know? You ought to think about it," he said, and I answered I'd put my mind to it. We were abreast of the Liberty Pole by this time, and I thanked the Doctor and jumped down. "There's chequit up in Peconic," he said, "and will you and Nat be available if we want you end of the week?'' I told him we would be, and said good-bye.

Fishing and taking out parties with the Discovery was just fooling around, boys' business, pleasant but not men's work. There were men, of course, grown men who made a living on the water with a lot less -- a sharpie, eelpots, and a clamrake, or even just a clamrake, some of them -- but not a Dimon. It wasn't enough. There was something too about having just one friend and he your partner. It made me uneasy. Fishing in a big way, that was another matter. I'd like that, but it meant at least another summer in a bunker-steamer crew, then taking my chances the second or third year for a shot at going mate, or pilot maybe, under somebody.

I stopped in the lane and looked at the home place, over the picket fence. That needed painting, but the rest was as shipshape as you'd want to see; even the woodpile was neat. Lace curtains in the parlor windows. I went around back, drew a bucket from the well, and drank from the piggin. Father had been talking about driving a point, and having a pump, or maybe just mounting a pump top of the old well, and boarding it over. His face was easy to see, and the sound of his voice easy to remember. Sometimes it seemed as if we hadn't had much to do with each other all those sixteen years, but that wasn't true. He'd taught me to swim, at Fresh Pond, gently; I hadn't been taken through the surf and dropped overboard by him the way the Leister boys had learned; to row; to gun; to fish; sail; plow; milk; about everything I knew I guessed, except how to read. And sew. Mother had taught me that, the time I'd had the measles, and she put me to quilt, patch-work. To keep me occupied, she said, and out of mischief. She used to make me sleep with my hands outside the covers, when I was little. I hadn't known why. That and whistling in the house bothered her. The not whistling she got from Father. He didn't like it inside or out. That was being a seaman, not whistling for fear of getting more wind than you whistled for. And not driving a knife into the mast, nor having Finns, women, or preachers aboard. Jonah. The Old Testament. That's what Father was, our Father. Hard and righteous. I could see him carrying that Whinhenny who'd wanted to sleep double-banked in his bunk up the ladder from the forecastle and across the deck and dumping her into the roadstead at Honolulu. Like Moses carrying the Tablets, white beard and angry eyes. Except his beard couldn't've been white then; I didn't know if he even wore one in those days.

Father never knew what I'd done in that line. Nor had I ever tried to explain to him what had happened on the islands. I couldn't live up to him; I'd already headed off on a different tack. Not that whalers, and fishermen, and farmers, and even the men in the Old Testament, didn't fornicate; I knew better. Some of them even did it on Sundays, but not the Patriarchs. I'd bit the apple, I thought, and wondered what I'd meant by that. Amagansett, the farm, wasn't the Garden of Eden, no, not by a long shot, and I wasn't being driven out, though I'd seen the old black snake from under the barn the day before, the first time since fall. I guessed, for my age, that my experience, and my knowledge, was about what Father's had been at that age, his without the womanizing, but there was something different. Maybe it was the times. Father'd turned seventeen before the Rebellion and in a backwards part of the nation at that. Lord knows we were still backward, compared to some. A.P. Blake was older than him, but there weren't any A.P. Blakes then. Nor anaesthesia, nor antisepsis. Maybe it was belief. Father had it; Mother believed too. I didn't know if I did or didn't. Not in Hell certainly. In the life everlasting. Together again in Heaven. How old were you in Heaven? I thought of Mother going up at ninety, with Father still a youngish man.

"What are you grinning about, young man?" I jumped near out of my skin; Mother was standing in the cold-pantry doorway, watching. I hung the piggin on the well-house nail and came in. "Nothing, Mother."

Nat sent me over a note from Springs late that afternoon by one of his dim-wit cousins, the one who'd been kicked in the head by a cow he was getting ready to milk. At least, he said he'd been getting ready to milk her; Nat claimed different. It was the first of Nat's spelling I'd seen since we were in school together, and he hadn't improved any. I guessed he'd written because he was afraid the cousin would forget the message, which was:

> "Jerry -- meat me in Habor Mon. a.m. D. Fordhams
> have chatred slupe for week fishing. Prty of fore. Yrs.
> Nat."

It took me a while to get outside of that. The "s" on Fordham was what everybody in Springs did with last names. The Field family was always Fields and their distant cousins whose name was really Fields were Fieldses, like this, Isaac Ludlow Fieldses. We couldn't cart around any four people for a week fishing, so he meant weakfish, chequit. If he wanted me to meet him there, instead of sailing over with him, it probably was because he'd gone off somewhere with the Discovery right after sending me the note. Cousin Mushmelon, they called him that for the shape of his head, he was really Ames, said that was so, that Nat had run off to Bostwick's Creek after long clams. He had that Accabonac way of talking so bad it was hard for me to understand, for all I'd been listening to it all my life. "Runawf Bawick lunclammnh" was what he really said, quick but deep. It made sense, long-clamming; Nat could probably get fifty cents a bushel in the Harbor, to forty in Springs. Even though he'd dared tar the sloop's bottom on a Sunday, he couldn't very well dig clams in the Creek on a Sunday afternoon, even if it was the best digging tide of the month. Nobody over on Gardiner's Island would mind, or like enough even see him, up to Bostwick's. The last time we'd been there, in March, there'd been water enough in the entrance to float the sloop; with this tide, low water springs, it wouldn't be much over your ankles. I thought of Squire Gardiner and Mr. Homidy standing there in the cold rain in the little meadow above the Creek, looking back at the gutway opening through the beach. That seemed longer ago than three months.

Ames was still there, expectant. I gave him a five-cent piece, and he popped it into his cheek and headed back to Springs, happy as a clam and about as smart. I dreamt that night about a girl, her face was something like Sam's wife,

and she was doing the sort of things in those French pictures, and I woke up wet again, without the excuse of the Columbiad's spicy meals. The clock at the bottom of the stairs
struck four, and I figured I might as well get up and get under
way. We were as caught up with the work as you ever were
on a farm, and neither Mother nor Sam had objected to my
going.

I got to Long Wharf before Nat did, and found the Doctor
and three other members of the Century. They had a big
bucket of small shrimps, little fellows like sandfleas, seined
in the Cove, and by early afternoon we'd worked up around
Hog Neck on the last of the flood, eating our sandwiches on
the way, and were anchored in Peconic Bay, chumming up
the weakfish. The men had what they called sporting gear,
and they'd brought along a sort of glorified crab net to dip the
fish out of the water with; you needed it with the sort of bast-
ing-thread tackle they were using, on weakfish.

My heart wasn't in it, the fishing. Ordinarily, an expedi-
tion like this was pleasant enough -- horseplay, a hamper of
good grub, sometimes champagne, not much work really,
gutting and scaling a few fish later was all. I did what I had to,
baiting hooks and putting the weakfish in the wet well and
dribbling shrimp for chum out of the bucket, and didn't say
much. I felt uneasy, as I had for a month, only more so. It was
the way I'd been at Inagua, unsettled about the gills, as if I
were homesick, but here I was at home, or close to it, and
among friends. It was a sort of out-of-place feeling, the way
I'd been once at a Methodist wedding. This was late in the
spring for it, but Mother would have prescribed sulphur and
molasses, no matter if I was regular as twice-a-day, like high
tide.

There was a schooner working oyster ground off Cow
Neck. I wouldn't have minded being back aboard the Lavolta
I thought; it was a comfortable feeling, setting off on an
ocean passage, taking your departure from one place on the
globe, longitude that and latitude this, trusting to the Cap-

tain to get you there the way you were supposed to trust in the Lord. Going to sea was not the safest life, but it was regular, you could say that. Starboard watch below, larboard watch on deck. Eat, sleep, work the vessel. It didn't matter, Atlantic or Pacific, you knew where you were headed, if not when you'd get there.

Charlie's father, Mr. Masters from the watchcase factory, was telling about the set-to the week previous when the mate aboard the new steam oyster-dredge shot his Irish cook, who'd been paid off for giving the mate lip and had come back aboard to continue the argument with a brick in his hand. When he jumped down off Long Wharf despite being warned the mate let go with a little .32 rimfire bulldog revolver and hit him in the head. The bullet bounced right off as you might have figured, doing no more than taking off some hide and knocking Paddy cold. The man was not arrested, nor was the mate; the Constable couldn't figure the legal ins and outs, the dredge being a documented vessel and so forth. A bunch of Hibernians met that night, got all worked up, and headed for Long Wharf to teach the mate that an Irishman was as good as an American, maybe better, and not to be shot in the head. The dredge crew heard them coming, and cast off her lines and let her drift out away from the Wharf, not having steam up and being lucky enough to have the breeze off the land. The Micks threw rocks at the dredge until the Constable, with the volunteers from the Murray Hill Hose Company, chased them home.

"A regular Draft Riot," Mr. Masters said. "They're good workers but I wonder sometimes if the country wouldn't be better off if we'd never let them in. They don't care a damnative about authority, and they treat the company houses like the sties they was raised in. The trouble is, though, we can't get help enough out of our Native Americans. Around here, they'd sooner make five dollars a week, just some weeks at that, clamming, than ten every week at a workbench. Inde-Goddamned-Pendent, too much so for their own good." Dr. Fordham coughed, and inclined his head forward, toward Nat and me, for all the Doctor was as native as either of us.

Mr. Watchcase Factory paid no heed, and went on. "There's something lacking in the people out here, the natives, present company excepted of course. Maybe the best blood went to the goldfields in '49, like they say. I dunno. They don't have any more use for the Irish than I do, but if they won't work the Micks will."

Mr. Masters had been brought in from around Bridge-port to run the watchcase factory as soon as it was built. You might not like what he had to say, about the local people, but there was truth in it. What he was going on to say about foreigners -- "What saves us is they aren't all Dutch-men, some is Russians, Polack Russians, or Silesians, or Austrians. . . ." -- I wasn't sure about. Once you got to know them people were pretty much the same, after they got over being uneasy about being strangers. No matter what their color, maybe even, though I wasn't so sure about that. God wanted to keep the races separate or He wouldn't have made them different colors. Or would He? He'd made them so they could breed without producing mules, like a donkey and a horse, that couldn't reproduce. Maria might have had my child, a mulatto. Might have. Well, she probably wouldn't, couldn't now. That was something to think about, having a half-colored child. Or having a child with Diana, who was a quarter-breed Indian, likely. For all I knew the white blood in Diana had been from one of the Dimons, or from any one of the old families; just about no matter who he was, if it was somebody from one of those families who'd climbed into bed with some squaw ancestress of Diana's a long time back, she'd have been related to me. It might just as well have been a buck Indian fornicating with a white girl, but that was hard to imagine in the old families.

What Mr. Masters had said about people out here not being willing to work didn't mean they were lazy. It wasn't that; they didn't want to work indoors, some of them, or they didn't want to work for somebody. They'd take orders from a captain or a mate, but that was different from taking them from a foreman. I'd heard old men say that the country was going to hell in a handbasket, that it wasn't what it was set up to be, a nation of independent farmers and fishermen, like the Roman Republic, each with his own holding and able to look any man in the eye and as good as the next man, blacks excepted, and that it was the Morgans and Blakes and Jay Goulds and all the rest of the Goldbugs had done the mischief, bringing in labor from abroad, setting up high tariffs, rigging railroad rates against the farmers too. That was one argument the mossbacks had against running the line out to Montauk; we'd get dependent on the railroad, and then they'd soak it to us. Silver and mortgage rates had something to do with it, and Manifest Destiny, whatever that was. But there were others who boomed the railroad, and the watchcase factory, and gold, and even bringing in foreigners, as part of progress, and the best things that could happen, and part of the Almighty's plan for the American people.

We'd been set on earth to do this, and help out those who couldn't do these things for themselves. Walker had said it was our duty, in a way, to help the Cubans, even if they didn't want us to. He hadn't thought much of missionaries, but he'd used that word once, mission, and had been embarrassed. It was like that, and the United States could no more leave its neighbors to live in poverty and disease than it had been able to let its Indian wards keep on running naked and scalping each other, or the courts could allow Montauk to remain in the hands of the Proprietors with everybody owning shares still reckoned up in shillings and pence, all contrary to progress. A.P. Blake and a missionary were a world apart from each other, but I guessed the Reverend Doctor Talmage could bring them together in your mind, and show how they weren't so very different, both engaged in the Lord's work. Unless of course he knew what I knew, that Blake had got rid of two men just because they were working for British interests rather than his own.

Dr. Fordham slid across the deck and laid down his tackle. "We've about clammed the tide out, Jerry," he said. "We'd best be thinking of heading home. Speaking of clamming, you made up your mind yet? You going to keep on clamming, or go to work in the watchcase factory?" He laughed; he didn't mean the watchcase factory, and he knew I knew. "You want to try doctoring, I think I can get you started, provided you'll tutor with the Hallocks this summer, and even arrange a loan for the fee, if need be. How about it?"

"All right," I said, without waiting to think. "I'll take a shot at it."

"You'll have to take more than a shot, young man. Four years of the hardest brain work you ever did or ever will do, it is these days, and two more years of residency. Blackwell's Island probably, ninety-eight hours a week. You think you can stick it?" I said yes, but thought maybe.

It was on toward dark by the time we'd unloaded the party, at Gordon's boatshop, and iced down the fish for them. Nat strolled up street for some excitement and I sat on deck, smoking in the dusk. What little wind there was was southerly, and sounds from the village carried across it. I'd never been able to figure out why noise should travel better across the wind than with it, but it was a fact. The rumble of wheels on the tollbridge to Hog Neck and laughter from someone on a porch up the hill came from the north and west; a quawker screeched above the marsh to the east, toward Little Northwest Creek. The quawk sounded again, closer, and you could hear his wings. He passed, and I saw the night heron's shape, black against the red sky over the village, stilt legs dangling down and his neck folded back against his breast.

A piano tinkled, like enough the one at the Fort. Nat

hadn't said, out of consideration for me I guessed, but he'd no doubt been bound there. I had a good smoke, here; the watchcase factory man had given us what was left of the box he'd brought for the Club. I'd be lying if I said I didn't like cigars and the sporting life, women and shooting and rum and the rest, I thought, and laughed at myself, seventeen taking himself so grown-up.

But it was true. And it was true that there was a pulling and a hauling inside, between the Century Gun Club sort of life, and what I'd learned at home. There was that, the old way, and the new way, business and progress and all, that went with being a sport. I didn't think the old way was mine, but doctoring could give you the best of both. At least it appeared that way. Dr. Fordham seemed to do well enough for himself at something he enjoyed, and still managed to straddle the two pretty well. The new people respected him, and so did the old, even though they knew of his sporting ways. If he'd been a big farmer and spent that much time gunning and fishing for pleasure, let alone visiting Mrs. Hetty Mack's, they'd have gossiped he was wasting his substance, and living above himself, and hardened their hearts against him. What was it he'd said? A doctor is the luckiest man alive, for his successes are there for all to see, and his failures are buried. People expected physicians to joke about themselves that way, when they wouldn't accept it in anyone else. Did you ever see a minister who didn't take himself serious, or a lawyer? You might find a farmer who didn't, but he'd be one of the sorry ones. The clock in the Methodist steeple struck nine, and I turned in. Nat came aboard a long time later; I woke for a moment as the sloop heeled to his weight.

He crawled out when I did, though, and we were well past Cedar Island before the tide turned in the morning. Nat wanted to go to East Hampton so we went up to the Head of Three Mile Harbor instead of to Accabonac Creek; six of one, half a dozen of the other to me. He'd heard me talking with

Dr. Fordham so I guessed he knew what was on my mind but neither of us brought it up. If I was going to tutor it meant making the arrangements right off, probably getting a half-day job in Bridgehampton and boarding with the Hallocks again. If Piersall's drugstore there needed anybody, that would be hard to beat. Most of it would be Latin, the summer's work, I didn't have to ask about that. Professor Hallock would know what I needed, for the Regents medical school examination. I got to thinking so hard about it I stood for a long time with a length of line in my hands on the dock without making fast to the piling until Nat started laughing. I sloped off to Amagansett as soon as I could to tell Mother what I'd decided. She seemed to take it all matter-of-fact, which surprised me some and irritated me more, until I realized she wasn't really herself these days.

It was all arranged inside of two days. On Wednesday, I rode over to Bridgehampton. Professor Hallock would take me, and a rich boy whose family had a summer place at Good Ground and wanted to enter him in Princeton, for two hours the latter part of each afternoon. What I'd saved up fishing would more than pay tuition, and room and board at the Hallocks', and give me a start on medical school. We'd commence the next Monday.

On Thursday, I caught up with Nat at Mulligan's livery stable in East Hampton -- he was watching a bunch of men playing at cards, which was an improvement over the dog-fights and cock-fights they sometimes put on there -- and we worked it out about the boat. I'd keep a half interest in it, but only a one-tenth lay in the proceeds. That would leave Nat with around seven-tenths after upkeep for himself and who-ever he took on to help out, probably not one of his Springs cousins and not Ames Mushmelon, he was too unhandy to be any use on the water. Nat let on he wasn't surprised, and said he'd always known I had a streak of laziness in me too broad for fishing. He was fooling, and it didn't bother me. I didn't tell him that although I trusted him as far as money went I wasn't entirely sure he had enough gumption to work the sloop and turn a profit without me along to stir him up. That was better left unsaid; in any event, I couldn't lose money by this arrangement, unless he went and put a rock through the sloop. We parted friends.

I rode over to East Hampton in the morning and bought a suit of clothes, the first I'd had first crack at since Cuba; two shirts; a hat; and a pair of shoes; as good as Van Scoy & Dayton had, first quality and twenty-two dollars in all. I'd figured to spend the whole morning at clothes-buying, but I'd felt awkward about being too choosy, and was back in Amagansett before noon. I decided to pack some sandwiches and go down to Fresh Pond for the Sunday School picnic. It was that time of year again. Mother didn't object; in fact she sort of smiled.

They'd mostly finished eating by the time I got there, and the young ones were chasing mummychoggs and crabs, pantlegs rolled, in the dreen where the pond lets out into the Bay. The teachers and the older girls were in the shade under the brush arbors, watching the boys choose up sides for a game of ball, the captains fist over fist on the bat, no eagle-claws. I got picked right off, though I never was much of a player, but I was bigger than most there, and played center field. We won; I'd got a two-base hit that drove home one of our runs.

I got to thinking about last year's picnic later, sitting in the boys' privy. The place had that mildew smell a privy gets when it isn't used regular; except for some of the picnickers that afternoon, the ones who hadn't gone in the bushes or water, I doubted anybody'd been in there since last summer. The squares of newspaper strung and hanging on a nail were from the year before, yellow and scratchy. I'd had a good lunch last year with the East Hampton Dimons, chicken and roast clams. Only twelve months back; it seemed longer. I'd gone off to Montauk afterward, the day we got the sloop.

I stood up and opened the door, and stepped out squinting against the light. This was the same sort of day, clear, light airs from the southwest, strawberrying weather. The Gardiner's Island mill was working again, arms revolving slowly. There were sails all along the horizon up past Plum Gut and Gardiner's Point. South of Cartwright Shoal, the Jud Field was steaming along toward the fish factories at Promised Land. There were steamers at the factories, and the black smoke moving slowly off to leeward in long banks showed the works were handling fish. The sheds at Promised Land were deep red in this light, and looked closer than they were. To the right of the factory, over the beach at Cedar Bush and across the sandhills, I could see the peak of the roof of Number Nine Station, and its flagpole and flag. Just past the Station was the ocean beach; down the beach was Montauk. I could be at Third House by dark if I started now, I thought. I wasn't going, though.

I finished buttoning my trousers and walked around the privy, back toward the picnic ground and Ranger, tethered in the shade near some new grass. The picnic was over, and the children were climbing into the wagons. The Dunton girl swung up into the one with the oldest girls, and I could see her ankles. Dr. Fordham had said those nurses on Blackwell's Island were some frolicsome.

Epilogue

If I'd dreamt I'd live to be one hundred plus years old and flat on my back in a so-called rest home being fed liquids with a spoon by a licensed practical nurse who couldn't stew rags for a midwife I wouldn't have believed it. No, you say, I won't live to be old. Won't happen to me. Oh, no, live hard, die young, and leave a beautiful corpse.

More like King Tut's mummy. Or maybe that's what I am right now, sixteen and asleep and dreaming I'm ninety-eight, or is it one-hundred and eight? Propped up against a palm tree on Inagua with my chin on my chest and my mouth open having bad dreams, a century's worth of imaginary happenings all charging through my head sixty miles an hour, mile a minute, wars and children and grandchildren and patients and nonsense.

Vanity, vanity, all is vanity. There's no vanity in hanging on, though they'll hang on when they haven't consciousness, haven't even a brain. Not that what I've got left is more than half a brain. Functioning. No. Vanity's gone when they're shoving a pot under your rear end, tubes into your arms, and talking about you in earshot as if you was deaf or three years old.

"God Rest Ye Merry Gentlemen!" Now isn't that a fine thing to be singing in the men's wing of a rest home. Christ on a crutch. Maybe if I ease this sheet up over my eyes they'll think I've died and shove off and leave me in peace. Not easy to do with one hand. I'd as soon be back in the Hospital, if it didn't cost an arm and a leg. Only one left of each now, for that matter. Seventy-nine dollars a day for a semi-private room! I was middle-aged before I made that much in a week. Oh, it's all right because the government pays it, or the insurance company, or somebody. Santa Claus.

Saving thirty or forty dollars a day here for my heirs. You never think it's going to come to that, no you don't. Well, I've left little enough for them to fight over. A few little Christmas presents for some of them if I go as fast as I expect I will. "Merry Christmas, dear; your Greatuncle Jerry has died and left you $500 and his library."

Leave that sheet be. I want to rest with it over my face. I'll have it over my face. Have to listen to that television caterwauling, but nothing says I have to watch it. Want to think. Close my eyes, and I can see the ocean beach. Warm.

Damn. It's Tiny Tim, the nurses call him. On his rounds. I'd give a lot to know how much he collects a head for strolling through here. Damned if I'll answer him. Wants to know how I feel, let him find out for himself. How does he think I feel, for God's sake? He goes after my bad arm for pulse 'cause he knows I can't move it away from him. I'd been practicing forty years before he was born. Forceps delivery by the look of that head.

Who's that sitting on the bedstead? Looks like me, but he's seventy if he's a day. Overweight, high blood pressure. My God. It's my son, Paul. He never took my hand before, not since he was six or seven, the age when he'd chase me in the Stanley down the driveway with his Irish

Mail. How he'd pump! Paul. New Testament names were coming in then. 'Twasn't my idea, but nothing would do but Paul. Clara generally had her way, with the children. He's not saying anything and I don't feel like it either. Looks sad. Well, well. Paul. In from California. He don't know it, but that's an Intimation of Mortality if ever there was. I'll be setting off soon, then.

Why doesn't he say something? I can hear. That's about all that works right, now. That and my recollection. Certainly not what's between my legs. A joke. I'd laugh if I could. Don't know but what I'd rather be there, in the city where Paul lives, than here, in this fix. In the city listening to the sirens and the jets and the traffic instead of that goddamned television set and that infernal gabble, gabble, gabble. Somebody ought to get a grant to find out why old men act like old women. Atrophy of the prostate most likely, unless it's enlarged, and then you could lay it to the fact that they're outnumbered, the males. And why should the average run of barnyard female last longer? Life is like a conversation with them, I guess; they want to have the last word. That being the case, I've won a lot of arguments. No more though. Even if some of the damage is repairing itself. Don't have to search as hard for words, thinking. But is thinking using words? I'm not talking, I'm remembering. Bock beer and Fresca, Cotolene, low-chloresterol salad dressing, wireless radio, videotape, Paul, Nat, Patton, Joe Wheeler, Earle Wheeler, two Roosevelts, two MacArthurs, General Pershing, Pershing tanks, high tariff, no tariff, low tariff, twenty cents on the dollar, veterans' bonus, veterans' march, Veterans' Day, Hooverville, Hoover Dam, Hayes office, "I am Curious," Hurricane of '38, Blizzard of '88, fall of Paris, shelling of Paris, Huns, Nazis, Werner Von Braun, Nurse Cavell, Lidice, My Lai, My God. Son of a _____, do you want to live forever? Hell No, We Won't Go, bathtub gin, GI gin, tonsils out, tonsils in, mastoid surgery, unnecessary surgery, socialized medi-

cine, medical economics, influenza epidemic, welfare, social services, poorhouse, overseer of the poor, scorchers, speeders, bicycle paths, Hudson Six, Steamer, Tiger in Your Tank, Herald Tribune, Herald, Tribune, Sun, World, Telegram, World Telegram and Sun, World Journal Telegram, Police Gazette, Puck, Life, Harper's, Life, Saturday Evening Post, "Sex," "Sex and the Single Girl," Brown's Mule, Helen Gurley Brown, Brown Bomber, San Juan Hill, Bull Moose, Bull Sheet, Mother, You Mother, "The Wall," the Berlin Wall, against the wall, "The Bridge of San Luis Rey," "The Bridges of Toko-Ri," "The Bridge at Remagen," Brodie, Brooklyn Bridge, Brooklyn Eagle, Brooklyn Dodgers, Trolley-Dodgers, Tralee, Roses of Picardy, Piccard, balloon ascensions, Cape Kennedy, Joe Kennedy, John Kennedy, Robert Kennedy, Edward Kennedy, Jacqueline Bouvier, Black Jack, Major Bouvier, major surgery, minor surgery, in the office, house calls, clinic, outpatient, in-patient, splitting fees, stock split, stock cars, stock yards, half a fathom, fathom and a half at low water, keep close to western shore until cupola bears NNE, Eastern Star, Easter, resurrection of the body. If that damned fool hasn't gone off on vacation he'll open that letter and it'll be cremation. Anybody feels like taking the time can sprinkle them in South End Cemetery, a little here and a little there. All run off into Town Pond eventually.

They could tell you how I pass my day, the nurses. Along after seven, after they've fooled around with the bedpan and set me sucking on a straw like a twelve-year-old in a candy kitchen, the old one with the Bellevue cap cranks the bed up and points me toward the television. I can't see it till they wind me up, only listen. In the afternoon, there's "The Dating Game," a lot here seem to enjoy that, and "General Hospital," that cheers them up. So does the evening news, although most of it's bad. There's people here so far gone upstairs they think it's the Filipinos we're chasing around with the heliocopters.

Aguinaldo and his men.

There goes the sound; just the picture's left. Some kind of a church that caroling's coming from. Like the Amagansett Presbyterian Church. Did you hear what they did with that Clark estate money? Walled in the balcony to pen the children up during the service, back of three sound-proof picture windows. So they could be seen but not heard. Only the only ones can see them is the preacher, and the choir. And the kids like enough carrying on behind the glass like monkeys in the zoo. They put in a set of electric bells to hector people with every hour on the hour too. What would Father say? I know what I say. Jesus Christ.

There goes the picture too. About time.

Afterword

Most novelists take for their first themes a moment in their experience and cram it full of autobiographical detail and attempts at psychological truth. The late Everett Rattray's first, and only, novel is different. While he used many of his own experiences to enrich his story, its basis was his knowledge of and appreciation for the thinking, customs, speech, and vocations of the people he knew best, those of eastern Long Island, and his understanding of American history.

Everett Rattray was, like many among older generations of East Hamptoners, closer to his roots than many of us now can imagine. He was intimate with the failings and prejudices, courage and strengths, of those who had been his ancestors; it was almost as if their characteristics and lives had been his own.

Knowing them, he knew the area's past. This was in part because the world of eastern Long Island had stayed more or less the same almost from its 17th century beginnings into the 20th century, when the stirrings of progress reached even into the backwaters. History was as much a part of Everett Rattray's character as humor and humanity, and the novel reflects this. The story is full of scrupulous detail about historic moments, the natural environment, and the people he describes, but his eye is affectionate.

Dimon was an old East Hampton name, although it disappeared from the region. Homidy will be recognized by those who know East Hampton history as inspired by the Dominy family. Many of those mentioned, such as Ephraim Byram and the Rev. T. DeWitt Talmage, are historical figures. In other cases, a character or an incident has been plucked from its actual place in history for the purposes of fiction.

This is a novel no one but Everett Rattray could have written. He had long experience on the sea, on naval ships and fishing and sailing boats, and he had been to the places of which he writes, even Mathewtown, Great Inagua. He knew family and local lore about shore whaling, oldtimers, and hunting and fishing, and he was there when men who had chased the whale guffawed over the film version of "Moby Dick." It was important to get things right. "The Adventures of Jeremiah Dimon" was a book, however, for which little research was necessary; he had almost all the information he needed at the ready.

His admiration for the medical profession, and particularly for his greatuncle, Dr. David Edwards, while important to the specifics of the story, also is important metaphorically. Unlike his father, and their fathers before him, Jeremiah chooses not to follow the family in farming and fishing. The world even at home, was changing, and the boy, having seen enough of the world to recognize that, breaks tradition. Ev used the title "Port of Entry" for the first draft of the novel. While the book recounts the hope of making Montauk a Port of Entry, it also describes the time when East Hampton was about to make its entry into the modern world and Jeremiah Dimon his entry into man-

hood.

In the late 1960s, with three small children at home, Ev would come home from a day's work as editor of the East Hampton Star with enough energy to work on the manuscript. He sat at a small desk in a part of his Amagansett house with a view of Gardiner's Bay. He thought his novel would break new ground. It is about a boy of 16, but it is not written for children or as a young adult book. It is not an historical novel, although steeped in history. It is old-fashioned, but it contains sex and violence. It is episodic, but it is more than an adventure story. It uses unfamiliar, sometimes arcane language, and, even though the author tries to instruct the reader, the reader often is left to figure things out alone. "Pightle," for example, is a word Ev knew when he was growing up, but it will not be found in every dictionary.

Perhaps because the novel is difficult to categorize, it failed to find a publisher among the several who saw the manuscript soon after its completion. One editor of a large New York publishing house said what the author may have dreamed but was too modest to have claimed: that the novel was something of a cross between Twain and Conrad, that it did not fit in the genre of most modern novels, but was startling in its evocation of time and place and perhaps even important.

The version published here is basically one that the author edited himself from his first draft, doing as good a job on his own work as he did at the Star for others. In his second draft, the old Jeremiah Dimon, who is "Heading Out," was eliminated from much of the text and relegated to a prologue. The epilogue, added for this printing, is from material culled from the first draft.

As the editor now of the East Hampton Star it gives me great pleasure to see the book published by Pushcart Press and to plan for it to be excerpted in the Star during the paper's 100th anniversary year, 1985. I only regret that

Ev, who died on January 14, 1980, did not see it published in his lifetime.

Although I am hesitant to predict the name of Jeremiah Dimon will become as well known as Huckleberry Finn, I anticipate the novel will find its place in our literature.

Helen S. Rattray
January 1, 1985

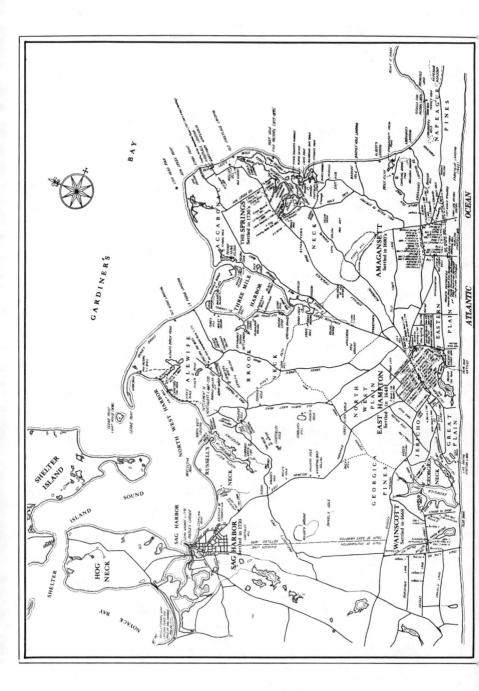

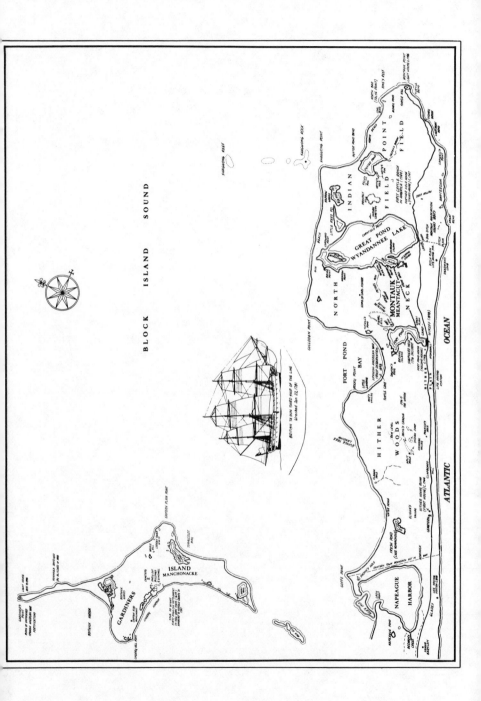